Pe...

Dalton's sm... ... ...
were full and parted over even white teeth. ... ...
of her depths as her eyes collided with his probing gaze.

Flustered, she turned her head. "You certainly impressed my son."

"But not you?"

Another question out of left field, but always at close range. Though his tone was casual, there was nothing casual about the tension that leapt between them. He was probing—delicately, with silken words—but probing, nonetheless.

He was dangerous, and she was defenseless. As long as she didn't pick on that weakness, she would be just fine.

*　　　*　　　*

"Simply captivating . . . a gripping, emotional tale and a wonderful love story."
—Julie Garwood on Sweet Justice

"Popular romance writer Mary Lynn Baxter makes a perfect ten-point dive into women's fiction. . . . Ms. Baxter has constructed a dramatic, riveting, and emotionally complex novel that should land on the bestseller list."
—Affaire de Coeur on Sweet Justice

"A tender and touching story that strikes every chord within the female spirit."
—Sandra Brown on A Day in April

Also by Mary Lynn Baxter

SWEET JUSTICE

Published by
WARNER BOOKS

MARY LYNN BAXTER

Priceless

WARNER BOOKS

A Time Warner Company

WARNER BOOKS EDITION

Cover design by Diane Luger
Cover illustration by Dominick Finelle
Hand lettering by Carl Dellacroce

Warner Books, Inc.
1271 Avenue of the Americas
New York, NY 10020

 A Time Warner Company

Printed in the United States of America

First Printing: March, 1995

10 9 8 7 6 5 4 3 2 1

Acknowledgements

A special thanks to Dr. Brenda Bordson for so graciously giving of her time in supplying me with invaluable information.

Thanks also to Becky Canterbury for her architectural expertise.

One

Bogalusa, Louisiana, June 1989

"Sonofabitchin' little pest!"

Parker Montgomery grabbed the flyswatter and slammed it against the table at the right of the swing. Seconds later he lifted the mesh weapon and laughed a deep belly laugh.

His gaze focused on the glass surface, where the giant mosquito had rested contentedly after feasting on his arm. Now the varmint was nothing but a splattered stain of red.

Parker chuckled again. "Told you what was going to happen if you didn't stop chewing on me."

Without bothering to clear away the mess, Parker laid the swatter down beside him on the swing. He knew it would only be a matter of time until he'd need it again. He'd swear the damned mosquitoes got bigger every year, or maybe it was that he was getting older and less tolerant. He suspected the latter was the case, especially when it came to his son.

He muttered a curse. Dalton was the last person Parker wanted to think about on a morning so glorious, despite the climbing humidity and annoying insects.

Parker sat on the back porch that ran the length of the tall columned house. The stately home had been in his family

1

since the early 1900s, and he had kept it in pristine condition over the years. He loved showing it off.

Parties, however, were mostly things of the past. Since his retirement from his long-held position as a Louisiana senator in Washington, that sort of hoopla didn't interest him anymore.

His retirement or his lack of social life, however, wasn't what had him out of sorts, and he damn well knew it. But he liked to play those mind games, which he'd decided made day-to-day living more bearable.

If only his son were someone he could be proud of and depend on. Was that asking too much? Hell, a man should be proud of his only living son. If only his elder son had lived. If only . . .

"Knock it off," he muttered to himself.

Still, chastising himself failed to plug the memories or the pain that sometimes nearly drove him over the edge. He knew that only death would relieve that sting.

Meanwhile he had to do something about his remaining son. Dalton Winslow Montgomery. He was the single biggest disappointment of Parker's life.

"Damn!"

Another mosquito sting forced him to reach for the swatter. It was too late. The mosquito had filled his belly to capacity and flown off.

Shoving back a lock of thinning white hair, Parker stood and stretched. He was a big man who had remained trim despite his sixty years and the good life he had led. While in Washington he had worked out in a gym every day, and that rigid schedule had paid off. Both his body and his mind were in excellent condition.

Shading his eyes, he surveyed his empire, though from his position he was able to see only a small portion of the land he owned. The Montgomery mansion, as it was known in the small town of fourteen thousand, was on the outskirts of town and sat atop a hill that was surrounded by huge moss-draped oak trees and pines that seemed to reach clear to heaven. Magnolias and dogwoods, both heavy with white blossoms, further enhanced the beauty of the landscape.

Bordering the land was the Pearl River with its hidden

bayous and heavy boating traffic. The river wasn't what had sustained the town, kept it alive and prosperous; rather, it was the lumber industry that his father had carved out of the virgin forest long years ago.

Though Parker no longer had any interest or stock in the company that had bought out the mill, closed it, then turned it into another money-making empire, he had the millions the deal had brought him. Too, he had the thousands of acres of land that could be farmed and filled with cattle.

A contented sigh broke through Parker's lips. He didn't know of another place on earth he'd rather be. Too bad Dalton didn't feel that way. But then Dalton's only interest was in himself.

Parker pulled at his thick white mustache, then barked another expletive, angry that his thoughts had returned to the son he wanted to disown but couldn't, not because he didn't want to, but because he had the Montgomery name to protect.

"Long time no see, my friend."

Parker swung around, taken aback by the sound of the voice. His old friend, Doug Chartres, a senator from the state of Georgia, leaned against one side of the French door, grinning like a Cheshire cat.

"Why, you old sonofagun, you!" Parker laughed and took a step toward him, his hand outstretched. "What the bloody hell brings you to this neck of the woods?" he asked, pumping Doug's hand up and down.

"Nothing much," Chartres replied in a lazy drawl, though he returned Parker's handshake with vigor.

Parker eyed his friend, whom he hadn't seen in a few years since they both had retired from politics. Chartres was a short man with balding red hair and freckles who accepted the ribbing he took for his coloring with good nature.

"Sorry if I intruded," Doug said. "I talked your housekeeper into letting me surprise you."

"Ah, you certainly did that."

Doug pushed away from the door. "Actually, I can't believe you didn't hear me." He grinned and cut Parker a side glance. "Your hearing gettin' bad?"

Parker returned his stare. "Hell, no. I was just lost in thought."

Before Chartres could respond, the housekeeper appeared in the doorway. "Mr. Parker, would you and your guest care for a mint julep?"

Parker looked at Doug with uplifted brows.

"Sounds good to me."

"Thanks, Thelma," Parker said to the woman, who nodded, then disappeared

"Well, have a seat on the swing here," Parker said, "and tell me what's brought you to Bogalusa."

"I had business nearby, so on the spur of the moment, I thought I'd stop in."

"Well, I'm glad you did."

"So what have you been up to since you retired?"

"Probably the same thing you have."

Doug grinned. "Which is not a goddamn thing more than we have to, right?"

"Right."

They both chuckled, while Doug slapped at a mosquito with the palm of his hand.

Parker cursed. "Let's go inside. I'd hate for you to get eaten alive."

"Hell, man, I can handle the mosquitoes; it's this heat that drives me nuts."

"Well, then, let's move."

"Nah, I'm not planning to be here that long." Doug pulled a handkerchief from his back pocket and wiped the sweat from his forehead and upper lip. "Looks like we're in for one helluva long, hot summer."

Thelma appeared once again through the French doors, carrying a tray bearing a plate of tea cakes and two tall glasses filled with a green liquid, shaved ice, mint leaves, and orange slices wedged on the side. She placed the tray on the table in front of the wicker couch.

"Enjoy," she said with a shy smile, then shuffled off.

After swallowing a mouthful of cake, Doug asked, "You seeing anyone, Parker?"

Parker paused just as he was about to take a sip of his drink. "You mean a woman?"

"Of course I mean a woman." He gave Parker a lurid grin. "Unless you've turned funny or something."

Parker grunted. "You haven't changed a bit, Chartres. You still let your mouth overload your ass."

Doug merely laughed as he reached for another tea cake, then took a generous bite. Only after the last crumb had disappeared did he ask, "Well?"

"It's none of your business," Parker snapped, though with a smile.

"Which means no."

Parker shrugged. "So what?"

"Well, I just figured a good-looking man with your money would have to beat back the women." Doug grinned.

"I've had my fair share who've been interested, I'll admit, but . . . " Parker let his voice trail off, loath to discuss his private life with this man or anyone else. But to keep from being rude, he added, "Frankly, I haven't found anyone who could replace Evelyn."

Doug shook his head. "That wife of yours must've been some woman."

A faraway look appeared in Parker's eyes. "She was."

"Well, as you know, my other half dumped me years ago, and once around that mulberry bush was enough for me."

Parker laughed and slapped his friend on the back.

They fell silent for another long moment, then after the tray was removed, they talked about their days in Washington, sharing stories and incidents that brought laughter as well as feelings of melancholy, for those days were gone and could never be recaptured.

Finally Doug stood. "Well, I have to say that this visit has been good for me. Like you, I'm fighting off becoming old and set in my ways."

"Glad you came. Stop by anytime."

"I'll remember that. And if you're ever over my way, you do the same. I'll even spring for dinner."

"No, you won 't, you cheap bastard."

Doug threw back his head and laughed.

"Come on," Parker said with an answering grin on his face, "I'll walk you to the car."

They rounded the corner and stepped onto the front lawn

when Doug paused. "By the way, I forgot to ask about Dalton. How's he doing?"

Parker knew his expression tightened, but it was a reaction he couldn't control. "Fine, I guess," he said in a clipped tone, not about to air his family's dirty laundry.

"Well, I know you've bailed him out of more than one jam—"

"What's your point?" Parker demanded, an edge to his voice.

Doug flushed. "There's no point, not really." He paused. "It's just that—" This time his words broke off altogether.

Curious in spite of himself, Parker pressed, "Go on. It's just what?"

"Something's been bothering me for a while, I'll admit."

"I'm listening."

"Actually, I saw Dalton myself a while back."

"Oh." Parker's tone dropped several degrees.

Doug hesitated, reached up, and wiped the sweat from the bald spot on top of his head. "Why the hell are we standing out here in the boiling-ass hot sun?"

Parker didn't respond.

"Anyway, what I was about to say is that I saw Dalton in Bristol."

"Bristol?" Parker shrugged. "As far as I know, there's nothing there that would interest my son."

Doug grinned his Cheshire cat grin. "Oh, but there is."

"Christ, Chartres, stop playing this cat-and-mouse game and tell me what the hell you're getting at."

As if realizing he'd pushed Parker too far, Doug cleared his throat and looked directly into his cohort's eyes. "The town's only claim to fame is their sperm bank."

Parker blinked, knowing he had a stupid look on his face. "Sperm bank?"

"Yeah, as in donor sperm bank."

"So?"

"So, that's where studs go into a room, look at girlie magazines, then jack off in a jar."

Parker's lips stretched into a disgusted line. "I still don't know what that has to do with Dalton."

Doug winked. "That's where I saw your son."

Parker felt the color drain from his face and his lips go slack. Yet he managed to wheeze, "Dalton? You saw my son there?"

"Yep. He was strolling out of the place with that satisfied look on his face which said he'd just blown his wad."

"Why, you . . . you . . . " The words stopped. Parker staggered, clutched his chest, then fell to his knees.

"Sweet Jesus!" Doug cried, catching his friend before he hit the ground.

"Help me," Parker whispered, then closed his eyes.

"Thelma! Thelma!"

Moments later the housekeeper appeared on the front steps. When she saw Parker cradled in Doug's arms, she screamed.

"For God's sake, woman, shut up and call 911!"

When she still didn't move, Doug bellowed, *"Now!"*

Thelma turned and dashed back into the house.

Doug cradled his friend in his arms, then lifted his head and whispered a prayer.

Two

Biloxi, Mississippi, June 1989

The loud blare of the horn didn't register with Leah Frazier until she twisted her head to the left.

A huge truck seemed to have come out of nowhere, and it was heading straight for her. In fact, within a matter of seconds no one would be able to tell where her Honda left off and the truck began. They seemed destined to merge as one, metal into metal.

"Oh, my God!" Leah whispered, blind panic forcing her to act.

In the nick of time she jerked the wheel to the right just as the truck veered to the left. Tires and brakes squealed before her vehicle shot off the shoulder of the road and careened down the grassy embankment. Aeons seemed to pass before it came to an abrupt halt.

Leah's head banged against the steering wheel, and while she saw stars and reeled from the blunted blow, she didn't lose total consciousness.

She did, however, bite her tongue; the salty taste of blood was on her lips.

"Hey, lady, you all right?"

8

Leah lifted her head slowly and through dazed eyes stared at a bearded man whose nose pressed against the glass. She managed to nod before fumbling for the door handle. He stepped back and helped her with the door.

"Are you all right?" he asked again, peering at her closely.

"I . . . I think so." Leah placed two fingers on her head, certain she would come back with blood on them. Surprisingly, she didn't. But there was already the beginning of a goose egg.

He looked as if he might want to argue the point with her, but then he said, "If you're sure, move over, and I'll get your car back on track."

Leah did as she was told, and in a matter of minutes the Honda was back on the shoulder of the road, facing in the right direction.

The man made no move, however, to get out of the vehicle. "Lady, are you sick or something?" He looked suddenly embarrassed. "I mean, you ignored the red light and just pulled out in front of me—"

"I know, and I'm sorry, so sorry." Leah licked her dry lips. "My . . . my mind was somewhere else. I simply wasn't paying attention."

"That's an understatement," he said. "Look, if you're sure you're able to drive, I suggest you go straight home. That knot on your head is bound to give you a whopping headache."

She forced a wobbly smile. "Again, I'm sorry for the inconvenience I've caused you. Thanks for helping me."

"No problem. But please, do us all a favor and keep your mind on your driving, okay?"

"Okay," Leah whispered, switching on the ignition. She didn't move, though. Even after the truck had long disappeared, she remained where she was, trembling all over.

God, she had almost been killed. How could she have been so careless? So stupid? Stress and fear. Those were the culprits. Not every day did a woman learn that her husband had a life-threatening illness.

Leah didn't want to recall the conversation she'd just had with her husband's doctor, but she couldn't stop herself, especially after what had just happened. His words flooded her mind like a gushing faucet that wouldn't turn off.

"Your husband is a very sick man." The doctor had paused then, as if searching for exactly the right words to continue. "He's never going to get well."

Leah's stomach had lurched, and she had a surge of nausea. She clutched at her middle as emotions charged through her at such a rapid rate that she wasn't sure she could remain upright.

Dr. Dan Bolton lunged out of his chair, but Leah waved him away, then took several deep breaths. When she could speak again, she asked, "Are you saying, Dan, that Rufus is dying?"

Dr. Bolton ran a hand through his full head of blond hair; his round, pink face creased with distress. "I'm sorry, but yes, that's what I'm saying.

"The fungus he picked up in 'Nam has attacked his lungs. Unfortunately, there's no cure." Dr. Bolton paused and looked at Leah as if he would do anything in his power to remove the stunned horror reflected in her face.

"In most cases, if it hasn't gotten a stronghold, the disease can be treated successfully with antifungals and other drugs. But in Rufus's case, with his history of inherited respiratory problems, the prognosis is not good."

Leah tried to swallow, but she didn't have enough saliva left in her mouth to manage even that simple gesture. "How . . . how long?" she finally choked out.

Dr. Bolton signed, then rubbed his chin. "It could take several years, or it could be much sooner."

"It all depends on how and if he continues to respond to the medication." Leah's words were a flat statement of fact rather than a question.

"Exactly."

Leah rose to her feet, walked to the window in the office, and peered outside with tear-glazed eyes. The people on the sidewalk, the cars swishing by, the hovering clouds, made little impression on her. They might as well as have been caricatures from an alien land.

In one sentence the kindly, middle-aged man sitting behind his massive desk had dealt her the severest blow of her life. Yet she could not, must not, think of herself. It was Rufus who was facing death. Again weakness threatened to buckle Leah's legs.

"Leah, are you all right?"

No, I'll never be all right again, she wanted to shout. Instead she turned her tearstained face toward Dan and whispered, "Don't worry about me."

"I'm worried about you both," he countered bluntly.

"Does Rufus know?"

"Yes, he knows."

"So you told him yesterday?"

Dr. Bolton nodded.

Leah turned back toward the window. "I knew something was bothering him last night, but he didn't want to talk about it, so I didn't push him."

"He wanted me to break the news to you, hopefully to soften the blow."

Leah reached into her bag, pulled out a tissue, and blotted the tears from her cheeks. "I'd rather it had come from him."

"We talked about that, but he simply wasn't capable of it. He said he couldn't bear to look you in the face and tell you something he knew would totally devastate you."

Leah almost smiled. "That's like Rufus, always wanting to protect me from the evil in the world."

"You're lucky, my dear. Rufus Frazier is a man in a million." Dr. Bolton paused again, this time with a deep-felt sigh. "It's times like this that I feel so frustrated with the limitations of my work."

A silence fell over the room as Leah walked back to the chair and sat down. She didn't lean back but remained reed straight, fearing if she relaxed, she'd break into pieces.

"Where do we go from here, in terms of treatment?" she had asked, her voice and eyes now direct.

Dan Bolton picked up a pair of glasses, plopped them onto his wide nose, and returned Leah's direct stare. "Besides the heavy amount of medication he'll have to take, he'll need rest. A lot of rest."

"Are you saying he won't be able to work?"

"It would be to his advantage if he didn't have to." The

doctor's eyes narrowed. "If I'm not mistaken, his job is fairly high-stress, right?"

Leah bit her lower lip. "Right, especially in the architecture firm where he works. He's under tremendous pressure."

"Well, we won't worry about the job aspect for a while longer."

"Does he know that you'd rather he curtail his work?"

"No, but I'm sure he suspects that's a reality."

Leah sighed and rose to her feet. The doctor followed suit, and for a moment they simply looked at each other, at a loss as to how to deal with the situation.

Dr. Bolton was the first to break the heavy silence. He came from behind his desk and placed one arm around Leah's shoulders. "Keep your chin up, you hear? We're going to do everything we can to keep him comfortable and to prolong his life."

Fresh tears gathered in Leah's eyes as she looked into his. "But not long enough for him to see our son grown. You can't promise that, can you?"

Dan Bolton's features twisted. "No, I'm afraid I can't."

That conversation had taken place only a short while ago. Now, Leah had the excruciating task of facing her husband. After taking several deep breaths, she shifted the gear into drive.

Highway 90 between Biloxi and Gulfport was not busy at this time of the morning, for which she was thankful. She couldn't have dealt with rush-hour traffic. Concentrating with difficulty, she stared straight ahead, unaware of the beauty of the tranquil waters of the Gulf to her left or the lovely antebellum homes, with lawns shaded by huge oak trees, on her right.

Suddenly and without forethought, Leah swung her Honda off the highway next to a deserted stretch of beach. She knew she shouldn't be stopping. She had promised her superior that as soon as she left the doctor's office she would return to work.

Thoughts of Cooper Anderson added to her misery. He hadn't been pleased that she had failed to report to the office promptly at eight o'clock. The firm she worked for was a rival to that of her husband. Founded by Anderson's father and several of his cronies, Anderson, Thomas, and Swain was a prestigious company. Because of that and because she was a woman in what had always been virtually a man's world, the pressure upon her was enormous, especially as she wasn't yet licensed as an architect.

Well, Anderson be damned, Leah thought as she parked her car and got out. The offensive odor of fish, accompanied by the smell of salty sea air, hit her in the face. Then the humidity robbed her of her breath. Although it was the middle of June, not yet officially summer, it was already unbearably hot. Or maybe her discomfort stemmed from the shock she had just received. Leah removed her patent-leather pumps and walked hose-footed through the sand.

After a moment she paused and stared at the sky, at the azure-colored clouds that were building over the Gulf. Hurricane season was imminent, a season that was dreaded, yet summer was looked forward to by the locals. Summer meant tourists. And both Biloxi and Gulfport relied heavily on tourism for their livelihood, especially now that gambling had come into play.

The sand felt odd as it shifted through her hose, but she didn't care. She could dust the white powder off the bottom of her feet with little effort. If only she could alleviate the humidity as easily. Even the few minutes she'd been walking had her bra under her suit stuck to her skin. She pulled her blouse away from her body, but that did little to relieve her discomfort.

Still, she kept on walking, her mind reeling. Rufus, her husband, the gentle, kind man who had taught her that love wasn't synonymous with jealousy and evil, was going to die long before his time. It wasn't fair; it wasn't right!

How could she face a future without him? Her thoughts returned to the day she had announced to her mother that she was going to marry him, a man fifteen years her senior.

Jessica Gentry's face had twisted into a stunned frown. Dramatically, she had placed her hand against her chest as if Leah had just dealt her a mortal blow.

"Marry him!" she'd screeched. "Why, have you lost your mind, child?"

Leah stared into her mother's livid face, and her stomach

had roiled. She felt an urge to slap that look off Jessica's face, a look that she'd seen more times than she cared to acknowledge.

"No, I haven't lost my mind," Leah replied in a voice that shook despite her efforts to keep it steady.

"Well, it sounds like it to me."

Leah's chin jutted. "I've made my decision."

Jessica lunged off the lumpy sofa, pushed back a clump of stringy hair as if to see her daughter better, and began to pace the floor. She stopped suddenly and whipped around.

"Well, just unmake it. I'm not about to allow you to throw your life away on a man who's too old for you and who can't make you a decent living."

"You mean make *you* a decent living, don't you, Mama?"

Jessica's eyes had narrowed until they were tiny slits. "You watch your mouth, young lady. I don't care how old you are, I'll not have you talk to me like that."

"I'm not changing my mind. I love him and he loves me."

"Love!" Jessica's lips curved into a sneer. "You don't have the foggiest idea of what love is."

"Look, I don't have to stand here and listen—"

"Oh, yes, you do." Jessica's eyes glittered. "You owe me, and don't you ever forget it. I've worked my fingers to the bone to see that you got an education and made something of yourself. Now, you want to throw it all away for a man who doesn't deserve you. And all in the name of lust."

"That's not the way it is."

"Well, then, just how is it?"

"He cares about me, not just about my body!" Leah heard her voice rise several octaves, but she didn't try to control it.

Again Jessica sneered. "We'll see. You just watch, in no time you'll be miserable just like me."

"No, Mama, I'll never be just like you." Leah's quietly spoken words failed to temper her mother's fury.

"If you marry him, you will be. I can promise you that."

She had married Rufus, and now, years later, her mother's promised threat had proved to be only empty words. Marriage to Rufus had made her extremely happy.

Life. Suddenly another pain shot through her, and she listened as thunder rumbled in the distance. She didn't care if a deluge of rain fell and soaked her. She couldn't have moved had she wanted to. Her thoughts had shifted to *their* child. For the second time her knees almost gave way.

After all they had been through, after all the tests, the unconventional methods, Rufus wouldn't live to see their child reach manhood.

"It's not fair!" Leah shouted, looking heavenward.

She knew she couldn't blame God. Dying was a part of living. And to live meant pain. She had learned that at a tender age.

Tears clogged her throat again, but Leah refused to give in to them. She pivoted and headed back toward her car; all the while a resolve built inside her. Even if she had only one day left with Rufus, she would make the most of it. Not for herself, but for him and the child who was her husband's most treasured possession.

Three

Biloxi, Mississippi, July 1994

Dalton Montgomery reached for the pillow beside him on the couch and pitched it across the room. With a grunt of disgust he shoved all five fingers through longish, dark blond hair. The water in the shower had just been turned off. He sighed. That meant his latest conquest was about to slink out of the bedroom and intrude on his privacy, which irritated the hell out of him.

When he'd walked into the condo fifteen minutes ago, he'd known he had company, even before he'd heard the running water. Perfume had permeated the premises. But then he had no one to blame but himself. He shouldn't have given her a key to his place.

Maybe someday he'd learn not to let his libido overrule his sound judgment. Or maybe he wouldn't. At least that was what his father thought. He smirked, then pitched the other pillow across the room. This time it bounced off the wall and nearly came back to him. He had no intention of thinking about his father, even if the old man was close to death. Talk about darkening his mood—thoughts of Parker Montgomery would surely do the trick.

16

He mumbled a curse as Tanya Delisle appeared in the doorway. Her full lower lip was stretched into what he knew to be her sexy "come on" grin.

Not tonight, babe, he thought. But he held back that comment simply because he knew his rude words would cause an immediate ruckus. After all, *he* had given her a key.

"Hi, darlin'," Tanya said, the words sounding like velvet rolling off her tongue. One thing he had to say in her favor was that she had a great voice. In fact, that outweighed her other attributes, though they weren't shabby, not by a long shot.

She was tall with hazel eyes, large breasts, and a relatively small waist. But her thighs were beginning to thicken, and he knew when she reached middle age she would be as broad as two ax handles. Thank God that wasn't his problem. When that happened, he had no intention of being around. A long-term relationship was the one thing he had avoided and would continue to avoid.

"What's the matter, darlin'?" she pressed when Dalton didn't respond to her greeting. "You had a hard day, huh?" She glided across the room, clad only in a towel that was secured above her cleavage. "If that's the case, I know just the solution to make you feel better."

"Tanya, what are you doing here?" Dalton squinted up at her, his forehead threaded into a frown.

She pursed her lips. "What do you mean, what am I doing here?"

"I don't recall inviting you," Dalton countered in a tired voice. For once his mind was on something other than sex. Only hours ago he'd had a verbal slugging match with his father. Following one of those bouts, nothing could soothe him.

"Why, darlin', you don't have to invite me." She winked. "I have a key, remember?"

"I want it back."

Her face paled slightly, but then she waved her hand and smiled. "You don't mean that. You're just in a bad ole mood."

Before he was aware of her intentions, Tanya dropped to her knees, which instantly loosened the towel. It seemed to drift from her body in slow motion. She smiled, then attacked his zipper with eager fingers.

Dalton stilled her hands.

She gazed at him, a stunned expression on her face.

"I want my key back," Dalton repeated.

Tanya scrambled to her feet, placed her hands on her naked hips, and glared down at him. "What the hell's going on? I'm not just some—"

"Yes, you are," Dalton said in a tired, bored voice. "But it's not your fault. Please, just go get dressed and leave the key on your way out."

"I hope you burn in hell, Dalton Montgomery," Tanya spat, huge tears rolling down her face.

"I'm sure you'll get your wish," he mumbled to her back, pressing his frame deeper into the cushions.

Five minutes later the front door slammed shut. Dalton winced but remained on the couch and concentrated on emptying his mind. He closed his eyes, but he couldn't keep them shut. His head buzzed like an electric saw. Finally his gaze ventured toward the French doors that led to his front deck and the ocean beyond.

Though he couldn't hear the waves lap against the shoreline, he pretended he could; the sound never failed to relax him.

He liked his condo, partly because he'd bought it for a song and partly because of the view. It had been a government repossession, and he'd saved a small portion of the money he'd finally inherited from his mother and made a bid. Lo and behold, he'd gotten the damn thing.

Dalton whipped his eyes back to the interior, which he knew could use some help, at least on the decorating end. But he wasn't interested in hearth and home. That was definitely not where his heart was. Still, maybe one of these days he'd fix up the place, make it more like a home than a hotel.

He especially liked the modern spiral staircase that led upstairs to the loft. He'd liked it so much, he'd made the loft his bedroom, leaving the master bedroom free for the company he never had.

The rest of the downstairs consisted of another bedroom,

bath, kitchen, and living room. That space was the most sparsely furnished of all, with only an entertainment center, a dark green leather couch, and two matching chairs. The walls were as empty as his personal life, he thought with a bleak smile. But then that, too, was of his own choosing.

He could have taken the marriage and family route. Lord knew, he'd had plenty of opportunities. Apparently that wasn't in the cards for him. He'd never found a woman to whom he felt he could remain faithful. He'd never even found a woman he wanted to wake up beside every morning. He'd decided no such woman existed.

All he cared about now was his latest business venture. At the thought of it, a surge of excitement rushed through him; he was close to owning his own business, which was a miracle in itself.

"You've nailed it this time, Montgomery!" he cheered himself aloud. "Just see that you don't fuck it up."

Next to women, gambling was the love of his life. It was also his downfall. He'd admit that. Now, however, with dockside gambling having been legalized in Biloxi, he had the chance to turn that passion into a legitimate business and make huge sums of money.

Maybe he might even make his old man proud. That was a laugh. He didn't give a shit if he made his father proud or not. He'd stopped trying to do that years ago. This business was for himself. He wanted to make himself proud.

Luckily, as in the case of his condo, he had stumbled on some property and a dilapidated private club that no one wanted. Now, two years later, the stretch of beachfront property along Highway 90, Beach Boulevard, had become the hottest and highest-priced property in the state, thanks to the emergence of dockside gambling. That piece of earth was a gold mine in itself.

Dalton had had offer after offer to sell it at triple what he'd paid. But he wasn't interested in selling the property or the club; he was interesting in renovating both.

In addition, he'd had the opportunity to purchase a paddle wheel boat that had been a three-story floating restaurant. The owner had been in the process of turning it into a casino when he'd declared bankruptcy.

For Dalton, opening a club with adjoining casino would be the ultimate high, but it wouldn't be a piece of cake. Competition was tough. Others along that strip had the jump on him. Floating casinos were strung along the beachfront farther than the eye could see.

Dalton never doubted that he was up to the challenge. He had the money to back him from the bank, though getting it had eaten into his pride because it had been his father's name that had secured him the loans.

First, though, in a moment of weakness, he'd gone to Parker and asked him for the money outright, thinking the bank wouldn't loan him a cent, much less megabucks. Approaching his father had been a mistake; he should've known better.

Any time he went to see Parker, he left with another chunk of himself missing.

This time it would be different, he'd told himself. He was finally doing something constructive, something that Parker could relate to—a sound business venture. With that in mind, Dalton had driven to Bogalusa. . . .

"Why are you here?" Parker had demanded the instant Dalton walked out onto the porch. "I know you want something."

Dalton hadn't said anything. First, he'd been taken aback by how awful Parker looked, how rapidly he'd deteriorated. Parker had sat on the swing shrunken like an old man of ninety instead of sixty-five. According to the doctors, Parker Montgomery should have already been dead. After four heart attacks in the past five years, he was a living miracle.

"You're right, I do want something," Dalton said, followed by a deep sigh.

Though his body had grown weak, there was nothing weak about Parker's mind. It was as sharp as ever, and so was that steely glint in his eyes that would make most men slither away in shame.

"Money. You've come with your hand out again, haven't you?"

Dalton opened his mouth, only to slam it shut as Parker interrupted, "What have you done this time? Knocked someone up, I suppose."

Dalton clenched his fists, then shifted his gaze to the huge pine tree next to the porch. A robin redbreast perched on a limb, cleaning himself vigorously. He watched the bird and silently envied its uncomplicated life.

Finally he turned back to his father. "I haven't done anything. This time it's business."

"Monkey business, I bet."

Dalton suddenly exploded. "I knew this was a mistake. Every time I come here I wish to hell I hadn't."

"That's because you always come with your hand out because you've gotten in over your damn head."

"Just exactly what do you expect from me?" Dalton retaliated, feeling his temper soar. "I'm not you. And I'm not my brother and never will be." He watched Parker's face grow ashen. He didn't care.

"Don't you dare speak of your brother in that tone!"

A long silence followed Parker's outburst, which did nothing to diffuse the heightened tension.

Parker was the first to break it, though his voice hadn't lost any of its venom. He merely sounded sick and tired. "For starters, I want you to settle down. Goddammit, boy, you're thirty-five years old and still behaving as if you were twenty-five."

"So?" Dalton goaded, knowing very well what the old man was getting at.

"So stop whoring and get a job that lasts longer than any of the women in your life."

"That's exactly what I'm trying to do."

"Sure."

Dalton ignored the sarcasm in Parker's tone and went on to explain about the property he'd bought with the trust fund from his mother and exactly what he wanted to do with it.

"As you know, the other casino managers are getting rich," Dalton added, his eyes gleaming. "It's a sure bet I will, too. What I need now is the money to renovate the club, buy that paddle wheel boat, then renovate it."

"No."

The softly spoken word hit Dalton like a brick upside his head. He blinked. "No? You're saying 'no' just like that?"

"No," the old man repeated. "I won't give you another

cent. I told you that the last time you came with your hand outstretched for money to pay another gambling debt."

"But this is different. This is—"

"No. That's my final answer. Now, get out of here and let me be."

Dalton was proud of himself. He didn't beg. He didn't plead. And most of all he didn't shake the old man into compliance. To do so would play into Parker's hands, give him ammunition to disown him. He wasn't about to give his father that satisfaction.

Now, as Dalton pulled his thoughts back from that ugly scene, he couldn't believe he'd had the guts to go straight to the bank. He had been sure that he hadn't a chance of getting a loan, but the bank had come through. It was only after he'd subdued his anger at his father that he had understood the reason. Everyone knew how ill his father was and that Dalton soon would inherit his father's millions, which would enable him to pay off *all* his debts. That didn't mean, however, that he wanted his father to die. The reality was that his father *was* going to die.

A sudden chill shot through Dalton. He *would* inherit his father's millions, despite Parker's threat to the contrary. He was sure Parker had been blowing hot air. Besides the fact that there was no one else to leave his fortune to, Parker wouldn't want his friends to know he despised his only living son.

To the world, father and son were one happy family.

Dalton closed his eyes and gave in to the sadness that washed through him. If only things had been different. If only his older brother hadn't died. If only . . .

Hell, crying in his beer wasn't the answer. He'd much rather be drinking one. Dalton rolled off the couch, stomped into the kitchen, jerked open the refrigerator, and grabbed a can of Coors. He popped the top, leaned his head back, and chugged it down. When that one was empty, he grabbed another.

And another.

"Hey, buddy, if you're there, pick up the phone."

Dalton shook his head several times to clear it. Finally he

realized the ringing in his head was not his brain blitzing apart, but the telephone, followed by a voice on the answering machine.

He fumbled for the receiver that was on the table beside his bed. "I'm here."

"Well, you damn well shouldn't be, you asshole."

In spite of his pounding head, Dalton smiled. His friend and soon-to-be assistant didn't mince words. He never had, and Dalton guessed he never would. For that reason Dalton thought him an invaluable ally and businessman. He always knew where he stood with Tony Watson.

"You were supposed to have been here an hour ago."

Dalton managed to sit up and swing his legs onto the side of the bed. "I know, but something came up."

"Yeah, something with big tits and a hot pussy."

"Go to hell."

Tony chuckled, then his tone changed. "You wanna make our meeting for later?"

"No. Just stay where you are. Give me ten minutes."

"Well, you'd better hurry. This place is hotter than nine kinds of hell."

"You'll live," Dalton snapped, then dropped the receiver back on the hook. "Shit," he muttered as the jarring sound turned that electric saw back on in his head.

Still, twenty minutes later he was dressed and on his way out the door.

Four

" 'Bout time you got here."

"Hey, calm down," Dalton said. "You're nagging like a fishwife."

Tony snorted.

Dalton's lips quirked as he studied his old friend. Most people would conclude Tony was just an average guy. Nothing could have been farther from the truth. When Tony smiled, the dimples in both cheeks completely shot down that assessment. In addition, his mind, sharp as a steel trap, was far above average. "Exceptional" was the word Dalton liked to use.

"So what's up?" Tony asked, flashing his dynamic grin.

"I went to the bank and got the money."

"In hand?"

"You know better than that."

Tony's thin face turned sober. "Then your request could still get the ax."

"It could, but it won't."

Tony reached up and wiped the sweat that trickled down both sides of his face. "How long am I going to have to endure this heat? It's getting to me."

Dalton smiled, displaying a row of even white teeth that accented his deep tan. "That's because you're wearing so many clothes."

"Well, I'm not about to run around half naked."

Dalton shrugged. "Suit yourself." Dalton himself had dressed for the heat in a muscle shirt and frayed cutoffs.

July in Biloxi was indeed hell. It was the hottest month of the year, when the temperature soared to ninety-eight degrees and above. On days like today, when the humidity was high, being without an air conditioner proved almost unbearable.

"When the hell is that new a/c unit coming, anyway?" Tony demanded.

"As soon as I get the dough from the bank."

Tony sighed. "I guess I'll live. Meantime, show me around."

"Thought you'd never ask."

"Smart-ass."

Dalton laughed, certain he'd made the right choice in selecting Tony to work for him.

Today was the first time Tony had seen the club. In fact, Dalton had only recently hired him, having heard that he was back in the area. He had met Tony at the University of Texas, and they had become friends. But after graduation they had drifted apart, especially after Tony had settled in the Northeast.

A few months ago Tony had been laid off from his job up north. He had come south to stay with his sister and had called Dalton, asking for his help in finding employment.

Dalton had worried about working so closely with a friend, then decided that would be the best course to take. He had interviewed a lot of strangers who had been more qualified, but somehow he had shied away from them. He'd opted for someone he trusted.

Besides, Tony knew him, knew what a wild cannon he was. After all, Tony had been in on some of those late night gambling parties that had landed Dalton in big trouble. Dalton felt he'd always know where he stood with Tony, and vice versa.

Now after they had walked around the club, Dalton asked, "Well, what do you think? Do you see the possibilities?"

Tony threw him a quick look. "Are you kidding? Of course

I do, but I have to say, it needs a helluva lot of work. An architect, a designer, and a small fortune should cure all the ills."

"That's my thinking."

Dalton surveyed the large dining area, kitchen, bar, and small but serviceable dance floor. Tony was right. The place needed renovation. The air of neglect inside was actually worse than the sweltering heat outside. It was gloomy, too, with heavy tattered drapes that hid the gorgeous view of the ocean. Why anyone would want to do that was beyond him.

The remainder of the club was not much better. The kitchen, while modern enough, was filthy. But it needed more than a good scrubbing to make it operational. A portion of the dance floor had buckled, making it impossible to use as well.

Dalton and Tony batted several ideas back and forth before Dalton said, "Let's get the hell out of here." Sweat oozed from every pore of his body, saturating both his shirt and his underwear. He could imagine what Tony was feeling, dressed in a pair of cotton Dockers and sportshirt.

"Halle-damn-lujah!"

Dalton laughed. "Wimp."

When they walked outside onto the deck that ran the entire length of the club, the heat hit them in the face like the blast from a furnace.

"Damn!" Tony choked.

"You'll get used to it."

"Not in this lifetime I won't. And to think I bitched about the cold up north."

"Well, then you're in a hellava state because it ain't gonna get any better, not for a long time. Maybe October."

Tony moaned in concert with Dalton's laugh as they both sat on deck chairs. Directly in their line of vision was a paddle wheel boat that was a replica of the ones that plied the Mississippi River in the 1800s. Though it too was in a sad state of disrepair, Dalton knew it could be renovated just as easily as the club. He smiled.

For a while neither man spoke. Despite the cloying heat, Dalton was content. For the first time in his life, he felt as if he was as close to heaven as he'd ever get. He had finally settled down and was prepared to shoulder responsibility.

He smiled.

"Care to share the joke?" Tony asked, adjusting his sunglasses on the bridge of his nose.

"Nah. It's just something crazy going through my head." Dalton paused. "So tell me your gut feeling about the boat."

Tony's eyes scanned the beachfront. "When it's refurbished, it'll fit in with all the others."

Dalton made a sound. "Hell, I don't want mine to fit in; I want it to stand out, be different."

"Now, why am I not surprised?"

"Because you know me."

"Yeah, I guess I do. You always did march to the beat of your own drum."

"Ah, but that's what makes life exciting, my friend."

"Did you by any chance approach your father for the money you need?" Tony asked in his usual direct manner.

Dalton hadn't told Tony of the deep animosity that existed between him and his father. First, it was none of Tony's business. Second, he didn't care to discuss skeletons in his closet. Still, he suspected that Tony knew all was not well on the home front. Dalton realized he had no choice except to level with him now.

"The old man doesn't trust me to make a go of it," he said at last.

"So when he turned you down, you were able to just waltz into the bank and get a loan?"

"That's right." Dalton paused and rubbed his chin, his whiskers beginning to itch.

"On the property alone?"

"Well," Dalton hedged, "not exactly. My father's name helped."

"And that galled you, didn't it?"

"You're damn right, but I had no choice. They know my old man is worth a fortune and that that fortune will soon be mine."

"Is Parker *that* close to death?"

A bleak look closed down Dalton's features. "He has been for months; he just keeps hanging on."

"Is his mind as good as ever?"

"It is, and so is his tongue. Still, he's a very sick man."

"For what it's worth, I'm sorry."

Dalton released a long sigh. "Yeah, me too."

They were silent for another moment, then Tony asked, though with more caution than before, "Are you sure you're going to inherit—" He cleared his throat, then went on, "I mean, if the two of you—" Again his voice played out, and his face turned red.

"It's all right. You might as well know my father despises me." Dalton shrugged. "I came to terms with that a long time ago, but I don't think he'd ever disown me."

"Apparently the bank thinks the same thing."

"Right. They aren't worried about getting their money."

"Well, if there's anything I can do . . . "

"There isn't." Dalton smiled. "But thanks for asking."

The cellular phone rang, startling them both.

"Hell, I don't want to talk to anyone right now," Dalton said, thinking of Tanya.

Tony stood. "I'll get it."

Moments later he came back outside, his expression subdued.

"Who was it?" Dalton asked, feeling goose bumps cover his neck.

"The hospital. It's your father. He's had another attack."

Dalton maneuvered his Mercedes up the long winding drive toward the Montgomery mansion. Just after he'd turned into the drive, he'd paused and considered backing out and heading in the opposite direction.

It wasn't that he hated the house. He didn't. He hated the memories that lingered, and that still caused him to have nightmares.

Nevertheless, he had to walk inside and listen to the reading of Parker's will.

Dalton braked in front of the white-columned house but made no move to get out of the car. A feeling he couldn't define washed through him. Despite the urgent call from the hospital, his father had again thrown medical science another curve and survived three more weeks.

His funeral had taken place two days ago, with at least half the state of Louisiana in attendance. There had been flowers galore. He'd known his politician father had been a man of great respect and influence, but he hadn't realized the extent of his power until his death.

The day after the funeral, Dalton had gotten blind, stinking drunk and hadn't been in any shape to meet with the attorney. Now, however, William DeChamp, the tight-assed family lawyer, had insisted that Dalton meet him promptly at ten.

Well, it was ten-thirty, and he knew DeChamp would be hopping mad at being kept waiting, but Dalton figured it would do him good to be crossed.

Smiling at the thought, Dalton opened the door and climbed out. He noticed how the leaves on the huge moss-draped oak trees drooped; it was as though the heat had sucked their vitality from them. He could identify with that, he thought, wishing he were wearing shorts rather than the pair of jeans and chambray shirt that clung to him like a second layer of skin.

He opened the door to find Thelma walking toward him, her eyes swollen from crying. "I thought I heard your car," she said, trying to smile.

He leaned over and pecked her on the cheek. "It's going to be all right. I promise."

Thelma gulped. "I don't know what's going to happen to me and Elvira and Mack now that Mr. Montgomery's passed."

"Hey, now, dry those tears, you hear? I told you everything's going to be okay." Dalton smiled. "You trust me, don't you?"

She nodded.

"Then be a good girl and bring Mr. DeChamp and me some iced tea."

"Of course."

As Dalton made his way across the gleaming hardwood floor, he smelled furniture polish combined with the strong scent of fresh flowers.

"It's about time you got here."

William DeChamp stepped from the library into the hall. He was in his sixties with a thatch of naturally curly gray hair, green eyes, and red-toned skin that had a tendency to turn fiery when he was angry. And he was plenty angry.

"It's nice to see you, too."

"Damn you," the attorney snapped. "Don't you know it's

rude to keep people waiting? You act as if you were raised in a barn. No wonder you were an embarrassment to your father. You're nothing but white trash."

Dalton stopped midstride. His jaw clenched, and his eyes turned hard and dangerously cold. "I'd watch my mouth, if I were you."

DeChamp stiffened. "You can't threaten me."

"We'll see about that," Dalton said in that same deadly, calm voice.

The attorney turned pale, but the smug look never left his face. "In here," he demanded, pivoting on his heel and walking back into the room.

Dalton sauntered in after him and plopped down on the chair in front of his father's massive desk. He kept his gaze pinned on the attorney. Dalton hated this room. It was here, on so many occasions, that he'd encountered his father's sharp tongue and the sting of his belt. Now he had to endure DeChamp's whining contempt, but not for long.

"Look, let's cut to the chase, shall we. You don't like me, and I don't like you, so the sooner we get this over with, the sooner we can go our separate ways."

DeChamp smiled, looking like a cat that had just swallowed a canary. "It won't be that simple, I'm afraid."

"And just why not?"

DeChamp ignored his direct question and instead reached for the official-looking document. "Are you ready to hear your father's wishes?"

"That's what I'm here for. Shoot."

Bill stared at Dalton for a moment, distaste in his gaze. "You didn't give a damn about him, did you?"

Dalton sat up straighter. "I've had about enough of your insulting bullshit. You don't have a clue how I felt about my father, and furthermore, it's none of your goddamn business. You're nothing but hired help, so earn your money and read the will."

Though DeChamp's face looked like a ripe tomato ready to explode, he reached for his glasses, then began to read:

"I, Parker Everett Montgomery, being of sound mind, leave twenty-five thousand dollars each to my long and faithful servants, Thelma, Elvira, and Mack.

"To my son, Dalton Winslow Montgomery, I leave this

house. I also leave him cash money, stocks, and bonds, but *only* in the event that he finds his firstborn child, fathered through artificial insemination, and assumes his legal duties and responsibilities toward that child."

Dalton sat stunned in paralysis. Even his mind refused to function; it was as if DeChamp's words had blown it to smithereens.

The attorney had no such problem. He sat back on the chair and chuckled. "Well, now, just what do you think about them apples, boy?"

All too soon both Dalton's body and brain surged back to life.

How had his father found out he'd donated sperm five years ago for quick cash?

DeChamp stood, tossed the will at a glazed-eyed Dalton, and smiled triumphantly. "Read it for yourself. Maybe then it'll sink in."

"But how . . . ?" Dalton croaked. His throat felt as if it had been scraped with a razor blade.

"Need I remind you that your father was a very influential man who had friends all over the state, any one of whom could have provided him with that information." The glee in DeChamp's face and tone increased. "And you, of all people, should know that if the price is right, nothing is sacred."

"But what . . . what if there's no child? I mean—" Dalton was floundering but couldn't help it. "Didn't he have a contingency clause?"

"Nope. I'm sure your old man figured there'd be a lot of brats, considering you're such a stud. Right?"

Without waiting for an answer, DeChamp pivoted and walked out of the room.

Dalton lowered his head, rested it in a pair of unsteady hands, and took deep, gulping breaths. He feared he might vomit.

What now? Without the money he was ruined. He stood to lose everything. But more than that, his father had won. And he knew that wherever Parker was right now, he was laughing.

Somehow Dalton managed to stand and cross to the door, where he met Thelma carrying a tray. He walked past her, but not before he noticed her frightened, troubled eyes.

He couldn't reassure her, not when he'd just had his legs cut out from under him. Only after he reached the car, climbed inside, and slammed the door did he come to life.

"I'll beat you at your own game, old man! I don't know how, but I swear I will."

Five

Gulfport, Mississippi, July 1994

Papers littered the breakfast room table in the modest Frazier home. Leah dropped her pencil, massaged the back of her neck, and sighed.

She needed a break from the tedious budget work, but a break wouldn't solve her problem. What little money she had must be juggled and manipulated to cover as many of the expenses as possible.

She toyed idly with a burnished brown curl while her eyes drifted to the buffet in the kitchen. They brightened as they settled on a picture of her husband, Rufus, and her son, Coty. Coty's dog, Jojo, was between them.

Leah smiled. Then, feeling the prick of tears behind her eyes, she turned to look out the bay windows. The day was shaping into a lovely one, though she knew by nine o'clock the heat, combined with the humidity, would be unbearable. As long as one remained indoors, there was no problem. Unfortunately that wouldn't be the case with her.

Although it was Saturday, she would leave soon for the special care facility ten miles outside of Gulfport, where she'd sit with her husband most of the afternoon. Her friend and occasional employee had agreed to look after Coty.

Leah heard a tapping sound and noticed a woodpecker trying to peck the side of the acrylic bird feeder in the backyard. "Stop that, dummy," she muttered.

As if the bird had heard her, it transferred its beak to the hole and latched on to some seed. She watched until it flew away. She shook her head, then turned back to the task at hand. The figures in front of her hadn't changed. No matter how she calculated it, there was not enough money to go around.

Frustrated, Leah again slammed the pencil down and stared into space. It had been five years since Rufus had been diagnosed with that killer lung disease, but she still found it hard to believe or accept, despite the pain he had suffered and the heartache she had borne watching him.

Her throat tightened as her thoughts suddenly focused on her son—darling, precious, rambunctious Coty, whom she loved more than life itself, whom *Rufus* loved more than life itself. It would be only a matter of time before Coty would be without his father. But then, he'd never had a father, not in the real sense of the word.

Shortly before she had learned of Rufus's illness, Coty had been born. By the time he was three years old, Rufus's health had deteriorated to such an extent that he couldn't enjoy his son. Yet there were rare good moments they had together, such as when that photo was taken.

"Stop procrastinating," she told herself. But she couldn't bear to continue. There was no use. She couldn't manufacture money where there wasn't any, and she didn't know how to remedy her situation. If she didn't get her newly opened architectural business on the road to success, she stood to lose everything, including the house.

She had been so proud when they had bought the small brick home on Hewes. Huge gnarled pin oaks spread their branches over the street like protective umbrellas. Her backyard had a gorgeous magnolia tree and a honeysuckle-lined fence.

The interior was equally as charming, she thought, with its

hodgepodge decor and open-air effect that made her plants grow lushly.

When the phone rang suddenly, Leah raced to the buffet and lifted the receiver. She hoped the noise hadn't wakened Coty.

"Hello." Her voice came out a whisper.

"Leah, is that you?"

Her heart nose-dived. Her mother, the last person she wanted to speak to right now, was on the other end of the line. But then she couldn't remember a time lately that she wanted to talk to Jessica Gentry. Some things never changed, and their relationship was one of them.

"Of course it's me, Mama."

"Well," Jessica said in her whiniest voice, "you didn't sound like yourself. Is something wrong?"

Leah pictured her mother sitting in the living room of the big rambling house that Leah feared would someday fall down around her mother's ears. Still, her mother refused to sell or do more than basic repairs.

Jessica would have a cup of coffee and a smoldering cigarette in a butt-filled ashtray on the table beside her. She'd have on a robe, and her brown hair, dusted with gray, which made it look dirty, would be in complete disarray. Her face, relatively unlined for a woman in her sixties, would be pinched into a frown.

Her mother was extremely bitter at the hand life had dealt her. No matter how hard Leah tried, she had never been able to please Jessica. Leah had stopped trying, just as she had stopped blaming herself for the incident in her childhood that had nearly ruined her life. She gave her mother full credit for that.

"Leah, for heaven's sake, has the cat got your tongue?"

"No, Mama, I've just got finances on the brain."

Her mother made a snorting sound. "Well, you can't say I didn't tell you that you'd regret marrying a man fifteen years older than yourself, who couldn't make you a decent living."

"Stop it, Mama! Rufus is my husband, and I won't listen to you bad-mouth him, especially when he's . . . " Her voice faded. Leah couldn't bring herself to say the word *dying*.

Jessica repeated the snorting sound, but she didn't offer a

comeback. "I know you're going to the nursing home. Do you want me to keep Coty?"

"No thanks. Sophie's coming in a little while. She's going to take him to the zoo."

"Well, all right."

Leah heard both relief and anger in her mother's tone. While she didn't particularly like to baby-sit her grandson, Jessica resented anyone else's doing so.

"Mama, if there's nothing else, I need to get back to work. I'll call you later, okay?"

"One of these days, maybe you'll have time for me." With that, Jessica hung up.

Leah held the receiver away from her ear and gave in to the fury that rushed through her. One of these days she'd pay her mother back.

"Yo, anyone home?"

Leah swung around to the door that led from the garage into the kitchen. Sophie Beauvoir bounced into the kitchen with a grin on her wide mouth and a twinkle in her eyes. When she saw the look on Leah's face, however, her expression changed abruptly.

"Hey, kid, what's the matter? Is it Rufus?"

Leah forced a smile at the same time she replaced the receiver on the hook. "No, thank God, only Mama."

Sophie rolled her eyes. "Her again. Why doesn't she go take—" She broke off suddenly, as if realizing what she was about to say. "Sorry, my mouth has a tendency to overload my you-know-what."

Leah's features cleared, and she smiled. "It's all right. You can say it. Most of the time, I wish the same thing. Isn't it awful to feel that way about your mother?"

"Not in your case," Sophie countered bluntly. "I've never met a more bossy, more domineering woman—" She stopped in midsentence. "There I go again."

Leah chuckled. "Sit down. Want a cup of coffee?"

"I'd love one, only it's not decaf, is it?"

"Bitch, bitch, bitch."

Sophie grinned. "That's me, your proverbial bitch."

"Hogwash," Leah said.

When she returned to the table with the coffee, her friend

was staring out the window. Sophie, Leah thought, as she often did, would be a knockout if she would lose about twenty-five pounds. Even with her weight problem, she was a woman who was noticed, especially by men. She had gleaming black hair and eyes, thanks to her French/Cajun ancestry, that were striking against her fair skin.

"Man, your flowers have really gone crazy this spring and summer," Sophie observed.

Leah eased onto her chair and, as unobtrusively as possible, gathered the papers with figures on them and pushed them aside. "Working in the yard has proved to be my best stress reliever. Heaven knows I've certainly had time enough lately to putter."

Today even the beauty of the camellias, black-eyed Susans, and pink-and-white Cherokee roses failed to cheer Leah.

Sophie's lips stretched into a tight line. "For the life of me, I can't understand why so few jobs are coming your way. It just doesn't make sense."

"You're absolutely right. There's no reason why my phone shouldn't be ringing off the wall. Why, thanks to gambling, this area is booming like it's never done before and never will again."

A year ago Leah had left her job at Anderson, Thomas, and Swain, and gone into business for herself. She had rented an office in a complex a mile from her house and, with Sophie's promised help, despite her lack of formal training in architecture, had been sure of success in her new venture. But that hadn't happened.

At the time Leah had made the move, the situation at the firm had become intolerable because her boss had made life miserable for her. Steady income or not, she couldn't put up with Cooper Anderson's groping hands another day.

"I think Cooper might have something to do with it," Sophie suggested.

"Why do you say that?" Leah asked cautiously. She had her own suspicions; but she hadn't shared them with anyone, and she didn't intend to now.

"Because of the way you react when I mention him."

Leah didn't respond.

"If I find that he is responsible, then I'll personally denut him."

"Sophie!"

Sophie didn't so much as blink. "Well, I will."

Leah laughed. "You're good for my soul."

"And right now your soul's hurting."

The smile deserted Leah's face. "Big time. If something doesn't happen soon, I'm going to have to give up the business. But worse than that, I don't know how much longer I can keep Rufus in that facility or keep the house. Right now I feel like Humpty-Dumpty, splattered into a million pieces, unable to glue myself back together."

"His insurance has run out completely, then?"

"The company went out of business, actually, and left us holding the bag."

"Sue the hell out of 'em!"

"Oh, Sophie, that would be a mess, too. Besides, that takes time and money, neither of which I have." Leah paused and bit down on her lower lip. "Our savings are gone, too."

"You know if I can help—"

"I know, and thanks, but no thanks."

"How is Rufus? Any change?"

Leah sighed. "Only for the worse. He's growing weaker by the day. I just don't see how he can last—" Her voice broke, and she turned away.

"Well, maybe he won't, for his own sake," Sophie said softly, her own eyes filling with unshed tears.

Leah cleared her throat, then changed the subject. "We both know what the real problem is, no matter how much I'd like to ignore it. Sure, I'd like to think that Cooper was so upset about my leaving that he's bad-mouthing me all over town. And while that might be partly true, it's not the real reason.

"It's that accusation hanging over my head. That's what's keeping me from getting work these last few months."

"Damn. That old bitch is another one I'd like to get my hands on."

A smile flirted with Leah's lips. "My, but you're on a tear this morning. Are you sure Louis didn't slip something into your coffee?"

Louis Appleby was Sophie's fiancé, with whom she lived. He seemed an okay fellow, though Leah didn't know him very well.

Sophie made a face. "No, he didn't, but it wouldn't have made any difference. That old woman's been nothing but Trouble with a capital T."

"I won't argue with that. She's certainly managed to make my life miserable."

"Are you any closer to settling the matter?"

"As far as I'm concerned, it was settled when I denied taking the jewelry."

"But you haven't had any luck getting that insurance investigator off your back, right?"

"That's it in a nutshell." Leah stood, then shoved her hands down into the pockets of her shorts. "Want another cup of coffee?"

Sophie stared into her cup, which was still full. "No thanks."

Leah crossed to the coffeepot, refilled her cup, then turned around. "You know the police think I stole the jewelry," she said in a forlorn voice.

"That's ridiculous."

"I agree, but it's a fact."

"I guess if you didn't have bad luck, you wouldn't have any luck at all. Isn't that how the adage goes?"

"It is, and it fits me to a tee."

The first well-paying job Leah had been hired to do after she'd left the firm had taken a quick and unexpected twist, thus landing her in her present predicament.

Ellen Thibodeaux, a woman with more money than sense, had hired Leah as an architect and designer to modernize her antebellum home. Leah had been thrilled with the money as well as the challenge. She'd also felt confident, sure of Sophie's help.

But Sophie's other job as a clerk in an interior design shop had taken precedence, and she hadn't been available. So Leah had tackled the project and done quite well. In fact, the job had been nearly completed when the unthinkable had happened. Several valuable pieces of Ellen's jewelry had been discovered missing.

Though work crews had been in and out of the house, Leah had instantly become the prime suspect because of her dire financial straits. Leah had been mortified and furious. Both emotions, however, had been wasted efforts because she continued to remain the insurance company's main suspect, even though neither her accuser nor the company had any proof.

"What's that bozo's name?"

Leah blinked. "Who?"

"That insurance guy."

"J. T. Partridge."

Sophie harrumphed. "How could I have forgotten? He even sounds like a jerk."

Leah didn't say anything.

"So just how much of a thorn is he?"

"A big one."

Sophie frowned, then glanced at her watch. "Oops, gotta go. I didn't mean to camp here. I just ran by to make sure Coty and I were still on for the zoo."

"If you don't mind?"

"I can't wait."

"I'll have him ready in a couple of hours."

Sophie stood. "Great."

Leah walked Sophie to the door and watched her drive off; then she saw him. She froze. Lounging in his car across the street was J. T. Partridge.

From where she stood, she saw the cigar dangling like a brown lizard from one corner of his mouth. She shuddered yet couldn't look away.

He watched her as well, while he puffed on his cigar as if he didn't have anything to do.

Leah knew better.

Six

Leah's blood pressure refused to settle. Even after she'd sipped her coffee and eased back onto her chair at the table, she remained light-headed.

Damn him, she fumed. Something had to be done about that loathsome man who was determined to make her pay for something she hadn't done. If only she hadn't been blindsided, if only she'd seen it coming, she could have been prepared. But how did one prepare for being accused of a crime? Still, that situation and J. T. Partridge were only the tip of the iceberg.

Worse was that her husband was slowly dying in a nursing home and she was powerless to do anything about it. Next in line was her career. Despite her high hopes, it was on the skids.

She'd sweated blood to obtain her present status in the work world. She had attended the university, where she had obtained her B.A. degree in business before deciding to major in architecture. She had gone to class, then to work, then back to the dorm, where she'd studied into the wee hours of the morning.

Then had begun the two-year master's program, which in turn had led to a three-year internship at the Cooper firm. She'd worked hard and had believed in Cooper Anderson's promises of promotions and higher pay until she'd realized that those promises came with a price she hadn't been willing to pay. That price was her sexual favors.

Why was it men always wanted something from her that she couldn't give? Thank God for Rufus, who had been the exception. Yet she had cheated him in a way. She had never been able to love him with the same passion with which he'd loved her. While she loved Rufus, she was not *in love* with him. Though she regretted that, she couldn't help her feelings.

The heaviness inside her drove Leah back to the window.

The insurance investigator was still there.

She clenched and unclenched her fingers, feeling her nails dig into her tender palms. Why was he tormenting her like this? Was that the way he derived his satisfaction, harassing innocent people?

She wished she had the guts to walk out the door, cross the street, and whack him across his ugly face. For a moment she was appalled at her thoughts; then anger took over again. He deserved more grief than she could possibly ever give him!

Suddenly and subconsciously, she heard Rufus's soothing voice saying, "Calm down, honey. If he knows he can rile you, he'll just do it that much more." Well, Rufus wasn't here to act as a buffer between her and this vile man. She was the one in charge; yet she didn't have a clue as to how to deal with him, how to make him disappear from her life.

He was aware of her watching him. She felt that in her bones. Those eyes didn't miss anything, despite the distance between them.

Leah remembered the first time she had met him. He'd come to her door accompanied by a policeman. It had been on one of Rufus's better days, and she'd brought him home from the nursing home. He had been outside in his wheelchair, watching Coty chase a ball.

She'd been inside, baking a cake, feeling unrealistically optimistic, telling herself that the doctors didn't know what they were talking about, that Rufus was indeed going to get well and would soon be able to return home.

That was when the doorbell had rung. She had wiped her hands on a towel and dashed to the door. She'd opened it without bothering to look through the peephole first. When she'd seen the strange man standing slightly behind a tall policeman, her jaw had sagged.

"Ma'am, are you Leah Frazier?" the cop had asked.

She could find no fault with his tone; it was polite. "Yes," she said hesitantly, with her heart pumping much harder than it should have.

"I'm Officer Michaels, and this is J. T. Partridge with the Mutual Life Insurance Company. May we come in and talk to you?"

Officer Michaels's appearance didn't bother her in the least. He was rather nice looking, clean-cut, with direct brown eyes.

His companion was another story. From the moment Leah laid eyes on him, her skin crawled. The insurance agent was short, with a receding hairline and a stomach that overlapped his belt. Still, she might have ignored the sloppy way he wore his clothes, the stain on the front of his shirt, and the foul-smelling cigar that seemed attached to his lip had it not been for the insolent gaze that roamed her body.

A jolt of fear held her transfixed.

"Ma'am?" the officer pressed.

Leah gripped the doorknob tighter. "What's this all about, Officer Michaels?" she asked in an unsteady voice.

"A theft."

Leah blinked. "Excuse me?"

"A theft, lady," Partridge put in rudely.

Officer Michaels threw him a look, then turned back to Leah. "You're presently employed by a Mrs. Ellen Thibodeaux. Is that correct?"

"Yes."

"She reported a theft in which three pieces of valuable jewelry were taken from her safe."

Leah blinked again, then managed to wheeze, "When?"

"She's not sure. She just discovered it yesterday."

Today was Saturday, her day off, Leah thought irrationally, before facing the solemn-faced officer once again. She pointedly kept her eyes off Partridge.

"So why have you come here?" she asked.

"We're talking to everyone who works there."

"But I didn't take the jewelry," Leah said, feeling her voice rise in spite of her efforts to keep it level.

"Are you sure about that?" Partridge asked.

"Yes, I'm sure," Leah snapped, no longer able to ignore Partridge as he removed the cigar from his mouth with nicotine-stained fingers. She shuddered, noticing that the end of the cigar looked as though it had been chewed on by a hungry dog.

Repulsed, she averted her glance.

"We have a search warrant," the officer said.

Leah's heart plummeted to her toes as she realized that this was not a nightmare from which she would awaken. Nor were these men simply going to disappear if she blinked her eyes. This scenario was frighteningly real.

"A search warrant, but—"

"Look, lady, why don't you stop playing games and get the nice cop here the jewelry. It'll sure save a lot of hassle in the end."

"Mr. Partridge, I'm in charge here," Officer Michaels said, his voice holding a definite edge. "You'll get your chance. Until then, be quiet."

The dressing-down of Partridge did nothing to calm Leah's scattered thoughts or calm her racing heart. How on earth could this be happening? How could she even be implicated? She hadn't even known the woman had any precious jewelry. Besides, she'd never stolen anything in her life, except a package of candy, and that had been only because she'd been dared to do so. Later, she confessed to her mother; and, after receiving a whipping, she'd had to return the candy and confess to the owner. The embarrassing debacle had taught her a lesson she'd never forgotten.

"Please, don't make this difficult," Officer Michaels said. "If you're innocent, you have nothing to fear. Step aside and let us in."

The search had yielded nothing, of course, except to upset Rufus and to taint her. After the two men had left, a cold kernel of fear had replaced Leah's fury, just as it did now as she continued to watch Partridge watching *her*.

What if the police were able to trump up charges against her and make them stick? After all, she was *desperate* for money. Stranger things had happened to innocent people. Weren't the prisons supposedly full of such people?

"Mommy!"

Leah swung around and watched as her five-year-old son raced through the door, his eyes bright with excitement. "Is this the day I go to the zoo?"

She gave him an indulgent smile and held out her arms. He ran into them. "That it is, cowboy." She hugged him tightly, all the while feeling her painful thoughts recede into the background and a wholeness return to her heart.

"Ouch, Mommy, you're hurting me."

"Sorry," she said, letting his squirming body loose. She smiled down at him, thinking that he was the most beautiful child on earth, with his brown hair lightened by blond streaks and his wide green eyes, a replica of hers. But he was much more than beautiful; he was a good child.

And right now he was the only stability in her life.

J. T. Partridge knew the instant she left the window. It was time he left, too. He'd accomplished exactly what he'd set out to do, and that was to unnerve Leah Frazier.

He cranked the car, and after chomping down on his cigar, he gunned the gas pedal and drove off.

A short time later he walked into the Mutual Life Insurance building, a confident swagger to his gait. He felt it was only a matter of time until he proved Leah Frazier's guilt. By accomplishing that feat, he would save his company megabucks, which would put him in line for the promotion that he'd had his eye on for a while now.

Yep, nailing the Frazier woman would keep the nail out of his coffin. Not only did he need the promotion, he needed the bonus that would go with it. The extra dough would provide him with the means to get rid of his estranged wife.

Any woman who would hit him in the head with an iron skillet was capable of anything. Besides, she was a whore.

"Hey, Partridge," one of his co-workers called out as he entered the main office complex, "the boss wants to see you."

"Shit," J.T. mumbled under his breath.

The other fellow heard him and grinned. "What'd you do this time? Man, your ass stays in the sling, doesn't it?"

"Drop dead, Montes," J.T. said as he stalked toward the boss's office.

Seconds later he sat in front of Joseph Seasack's desk, stared into Cajun black eyes, and listened to a strongly accented voice.

"How's this case shaping up?"

"Good," J.T. said, trying to ignore the sweat that saturated his face and body.

"It damn well better be," Seasack countered.

"That Frazier woman is the one, only I haven't been able to prove it."

"What the hell are the cops doing?" Seasack stood, his big, beefy frame seeming to dominate the room.

J.T. scooted deeper onto his chair. It wasn't that the man intimidated him, it was just that the stakes in this case were so high, especially for him. If he could find that jewelry . . .

He cleared his throat. "They're talking to everyone who's been in and out of the house since day one. The problem is the job was nearly finished when the theft occurred, and most of the workers have scattered hither and yon."

"Except for Leah Frazier."

"Yeah. But she's got to be the one. She's in deep yogurt financially.'

Seasack sneered. "Deep yogurt? Jesus, Partridge."

J.T. flushed. "So, deep shit, if you will."

"Deep yogurt, deep shit; it makes no difference to me." He pressed both hands on the desk and leaned toward J.T. "I don't particularly like you, Partridge. I don't want to even be around you. But what I *do* want is the person who stole that jewelry."

Partridge stood. "I understand, and I'll take care of it. You can count on it." With that promise still hanging in the air, he turned and made his way toward the door.

"Oh, and Partridge."

J.T. turned around. "Yeah?"

"Just remember: If you don't do what's expected of you, it's not just the promotion that's at stake. It's your ass."

J.T. cleared a glob of sweat off his forehead with two unsteady fingers. "I understand."

"So I suggest you nail hers and save yours."

Seven

The summer day was glorious. Mother Nature seemed to have outdone herself as the sparkling waters of the Mississippi Sound lapped gently against the bleached white sand. Although Dalton stood at the French doors and faced that lovely sight, its beauty was lost on him.

Turning, he walked back to the couch, sat down with his long legs sprawled in front of him, and reached for his beer. He tipped his head back, gulped the last of it, then tossed the empty can in the direction of the wastebasket. He missed. It pinged against the wall.

"S-h-i-t," he drawled, slinking farther down on the couch. Then, realizing that if he shifted any more he would be on the floor, he dug the heel of his bare feet into the carpet and forced himself upright.

He was drunk, stinking blind drunk. His head reeled, and every muscle in his body protested. Yet his mind wasn't dulled to the point that he was unable to think. Damn shame, too. He wished he could reach inside his head, dig into his brain, and remove the evilness that lurked there.

He hated his own father. He hadn't admitted that unvarnished truth to himself until now. Nor had he faced the fact that his father had hated him, too, and even from the grave still had the power to hurt and control him.

"How the hell did he know about the sperm bank?"

Although Dalton asked that question aloud for the hundredth time since the funeral two weeks ago, he knew the answer: Parker Montgomery had friends in high places. At one point in his life Dalton had thought his father could walk on the water. He was in awe of Parker, as were his constituents. He had power and influence and knew how to use them.

After Dalton's mother had died giving birth to him, Parker had reared him and his older brother, Michael, alone. The brothers were complete opposites. Michael, the elder by two years, was serious like Parker and determined to follow in his father's political footsteps. Dalton was anything but serious. He was fun-loving and sensitive, until he learned that the only way to get his father's attention was to cause trouble.

Then one day that pattern of behavior had cost him dearly. He and his brother had taken their new speedboat on a trial run. Dalton had been driving the boat when another one had darted into his path. . . .

A deep moan, like that of a wounded animal, suddenly tore from Dalton's gut past his lips. The sound shattered the silence.

To this day Dalton had difficulty reliving those moments, those hours, those days, that followed the accident that had taken his brother's life. The remorse he'd felt, along with the awful things his father had said to him, were too painful to recall.

Parker had blamed him, not just for the accident, but for other things as well, such as his mother's death and his lack of ambition. But it had been the accident that had brought Parker's hostility into the open; his grief had known no boundaries.

Dalton, shouldering that blame, had pinpointed that moment as the day he died inside, the day he stopped feeling. The breach between father and son widened so that life at the mansion became unbearable. As soon as he graduated from high school, he left home and entered the University of

Texas, where he graduated five years later with a degree in business.

During that time he began to gamble with a feverish passion—much to his father's disgust because he lost far more than he won.

Even though Dalton knew he couldn't make a living as a professional gambler, he still wasn't ready to settle down behind a desk. A buddy finally talked him into working offshore on an oil rig. From there he moved to the rodeo circuit. He did that for several years, but because of his obsession with gambling, he stayed in trouble, and Parker had to bail him out.

Only after Parker suffered his first heart attack did Dalton return to Louisiana to oversee the running of the estate. Father and son fought continually, so Dalton moved into a condo and dabbled in construction work. Still, gambling kept him short of money.

He was lamenting this shortage of cash one evening with three of his friends. They had been drinking heavily, but none had been drunk, or at least Dalton hadn't thought so until ruddy-complexioned Lance Peters said, "Say, Montgomery, I know a way you can make some quick cash."

Rusty McKelvey, sitting next to Peters, threw his head back and laughed. "Jesus, Peters, don't start on that again, *pleazze.*"

The third man, Marv Sutton, who had rodeoed with Dalton and was his closest friend of the three, stared at Dalton. "You know what the hell these blubbering idiots are talking about?"

"Haven't the foggiest," Dalton said, his own lips twitching. "But if it has to do with money, then I'm all ears."

McKelvey, flexing his huge biceps, nudged Peters on the arm. "Go on, you started this shit. Tell 'em."

Peters's grin widened as he leaned forward on the table and lowered his voice. "Sperm banks."

Marv Sutton looked at Dalton with a blank face, while Dalton looked back at him, his face equally blank. Then both men stared at Peters, whose features were as innocent as a newborn baby's.

Rusty McKelvey was laughing outright.

"Hell, Peters," Dalton finally said, "I think you've finally lost it."

"Hey, man, this is serious shit. *I'm serious.*"

Before Dalton could respond, Sutton leaned closer to Peters and said, "Are you talking about what I think you're talking about?"

"Yep."

"Which is?" Dalton pressed.

"Jacking off in a jar for money, for chrissake! Hell, Montgomery, do I have to draw you a picture?"

Dalton felt his mouth go slack, then recovered only enough to throw Peters an incredulous look. "You mean to tell me that you—"

"That's right, asshole, I did. And I made seven thousand bucks doing it, too, in one year."

The silence around the table would have been total had it not been for Peters's set of dentures clicking. Whenever he got excited, they wouldn't stay in place. His original perfect set of white teeth had been lost in a motorcycle accident.

"Seven thousand dollars!" Sutton yelped, bug-eyed.

"You've got to be kidding," Dalton said, staring at Peters. "You mean someone actually paid you that kind of money to jack off?"

"You betcha—a hundred and fifty bucks a week. Healthy specimens like me donate sperm so that people who otherwise couldn't, can have babies."

"I know what the hell it's for, Peters," Dalton said, his tone filled with sarcasm, "but I didn't realize that kind of bread went along with it."

"Well, it does. But, like I said, you have to meet rigid criteria. You'd have no problem, though, not with your muscular build and those bedroom eyes."

McKelvey snickered, then slapped Dalton on the back. "Bedroom eyes, huh? Better watch ole Peters. Sounds like he might have the hots for you himself."

"Drop dead, McKelvey," Peters said.

"Let's cut the crap, okay?" Dalton said, "So you've actually been a donor?" He still wasn't convinced that Peters was telling the truth.

"I can verify that," McKelvey chimed in again. "He paid

me back some money he owed me. And hell, I knew he hadn't worked for it."

Dalton took a swig of beer. "How much can you make a month?"

"It varies," Peters said. "A fellow told me that he made as much as twelve hundred, but I never did. The most I made was eight hundred."

Dalton's interest piqued. He was desperate for money but wasn't eager to approach his father. Besides, the old man probably wouldn't give it to him.

"Hell, that blows my mind," Sutton chimed in, an amazed expression on his face.

McKelvey laughed. "Hell, it's not your mind that's supposed to blow, you idiot."

They all laughed again, except Dalton. His eyes narrowed on Peters. "So where'd you do this?"

"In New Jersey. But there's a clinic near here in Bristol."

Bristol was a suburb of New Orleans, which meant the possibilities of being seen there would be slim—if, he told himself, he decided to check out the possibilities at all. If he did, he sure as hell wasn't about to tell these men. He might as well announce it to the world.

Still, he found himself asking more questions.

"So how does it work?"

"Shit, Dalton, are you hard of hearing?" McKelvey chimed in, "Lane told you that you jack—"

"Shove it, McKelvey," Dalton snapped. "I'm asking Peters, not you."

McKelvey shrugged, then took a generous draw on his beer.

"Well," Peters said eagerly, apparently liking all the attention he was getting, "for starters, you gotta be healthy. You know, no diseases."

"Go on," Dalton pressed, his tone irritated.

"Well, if you pass the doctor's scrutiny and are accepted into the program, then there's a trial period in which your sperm is checked and rechecked."

"How long?" Dalton asked.

"That depends, I think, on the clinic. In Jersey, it was three months. In Bristol, who knows. Anyhow, you fill out a long questionnaire, including a medical history. Man, they ask you everything, practically how many times a day you take a crap."

Dalton frowned. Everyone else laughed.

"I mean those doctors take this shit seriously," Peters continued.

"So once you've passed inspection, so to speak, what happens next?" Dalton's eyes never wavered.

"It's more complicated than I'm making it. But bottom line is you're given a number, and that number, along with all your qualifications, is filed in a catalog."

"Kinda like home shopping," Marv Sutton said drolly.

Dalton ignored him, his gaze concentrated on Peters. "So in a nutshell, you donate your sperm and get paid. Then someone who wants a child might pick your number."

"Bingo. But it doesn't matter whether your number is picked; that's not your concern. You still get paid for donating your sperm."

McKelvey jabbed Peters on the arm again. "Hell, man, I can't think of anything worse than a bunch of kids running around with your ugly mug."

"Go to hell, McKelvey," Peters shot back.

"Now, now, boys," Sutton drawled. "How'd we get on this subject, anyway? No one in his right mind would do such a thing. But then we all know that Peters doesn't have a mind." When the chuckles ceased, Sutton faced Dalton. "Hell, man, you're not seriously considering—"

"Nah," Dalton interrupted. "It's interesting, but it's not for me. I'm just sorry I ever opened this can of worms."

Peters beckoned for the waiter, as if totally unaffected by their putdown, then turned to Dalton. "So, Montgomery, stay broke. Hell, it ain't no sweat off my balls."

McKelvey smirked. "I doubt you still have any balls, after all you've put 'em through."

"Shut up," Peters said, but his gaze was on Dalton. "You sure you aren't interested?"

"I'm sure," Dalton said flatly.

"Can I get you boys another pitcher?" the waitress asked, slipping up unobtrusively and thereby closing the subject.

Yet several weeks later Dalton found himself still thinking

about what Peters had said, despite his revulsion at the entire scenario. He had overcome his objections, however, and checked into the possibilities on the sly, because his financial situation worsened by the day.

It wasn't until after he suffered heavy losses, a beating in Vegas and hadn't been able to pay his debts that he'd actually gone to the clinic.

Still, it hadn't been easy, and although it had been five years since he'd walked through that door, he remembered it as if it were yesterday.

He had waited in the reception room for only a few minutes, but it seemed like a lifetime. Finally a nurse appeared and gave him a folder filled with literature on donor insemination as well as information about the clinic itself.

Finally the nurse reappeared and escorted him into the office of Dr. Jeff Hamilton, who was a big, robust fellow with twinkling gray eyes. Dr. Hamilton picked up on Dalton's nervousness, smiled, and told him to relax. Dalton tried to comply, but his stomach was tied in a tight knot.

"Think of what you're about to do as a service to humanity," Dr. Hamilton said.

Dalton almost laughed out loud at the irony in all of this. The only service that he was concerned about was getting his own ass out of trouble. But out of courtesy, he listened.

"There are many, many couples who aren't able to have children of their own for one reason or another. Young men like yourself are their only hope. Because of you, they can have a child and rid themselves of the bitterness, and oftentimes divorce, that infertility brings to a couple's life."

"That's what I hope to accomplish," Dalton responded, eager to impress the doctor and move the process along.

He must have succeeded, for Dr. Hamilton moved to the question-and-answer stage concerning his life-style, his past and present medical condition, and his use of drugs and alcohol.

After it was noted that Dalton only drank socially, the doctor smiled, then handed him a raft of papers to fill out. As Peters had said, they wanted to know everything there was to know about him and more.

Once he completed the forms, Dr. Hamilton explained that

he must take a sperm test, to check his sperm count and motility.

He passed the trial period with flying colors, and before he could come to grips in his mind with what he was doing, Dalton found himself back at the clinic, being ushered into what was referred to as the "boys" room.

"Are you all right, Mr. Montgomery?" a gray-haired nurse asked.

He couldn't bring himself to look at her. "Uh, sure. I'm fine."

"Good," she said in a professional tone. "When you're finished, leave the jar on the table. I'll be back to take care of it."

"Yes, ma'am." Dalton swallowed, then waited for her to leave before actually perusing the room, which turned out to be as big a mistake as walking into it in the first place.

"Shit," he muttered as his eyes took in the tastefully decorated room equipped with a comfortable cot, a wicker étagère piled with white fluffy towels, a large supply of sample jars, and an adjacent bathroom. Then he noticed the "inspirational" literature displayed on a table in front of the cot. Hell, he hadn't read *Playboy* and *Penthouse* since his teens.

At that moment he seriously considered bolting from the room. Everything the doctor had prepared him for in this world of emotional high tech collapsed. What it boiled down to and what he had to accept was that he was locked in a strange room where he was expected to produce semen on demand.

Dalton's hand froze on his zipper while he fought with himself to honor the commitment he'd made to these people. Granted, he was an arrogant, self-centered sonofabitch who would stop at nothing to get what he wanted, but when he gave his word, he honored it.

"So do it, Montgomery," he said, "then get the hell outta here."

With a muttered expletive, he reached for a jar, then slowly unzipped his pants. . . .

He'd kept his word, but only one time. He hadn't been comfortable with the procedure. Broke or not, he hadn't been able to continue, even though the clinic would not have accepted him had they known he would donate only once.

Jacking off in a bottle was not for him. . . .

Cursing, Dalton jerked his thoughts out of the past and back to the present. He shouldn't have been surprised by his father's will. He should've expected Parker to object to his donating the patrician Montgomery "seed" to persons unknown. And "getting Dalton to shoulder responsibility for his actions" had been one of his father's most frequent lecture topics. Now he was pursuing that tack from the grave.

Wallowing in self-pity wasn't going to fix his dilemma. Dalton forced his battered body upright, walked gingerly into the bathroom, and stepped into the shower.

Twenty minutes later he was dressed, drinking strong Cajun coffee guaranteed either to sober him or kill him. He frowned into the cup. Dammit, he had to do something. He couldn't continue to lie down and let his father get away with robbing him of his inheritance. He wasn't about to let go of his dream of owning his own casino and club. If he didn't act *now* before the field became too crowded and the competition became too intense, he might as well chuck it all.

So, what was the answer? Dalton lumbered to the window, stared out at the ocean, and tried again to push back the thought that continued to fester like a boil ready to erupt. Could he do it? Could he pull it off? Could he actually find the firstborn he had fathered? He had to try. There was no other choice.

Eight

The office was on the fifth floor of a fairly new complex in downtown Bogalusa. Two side-by-side windows overlooked the busy downtown scene. The remaining walls were covered with autographed pictures of politicians from practically every state in the Union. Some dated far back into history. At a massive desk near the window Bill DeChamp sat thumping a pencil against the wood and staring down at the sea-foam green carpet, lost in thought.

Dalton wasn't late—not yet, anyway. But the appointed time was nearing, and one of DeChamp's pet peeves was someone who wasn't punctual. He glanced at his watch, feeling his impatience mount. He figured Dalton was lollygagging on purpose. He simply had to irritate everyone just as he had irritated his father.

Because of the bad blood between Parker and Dalton, DeChamp was in danger of not getting his cut of the money. Parker had stipulated in his will that only the servants (which excluded himself, DeChamp thought with a twisted smile) were to receive their rewards immediately.

At this moment DeChamp felt as much anger toward Parker as he did toward Parker's renegade son. Dalton should've remained on the rodeo circuit in Texas. Maybe then he might have broken his neck, and none of this craziness would've happened.

DeChamp didn't feel the least remorseful for those un-Christian thoughts. The cocky bastard needed to be brought down a peg or two. Yet DeChamp had to be careful. He considered Dalton a lit fuse just waiting to go off. And if he could have avoided this meeting, he would have. When he'd read the will, he had deliberately not told Dalton that Parker had put the screws to DeChamp as well. He hadn't wanted to dilute the bombshell he'd dropped in Dalton's lap.

Now he had no choice. Dalton had to be prodded to find a brat he'd sired, so that the will could be probated, and so that DeChamp could get his money. He *needed* his money.

He glanced at his watch again just as the door opened and Dalton sauntered in, a cocky half grin on his face.

DeChamp longed to knock that grin off but refrained from letting Dalton ruffle him. He had to remain calm and rational.

"What's up, Billy?"

DeChamp cringed inside at the flippant use of his nickname. But again he held himself in check. "Serious business, that's what. Something I'm sure you wouldn't know anything about."

Dalton's eyes narrowed, but that was the only indication he gave that DeChamp's sarcastic words had struck a nerve. "Let's just get to the point, and I'll be on my way."

"All right, if that's the way you want it." Even to his own ears, DeChamp's voice sounded stuffy and unbending.

Dalton sat down and stretched his legs in front of him. "Why don't you give it a rest? You're always so damn uptight."

DeChamp jammed a hand through his thick gray hair and glared at Dalton. "Too damned bad your mama didn't live long enough to teach you some manners. Better still, your daddy should've washed your mouth out with soap long ago, then perhaps you would understand the word *respect.*"

Dalton rolled his eyes. "Look, DeChamp, we've been down this road before. It's a given that we dislike each other, but we still have to communicate on this will. So I suggest again that you get that burr out of your butt, and give your bad attitude a rest."

DeChamp's face changed from white to fiery red. "One of these days you're going to get what's coming to you."

"I'd say I already have."

A smug smile crossed DeChamp's lips. "Yeah, and I could get real excited about that, too, except it affects me and my livelihood."

"Meaning?" Dalton crossed one jeans-clad leg over the other as if he didn't have a care in the world.

"It means that at the last minute, on his deathbed, your father added a clause that stated I couldn't get a cent in legal fees, which I might add are considerable, until the child is found and you uphold your end of the bargain."

Dalton stared at him blankly, then tossed his head back and laughed. "Well, I'll be damned. So I'm not the only one whose balls the old man put in a vise. What do you know about that?"

"You're despicable," DeChamp said with venom in his voice. "But that's beside the point. All I care about is getting my money. So I've decided to do what I can to find the child—"

Dalton bolted out of the chair, sprang forward and planted both hands on the desk. His face was suddenly so close that DeChamp felt Dalton's warm breath spray his face. "Don't fuck in my business! Is that clear?"

When Dalton slammed a fist on the desk, DeChamp jumped. "If there's a kid out there who belongs to me, I'll find it in my own way and in my own good time." Dalton paused and leaned closer into DeChamp's face. "Meanwhile, you keep your nose out of it and your mouth shut. I don't want to hear that you've blabbed about this to anyone."

"Are you threatening me?"

Dalton straightened. "Yeah, I'm threatening you. Things are already fucked up enough without your bungling interference. Besides, I think you're already dipping your sticky fingers in the till."

He paused as if to let that remark soak in. "If that proves to be true, when the estate is settled, you're dead in the water. You won't get a dime."

With that he turned and stomped out of the room.

DeChamp slumped in his chair then slapped his hand against his pocket, looking for his bottle of high blood pressure medicine. It wasn't there. He fought the panic that rose like bile in the back of his throat.

Sweet Jesus. Was Dalton clairvoyant? DeChamp hadn't taken a penny from the estate, but he had considered doing just that. No longer. He'd best forget that idea for now.

Damn Parker for punishing him along with his renegade son. He shouldn't have been surprised; after all, he wasn't from the house and lineage of David.

DeChamp smirked at his analogy. But it was the truth. He'd been a pauper before he'd married into money. That hadn't counted with Parker. In his own way Parker had been as snobbish as many of the other s.o.b.'s in this town who thought he wasn't good enough.

DeChamp gritted his teeth. As if this latest debacle weren't enough, he had his mistress to worry about, along with his wife, who was behaving strangely, as if she might have caught on to his latest shenanigan.

He had to do something about Sylvia, his mistress, now that their relationship had turned sour. But what? His indecision stemmed from the fact that he hadn't wanted the affair to end; she had the best tits of anyone he'd ever been with, and she knew how to use them to full advantage. His just thinking about their ripe fullness brought on an erection.

But pregnant!? The thought of that caused his erection to shrivel. "Dammit," he muttered, furious that he was put in this position.

If Sylvia was indeed pregnant and went through with her threat to tell his wife, Terri, he was in trouble way over his head. He had assumed things couldn't get worse, when some recent bad investments had put his finances in serious jeopardy. If his wife found out about that, she'd make him wish he were dead. Terri showed no mercy where money was concerned, since she had been the one with all the capital initially.

This crisis with his mistress would certainly send her over the edge. He couldn't let Dalton intimidate him. *To hell with Dalton!*

DeChamp had to do whatever was necessary to get his money.

Leah stared at the shrunken figure of her husband as he lay on the bed, his eyes closed, though she wasn't sure he was asleep. When she had married him, he'd been a robust man with dark hair, calm gray eyes, and a gentle smile. Now he was a shriveled man in both body and spirit.

His mind was still sharp, but he had told her several weeks earlier that he was ready to die, that he was tired of fighting a losing battle.

Leah blinked back the unwelcome tears, stood, and walked to the window. Early on, she had cried until she'd been sure there weren't any more tears inside her. But now she wouldn't give in to them. Rufus wouldn't want that. Seeing her cry would upset him, and the last thing she wanted to do was add to his pain and grief.

The thought of giving Rufus up became more unbearable by the day. He was her rock, her mainstay. Until he had come into her life, she hadn't had any stability. Her family was poor and, partly because of that, totally dysfunctional.

As a result, her formative years had been a nightmare. Her father had died of emphysema when she was in her teens. Her mother had worked in a school cafeteria to earn a meager income. She had also taken boarders into their rambling old home.

It had been shortly after that that the unthinkable had happened. . . .

Rufus moaned. Leah forgot the past, swung around, and rushed to his side. By the time she sat on the chair beside the bed, he had quieted.

"I'm here, darling," she said soothingly, stroking the side of his face with the back of her hand.

If only she had been able to talk to him, *really* talk. There was so much of herself she had kept from him, including her traumatic childhood. Only her mother knew, and to this day, that subject between mother and daughter was taboo.

Jessica's only concern had been that Leah make something of herself, that she succeed at all costs. Jessica had worked hard to make sure that Leah had the chance to go to college. Jessica had dreams of Leah's becoming a high-profile attorney.

That, however, hadn't been Leah's dream. She had found her niche in the arts, concentrating on architecture and interior design. It was only after she had graduated from architectural school, landed her first job, and met Rufus, who worked in a rival firm, that she had learned to trust a man.

Her mother, however, hadn't wanted her to marry Rufus.

"Have you lost your mind, child?" she remembered her mother asking. "Why, he's much too old for you. Fifteen years, for heaven's sake."

"That's not important," Leah had responded.

"Well then, what about the fact that he's unable to support you as you deserve?"

"I can support myself."

"Not on what beginning architects make, and you know that."

Leah had known exactly what she was getting at. Jessica felt that Leah owed her some of life's amenities for the sacrifices that she had made on Leah's behalf.

Leah had refused to capitulate, although she planned to help her mother financially when and if she could. Material things had never been important to Leah, so she had married Rufus anyway and had never been sorry. His gentleness had taught her that love wasn't synonymous with fear and pain. He loved her with all of his heart and yet demanded little.

However, when he wanted a child, she was willing to have one, only to find that his low sperm count prevented her from getting pregnant.

Finally, after agonizing over alternate choices, they had decided to go the donor route.

"At least a part of you will live in the child," Rufus had reasoned with a brave smile.

Leah had never regretted having a child, even though she would soon be left with the responsibility of rearing him alone.

"Mrs. Frazier."

Leah hadn't realized the door had opened. She looked up

into the face of one of the nurses who regularly attended to Rufus.

"Hello, Debbie." Leah forced a smile.

"I'm sorry to disturb you, but you have a phone call at the front desk."

"I do?" she asked inanely, her mind scrambling to think who could be calling her besides her mother. Oh, God, had something happened to her son? Rarely did Jessica keep Coty, but this afternoon, out of the blue, Jessica had called and asked if Leah would bring Coty over, that she planned to make a batch of cookies and wanted his help.

Leah wasn't about to look a gift horse in the mouth, as it would give her a chance to spend more time with Rufus.

"Is it a woman?" she asked, her voice trembling.

"I don't know. Emily, at the front desk, asked me to pass the word to you."

"Thanks, I appreciate it."

Leah followed the nurse out of the door and made her way toward the office.

"Thanks, Emily," Leah mouthed before saying a cautious "Hello?" into the receiver.

"Mrs. Frazier?"

"Yes," Leah said cautiously in response to the man's voice, which she could not readily identify.

"This is Larry Mason, at the bank."

Silence.

"Er . . . I've been instructed to call and tell you that if you don't pay us some money soon, we're going to foreclose on your home."

Leah's first reaction was red-hot fury. How dared he call her *here* and tell her something like that? The nursing home was not the place to conduct personal business.

"I can't discuss that now," she responded in a terse tone.

Mason sighed. "I do apologize for calling you at the nursing home, but we've had no luck in reaching you at home."

Like hell you haven't! she wanted to shout. "Look, I'll come to your office tomorrow. Will that suffice?" Her tone was cold.

"Uh, yes, that will be just fine."

Without bothering to say good-bye, Leah hung up, feeling

her face suffuse with color under Debbie's watchful eyes. "Is everything all right?"

Leah bit down on her lower lip. "No, but it's nothing I can't take care of." Which is a bold-faced lie, she added silently as she made her way back down the corridor toward Rufus's room. She took several deep breaths and felt her control return.

What was she going to do? Some way, she had to keep Rufus in this facility. She couldn't take care of him at home, nor could she afford around-the-clock care, which was more costly. Besides, this place was perfect. It was close to the house; it was small; and patients were treated as they ought to be treated. For those who still had the mental and physical capacity to appreciate beauty, the grounds were landscaped with flowers and trees.

Inside the rooms were tastefully and brightly furnished, unlike the typical hospital setting of most facilities. To add to the warmth, Leah tried to keep fresh flowers in the room at all times.

Oh, Rufus, I want you well again, her heart cried. I want us to laugh again, to make Coty laugh, to take the dog and run with our son on the beach, to picnic, do all the things we used to do. Dear Lord, I don't want our life to change!

It had changed, and nothing would ever be the same again. Her husband was dying. Her child would be fatherless. She didn't have any work. And she didn't have any money.

She was down, and her life was in total disarray. Somehow, though, she would find a way to survive. She always had.

Mustering all her courage, Leah calmly walked into Rufus's room, lifted his hand, and cradled it against her damp cheek.

Nine

Dalton had almost walked out of Eddie Temple's office. Later he didn't know why he hadn't, except there had been something solid beneath the detective's sloppy, sleazy appearance that had kept Dalton on his chair. Maybe it was the man's sharp, hungry eyes and confidence in himself. Dalton had never been one to judge a book by its cover because he himself had so often been prejudged that way. That was why he gave Eddie Temple the benefit of the doubt and kept his butt on the chair. Besides, this tall, thin, private dick had come highly recommended.

"So, what's on your mind, Mr. Montgomery?"

Dalton knew that what he was going to say sounded strange. Hell, it was bizarre! But he needed help. He couldn't accomplish this awesome task by himself. He needed *professional* help.

"You having second thoughts?" Eddie asked, patting the longish hair that was plastered to his head except where his earlobes poked through.

Dalton fought the urge to smile. "Yeah, you might say that."

"It's a woman, right?"

"What?"

Eddie grinned, then shifted on his squeaky chair. "A woman. You want me to get you out of a jam with a woman."

"Is that your area of expertise, Mr. Temple?"

"Ah, hell, call me Eddie."

"All right, Eddie."

"That and others, too. Listen, I'm a jack-of-all-trades, and if the money's right, I'll do most anything."

"Even if it's illegal."

Eddie held out his hands. "Like I said, if the money's right—"

Dalton got the message. Still, he hesitated, letting his eyes roam around the room. Typical detective office, he thought, except a little dirtier and more disorganized than most. Again the word *sleazy* came to mind, but if the man did indeed know his business, then it didn't matter if he worked in a pigsty or a palace.

"I have to tell you," Dalton finally said, "that what I'm about to ask you to help me with is clearly off the beaten track."

"How so?"

Dalton figured he'd dilly-dallied long enough. "Five years ago, I earned money by donating sperm to a donor bank."

"So?" Eddie said.

Dalton went on, "Anyhow, the upshot of it is that now I need to find a child that was conceived from my sperm."

This time Eddie Temple's mouth opened wide enough to catch most anything. Then he whistled.

"I warned you. So, you still interested?"

"You bet your sweet ass, 'cause it's gonna cost you."

"I'm used to that," Dalton said sarcastically.

"I need to know everything you know."

Dalton snorted. "You just heard it. Like adoptions, donor programs are almost always anonymous. Donors and parents never even learn each other's names. Donors are just numbers."

Eddie's expression perked up. "You said almost." He stressed the word *almost*. "You did say that, right?"

Dalton nodded.

"So that means that it's not impossible, just damned near it. Tell me, why do you want to find the child? Usually it's

the other way around—the child wants to find the parent."
Eddie grinned. "You know what I mean."

Dalton didn't share Eddie's humor; his face remained
tight. "For me, it's a matter of life and death."

"The death being that of your father, right?"

"So you do read the newspapers?"

Eddie's grin widened. "Every single day."

"So can you help me?" Dalton asked, his tone sharp, suddenly tiring of this weird man.

"Don't know, but I can do some snooping around the medical community, then talk to a lawyer friend who specializes
in tracking down adoptee's real parents. I'll see if he can
help."

"Meanwhile, any suggestions as to what I can do?" Dalton
asked. "I can't just sit on my butt and do nothing."

"Use your connections—doctors, lawyer, anyone
who might help. Call 'em, see what they have to say, if anything. I'll also visit the clinic, though I figure it'll be a waste
of time. They'll be as tight-lipped as a virgin on her first
date."

"Funny."

Eddie laughed. "Kinda thought so myself. But I'll make a
stab at the clinic, nevertheless."

Dalton didn't respond, except to get up. "I'll expect to
hear from you soon."

When Dalton reached the door, Eddie said, "What about
my money? We never—"

"If you come through, I'll come through with plenty."

Three days later Dalton walked into his condo to the ringing
of the phone. He dashed across the room for it, hoping it
was Eddie Temple or his doctor friend, Kirk Philemon, from
Austin.

"Yeah," Dalton said into the receiver.

"Hey, old buddy."

"Kirk, is that you?"

"Yep."

"The connection's not too clear, and I wasn't sure."

"It's probably the cordless phone. Half the time the damn things don't work."

"It's okay; I can hear you well enough."

"So what can I do for you? Sorry I wasn't available when you called the other day. I was at a convention in Frisco. When my nurse said you called, I couldn't believe it. It's been a long time."

His friendship with Kirk went back to their University of Texas days. They had gotten drunk and into trouble together. In fact, it had been Kirk who'd introduced him to gambling. Even though they hadn't remained in close contact over the years, the relationship had remained intact.

Besides, Dalton had pulled Kirk's chestnuts out of the fire on many occasions, so it shouldn't have been difficult to ask him for help. But it was; it galled him, actually. Damn his father.

"I hope it's not been too long to ask you to do me a favor," Dalton said at last, hearing the uneasiness in his own voice.

"Never. After all, I owe you."

"Well, I'm going to sound like I've gone off the deep end, but bear with me. I need to know if you or maybe a colleague might be able to give me some ideas on how I could break or penetrate the code of silence on donor insemination?"

Kirk whistled.

"I warned you. When I fuck up, I do it up right, don't I?" Dalton muttered into the silence.

"That you do, my friend, that you do."

Dalton sighed. "So are you saying forget it? If you are, don't bother, because I can't. My inheritance's at stake."

"Your old man socked it to you this time, huh?"

"That's putting it mildly. I owe the bank megabucks, and without Parker's money, I'll lose everything."

This time Kirk's sigh filtered through the receiver. "I'll do what I can, but I won't promise anything. This donor business is a hard nut to crack." He chuckled. "No pun intended."

Dalton didn't return the laughter. "Anything you can do will be more than appreciated."

"I'll be in touch. Meanwhile take care."

"Thanks for everything."

Dalton hung up, marched into the kitchen, opened the refrigerator, and grabbed a beer. He was drinking too much, he knew, but right now he didn't give a damn. It dulled the pain of his father's betrayal, and at the same time, reinforced his determination to find his child, *if there was one.*

He could only pray that there was.

Ten

Rain dripped through the canopy of the oak leaves as Dalton pulled into the parking lot at the donor clinic. The town, a bedroom community of New Orleans, was modern and charming.

He'd had a woman friend who had once lived here, and he'd spent a lot of time in her company. But the town didn't hold any appeal for him; in his mind it was associated with the donor clinic, which was a period in his life that he had hoped he would never have to think about again.

If only he'd stopped to think what Parker would do if he had ever uncovered his secret. Would he have done things differently? Probably not. One of his faults was his impatience. He'd needed money at the time, and donating his sperm had seemed an easy enough way to get it.

Dalton remained behind the wheel of his Mercedes for another moment and watched as the rain pelted against the windshield. The flash flood wouldn't last long, then the sun would come out and parboil everyone it touched.

A bitter taste invaded his mouth as his thoughts rehashed the reason he was at the clinic. Last night he had received a phone call from the detective.

"I dropped by the clinic," Eddie had said without preamble.

Dalton had just returned from the club, where he and Tony had been in a long business discussion. He'd been tired and hungry and restless. But when he'd heard Eddie's words, he had almost bolted off the couch, his weariness dropping off him like a frayed coat.

"And?" Dalton asked.

"Zilch."

"Damn."

"Ah, but it's just strike one. We're not out yet."

"That's easy for you to say," Dalton snapped, feeling the weariness wash through him again.

"I figured I wouldn't get to first base with those people. I pointed that out, remember?"

"So you did. Now what?"

"Well, I've still got my other sources working. Meanwhile, I think you oughta drop by the clinic and see what impact that has on them."

"I can tell you that already. I more or less welshed on the deal, which didn't exactly endear me to them."

"I'm sure that's true," Eddie said on a sigh, "but it's worth a try. The clinic is the key here. Unless we get their cooperation to some extent, cracking this thing is going to be well nigh impossible."

"No shit," Dalton muttered, more to himself than to Eddie.

The detective merely laughed, then said, "Drop by there tomorrow. Call me."

That ended the conversation, and here he sat, staring at the clinic as if it were some kind of monster who would swallow him the instant he walked through the door.

"Get a grip, Montgomery."

Following those terse words, Dalton jerked open the door and made his way toward the building.

The doctor's face was hostile when Dalton stated his purpose. They stared at each other for another long moment.

"I should have you thrown out of here."

"Why don't you?" Dalton asked.

"Because that's not the way we do things around here,"

Dr. Mayo said, "but the information you're demanding is not available under any circumstances."

"I could get a lawyer, you know," Dalton said, hoping the bluff would have an effect.

Mayo shrugged. "Go ahead, get ten lawyers. None of them will do you any good." His eyes narrowed. "Mr. Montgomery, the law is on the clinic's side. The records are private and cannot be opened unless it's a life or death matter. And I doubt that's the case with you, even though you say it is. But let's say it was, then a judge would still have to order the records unsealed." He paused. "If you'll recall, you signed an agreement to that effect when you participated in the donor program. That agreement also called for you to provide a series of donations, which according to your file, you failed to deliver."

"Look, Doctor, save the rhetoric. I know the drill, and I know how you feel about me. I also know my request is unorthodox. Still, when it gets down to it, the sperm is mine, and maybe, just maybe, a court in this land might recognize that."

"Maybe, but I can promise you that you'll be an old man before that happens."

Dalton blanched, then doubled his hand into a fist.

"Give up this crazy idea, Mr. Montgomery. I don't know why you want to know who your offspring is, and I don't care. The law is the law, and that's that."

A muscle ticked in Dalton's jaw. "We'll see about that, Doc. We'll just see about that."

Dalton, walking out toward the reception area, experienced the same mix of feelings he'd felt years ago after donating his sperm. Those feelings ranged from fury and pain to fear and anxiety. His back was against the wall, and he well knew it. But that didn't mean he wasn't going to stop trying to knock down that damn wall.

The waiting room was deserted. The receptionist looked up with a smile, only to have that smile disappear when she saw the scowl on his face.

"Is there anything I can do to help?" she asked in a husky voice.

Out of the corner of his eye, he caught the woman's sympathetic expression, and something made him stop in his tracks and stare at her. His gut churned.

She attempted another smile. "Apparently your visit didn't go well." Then, as if she realized she might have overstepped her bounds, she lowered her head, which was too bad, Dalton thought, as her blue eyes were large and expressive.

He sidled up to her desk and made himself smile. "As a matter of fact, it didn't."

Her smile eased into a frown. "Sorry about that."

She was pretty enough, with stylishly cut hair and a nice figure, as much as he could see of it. He eased onto the edge of her desk and casually swung his booted foot, his smile still intact. They stared at each other for a moment, then he said, "Me too."

She tipped her head sideways. "You sure I can't do anything to help?"

It was in that moment that a siren went off inside Dalton's head. Maybe she could get into those files for him. No, while he was definitely intrigued by the prospect of eliciting her help, he couldn't do it. He didn't want to get her into trouble and cause her to lose her job.

"You're sweet, but no."

She cocked her head to the side, and her smile widened. "Are you sure? Who knows what I might be willing to do if . . . " Her voice trailed off.

Dalton's lips twitched at her obvious meaning. He'd have to be a monk not to be flattered by the signals that radiated from her. "What's your name?"

"Joan Simmons."

"Well, Joan Simmons, maybe some other time."

This time her smile turned to a pout. "You don't know what you're missing," she said boldly.

"I'm sure." Dalton winked, then added, "Stay outta trouble, you hear?"

Later, as he entered his condo, his thoughts were still on the young woman. Too bad the circumstances and the timing were off. She might've been fun to date, but the last thing he wanted was to get involved with a woman, even for one evening. His sexual urges would definitely have to stay in cold storage until this matter was settled.

The phone rang, jarring him back to harsh reality. He reached for the receiver.

"Hey, Dalt, it's Kirk."

His heart missed a beat. "Find out anything?"

"Are you kidding? Hell, it'd be easier to break into Fort Knox than get information on donors. That's top-secret stuff. Now, if you were the child looking for the parent, then you'd have a whole helluva lot more leverage.

"But this way, I'm afraid you're screwed. I couldn't get to first base. I know two doctors who work in a clinic, and both said to tell you to forget it, that you'd be wasting time and energy." Kirk paused and took a deep breath. "Sorry, old buddy. I knew you were counting on me, and I hate like hell to let you down."

"I appreciate all the trouble you went to," Dalton said, feeling frustration lodge in his belly like a stone.

"What are you going to do next?"

"I have a detective helping me, not that I think he's worth a shit."

"I know patience is not your strong suit, but in this case, you're going to have to develop some."

"I know, I know."

"Look, again, I'm sorry I struck out. Keep me posted, okay?"

"Sure," Dalton said, though he knew he wouldn't. "Thanks for trying."

Once the conversation had ended, Dalton paced the floor. Two strikes, but it wasn't over till the fat lady sang; she hadn't sung yet, but a perky brunette had. In fact, she was singing in his ear loud and clear.

He lifted the receiver and punched out the clinic's number. After two rings he heard her say hello.

"Joan?"

"Yes."

He heard the hesitancy in her voice. "This is Dalton Montgomery."

"Oh, hi."

Dalton smiled, picking up on the sudden warmth in her voice. "How 'bout dinner tonight?" he asked without preamble. She was hot and ready, and he saw no reason to beat around the bush.

"I'd love that." She told him where she lived.

"Good. I'll pick you up at eight."

Joan eased down onto his lap, then lifted his hand to her breast. Dalton felt it swell and the nipple poke into the palm of his hand.

He'd been seeing Joan for over a week now and had yet to take her to bed. That must surely be a record for him, especially as she'd come on to him with every weapon in her arsenal. Despite her great body, her gift of gab, and even her sweetness, he simply wasn't interested in taking her to bed. He wanted one thing and one thing only from her, and that was help in obtaining his files.

Which proved he was a first-class shit.

But that couldn't be helped. He had reached the desperate stage, and so apparently had she, only in a different way. She squirmed in his lap.

"We could make love right here in the office, you know," she whispered against his lips.

They had been to dinner, and the fact that she'd had to stop by the office to pick up a package that she had forgotten to mail had played into Dalton's hands. That was the break he'd been waiting for.

"Yeah, I guess we could, only I don't think that'd be a good idea."

She pulled back. "I'm beginning to think I don't turn you on."

Dalton held back a sigh. "Look, Joan, you turn me on all right, only—"

She bounded off his lap, then glared down at him. "Only what?"

"I need your help."

She gave an unladylike snort. "Is that what we're all about?"

"Partly."

Her eyes widened. "Well, at least you're honest."

"You did say that you'd be willing to help me, didn't you?"

"Only because I was lusting after your body."

In spite of himself, Dalton's lips twitched. "So does that offer still hold?"

She hedged. "What exactly do you want from me?"

"I donated sperm here about five years ago."

She didn't look surprised at all. "I figured as much. So is that a problem? I mean—"

"I regretted it, so I sorta didn't live up to my contract."

She looked confused. "So why are you worrying about this now, after five years?"

"Because if I've fathered a child or children, I want to know it."

"Why?"

"My conscience," he lied. "If I've fathered at least one child, I want to know it. I can't speak for other men who've been in this situation, but for me, I feel responsible for the kid or kids who were born with my genes. In fact, the thought is working on my psyche big time. That's all I think about. So, I want to find at least one of them, the firstborn, preferably, and get to know him or her."

Joan's eyes widened. "You're kidding me?"

"I've never been more serious in my life."

He must've done a good sales job because her expression changed from one of blatant skepticism to cautious sympathy. "Somehow I never pegged you for fatherhood and the white picket fence bit."

"At one time, I wasn't interested in those things. Only now, I'm having second thoughts. I can't help wondering if my child is well and happy." He looked at her. "It's that simple and just that complicated."

She sighed. "What do you want me to do?"

"Help me find my child." When she didn't respond, he pressed on, "This clinic is bound to have the information. In a lot of clinics, I know the records aren't up to par, that they are either nonexistent or destroyed. But not here. This clinic seems to go by the book. I'm right, aren't I?"

"Yes." The warmth in her tone had cooled considerably.

"So, how does one go about finding the match?"

"You don't, not here," Joan said. "Not all of it, that is."

Dalton's stomach twisted. "What does 'not all of it' mean?"

"We know the donor by number only. The doctor who ordered the sperm knows the patient by name. That way everyone is protected."

His stomach twisted again. "Are you saying there's no way to match the two?"

"No." She wet her lips. "Not entirely. In that locked cabinet over there is a book with your donor number. That's the first step."

Dalton went weak all over. "Do you have the key?"

"It's in the top drawer of the desk where you're sitting," she answered with a slight quiver in her voice.

You really are a shit, Montgomery, he told himself again. But that didn't stop him from asking, "Will you open it?"

"Yes."

Except for the ticking of the wall clock, the room was silent as she bent next to him, pulled open the drawer, and removed the key.

He watched as she opened the file cabinet, removed a large ledger-type book, then scribbled a number on a notepad.

"What's next?" Dalton managed to ask, his heart hammering so loudly inside his chest, he suspected she could hear it.

"We check the safe to see if there's a postcard confirming a pregnancy that has your donor number beside it."

He must have looked as stunned as he felt.

Joan sort of smiled. "Yeah, Dr. Mayo receives a postcard from the doctor who gets sperm from this clinic each and every time one of his patients gets pregnant."

Dalton swallowed. "Does the doctor's address happen to be on that card?"

"Of course."

He blew air from his lungs. "So how are they filed, those postcards you're talking about?"

"By dates. We'll have to look for the earliest postal date for your firstborn. If you scored, that is."

"Scored?" His voice sounded nothing like his own. "You mean it's possible I might *not* have fathered a child?"

"You bet that's possible. Happens a lot, actually. For some women, AI simply doesn't work. Even if it does, they sometimes miscarry. Another possibility is that your number just didn't get chosen. Those are just some of the reasons why there may not be a postcard with your number on it."

Joan turned then and walked to where a picture hung on the wall. She swung the picture back to reveal a small safe. After opening it, she withdrew two long boxes.

Dalton stood beside Joan as she thumbed through the cards dated approximately one year after he'd donated his sperm.

When she neared the end of the stack with no results, Joan faced Dalton. "Looks like we're going to come up empty-handed."

"Keep looking," he said, sweating. "There are a few more in the file."

"You know I can get canned for this?"

"I know, and I promise I'll make it up to you."

"If I get the ax, it'll take a hell of a lot of making up."

"Keep looking," Dalton said again, hating that desperate note in his voice.

Joan lifted out the last card, her eyes widening.

Dalton went rigid. He opened his mouth, but nothing came out. He could only stare at her, but she wasn't staring back. She was reading the card, then she looked up and smiled.

"Paydirt! You're a father!"

Dalton's legs almost buckled beneath him.

Eleven

The next day Dalton stood on the deck of his boat, trying to envision what the ship would look like when it was converted into a casino, but his attention span was short; he couldn't keep his mind on business. His mind and body were in a state of heightened excitement.

He had a *child,* someone who was not just a figment of his imagination, but a flesh-and-blood human being charging around someone's household. Though the words Joan had read from the card were branded in his memory, he still couldn't quite come to grips with the hard, cold facts.

"Dr. Todd Raymond from Forest County, Hattisburg, Mississippi, confirmed a pregnancy from donor number 4173."

Dalton had remained upright on willpower alone. Then he'd taken several gulping breaths, frantically telling himself that grown men didn't faint; but he'd wanted to sink to his knees, though for what exact reason he couldn't have said. He hadn't know if he was relieved or disturbed that he'd sired a baby.

Now, as he continued to look over the water and the bodies already sunning on the white sand, he still didn't know. Maybe it was because he continued to reel from the knowledge that the doctor who had inserted his sperm into a strange woman was only about a hundred miles away.

Talk about fate smiling on him for once in his life. Still, a
niggling voice at the back of Dalton's mind warned him not
to get too cocky, that the recipient of his sperm might actually live in Kalamazoo, Michigan. Somehow, he didn't think
so. He suspected that she, too, lived nearby.

At the moment, he was waiting for Eddie either to call or
show up with information on the doctor. Once he had that
information, he could concentrate on the next move, which
was to find the woman. "Hey, Dalt, there's a man here to see
you."

Dalton swung around. Tony stood in the doorway of the
club. All morning they had been going over plans and ideas
for renovation.

"Tell him to come out here," Dalton said.

Seconds later Eddie Temple lumbered across the dock and
onto the deck of the boat, all the while wiping sweat from his
face with a less-than-white handkerchief.

"God, it's hotter than hell."

"A little sweat's good for the soul," Dalton said, unaffected in his standard attire of cutoffs and tank top. "You're
as bad as my assistant; you wear too many clothes."

Eddie grimaced while perusing Dalton. "If I dressed like
you, how many jobs do you think I could get?"

"You got a point. So what did you find out?" Dalton
cleared his throat, his voice sounding as tight as his gut felt.

"For starters, Dr. Raymond is dead."

"Damn!"

"Now, don't go gettin' yourself riled."

"Tell me one good reason why not," Dalton demanded,
cursing the sweat that popped out on his forehead.

"Well, for one thing he was just a family doctor who prac-
ticed alone."

"You mean a regular GP can do that sort of thing?"

"Of course he can. According to my source, donor insemination is a simple and easy procedure. It doesn't take an ex-
pert or high-tech equipment to do it."

"Is that good or bad?"

"I'd say it's good, because we only have one person to
deal with."

"Only that person happens to be dead." Dalton couldn't
mask the frustration or the anger in his tone.

"Still, all isn't lost. I found out that when Dr. Raymond

became ill, he moved his practice from a strip mall to his house. He saw very few patients during that time, but apparently your sperm recipient was one of them."

Dalton's insides jolted back to life. "How did you find that out?"

"How many times do I have to keep reminding you that snooping is my job?"

"Right."

Eddie cut him a sharp look, then went on, "Since he wasn't part of a group of doctors, his records are still at his house." Eddie's chest now protruded as if the information he'd just imparted were worth its weight in gold.

"No shit?"

"No shit."

Dalton grinned. "You know, for a little nothing I could kiss you."

Eddie backed up. "You do and I'll deck you, you sonofabitch."

Dalton laughed outright. "Don't go gettin' your dander up. It's just a figure of speech. So go on. How do you know the records are there? You couldn't have seen them."

"I didn't, but I did go to his house. When his widow, who by the way is still a sharp old broad, came to the door, I made up a story."

"What kind of story?" Dalton put in, his head beginning to pound like a sledgehammer.

"Well, I told her that my wife had been one of his patients and that I'd like to have her records because she has other problems now that her past problems might have a bearing on."

"And what did she say?"

"She said that she was leaving town and that when she came back, she'd talk to her attorney about releasing the records."

"Thank God she didn't destroy them when he died."

"That's definitely in our favor, but getting in to look at them is a horse of a different color."

"You don't think you'll ever set foot inside the door, do you?"

"I figure about the same chance as a snowball lasting in hell. When she calls her attorney, he'll tell her that my wife's doctor will have to request the records."

"Or," Dalton added, "he might say don't do one damn thing because you and your wife might be considering a lawsuit."

"You hit the nail on the head."

"So that only leaves one thing."

"And what is that?" There was a suspicious edge to Eddie's voice as he smoothed down a piece of plastic-looking hair.

"You're going to have to break in and get the info I need."

Eddie's face lost its color. "Like hell!"

Silence fell between them. In the distance Dalton heard a seagull's cry and a woman's shrill laugh, but he didn't let those noises distract him from his eye contact with Eddie. "Are you saying you refuse to break in?"

"You bet your sweet ass I am. Man, breaking and entering is a felony, in case you didn't know." Eddie was visibly upset.

"If I remember correctly, you told me if the price was right, you'd do anything."

"Not if it costs me my license and lands me in the slammer, I bloody well won't."

Dalton stared at Eddie speculatively before saying in a hard but emotionless tone, "If you won't break in, then I will. But as far as getting paid, forget it. The way I see it, I wasted my time hiring your chickenshit ass."

"You can't cheat me outta my money," Eddie said frantically.

"You hide and watch, pal."

Dalton hugged the commode while his stomach lurched, then gurgled, but there was nothing left to come out. He was positive only the lining of his stomach remained, but he wouldn't swear to that.

Somehow he mustered the strength to get to his feet and lean over the bathroom sink. Only after he'd splashed his face with cold water and brushed his teeth did he dare look at himself in the mirror.

His eyes were sunk so far back in his head that they were

almost impossible to see. His skin . . . well, it seemed no longer tanned and healthy. Instead it appeared pasty and drawn, as if he'd been locked in a closet for weeks.

He looked like warmed-over piss, he told himself before turning back on his image and making his way into his makeshift office in the club. He picked up his car keys and headed for Eddie's place to hear the detective's latest news.

As he drove, he reviewed the recent events again and again. He had to get hold of himself and begin to think logically.

It had been several days since he'd broken into the deceased doctor's house in the middle of the night and rummaged through every folder in the cabinet. Finally he found the file with his donor number and the recipient's name. He was still a basket case, considering the chance he'd taken.

His announcement to Eddie that he would break into the house had been a knee-jerk reaction. But when Dalton had thought about it, dissected the idea from every angle, he'd found he had had no choice but to go through with it. He'd been scared, though, terribly scared.

He couldn't believe he had stooped that low and broken the law. He wished now he hadn't been so desperate for money that he'd walked into that clinic. He wished that he'd been turned down flat. He wished that he'd known that that time in his life would come back to haunt him. God, he wished for so many things.

But there was nothing to be done about all that now. The past was past. Only it wasn't—not really.

It had caught up to him, with the potential to destroy his life.

Dammit, he couldn't go soft now. This was business, nothing more, nothing less. If he finally found the child, he had no intention of becoming emotionally involved. Attachments, mental or physical, were not for him. Holding himself aloof was the only way he could handle life.

Love had been thrown back in his face too many times. He'd tried to love his daddy; he'd tried to love his brother. Both had shunned that love, ignored it and ignored him. No, love was for the weak, not for him. He had adopted the philosophy so long ago, he saw no reason to change it now. In fact, he couldn't imagine being in love and wanting to consider the feelings of someone other than himself.

Yet he realized he wasn't as hard-assed as he'd thought. Sneaking up to that house in the dead of night, dressed in black, carrying a tiny flashlight and a small bag of tools, had shaken him to the core. The fact that he'd pulled it off had amazed him, especially as he'd had a helluva time removing the screen, then prying open the window. He'd been drenched with sweat from head to toe.

Only after he'd gotten inside had his stomach, which had quivered like Jell-O, tightened. The files, located in the tiny office off the den, had been in order. It had taken him only thirty minutes to find his file. He'd clutched it against his chest and made his escape.

From there he'd gone straight to Eddie's, awakened him, given him the file, and told him that if he wanted to redeem himself, he'd best find out all he could about the woman who had borne Dalton's child.

Now, several days after that visit to Eddie, Dalton looked up and watched as Eddie entered his office.

"It's about time you showed up," Dalton said.

Eddie took one look at him and grimaced. "God, you look like—"

"Warmed-over piss," Dalton finished for him. "I know."

"Did committing a felony do this to you?"

"Does counseling go along with detective work?"

Eddie raised his eyebrows. "Okay, I'll get straight to the point."

"Good. So what did you find?"

"Something that will definitely brighten your day. Leah Frazier lives in Gulfport."

"You're kidding," Dalton whispered. "Right here in my own backyard?"

"You shouldn't be surprised."

"I'm not, but the thought still blows my mind."

"It stands to reason that if the doctor was near, the patient would be, too. And we already know that practically any GP in any small town can do the procedure."

"So why do you think she went to Hattisburg as opposed to staying in Gulfport, where she lives?"

Eddie shrugged. "Probably because she didn't want anyone to know what she was up to. You know how women gossip."

"Yeah, guess so. But the reason doesn't matter. Nothing matters except that we've found her."

Dalton suddenly felt the urge to shout to the heavens. Fate, for the second time in his life, had smiled down on him. Instead he let out a controlled breath and said, "Let's have the rest."

"Okey dokey." Eddie plopped down on the chair in front of the table and opened the file. But he didn't start reading immediately. He fished a pair of glasses out of his pocket and shoved them on the bridge of his nose.

Dalton drummed his fingers on the Formica-topped table.

"She's married to a Rufus Frazier, who's ill and in a nursing home."

"Go on."

"She's a licensed architect and interior designer who recently left a large firm to go into business for herself."

"Was that information hard to come by?"

"Not really. But there's more, and it ain't good."

"What do you mean?"

"Well, she's gotten herself into some trouble. She's been implicated in a theft at the place she last worked. So far, she hasn't been arrested."

Dalton whistled. "Sounds like she's up the proverbial creek without a paddle."

"You're right. She's also in dire straits. She needs money, which is why she's the insurance company's number one suspect."

Dalton leaned back on his chair and twined his fingers behind his neck. "I'm impressed, Temple. Makes up for your not breaking into the doctor's house."

Eddie's face turned red. "I told you—"

"Yeah, yeah, I know what you told me."

Following Dalton's harsh words, the room fell silent. Then he asked, "What about the child?" He hoped he sounded nonchalant and not as twisted up as he actually felt inside.

"Ah, yes, the child. It's a boy, and his name is Coty Michael."

A surge of electricity shot through Dalton. A son. *He had a son.* A woman he'd never laid eyes on, whom he'd never even *touched,* had had his child. That thought was fucking mind-boggling.

"There's more, but it's all here in the file." Eddie closed the folder, then laid it in front of Dalton. "So what happens now?"

"You get paid and hit the road."

Eddie grinned. "You're an s.o.b., Montgomery, but I have to say, I like your style."

Dalton snorted as he wrote a check and handed it to Temple. "If there's anything else I need later on, I'll be in touch."

Eddie rose, looked down at the check, then grinned. "You just holler, now, you hear?"

With that he sauntered out of the room, leaving Dalton alone with his thoughts and a dwindling bank account. So what next? he asked himself. How did he go about meeting Leah Frazier?

Damned if he knew.

Then, suddenly, he sat straight up on his chair, feeling his heart palpitate and his mouth turn to cotton. The answer was simple, another sign of fate smiling on him.

Grinning like an idiot, he picked up the phone, punched out the number, and waited.

"Tony, Dalton."

"Hi. I was just about to call and see if you wanted to work on those plans today."

"Yes and no," Dalton responded.

"Come again?"

Dalton's grin covered his face. "Instead of busting our balls, I think we ought to hire an architect and interior designer."

Twelve

"Mommy, I have something to tell you."

Leah peered down at her son at the same time she set the sack of groceries on the cabinet. "All right, darling, I'm listening."

Coty tipped his head to one side, his green eyes pensive.

Instead of putting up the groceries as she'd intended, then starting their dinner, Leah leaned against the cabinet and smiled. "So shoot, cowboy."

The five-year-old lowered his head and pawed the floor with the tip of his scuffed boot.

"Coty?"

He looked up. "I hit Terry at school today."

"Mmm, want to tell me about it?"

Sudden tears welled up in his eyes. "He said my daddy was a sick old man who'd never be able to play ball with me."

If she hadn't been anchored next to the cabinet, Leah felt certain her legs would have buckled. God, how much more could she take? The one thing she'd prided herself on was her son's stability and his acceptance that their family was not like all other families. Now, as she stared into his pinched little face and saw his lower lip quiver, she knew she had failed. She dropped to her knees and hugged him.

He remained stiff at first, then he hugged her back. She fought off tears and pulled away so as to look directly at him. "Terry's right. Your daddy won't be able to play ball with you." She paused, then added softly, "Remember when we talked about that?"

"But—"

"I know what you're going to say. And you're right, it was mean of Terry to tease you about something that's so serious and makes you hurt." Leah paused again. This was so hard to explain to a child who wore rose-colored glasses, that life wasn't fair, that it had never been fair and never would be. "But it was also mean of you to hit him."

Coty stretched his lips into a mutinous line. "I'd do it again."

"No, I don't think so. That's not the way your daddy or I want you to behave. Just because Terry's an insensitive goon—"

Coty squirmed out of her arms, giggling.

"Well, he is a goon, and because of that you have to ignore him rather than beat up on him. Okay?"

"Okay. Can I go outside?"

"First, tell me what your teacher did."

His face clouded again. "She made us both stand in the corner."

A shudder went through Leah. "Well, the next time anything like that happens, *I'm* going to take a paddle to your bobo when you get home."

Coty stared at Leah as if testing her words by the look on her face. She must have convinced him. "Yes, ma'am," he mumbled, once again digging at the floor with his boot.

Leah flicked his chin up and smiled. "Take off. I'll holler when dinner's ready. Afterward, if there's time, I'll play catch with you. All right?"

"Yea!" Coty raced out the door.

Leah straightened and turned her attention back to the groceries. But her enthusiasm for doing anything was gone. She had done her best to prepare Coty for the change that had taken place, especially when she'd placed Rufus in the special care facility. The doctor had encouraged the move, as she couldn't handle Rufus or take care of his special needs. She had tried outside help, but that had been disastrous. One had stolen money, and another had been short-tempered with Coty.

In the end it had been Rufus himself who had broached the subject of entering Brookshire House, only to later make the final decision, reasoning that he'd rather Coty not see him grow weaker by the day. Leah had tried to talk him out of it.

"Darling, no," she'd said. "Coty will adjust. He loves you and understands."

Rufus had smiled. "No, sweetheart, he doesn't understand. He's a child and shouldn't be faced with life's harsh realities yet. I want to spare him that."

"What if I moved the business back home? Then I could watch the sitters—" She'd broken off, hearing the crack in her own voice.

"Shh, don't you dare think about moving your office. With Sophie as a part-time employee, this house is too small. Besides, you're hardly there anyway; you're always with me. You need some space, too, my darling."

She hadn't needed space, but she hadn't been able to convince him. Even though he was only a mere shell of the man she had married, she still coveted the time she spent reading to him, talking to him, stroking him. Yet he seemed to be losing his fighting spirit, and at times she wondered if hers wasn't diminishing as well, especially in the present climate.

What money they had was now gone. Soon she would have no choice but to bring Rufus back home. Then what? she asked herself.

Leah shook her head, then went about the task at hand. She was about to call Coty in for an early dinner when the phone rang. She stared at it for a moment, never knowing if it was a prospective client calling, as her business and home number were the same, or if it was the nursing home. Fearing the latter, she paused to collect her wits before answering it.

"Hello," she said hesitantly.

"Mrs. Frazier?"

Leah didn't recognize the man's voice, but it was deep and— The word she searched for wouldn't come to mind. Sexy? Was that it? Then, mortified at her thoughts, Leah replied more sharply than she intended, "Yes, this is she."

"I'm Dalton Montgomery."

When she didn't respond, she thought she heard a sigh on the other end of the line, but she wasn't sure.

"You're an architect as well as an interior designer, right?"

"Right," she said, caution lowering her tone. "Why?"

"I'd like to talk to you about doing a job for me."

Leah was so taken aback that for a moment she was speechless.

"Mrs. Frazier, you still there?"

"Yes, I'm still here. How did you get my name?"

"A friend of a friend recommended you."

Sounded truthful enough. So why didn't she believe him? "What kind of job do you have in mind?"

"Well, it's much too complicated to go into over the phone. Would you be free to meet me at Windsor's Restaurant for coffee tomorrow in Biloxi, say, around five o'clock?"

If Leah hadn't known the restaurant as one where the climate was conducive for business, she would've said a flat no. But when one needed work, one had to take a few chances. Besides, what could happen to her in a restaurant full of people?

"All right, Mr. Montgomery. I'll meet you."

"Good. See you tomorrow, then."

He hung up. Leah stared at the receiver, a strange feeling slithering through her. Now, just what was that all about? she wondered.

Sighing, she replaced the receiver, then walked to the door. "Hey, cowboy, supper's ready."

Coty ran up the steps. "Are you still gonna play catch with me?"

Leah ruffled his hair. "Wouldn't miss it for anything."

When Dalton parked his car in front of the restaurant, the sky was still as orange as a robin's breast. After easing his six-foot-plus frame from behind the wheel into the blistering heat, he paused.

Dammit, he was trembling, but his entire future hinged on this interview, and if he blew it— He shook his head, refusing to dwell on the negative. Hell, he wasn't going to blow it. She was a woman, wasn't she? Once he set his mind to it, there wasn't a woman alive he couldn't charm.

The fact that she was the mother of his son didn't play into this meeting at all. It was business. Strictly business.

He walked out of the sunlight into the shadowed interior of the restaurant. While he waited for the hostess, he saw her. Gut instinct told him she was Leah Frazier.

She sat at an out-of-the-way table by the windows. Her profile was all that was available to him, but some profile it was. She was small and had finely drawn features. Her cheekbones were high and her complexion flawless, despite the fact that she was thirty, as he knew. Her burnished brown hair was fashionably tousled. He'd bet the rest of the package was there as well—a slim but rounded figure that was sexy in a subtle way.

But her figure wasn't what fascinated him. "Cool"—that was the word that came to mind. "Unapproachable" was another. She had on a gold linen suit, but that warm color did little to alleviate that cool demeanor. Yet she was married.

Still, he'd bet everything he owned that she'd never been fucked on the kitchen stove. Now that was an intriguing thought, he told himself, one certainly worth exploring. . . .

He quickly derailed the thought. Talk about a fatal attraction. If ever his libido needed to be shut down, it was now.

This was business, he reminded himself again. *She* was business and nothing else, which wasn't quite the truth, either. His entire future rested on those slender shoulders.

What a pity, too. Under any other circumstances he'd love to dive into that forbidden water. Sanity rescued him, but he couldn't look away.

As if she sensed his presence, she turned. Smoky green eyes that seemed to fill her face stared back at him. He was captivated, not by their beauty, but by the immeasurable pain reflected in them.

She looked so lost, so forlorn, so vulnerable, that he didn't move. Was her ailing husband responsible for that kind of pain?

As though embarrassed at having been caught staring back at him, she reached for the glass of water in front of her and sipped from it.

Dalton gave her a minute longer to compose herself, then he bypassed the hostess with a smile and made his way toward her table. The only reaction he received to the fact that their eyes had touched moments ago was a slight tensing of her body.

"Hello, Mrs. Frazier."

She smiled, which made her even lovelier.

Dalton pulled out a chair and immediately motioned for the waiter. "What would you like?"

"Just coffee, please."

When the waiter reached his side, Dalton said, "Coffee for the lady, and I'll have a beer."

The waiter nodded, then walked off.

"This is a nice place," Leah said, looking around. "I've never been here."

Her voice was nice, too, kind of husky but lilting. "I'm not a regular myself, but on occasion, I have been here. They say the food's delicious, although it's the atmosphere I like."

And he did. While tastefully decorated, the restaurant was quiet, thus allowing one to enjoy the meal and/or conversation without a lot of unnecessary noise. At the moment the main dining area was practically empty.

The waiter returned with their drinks. After Dalton explained that they weren't going to order dinner, the waiter discreetly disappeared.

Dalton sipped his beer and looked at Leah over the rim. She was watching him, her eyes large and questioning.

He lowered his glass and said in his most businesslike tone, "I'm about to undertake a huge renovation project."

"That's what I do, Mr. Montgomery."

"And that's why I asked you here," he lied. "So, here's the deal. I own a club on gambler's drag." She smiled at his terminology, and for another moment that smile hit him in the gut, silencing him.

"Go on," she prodded.

He took another sip of beer. "In a nutshell, what I have in mind is first to upgrade and redecorate my club. I'm also considering adding an apartment above, though I might put that on hold because there's already a large room with an attached bath which will suffice for now.

"Anyway, the club is presently linked by a dock to a paddle wheel boat, which I recently bought from a fellow who went bankrupt. He was in the process of remodeling it for a casino. The problem is, I don't like the decor or anything else about it and want to make a lot of changes."

"Ah, so you're a gambler, Mr. Montgomery?"

"That's right." Dalton paused and watched as she placed the coffee cup against her red lips. He cleared his throat, then said, "I sense you don't approve of gambling."

Color tinted her cheeks, and when she breathed, her breasts rose and pressed against her blouse. He turned away and focused his attention on a bed of periwinkles outside the glass window. He watched as they ruffled in the gentle breeze.

"Whether I approve or not doesn't matter."

He looked back at her. "That's not entirely true. You'd be working on a casino; and if you don't approve, that might affect your judgment." Not that he gave a damn, he reminded himself. This wasn't about architecture, but rather his curiosity about her. Hell, he could've told her all this over the phone.

"I disagree," she said emphatically.

"So you would be interested in the job?"

"Of course, any architect in her right mind would be. It sounds like a wonderful opportunity as well as a challenge."

Dalton eased back on his chair. "That it will be, Mrs. Frazier. That it will be."

She flushed again, and this time the rosiness spread to the open V of her blouse, yet her gaze never wavered; and they stared at each other for a guarded moment.

If things had been different, he figured she was the type of woman his father would have chosen for him to marry—regal, confident, and aloof.

Earlier, in that flash of insanity, he'd been interested. No longer. He liked his women a trifle tougher around the edges. There was nothing tough about this woman. Or was there? Like the rarest of porcelain, she looked delicate, but he sensed that she wouldn't crack easily.

"Any questions?" he asked, forcing his mind back on business.

"Yes. Surely there are others who are much more qualified in this particular field than I am. I've had absolutely no experience in designing casinos, so why would you consider—"

"True," he cut in, "but as I said before, you come highly recommended."

She looked far from convinced, but she didn't say anything. He perceived her to be both intuitive and smart. He'd have to be damn careful or she'd see through this ruse.

Their eyes met again, and for a reason Dalton couldn't pinpoint, the tension in the air turned so thick that it was smothering.

"I really have to be going," she said suddenly, the lilt in her voice a decibel higher. "You have my number, if you'd like to pursue the project further. I really am interested."

She stood, and he followed suit. "Thanks for coming."

He held out his hand, and though she placed her soft one in his, the contact was so brief, he might have imagined it. But he hadn't imagined the trembling in that hand.

After she left, Dalton downed two more beers.

He smelled her cheap perfume. The instant J. T. Partridge opened the door to his apartment, the scent hit him in the face. He fought the urge to flee. God, his wife, Josephine, was the last human he wanted to see. He only wanted to drown his problems in a bottle of booze, then pass out.

J.T. didn't bother to switch on the light. The moon, whose brightness streamed through the open curtains, allowed him to see her sitting on the couch as if she belonged there. Well, she sure as hell didn't, not anymore.

"What are you doing here, Josephine?" he asked without mincing words.

She wrinkled her nose. "Why, is that any way to talk to your wife?"

"Soon to be ex." J.T. stressed the "ex."

Josephine laughed an ugly laugh. "That's where you're wrong. I've changed my mind. I don't want a divorce."

J.T. laughed, too, but in desperation. "Sure you do."

Josephine stood, and when she did, J.T. noticed she'd been

drinking. She actually needed to hold on to the arm of the sofa to stand.

She wasn't a pretty woman; hell, she wasn't even attractive. Her face was too long and her chin too pointed. But at one time she'd had the best set of boobs he'd ever seen on any woman. Now that alcohol had put weight on her, he was sure they hung to her waist. Overall, she was a mess, and J.T. turned away, repulsed.

"Don't you dare!" she said in a seething tone.

"Don't what?"

"Turn away from me, you prick."

"If you came here just to indulge in a verbal slinging match, then you're wasting your time. I'm dead tired, and I want to go to bed."

"Actually, that's what I had on my mind, too. I came to fuck."

J.T. rubbed his bulging stomach, then reached for the switch to his right. Instant light flooded the dingy, mussed-up room. They squinted at each other, trying to adjust to the abrupt change.

Josephine covered her eyes. "Turn that damn thing off."

"No. I want you outta here. Now!"

She stepped closer. "Liar."

"I'm not lying. We're through, as in finished."

She twisted her face into an ugly expression of mockery. "Whatsa matter, honey, you can't get it up no more?" She took another step closer.

J.T. wanted to back up, only he couldn't. Once again she seemed to know exactly which button to push to intimidate him, to make him feel like a trapped animal with a net over it. The more he struggled to free himself, the more the net tightened.

He needed a drink. He eyed the bottle of whiskey on a table across the room. He took a step toward it.

"Uh-uh, lover," she said, placing a hand on his arm.

J.T. shook it off and headed toward the bottle. He raised it to his mouth and poured the whiskey down his throat. But the hot, stinging liquid did nothing to dissolve the lump of fear lodged there. It turned solid instead of dissolving.

He hated this woman and rued the day he'd ever married her. She had made his life miserable, bitching from daylight till dark about how he was a loser who never made enough money, who never gave her the pretty things she'd always wanted.

She'd finally walked out on him, telling him she planned to divorce him. That had been one happy day in his miserable existence. Now, all his hope for a better future was threatened.

"Why did you really come here?" J.T. demanded.

"I told you, honey, I wanna fuck."

"Cut the crap, Josephine. We both know you've had all the nooky you can stand. Why, I bet you just crawled outta some dude's bed to come here."

Her eyes flashed and her voice shook. "You're a swine. I don't know what I ever saw in you."

"Then leave."

"No, not until I get what I came for."

Before J.T. realized her intention, she reached out and unzipped his fly. His limp penis spilled out.

She looked down at it, then back up at him. "My, my, but it does appear dead."

J.T. slapped her hand away, then zipped his pants. "Go fuck yourself."

Josephine smiled again, a transparent smile, menacing and dangerous. "No, I don't think so. I prefer to fuck you. So you'd best get used to having wifey-poo around again. You see, I heard about your pending promotion and the bonus you'll get. And I want my fair share. Of both."

"That ain't gonna happen."

"Oh, I think it will. So why don't we let bygones be bygones? We were always good in bed. I know I can bring that poor limp thing back to life."

J.T. trembled so with rage, he couldn't think of a comeback. All he could do was sweat like a pig, but he knew he was close to the edge. Finally he reached for the bottle of whiskey and headed for the door. There he paused and said, "If you won't leave, then I will. And as far as our getting back together, I'll see you in hell first."

He slammed the door on Josephine's raucous laughter.

Moments later and still shaking, J.T. climbed into his car and drove off.

He didn't stop until Leah Frazier's house was in sight. He

blamed her for this latest screw-up in his life. If only she had fenced those jewels, then he'd be sitting on easy street.

And until she did just that, he'd never have the means to dump that greedy bitch he was married to.

He leaned his head back on the seat and stared at Leah's bedroom window.

Thirteen

"Mommy, when's Daddy coming home?"

Those words tore at Leah's heart as she held Coty's hand and led him into Rufus's room.

"It'll be a while, son," Rufus answered in a weak, croaking voice, but his face bore a smile as he held out a hand to his son.

She had called earlier to see how her husband's day had begun. The charge nurse had told her he was sitting up in bed, which was rare. Since Coty had been asking to see his daddy, she decided to chance today.

In addition, she'd felt guilty; it had been a while since she'd brought Coty to the nursing facility. During that time, Rufus's health had worsened. Coty seemed to sense this as he looked up at Leah. "It's okay."

She smiled around her broken heart. "It's okay."

Coty scooted to the bedside and placed his tiny hand in Rufus's large but thin one. "How's my boy?" Rufus asked with difficulty.

"Okay. Mommy played ball with me." Coty's eyes were bright, then they dimmed. "But I wish you could play. Mommy's not very good." He cut his eyes toward Leah. "She keeps missing the ball and having to chase it."

That last sentence was spoken in such childish disgust that Leah chuckled. So did Rufus, which made her heart soar. Coty was what kept him alive. He loved her; she had no doubt about that. But his son was the star in his life, which was why he fought so hard.

"I'm sorry, cowboy, I wish I could—" Rufus broke off and went into a fit of coughing.

A look of fear crossed Coty's face; he backed away as Leah rushed to Rufus's side. Finally the spell passed, but Rufus was so weak, he sank his head into the pillow and closed his eyes. "I'm sorry. I—"

"Shh, darling, it's okay," Leah whispered, soothing his damp forehead with the palm of her hand.

"Mommy—"

Coty never finished his sentence. The door opened, and a large, rawboned nurse walked in. "Why, hello there, Coty," she said with a smile.

"Hi," he responded shyly.

"Good morning, Hazel," Leah said to her favorite staff nurse.

"Uh-oh, Mr. Frazier, looks like you've had another one of those nasty coughing spells."

"That he did," Leah confirmed, her brows knitted in a frown.

"Well, this should help." Hazel braced Rufus's head against her solid chest and held him while he swallowed a pill. She then turned her attention to Coty. "Mr. Riley has a puppy from the animal shelter visiting him. Would you like to see it?"

Coty's eyes lit. "Can I, Mommy?"

"I don't mind."

"How 'bout that, son?" Rufus said, making a valiant effort not to cough.

Leah knew how difficult that was for him, as he kept swallowing. She wished there were something more she could do, but there wasn't. Everything possible was already being done.

"I'll be back shortly," Hazel said, jarring Leah back to the moment at hand.

The nurse held true to her words. Moments later she walked back into the room.

"Looky, Mommy," Coty cried. "Looky what Nurse Riley has."

"Oh, my goodness." Leah stared at the tiny, squirming puppy in the nurse's arms.

Rufus chuckled, then coughed.

Leah gave him a quick glance. "Are you all right?"

"I'm fine." Then to Coty, "Go ahead, son, take him. I think he's more than Nurse Hazel can handle. He reminds me of my dog when he was little."

Grinning, Coty reached for the puppy, then laughed as a red, wet tongue licked his cheek, then his lips.

"Coty!" Leah cried, dismayed. "Don't let him lick you on the mouth."

"Why not? He doesn't have bad breath."

Leah looked heavenward.

"How would you like to play with him a few more minutes?" the nurse asked, hiding a smile.

"That'd be neat."

Hazel's smile broadened. "I'll be back later."

Once the nurse left, Coty sat on the floor and tried without success to hold on to the wiggly puppy. "Here, puppy," he called. "Here, puppy."

Leah eased down on the bed beside Rufus, and together they watched Coty scoot on the floor toward the dog. Leah squeezed Rufus's hand and smiled. Rufus managed a squeeze and wink in return.

"Uh-oh," Coty said suddenly.

Leah looked up just in time to see the puppy hike his leg.

"Oh, no! Coty, stop him!"

"Well, he just has to pee, Mommy."

"Where did you hear that word, young man?"

"Pee?" Coty asked innocently.

"Yes."

Coty shrugged.

Leah swallowed a retort when she felt Rufus tug on her hand. "Hey, it's all right. It's no big deal."

Leah smiled. "You're right, it's not. I'll just get a paper towel and clean it up."

"No, you won't," Nurse Hazel said, breezing into the room. "I'll take care of that myself." She grinned at Coty who once again had the dog in his arms. "Your friend had an accident, I see."

"Yes, ma'am, he p—"

"Coty!"

Everyone laughed.

"Want to take the pup back to Mr. Riley?" Hazel asked Coty.

"Yes, ma'am."

"Go ahead," Leah prodded with a smile.

The minute they left the room, Leah sat down next to her husband's bed and reached for his hand. "Feeling better?"

Rufus tried to squeeze her fingers. "Much."

"Good." She fought back tears.

His features contorted into a half smile. "You look beautiful."

Leah felt a flush stain her face. "You know better than that. I look like Mrs. Frump, actually."

"Never," he rasped.

She smiled again, but only with her mouth. Her eyes remained shadowed and pain filled, even though his brimmed with pride and love as he continued to look at her, as if memorizing her features.

Leah couldn't hold back the tears. "It's not fair," she said tersely. "You're too young; it isn't fair." She couldn't control the anger that rose to the surface.

"Don't, my darling. Just take care of yourself and our son."

"Rufus, let me take you home, so I can—"

"No," he interrupted. "You know how I feel about that. I don't want Coty to see me like this every day. It's not good for him or you. You need to concentrate on your work."

If only I had some work to concentrate on, she agonized silently. She had no intention, however, of sharing that burden, nor could she muster the courage to tell him that she might *have* to bring him home, because the insurance company had gone out of business and they were down to their last drop of savings.

"By the way, how is your work? Is it going great guns?"

"As a matter of fact, it is," she lied, forcing a bright smile.

Rufus lifted her hand to his lips and kissed it gently. "I love you," he said. Tears now flooded his eyes. "And I'm so sorry—"

Leah shook her head as the tears trickled down her cheeks. "Don't say that. Don't ever say that. You have nothing to be sorry about."

"Dry those tears, you hear? You have to keep your chin up for Coty's sake."

"I'll try." Her smile was tremulous at best.

"Try a little harder." He smiled and squeezed her hand again. "Promise."

"I promise," she whispered, easing her hand out of his as he drifted off to sleep.

Leah raised her head, feeling as if she were about to drown in sorrow. The futility of it all was almost more than she could bear.

Moments later she rose and walked out of the room, closing the door softly behind her.

Later Leah sat in her office and stared at the list of companies in front of her. She had called all but two, and without exception they had already hired an architectural firm.

As discouraging as those phone calls were, she wasn't in total despair. In the back of her mind she nursed a small hope that the Montgomery job would come through.

She shouldn't think that; she was just asking for more heartache. Common sense told her that he wasn't about to hire someone with no experience for his project.

Yet she couldn't control her thoughts about the job or the man himself. Dalton Montgomery had caught her completely off guard. She hadn't liked the way he had looked at her, as if he'd like to undress her; but then, she had rationalized her paranoia stemmed from what had happened at the architectural firm.

Too, maybe she was down on herself for the sudden awareness she'd felt toward him. She'd noticed him the moment he'd entered the restaurant. Still, if she could get that job, she knew she could cope with her paranoia and his cockiness.

Leah stood, stretched her back, then jumped as a bolt of lightning flashed, followed by a boom of thunder that shook the room. She turned anxious eyes toward the window. She should be used to this weather, but violent storms still spooked her. Coty had gone to visit a friend; she wished now she hadn't let him. She'd feel better if he were at home with her.

She reached for the remote control and was about to flick on the television when the doorbell rang. Frowning, she made her way into the living room and opened the door to find Sophie, soaking wet, standing on the front porch.

"Jeez!" Sophie skirted past Leah and didn't stop until she was in the middle of the room. "When I left the house this morning, I had no idea the bottom was going to fall out of the sky."

"That makes two of us."

"And the weather channel predicted showers."

"Figures."

Sophie chuckled. "Mind if I borrow a towel?"

"Oops, sorry. I should've notice that you looked like a drowned rat."

"Thanks," Sophie muttered before she tromped toward the bathroom. A few minutes later she faced Leah across the dining room table, a steaming cup of French vanilla coffee in front of her.

"Mmm," Sophie said, inhaling the fumes. "Thanks. A lady after my own heart, though I thought you'd be drinking iced tea. It's so damned humid out."

"It's my mood, I guess."

"You've been to the nursing home, huh?"

"I took Coty."

"How did that go?"

Leah swallowed a sigh before swallowing a sip of coffee. "Every time I take him, my heart cracks a little more."

"I can imagine the hell you're going through."

They were silent for a long moment, then Leah said, "I've been on the phone all afternoon. So far, I've struck out."

"That's not your only problem."

Leah's cup froze midway to her mouth. "What're you talking about?"

"That royal pain in the butt's still hanging around."

Leah's eyes widened. "J. T. Partridge, the insurance man?"

"Yep."

"You mean he's outside my house in this nasty weather?"

"Just step out the door and smell the foul odor in the air and you'll believe me."

"That bastard."

"He's that and more."

"Oh, Sophie, what if I get arrested for that theft?" Leah's eyes were filled with fear.

Sophie waved a hand. "Ah, that'll never happen. My advice is to ignore the creep and concentrate your energy on finding a good job, not some penny-ante one."

"Funny that you should say that." Leah looked at the rain that hit the window like spears before she returned her gaze to Sophie. "Actually, I had an interesting meeting a couple days ago about just such a job."

Sophie's mouth flopped open. "Why didn't you tell me?"

"Because I don't think anything will come of it, that's why."

"Well, you should've said something, anyway. So who'd you meet with?"

"Dalton Montgomery."

"Dalton Montgomery. Dalton Montgomery. I know that name." Suddenly Sophie's face came alive. "He's the guy, I'm almost sure, who dated my friend Cynthia for a while, then dropped her flat."

"I wouldn't find that hard to believe. He has the words *ladies' man* tattooed all over him."

"So he's good-looking, huh?"

Leah shrugged. "He's okay."

"Define okay."

"Interested?" Leah smiled. ·

"Why not? I'm neither dead nor married."

"Not yet, anyway," Leah teased.

"Right, so what's he like?"

"Somehow I don't think Louis would take too kindly to your curiosity about another man.

"Like I said, I'm not dead or married yet."

Leah merely shook her head. "Well, he's tall and blond and has sort of uneven features that if analyzed separately wouldn't be attractive. But together they make an intriguing package." What she failed to add was that it wasn't fair that a man should have eyes like his, deep set and black, with heavy lashes and strong brows.

"Intriguing, huh?"

Leah pursed her lips. "It's just a figure of speech."

"You know who he is, don't you?"

"I haven't the foggiest."

"Sure you do. Think. Doesn't the name 'Montgomery' mean anything to you?"

"No."

"Oh, come on. His father, who's now dead, was a senator from Louisiana. He was so powerful, many thought of him as another Huey P. Long."

"Ah, so that's where Dalton Montgomery is getting the money for this project."

"Which is?" Sophie demanded, her features animated.

Leah told her the gist of her conversation with Dalton.

"Wow! Do you realize that a job like that will figure in the millions?"

"That's why I know I'm not about to get it, especially when he checks the references I gave him."

"Surely you didn't put that bastard Cooper Anderson down for a reference?"

"Not as a reference, but I had to tell him where I'd been working. Besides, he knows that from a friend of a friend."

"Right. Still, it'll be a damn shame if he talks to him."

"I know. And don't forget about Ellen Thibodeaux and her accusation."

"So you didn't mention the theft?"

"No, I just couldn't bring myself to mention it; why humiliate myself for no reason?"

"That was probably smart." Sophie was quiet for a moment. "What do you think made him call you? After all, you don't know beans about casinos and clubs."

"Beats me," Leah said, her mouth turned down. "He just kept saying that I came highly recommended."

Sophie shrugged. "Well, maybe your luck's about to change."

"Nah. Some big firm, probably my old one, will likely get the nod."

"You never know. We can keep our fingers crossed and everything else, I guess."

"Meanwhile, *I* have to find some work," Leah said in a dejected tone. "Any ideas?"

"I see two names on that list not crossed off."

"Right."

"Then call them."

Leah picked up the phone.

The office on the top floor of the architectural firm Cooper, Thomas, and Swain fell silent as two men looked at each other.

"So what's the verdict?" Cooper Anderson, the senior partner, asked.

"I've interviewed a dozen applicants and none are suitable." Darwin Thomas, second in command, sounded clearly put out.

"We'll just have to keep on trying."

Darwin stood and walked to the window in the plush office. Frowning, Cooper watched him, thinking what a paradox he was, with his balding head and bulging biceps. He wanted to smile but didn't.

"What I'd like to know is why in hell you let Leah Frazier walk." Darwin had turned now and was glaring at Cooper.

Cooper tensed. "You have that all wrong, my friend. She just waltzed in one day and said adios."

"Oh, come on, Cooper, since when did you let a slip of a woman like her put one over on you? There must've been more to it than that. Hell, man, she made this firm a lot of money. Besides that, she was up for a hefty raise."

"It was her choice, Darwin," Cooper said coldly. "And I don't like it any more than you do."

"Then get her back." Darwin tossed the folder on Cooper's desk. "None of these measure up to her." He turned and walked to the door, only to pause there. "By the way, Walter feels the same way I do."

He slammed the door behind him, and Cooper winced. Great, just great, he thought. Two partners against one, which spelled trouble for him. If they found out . . .

He cursed aloud.

Fourteen

DeChamp's penis was rock hard.

He groaned, then shifted as Sylvia's tongue and teeth continued to torment him. He shouldn't be here, he knew that, but he hadn't been able to stay away.

Pregnant or not, this woman was an addiction he couldn't seem to shake. Besides, he figured on convincing Sylvia not to tell his wife, Terri, about the baby by promising he would divorce her.

But first things first, DeChamp told himself, twisting his fingers in Sylvia's black hair. "On top," he urged in a guttural tone.

"Uh-uh, honey," she whispered, peering at him from under wispy bangs.

His hold on her tightened. "What do you mean, uh-uh?"

She smiled sweetly. "I don't intend to fuck you until you either tell your wife or give me some money."

He shoved her away at the same time his penis collapsed. "You little slut! I told you I won't be blackmailed."

She laughed. "I'd be careful what I said, especially when I own all the cards in the deck."

"How much money would it take to get rid of you?"

"Fifty thousand."

DeChamp almost choked. "You're crazier than hell! I don't have that kind of money, and even if I did, I wouldn't give it to you."

Sylvia's expression changed, yet the tone of her voice didn't. It was as soft as ever. "It's your balls that are in the vise, lover boy, so I'd suggest you rethink what you just said." She paused and flicked his limp penis. " 'Cause if you don't, you'll be real sorry. I promise you that."

"Go to hell!" DeChamp leapt out of bed and into his clothes, fearing he wouldn't make it out of the door before he lost the contents of his stomach. He didn't, and Sylvia merely laughed.

Once outside, he leaned against the apartment building, still heaving. He didn't love his wife, but he damn sure didn't love Sylvia. And the thought of a squalling kid in his life repulsed him. Whether he wanted to or not, he had to buy Sylvia's silence. The only means to that end was to build a fire under Dalton and force him to find *his* brat.

DeChamp wiped his mouth with the back of his hand as he stumbled toward his car. He couldn't dally any longer. Tomorrow he would take action to see what progress Mr. Montgomery had made.

"No, Mama, I won't be by this afternoon."

"Why not?"

"Because I'm trying my best to find work," Leah said with guarded patience. "I'm making a lot of phone calls. You know the drill."

"No, I don't know the drill, as you put it."

Leah sensed that Jessica was geared to pick a fight as she sat alone in her house, brooding, puffing on one cigarette after another. Although Jessica had confessed to having stopped that lethal habit, Leah knew better. Jessica simply no longer smoked in her presence.

Leah sighed. "It's like this, Mama, if I don't get a good job soon, I'm going to have to bring Rufus . . . " Her voice played out. She took a deep breath and went on, "He'll have to come back home."

"If you'd only listened to me," Jessica said in a biting

tone, "you wouldn't be in this god-awful predicament. You'd have a lovely home and plenty of money—"

"Look, I have to go. I hear Coty." Leah had heard enough, no longer willing to listen to another verse of the same old song. "If you really need anything, call me."

"I don't know what good that would do. You wouldn't help me."

The next thing Leah heard was the offensive dial tone in her ear. Her initial reaction was to scream her frustration, but she knew that wouldn't accomplish anything except alarm her son, which she couldn't do. His life was already too much out of balance.

Damn her mother. One of these days . . .

That thought was put on hold as the phone jangled under her hand.

"Hello," she all but snapped, thinking it was her mother again.

"Leah?"

She recognized the voice. It was Cooper Anderson, her old boss. Instantly wary and alert, she gripped the edge of the table and said, "Yes?"

"Is something wrong?" he asked in his smooth, confident voice.

Leah curbed her initial response to tell him to go to hell, then slam down the receiver. Instead she ignored his question and asked one of her own. "What do you want?"

"Actually, I'd like to talk to you."

"Oh?"

"I have one o'clock free today. Would that be convenient for you?"

She was probably wrong, but she thought she heard a groveling note in his voice. For a moment she was again tempted to tell him to go to hell. But why spite herself? Why not listen to what he had to say? She might find answers to questions that had plagued her since she had left his firm.

As she'd said to Sophie, she suspected that Cooper's influence had had something to do with her not getting any jobs, that he was sabotaging her name and work behind her back. If so, she wanted proof.

"So?"

"So, all right. I'll be there."

"Fine. You won't regret it."

Once Leah was off the phone, she tried to make the most of a bad start to the day. First her mother, then her disgusting ex-boss. How lucky could she get?

Cooper's office hadn't changed, nor had the man himself. But what had she expected? Leah asked herself. It hadn't been all that long since she'd left his employ. She sat on a chair in front of his expensive cherrywood desk, in his plushly decorated office, and continued to stare at him.

On closer observation, he *had* changed. Although his handsome features were still intact, he'd grown a mustache that was not at all flattering. Also, he appeared to have put on additional pounds, or was that extra bulk muscle? He looked as if he had been working out with weights, which would be just like him. That he might not appear as if he'd just stepped off the pages of *GQ*, even at the age of sixty, would be a blow to Cooper. His flashy pin-striped suit and tie reflected that attitude.

"Well, do I pass muster?" he said with a grin that displayed a set of perfect white teeth.

"Don't flatter yourself." Leah didn't bother to mask her contempt.

His face hardened, then he chuckled.

"What did you want to see me about, Cooper?" she asked, impatient for the interview to end.

His face hardened again, but when he spoke his tone was pleasant enough. "We've missed you here."

"Oh, really. How's that?" Leah idly smoothed a wrinkle out of her magenta cotton skirt yet kept her eyes directly on him. She wasn't about to make this encounter easy or give him an inch of leeway.

"You've changed, Leah," he said bluntly. "You seem . . . " He paused, as if searching for the right word. "Bitter, maybe that's what I'm trying to say. And it certainly doesn't become you."

"I'm not the least interested in what you think of me,

Cooper. But in case you haven't heard, my husband is dying."

Her soft but cold tone seemed to have dented his self-confident armor. For a moment he appeared as if he didn't know how to respond. But as usual, he rebounded and said in a sympathetic tone, "I had heard, and I can't tell you how sorry I am about that."

"Thank you," she said, not believing a word he said. "But that's not what you wanted to talk to me about." Her words, a flat statement of fact, placed the meeting back on a formal footing.

Cooper shifted on his chair. "No, no, it isn't."

She waited.

He sighed, looked out the window, then back at her. She noticed a film of perspiration on his forehead, though the room was so cold, it could have been used as a meat locker.

"I—we want you to come back to the firm."

Leah almost laughed out loud, only she caught herself in time. She didn't give a whit whether she insulted him or not, but again she was curious as to what had brought all this about.

"Who's 'we'?"

"My partners and I, of course."

Leah raised one perfectly arched brow. "Of course."

Cooper flushed, then toyed with his mustache. "All right, Leah, you've had your fun at my expense, so let's just get down to the bottom line."

"And what is that?"

"Money." He leaned forward. "How much will it take to entice you back?"

"More than you have."

He smiled and relaxed back onto his chair. "Oh, I don't know so much about that. Anyway, you're not in a position to quibble, I wouldn't think."

"And just what would you know about my business?" Her voice was tightly coiled.

"I know that you're in deep financial trouble, that you're having trouble getting work."

Leah seethed inwardly at his outward arrogance. She would take delight in bringing him down a peg or two.

"Somehow, I suspect that's partly your fault," she said with quiet but brutal frankness.

Cooper blinked, then stared hard at her as if to make sure he'd heard her correctly. "Pardon?"

"You heard me, and you know exactly what I mean."

"I'm afraid I don't. If you haven't found work, it's probably because you've been implicated in that theft. That's an unfortunate thing to have happened so early in your push for independence."

"Spare me the false sympathy, Cooper. But we both know that's *not* the only reason I can't get work."

"Well, you certainly can't blame me or this firm," he countered in a blustery tone.

"I think I can."

His lips stretched into a thin line. "I didn't ask you here to argue with you. I think your future is here, at Cooper, Thomas, and Swain. Why don't you just give up trying to make it on your own and come back?"

"Thanks, but no thanks."

"Just why the hell not? We're prepared to make it worth your while."

He named a figure, and it was all Leah could do to keep her mouth from flying open. Somehow, though, she managed to keep her features blank, though her heart was hammering.

"The answer is still no."

Cooper's demeanor turned ugly. She wasn't surprised; it always did when he was crossed.

"You'll regret that."

She stood and inched closer to the desk. "I don't think so."

"This firm has a lot of power."

"Ah, so now you're admitting that you've used that power to sabotage me?"

Cooper's face lost its color. "You deliberately misconstrued my words. I didn't say any such thing."

"Well, you implied it," Leah said, "and that's good enough for me. So back off, Cooper."

He sneered. "You can't threaten me. I have so much influence that if I choose to, I can fix it so you'll *never* get a decent-paying job."

Leah leaned over his desk and placed her face as close to

his as she could stomach, then said in a soft voice, "And *I* can fix it so you'll go to prison for sexual harassment."

He opened his mouth, but no words came out.

"I haven't forgotten the time you backed me into that closet." Leah's eyes looked him up and down. "I'd think about that before I made another stupid move."

With that she pivoted and walked calmly to the door. Just as she closed it behind her, Leah thought she heard a choking sound.

She kept on walking.

"Thanks for stopping by, Mr. Anderson."

"Call me Cooper, please."

"Cooper it is," Dalton said as he took the architect's extended hand.

"I'll look forward to hearing from you soon." Cooper's voice matched the excitement in his face. "Your project will be a sizable undertaking, and again, I'm convinced my firm is the right one for the job. We can make it into something special, a real showplace."

"I'm sure you're right," Dalton said, his voice devoid of emotion.

"Good, sounds like we might indeed be working together."

Although the anxiety was evident in Cooper's voice, Dalton remained noncommittal. "I'll give you a call."

Cooper was just about to open the door and leave when Dalton said to his back, "Uh, what about Leah Frazier?"

Cooper swung around. "What about her?" His tone was as rigid as the set of his shoulders.

Interesting, Dalton mused. "What kind of architect is she?"

Cooper grinned a smug grin. "She's certainly not of the caliber you need for this job."

"She used to work for you, right?"

"Right, only she couldn't quite cut it. When she left to open her own business, we were relieved."

"So what you're saying is that she's not good at her job?"

"That's exactly what I'm saying." Cooper stepped farther

into the room and spoke in a conspiratorial tone, "Actually, she's in trouble with the law over some jewelry that turned up missing from the house where she last worked."

"Oh, really?"

"Yeah." Cooper's smug grin turned smugger. "Forget about her. You need someone who's in the big leagues." He paused. "But I'm curious, how did you hear about her?"

"I'm checking out several firms," Dalton said in an even tone, "both small and large."

"I see." Cooper was clearly ruffled. "When the chips fall, I still think you'll find *my* firm is the best for the job."

Dalton smiled. "I'll certainly keep that in mind."

"Good, good." Cooper reached for the knot on his tie and loosened it. "I'll expect to hear from you."

Dalton didn't respond.

Dalton stared out the window at the ocean and wished he were riding those waves alongside those other surfers. He couldn't allow himself that luxury, not yet, anyway.

Hearing a noise, he turned and looked on as Tony sauntered into the makeshift office.

"Who was the fellow that just left?"

"An asshole."

Tony raised his eyebrows, then grinned. "That was exactly my thought."

"Well, it goes to show you that great minds think alike."

"I hear you."

Dalton's grin faded.

"Look," Tony said, "if there's nothing pressing at the moment, I have some personal business I need to take care of."

"No problem. Go ahead. I'll talk to you later."

Dalton wasn't even aware when Tony left. His mind was back on Leah and what to do about her. He looked over the résumé that she'd mailed him. He'd already checked out her other references and had received nothing but glowing reports on her ability as an architect.

Still, he'd wanted to talk to Cooper Anderson, for no reason except to get his reaction toward Leah. He didn't know what had happened between them, but whatever it was, it wasn't good.

But of the two, he was much more inclined to side with Leah. As far as the theft was concerned, he didn't believe for a second that she had anything to do with it.

Should he hire her? That was a big question. Should he go through with this crazy scheme? Yes. He had no other choice, since Parker had fucked up his plans. He had to get close to that kid. The only way to do that was through Leah. But all was not lost. He believed that Leah was the best architect and designer for the job. She seemed enthusiastic, savvy, and intelligent. He couldn't ask for more. Yet he remained leery of hiring her, and he didn't know why.

Dalton leaned back on his chair, his forehead wrinkled in a desperate frown.

Fifteen

Forget it, Leah. *He's* not going to call.

It had been a week since she'd met Dalton Montgomery. She had known she hadn't a prayer of getting that posh job. Still, on this bright, sunny, humid afternoon, she didn't want the truth slapping her in the face.

All wasn't lost, however. Her diligence in looking for work had paid off. She had gotten a job restructuring a small office complex. Though she was thrilled to be working again, the profit was nonexistent because she'd had to bid so low to get it.

Leah glanced up from the mess strewn across her desk, then massaged the muscles in the back of her neck; they were tight and sore. She winced before turning her attention back to her work.

Basically she was an organized person. There was no "basically" about it—she *was* organized, or at least she had been until Rufus became ill. Now, nothing was the same.

She'd always thought of herself as weak, one who never wanted to cause friction, who wanted everything to remain on an even keel. That was how she had survived her childhood, agreeing with others—mainly her mother—letting them make her decisions. But that had changed when she'd crossed her mother the first time, refusing to study law. The second time had been when she'd married Rufus.

While some now perceived her to be an iron lily, she knew better. Under that facade of strength remained that fragile butterfly of long ago. Somehow, though, she managed to make the decisions that had to be made. But she didn't like that responsibility. She had liked being cherished and treasured.

She had liked being a *wife*, which she no longer was. She loved being a mother, only now she was both mother and father. She feared she wasn't good at either anymore, nor was she sure she even liked herself.

Leah ached for strong arms to hold her, to soak up the misery that surrounded her like soured perfume, strong arms such as those of Dalton Montgomery.

Horrified by that thought, Leah lunged out of the chair and strove to get control of her emotions. She wouldn't crumble; neither would she let someone like Dalton Montgomery and the lure of his plum job further depress her.

Hoping to find solace in the lovely day, Leah walked to the window, only to find her eyes unconsciously sweeping the street. All she needed was to catch J. T. Partridge hanging around. She saw nothing suspicious, however. Her relief was strong as her gaze turned to the driveway, where a basketball goal was located.

Leah's eyes softened on Coty, Sophie, and her fiancé, Louis Appleby, as they attempted to teach her son how properly to shoot the basketball.

She couldn't hear all that was said, but she knew they were having fun. Coty's laughter, when Louis lifted him so that he could make the goal, warmed her heart. She actually laughed out loud. Then the laughter faded. Rufus should be doing that.

Leah shut down those thoughts and emptied her mind of everything except watching the three of them have fun. She liked Louis, although she didn't know him well. Maybe it would be good if Sophie married him. But Leah had her doubts about that.

Sophie simply wasn't ready to settle down, though Leah knew that eventually she would be, especially as Sophie had made the statement that she wanted a dozen children, having been reared as an only child. Apparently Louis felt the same way, as he, too, was an only child.

Sophie adored Coty. Leah shuddered to think how she would have coped had it not been for Sophie's unselfish help. Deciding to join the fun, Leah turned and walked toward the door, only to stop as the phone caught her midstride.

"Great," she muttered, and raced to answer it.

"Mrs. Frazier?"

Her pulse jumped several points. Even though she had talked with him only briefly, she would have know that voice anywhere. Like his eyes, it belonged exclusively to Dalton Montgomery.

"Yes?"

He chuckled. "You sound out of breath."

That deep husky voice brushed her nerves like sandpaper. She had the urge to slam down the phone and never talk to this man again. Then she saw the absurdity of her thoughts for what they were and regained her composure.

"Actually, I was on my way outside."

"Sorry. Did I catch you at a bad time?"

"No, no, that's all right. I was just going to watch my son play ball." Now why had she said that? He couldn't give a fig about her son or whether he played ball or not. Nervous chatter, that was all it was.

The silence stretched. "Mr. Montgomery?"

"I'm here. Look, I'd like to talk to you again. Soon."

Leah licked her dry lips. "Does that mean I'm being considered for the job?"

"It means you've got the job, if you want it."

Leah was dumbstruck. Surely she hadn't heard him correctly?

"Mrs. Frazier, are you still there?"

"Yes, and of course I want it," she said breathlessly.

"Sounds like you really mean that."

Did she detect a slight mockery in his tone, resulting from her almost childlike excitement? If so, damn him. But then it was obvious that he'd never wanted for a thing in his life. Apparently silver spoons were plentiful in his household.

"I do, Mr. Montgomery," she said, forcing a professional coolness into her tone. "For an architect who's just getting started on her own, your job is the chance of a lifetime."

"When can we meet again?"

"When it's convenient for you."

"How 'bout tomorrow around three?"

"Where?"

"At the club." He gave her the directions.

"Fine. I'll be there." Leah paused. "Do you mind if I ask why you chose me? I mean . . . "

"Let's just say I didn't want to deal with a big firm." He paused this time. "And let's just say, too, that I didn't like Cooper Anderson."

Leah was flabbergasted and couldn't utter a word.

Apparently nothing was expected because Dalton continued, "Three o'clock, Mrs. Frazier."

With that he hung up.

Leah didn't know how long she stood there in a daze before her wobbly legs took her toward the door. Once there, the impact of the conversation hit her. She literally hugged herself, laughed out loud, then flung open the door.

"Hey, gang, get your buns in this house. It's celebration time!"

Coty's hand went to his mouth. "Uh-oh, Mommy said an ugly word."

Louis ruffled his hair. "No, she didn't, pal. Now, if she'd said a—"

"Don't you dare!" Sophie interrupted, punching Louis on the arm.

Coty looked from one to the other.

Sophie turned her attention to Leah. "What on earth do we have to celebrate?"

Leah laughed again. "Come on in and you'll find out."

"You really have a great ass."

Sophie sent Louis a look. "What's this fixation you have all of a sudden with asses?"

Louis chuckled, his gaze leering. "It's not all of a sudden, and you know it. Since I first met you, I've been intrigued with *your* ass."

"You're perverted."

Louis laughed. "And horny."

"No way, not after—"

"Want me to show you?"

"No, what I want is something to eat. I'm in the mood for a midnight picnic."

Louis sighed. "All right. I'll see what I have in the fridge."

"I'll be waiting," Sophie said airily. "Oh, by the way, your ass isn't half bad, either."

Louis paused and swung around, a spark in his eyes. "We'll continue this conversation when I return."

Sophie smiled, then lay back on the bed and waited, never having felt so content in her life. Part of her euphoria stemmed from the lucrative job that had practically fallen into Leah's lap. Sophie couldn't believe it, nor could Leah. Nor could Louis, for that matter. But none of them were about to question the reason behind Dalton Montgomery's choice.

Sophie's part of the project would be to oversee the office refurbishing job. She knew she was up to the challenge, even though she had decided to go back to school part-time and work on her architectural degree. She hadn't told Louis that yet.

Ah, Louis—the best thing that had ever happened to her. Although he was from upstate New York, a dyed-in-the-wool Yankee, she didn't hold that against him. She paused in her thoughts and smiled. Actually he was a gem, much like Leah's husband, Rufus, except a lot younger.

Louis had followed a girlfriend to Mississippi a couple of years ago. But their love affair hadn't worked out. He'd been on the verge of returning to the North when he and Sophie had met at a party of a mutual friend. Sophie had liked him immediately; he'd taken her teasing of his accent in stride. Later she'd concluded that it had been love at first sight, though she'd never voiced that thought because it sounded so corny.

He was tall and good-looking with blond hair and blue eyes. More important, he was easygoing and treated her like a queen. He also had a great job as an assistant administrator in the local hospital. His only fault was his desire to get married right away and have a passel of kids.

The passel of kids she didn't mind—she wanted that many, too; it was the marriage part that scared her. She'd been down that road once before, and she wasn't eager to travel it again, at least not anytime soon.

"So what's going on in that evil mind of yours?" Louis asked, sauntering back into the room, carrying a tray filled with cheese and crackers, fruit, and wine.

Sophie scooted upright and watched as he set the platter in the middle of the bed, then sat down himself.

"So, what's the verdict?"

"Mmm, looks delicious, and I'm famished."

"Only because you were a glutton a while ago."

Sophie threw a strawberry at him. He laughed, then his features turned sober. "I have a surprise for you," he said.

"Oh?"

"I'm being considered for hospital administrator at another hospital."

Sophie's eyes widened, and she let out a cry. "That's great!" She leaned over and kissed him.

After a moment he said, "So, if I get it, will you marry me?"

Sophie didn't mince any words. "No. You know how I feel about that."

"I know, but I want kids, and I'm not getting any younger."

"That's supposed to be the woman's line." She paused and cocked her head to one side. "Who says we can't have a kid without a marriage license?"

He lifted both eyebrows. "You'd be willing to do that?"

"Maybe."

"You're something else, Sophie Beauvoir."

"So are you, Louis Appleby, even if you are a damn Yankee and don't know how to talk southern."

"Oh, but I'm learning."

Her eyes turned dreamy as she munched on cheese and crackers. "Yeah, we're so lucky." She paused. "I wish . . . "

"I know what you're thinking. I wish that, too. Leah's life is the pits, and I feel so sorry for her."

"Me too. And there's no telling when it's all going to end. Even when Rufus dies, she's left with that emptiness inside her."

"She spends hours with him every day, doesn't she?"

"Yes, more than I think she should," Sophie responded. "The strain is telling on her. She'd determined to be super-wife and supermom and superbreadwinner. Something has to go; yet she's unwilling to give an inch on any of it."

"Well, now that she has this job, the financial burden will lift."

"*If* this job turns out to be all that it's cracked up to be."

"What do you mean by that?"

Sophie's eyes clouded. "I don't know; there's just something about the whole thing that's almost too good to be true."

"Yeah, I heard you tell her that."

"But we'll see, and soon. We'll just have to keep everything but our legs crossed—" She broke off and grinned mischievously. "Speaking of uncrossed legs—"

With a light flaring his eyes, Louis shoved the tray aside and reached for her. "You can cross anything you like, honey, but never your legs."

Sophie giggled as his mouth meshed with hers.

Sixteen

Was she dressed okay?

Leah had asked herself that question five times already, which was ludicrous. The job was hers, so why was she in such a dither as to how she looked? She guessed she wanted to prove that she was indeed the best choice. Therefore she was determined to portray the cool, composed business-woman who knew how to function in a man's world.

This job was such a one-in-a-million opportunity that she couldn't afford any mistakes. Not only would it ease her financial burden, but it would reestablish her reputation and restore her self-confidence in herself as a legitimate architect and designer.

Leah's thoughts jumped to Rufus, who lay in bed, dying. For a moment feelings of guilt and hopelessness washed through her that were so strong, she held on to the nearest chest for support. How could she think about her vanity?

Rufus was the reason. If this job panned out, then he could remain in the nursing facility a while longer.

Leah forced back her sadness and reached for her large gold loop earrings. She had decided to wear a three-piece walking-short outfit, complete with panty hose, even though the day promised to be sweltering. One last glance in the mirror and she was ready to go, thinking she didn't look half bad in the pale aqua. It added some color to her pale features.

Coty had spent the night with a friend, so she didn't have to take him to play school, which had been a blessing. She felt she needed the extra time that would've been allotted to him. The rambunctious child liked to dash in and out of her room while she dressed and distract her with a stream of questions. With a smile on her lips as she thought of her son, Leah picked up her purse and left the house.

When she walked into the blinding, searing sun, she glanced at her watch and noted that she was leaving forty minutes early. She felt like a complete imbecile and was about to turn and go back inside when she saw him, or rather smelled him.

Leah jerked up her head and watched as J. T. Partridge meandered up the sidewalk, his cigar more intact than his clothes. Though his shirt appeared to have been pressed, there was a spot that looked like grease on his protruding belly. Her stomach revolted.

"Well, well, look who's all gussied up. Wouldn't by any chance be going to do a little fencing business, huh?"

Leah went cold at the evil that eroded off this man. What she couldn't understand was his apparently personal vendetta against her. Nevertheless, he frightened her. But she refused to let him see her fear. That would be playing into his hands.

"I'm late for an appointment, Mr. Partridge," she lied. "Would you mind stepping out of my way."

He grinned. "Ah, always the perfect lady."

"What do you want?"

"Why, I think that's obvious."

"Only to you, Mr. Partridge."

He stepped closer. "The jewels, honey. I want the jewels that belong to that crazy, fat old woman."

His breath stank, a combination of onions and tobacco. Leah took an unconscious step backward. He followed her. This time she stood her ground and didn't so much as flinch.

"You know I don't have those jewels," she said in the iciest tone she could muster. "You also know that I didn't take them."

"That's your happy ass," he spat.

She reeled against the nasty words and tone. "If you don't leave me alone, I'm going to report you, not only to your immediate boss, but to the insurance board." She paused. "Now, get out of my way."

He inched still closer. "You listen to me, little lady," he said, sneering, "you can report me to the devil himself, if it'll make you feel better. But we both know the truth. And one of these days when you get really desperate, probably when your old man buys it, you'll try and get rid—"

Leah's hand came up, and she slapped him hard—so hard, in fact, that he reeled backward.

"Why, you bitch! I'll—"

Leah didn't wait around for him to finish his sentence. She skirted past him, dashed to her car, and got inside.

It wasn't until she had backed the Honda into the street that she looked into the rearview mirror. J.T. stood massaging his cheek, watching her. She saw the twisted hatred on his face and knew that she hadn't heard the last from that man.

Heat rose in waves off the concrete as Leah made her way from the deserted parking lot to the front of Dalton's club. She knocked lightly. While she waited she glanced again at her watch. She was still early, twenty minutes, to be exact. To her way of thinking, it was better to be early than late.

Had he not heard her? She knocked again. Louder. Nothing. She turned the knob and was surprised when the door opened. She walked into the waiting area that was part of the restaurant. Though it was cool, the smell inside was musty. Her eyes scanned the area. Immediately in front of her was the bar. To the right of that was the restaurant. It was bare, only a shell.

To the left was an empty room with a central dance floor. She could imagine tables surrounding that floor filled with chattering, laughing faces.

Shaking herself mentally, and realizing she was getting way ahead of herself, Leah ventured to the right of the bar, and walked down the long hall to a door marked "Office." Though it was partly open, she paused and rapped on the wood. No response. She frowned, knowing that Dalton Montgomery must be on the premises. His black Mercedes was parked out front.

She pushed on the door, opening it wider. "Mr. Montgomery?"

Silence.

Brazenly she walked inside, only to freeze.

Dalton Montgomery had chosen that moment to waltz into the room half naked. His upper torso was shirtless, and he was in the process of snapping his cutoff jeans. Her eyes never made it to the zipper.

Leah gasped. Dalton jerked his head up. He grinned as he proceeded to snap his jeans and zip them, as if her presence were no big deal. It probably wasn't to him, she thought snidely. But it *was* a big deal to her; she knew her face was red as fire.

"Good afternoon," he said, that grin still intact as he strode closer to her.

"I'm—sorry, I didn't mean . . . " Words failed her.

"It's okay. I'm running late and you're running early. I like that in an employee."

"I knocked . . . several times, but—" Again Leah lost her voice in embarrassment. What a terrible way to start a new job!

"Hey, it's no big deal. I should've been ready, but I've been here since dawn, on the boat, actually, helping the carpenters gut the damn thing."

Leah bit down on her lower lip. "I see." Even her voice sounded odd.

He looked at her for a minute.

She flushed and felt more foolish than ever. After having acted so violently to his state of undress, he must think she was a prude. But the only man she'd ever seen without his clothes was Rufus, and he'd never looked that good. . . .

"You look nice," Dalton said, "but from now on, come in shorts or jeans—" He paused with a shrug. "Hell, whatever you're most comfortable in, is what I'm trying to say."

Discussing clothes or the lack of them made Leah even more uncomfortable. Maybe it was because of what had just happened, or maybe it was because she was so sensitive about everything these days.

Or maybe it was because he still hadn't put on a shirt.

"I'll keep that in mind," Leah said, relieved to find that her normal voice had returned and with it her composure.

Dalton reached for a blue T-shirt that hung over the back of the nearest chair and slipped it on. "Now we can get down to business."

Leah picked up on the mockery in his tone, as if he got a kick out of her prudish reaction to his near nakedness. Or perhaps her imagination was playing tricks on her. She doubted that, especially when a rakish light appeared in those dark eyes that were shaded by unusually thick lashes.

Immediately the words *free spirit* sprang to mind, only a free spirit with a brooding, outlaw edge. Yet he reminded her somewhat of a little lost boy—the James Dean type, only taller, more muscular, and wearing leather boots instead of a leather jacket. A charismatic accident waiting to happen.

Dalton Montgomery was all the above and more.

"There's a lot of business we need to go over this afternoon," he was saying, "though I don't wanna overwhelm you."

Leah shook herself mentally. "No problem."

"First, I'll give you the grand tour, then we'll talk some more."

"I'm ready when you are."

He motioned for her to go ahead of him, and for the next twenty minutes they toured the building, then crossed the plank to the paddle boat, which appeared in total shambles.

Dalton voiced her thoughts. "It's a mess, isn't it?"

"Why are they ripping it apart?"

"I told you I didn't like anything about it."

"Well, I can't say I blame you. That carpet is about the gaudiest pattern I've ever seen."

"That's why it'll soon be history, on all three floors."

Leah raised her head. "You don't plan to change the detailing around the edges and the ceiling, do you?"

"No way. That's real mahogany."

"It's lovely."

"Think it has potential?" Dalton asked, following her line of vision.

"Definitely, only I'll have to wait until the cleanup is complete before I can even think of beginning my creative processes."

Dalton smiled. "I can identify with that."

"What about equipment? Had the previous owner bought any?"

"Actually, he'd ordered some of the slot machines, which I bought and stored below."

When Leah didn't respond, he added, "Let's get out of here before we melt."

Leah nodded, as her clothes were so damp they stuck to her skin.

"As hot as it is here," Dalton said, "I'm sure I'll be real comfortable in hell."

Leah threw him an astonished look.

"Just a figure of speech," he said with a grin.

Nothing else was said until they were seated at Dalton's worktable. After announcing his thirst, he disappeared, then returned with two frosty mugs of iced tea.

They sipped the cold liquid for a moment, then Dalton asked, "So what'dya *really* think?"

"I think it'll be quite an undertaking."

"But you're up to it?"

"Let's hope so, only I still can't figure out why I got the job. I know there are firms here who've done several of the other casinos and very successfully, too."

"True, but I told you I didn't want to deal with a big firm. I wanted someone I could work with on a personal, one-to-one basis." He paused. "Speaking of personal, do you mind if I ask a couple of questions?"

Leah minded. She minded very much. Her response was taut. "Depending on how personal."

"Fair enough. So why did you leave the Anderson firm?"

"Money, or the lack of it," she said hesitantly, not about to tell him the *real* reason behind her exit. Apparently Cooper Anderson hadn't told him, either. But then she hadn't expected the rat to air his dirty secrets.

"They wouldn't pay you what you thought you were worth, huh?"

"They wouldn't pay me what I *am* worth."

Dalton grinned. "I stand corrected. Don't worry. I believe in your worth or you wouldn't be here."

There was another moment of silence. Then he asked, "What about your husband?"

Leah stiffened. "You've been checking into my personal business." It wasn't a question, but a flat statement of fact.

"If you mean that I checked on your references, then the answer is yes."

Leah felt foolish again. Of course someone would have mentioned that her husband was ill, that someone being Cooper Anderson. There was probably very little this man didn't know about her, in light of the magnitude of this job. So why did that unsettle her? Was it their unorthodox meeting?

"Look, I'll be very up front with you," Leah said. "Besides the challenge this job offers, I need it financially."

"Why?" he asked bluntly.

"I think you know why, Mr. Montgomery."

"Dalton. I can't go that 'Mr.' crap."

She nodded, but she didn't say his name. "I'm sure Cooper enlightened you."

Dalton didn't respond.

Leah's lips thinned. "I'm sure he also told you about my being questioned concerning some missing jewelry where I last worked."

"That he did. But I don't believe for a second that you're a thief."

"Thanks." Relief washed through Leah. She was glad the incident was out in the open. At least he hadn't asked for any humiliating details.

Still, she had to make her point. "If you know that, then you must know that my husband is ill and in an expensive nursing home that's very financially draining."

"If that's the case, then why not bring him home?"

It wasn't what he said, but what he didn't say, that sent hot fury stampeding through Leah. "I can't give him the care he deserves, that's why!" she replied hotly. How dare he judge her or her situation?

A heavy silence fell between them.

"Sorry," Dalton said at last. "I was out of line. I'm sure you're doing what's best for him."

His eyes were now direct and filled with unsuppressed sympathy. She swallowed hard and turned away. She didn't want his sympathy. Yet . . .

"So what about your son?"

Relieved to be once again on safe ground, Leah turned back to him with a smile that completely changed her features. "He's the delight of my life."

"I bet he's a handful."

"That's an understatement." She didn't say anything else for a moment, then she said, "What about you?"

He shrugged. "There's not much to tell."

"Oh, come now, I doubt that."

He shrugged again. "Let's just say all I'm interested in is completing this project. That's the delight of *my* life."

She knew there was more, much more, to this multifaceted man. But if he didn't want to talk about himself, then so be it. As long as they could work together, and she received a paycheck every month, then his personal life was no concern of hers.

"So how 'bout reporting to work day after tomorrow?" Dalton was saying. "Any problem with that?"

"None at all."

"Good. The first thing I want operational is the club." He walked around the table, then moved closer to her as he spread the architectural plan of the club, along with one of the paddle boat, on the table. "These you'll want to take home and study."

"Without a doubt," Leah said in a small voice, aware of the nearness of his body, the unique scent of his skin that drifted to her nostrils. That combination of body warmth and scent proved lethal to her concentration.

She pulled back, furious that she'd even noticed.

An eyebrow quirked, then he asked, "Have you ever gambled, Leah?"

"No."

"Ever been to a casino?"

"Once."

"Well, in the last year, with the riverboats, gambling's really come into its own, and the competition's fierce."

"When do you want to open yours?" Leah asked.

"Is tomorrow too soon?"

She smiled. "That eager, huh?"

He smiled back. "That eager."

Suddenly the room was too small, too confining, and an absurd stifling feeling made her skittish as they discussed their basic financial arrangements. They came to terms without difficulty. Relieved, Leah began to spread out the blueprints.

"I suggest we call it quits for today," Dalton said abruptly. "I'll set you up in an office, then we'll take it from there."

Leah stood. "Sounds good."

"I'll be in touch, okay?"

She nodded.

When she slid into her car a few minutes later, Leah felt limp, and not only from the heat. She started the car and pulled into the street, admitting that her day hadn't started off well. First that slob insurance investigator had confronted her. Then she'd stumbled onto her half-naked boss, a man who both intrigued her and fascinated her, which made for a very dangerous combination. But the day had not ended badly at all. She was working—and she'd have money enough to cover her expenses.

Deliberately setting aside her doubts, Leah forced herself to concentrate on nothing but the road ahead.

Seventeen

"Good morning, Dan."

Dr. Bolton halted in the hallway and smiled. But the smile lasted only briefly, especially after he saw Leah's face.

"Rufus feels . . . terrible." Leah's voice was barely audible, and there were traces of tears on her cheeks. "I'm sorry. I promised myself that I wouldn't cry, but every time I see him . . . " Her voice trailed off into nothingness.

"Come on, I'll buy you a cup of coffee." Dr. Bolton's round face broke into another short smile as he nodded to the charge nurse. "I'll be back shortly."

"Fine, sir."

A few minutes later Leah raised a cup of hot liquid to her lips and blew on it, then set it back on the table. Dan was already drinking his.

"I don't know how you can do that," she said inanely. "If it's too hot, it invariably burns the skin off the roof of my mouth."

"That's because you don't wear dentures."

"And you do?"

Dan chuckled. "Yep. It comes with the territory."

"You're not old."

"No, but I'm not young, either. Still, I have dentures."

Small talk, instead of getting to the point of the pain that brought them here. Leah smiled, but it never reached her eyes. They remained tormented.

Dan reached across and clasped her hands. "I know I don't have to tell you this, but he's going down fast."

Leah's chin wobbled. "I know. He could hardly talk to me this morning, though he managed to ask about Coty and me, of course."

"That boy is what's kept him going this long."

"Dammit, Dan, he's such a good man. Why did this have to happen to him when rapists and murderers stay perfectly healthy and continue to prey on innocent people?"

Dan let go of her hands, leaned back, and sighed. "Sometimes it's best if we don't ask why. Through the years I've learned that the hard way."

"Seeing so much pain and dying must work on your psyche."

"And on your heart as well."

Leah dug in her purse for a tissue and dabbed at her eyes, then looked back at the doctor. "You're a good man, Dan; I don't know how I would've managed without your support and wonderful care of Rufus."

"That's my job, my dear."

"True, but you have such compassion for your patients; so many doctors don't. Again, thanks."

He nodded, then said, "I didn't ask you here just for coffee, although Lord knows, you looked like you needed some."

"I did." Leah took another sip, feeling the heat calm her jittery stomach.

Dan was quiet for a moment, then he asked, "Have you thought about life support?"

Leah blinked while the bottom dropped out of her stomach.

"What do you want to do about that, if the time should come? Rufus doesn't have a living will, does he?"

Leah didn't want to be having this conversation. She wanted to get up and run out of there as if the devil himself were after her. "No," she said, swallowing around a lump in her throat, "but maybe he'll rally enough to make one out."

"Don't get your hopes up." The doctor paused. "He's slipping into a coma."

"I . . . I was afraid of that."

"So, unless things change drastically, and I don't foresee that happening, you'll have to make that decision."

"Exactly what does it involve?" Leah feared the answer to that question almost as much as she'd dreaded asking it.

Dan sighed again before drinking the last of his coffee. "In a nutshell, do you want him kept alive by machines?"

Leah didn't hesitate. "No. First, he wouldn't want that, and second, neither do I." She looked off into the distance and tried to compose herself. "And . . . and it wouldn't be good for Coty. Rufus wouldn't—" Her throat was so clogged now that she couldn't go on.

"You needn't say more. I understand."

Leah faced him again. "So where does that leave us? And Rufus?"

"In God's hands, my dear, in God's hands."

Coty ran across the room and hugged Leah around the legs the instant she walked into her mother's house. After she'd left the hospital, she'd gone to her office and buried herself in her work, her palliative for heartache.

She'd worked with Sophie on the small office job, then she'd studied and restudied the plans that Dalton had given her. After working for several hours without so much as a lunch break, she had a lot to talk over with Dalton.

Finally she'd had to bring her workday to a close and pick up her son, who was spending another afternoon with her mother.

Now, as Leah glanced down at the top of Coty's head, she smiled and tangled her hands in his thick hair.

He peered up at her. "Guess what, Mommy?"

"What?"

"Sammy brought a lizard to school today."

"A lizard, huh?" Leah made a face.

"Ah, Mommy, you look just like those dumb girls. They squealed and ran."

Leah laughed and hugged him closer. He wiggled out of

her arms, his face having lost its animation. "Grandma said you wouldn't let me have a lizard."

Always negative, that was Jessica. "Well, maybe not a lizard, but maybe some type of bug. We'll see about catching something later, okay?"

"Yippee!"

"I didn't hear you come in."

Leah turned and looked into her mother's face, which was completely devoid of a smile. Leah smiled anyway. "Hello, Mother."

"You're late."

Leah curbed the anger that threatened to surface. "I was busy, and time got away from me. Did Coty give you any trouble?"

"No, it's just that I like for you to do what you say you're going to do."

"Coty, run and take your things to the car while I talk to Grandma a minute."

"Okay." He turned and ran to what he called "his" bedroom.

"Why don't you sit down before you fall down," Jessica said, pushing a strand of her limp, brown-gray hair behind one ear.

Leah sank onto the couch, thinking that if only her mother would take pride in her appearance, she would be a striking woman. She had good bone structure, and for someone in her sixties, her skin was relatively unlined.

Jessica had no interest in appearances. Besides, as long as she had that bitter twist to her lips, no amount of makeup and not even the finest hairdo could improve her looks. Jessica felt that life had dealt her an unfair hand, and she was determined everyone would pay, most of all Leah.

"Want something to drink?" Jessica asked, not looking at her.

"No thanks, but I would like to talk."

Her mother sank on the edge of the nearest chair. "It's Rufus, isn't it?"

"That's part of it. He . . . he's in a coma."

"It'd be best if he just went on."

That's easy for you to say! Leah wanted to scream. She

took a deep breath and went on, "I've decided to move my office back home. I simply can't afford the extra rent."

"Well, it's about time," Jessica said flatly. "You should never have moved it out of your home in the first place."

Leah gritted her teeth. "I have a new job, a good one, too."

"So who hired you?" Jessica pressed.

Leah hedged. "A man who's renovating a club and—" She broke off, hating to say the word *casino* for fear of the fireworks it would set off. Nevertheless, her mother had to know, so it might as well be now.

"Well, go on. A club and what?"

"Gambling casino."

Jessica looked horrified. "Surely you're not going to get involved with a low-life gambler?"

Leah rose. "It's a done deal, so save your breath."

"I just hope you know what you're doing, young lady."

Me too, Leah thought, then said aloud, "Will you pick up Coty from school and keep him until I can get off? I'll pay you, of course." She wouldn't have asked had she not been desperate.

"I'll keep Coty, but I won't take any money, at least not now."

Leah would've loved to hug her mother, but she knew she'd be rebuffed. Some things never change, Leah thought sadly.

"Mommy, I'm ready to go," Coty called.

"I'm coming."

"See ya, Grandma," Coty added before banging the door shut.

Both women winced. "I'll speak to him about that," Leah said as she turned and made her way to the door. "Thanks. I'll talk to you later."

"I still say if you hadn't married Rufus, you wouldn't be in this situation."

Leah's throat constricted so that she couldn't retaliate, not that she would have anyway. She had learned long ago that with her mother she would never have the last word.

Leah stared at the untouched cup of French vanilla coffee on the table beside the couch. Frankly, she was too tired to enjoy it. More than that, she couldn't shut off her thoughts. She leaned her head back and closed her eyes. She knew it would only be a matter of time now until her husband passed away. But she couldn't think about that at this moment or she would sink into such depths of depression that she wouldn't be able to climb out. She had Coty to think about.

She forced her thoughts onto her new job, a job that she still couldn't believe was hers. If only her boss weren't Dalton Montgomery.

Was Sophie right? Was *he* too good to be true? Would this job end up in the drain like the last one?

"Are you sure that job's on the up and up?" Sophie's words came back to haunt her. "More important, is *he* on the up and up? My gut tells me there's something about both the job and Dalton Montgomery that doesn't quite add up."

Leah felt the same way, only *not* for the same reason. She couldn't forget her reaction to him in his state of undress or how his blatant display of masculinity had affected her.

Unwittingly, her eyes had strayed over his torso, which was covered in wiry hair, only not enough hair so that she failed to see the muscles that surrounded his navel, or the way his denim cutoffs strained across his sex. She was just lonely and missed her husband, she told herself. That was what this soul-searching was all about and nothing more.

For the most part, Leah was the typical wife and mother. Yet as a woman she believed in herself and her ability to compete in what she considered a man's world, if she chose to do so. Sometimes the traditional view and the emancipated one were in sharp conflict, as they were now. And all because of a man she'd just met, a man who unfortunately was to be her boss.

But she had no intention of being unfaithful to her husband, now or ever. Adultery was not something she was prepared to add to her list of troubles.

Leah heard a noise and swung around. Coty stood in the doorway, rubbing one of his eyes.

She rushed toward him, her mouth dry. "Coty, honey, what's wrong?"

"Something got after me, but he . . . he didn't get me."

She knelt in front of him. "Whew, am I glad about that. I wouldn't know what to do without you."

Coty leaned his head to one side, traces of fear no longer evident on his face. "Will you read me another story?"

Leah winked at him. "I don't see why not."

He kissed her on the cheek, then grabbed her hand. "I love you, Mommy."

"I love you, too," Leah whispered, rising to her feet.

With his tiny hand nestled in her soft one, they walked toward the bedroom.

"Montgomery."

Dalton had just walked into the office when the phone rang. He swallowed an expletive, recognizing DeChamp's voice. "Whatcha want, Billy?"

He heard DeChamp's swift intake of breath and knew his disrespectful tone had touched a nerve. But that gave him little satisfaction. DeChamp was a wimp, but he could be a lethal wimp if he were allowed to talk too freely. Dalton didn't intend to let that happen.

"What I want is my money, damn you."

"All in good time, if you've been a good boy, that is."

A pointed silence followed before DeChamp said, "I know you've hired a woman who has a kid."

This time it was Dalton who sucked in his breath before he managed to ask in an arctic voice, "Have you been spying on me, DeChamp?"

DeChamp merely laughed. "You figure that out. Later, Dalt."

Dalton heard the click in his ear just as he shouted, "I told you not to fuck with me!"

Eighteen

J. T. Partridge gnawed on his cigar like a dog with a juicy bone. Actually, he figured he was close to biting it in two. Rather that, he told himself, than punch out the lady who sat across from him.

Normally he didn't lose his cool. It took a lot to rile him to the extent that he'd consider hitting a woman—even his wife. But Ellen Thibodeaux, this rich bitch from the right side of the tracks, was enough to make any man lose control. Her mouth was her problem; she didn't know when to keep it shut. What she needed was an attitude adjustment, but then so did someone else—Leah Frazier.

"Well, Mr. Bigshot, aren't you going to answer me?"

J.T. sat behind his desk and scowled at Ellen, taking in her large frame, big breasts, and heavy thighs. She had nice, hazel-colored eyes, he conceded reluctantly. And her black hair was okay.

Overall, though, she was unattractive and rather pathetic. She had the most grating voice he'd ever heard, which was making this meeting more unpleasant. She'd been giving him hell for the past twenty minutes, and it didn't appear she was through.

Maybe he ought to teach her a lesson, he told himself, ignoring her tirade. That thought made him feel considerably better, but only for a second. If he even looked as if he were going to touch her, she'd have his ass hauled to jail so fast, he'd never know what hit him.

"Well?" Ellen pressed.

"Look, Mrs. Thibodeaux," J.T. said, mopping his face with a handkerchief, "these things take time."

She gave an unladylike snort. "I want my jewelry back, and I'm tired of pussyfooting around with incompetent jerks like you."

J.T.'s face turned fiery red, and he almost bit the end of his cigar completely off. But when he spoke his voice was reasonable, though he knew it was less than steady. "Look, I'm doing all I can, you hear? Why don't you go down and hassle the cops."

She made an ugly face. "Why, they're about as useless as my husband, and he's not worth killing."

"I don't know about your husband and don't give a damn, either, but what I do know is that I'm doing all I can. Hell, I got a better idea. My boss is issuing the orders; if you don't like the way the investigation's being handled, go hassle him." The minute J.T. uttered those words, he wished he could retract them.

"I already have."

J.T. swallowed against his throbbing Adam's apple.

As if she'd caught him in his own trap, Ellen smiled a syrupy smile that was anything but sweet. "And you know what he told me?"

She was toying with him, and J.T. knew it. Damn bitch. "No, I don't know what he told you."

"He said that *you* were in charge, and if I had any complaints, to take them up with you, that he was sure you'd be glad to talk with me."

J.T.'s nostrils flared; he felt as if he'd just stepped in a pile of cow manure and would never be rid of the stench. "It's not that I don't want to talk to you; it's just that at this point there's *nothing* to talk about."

"And just whose fault is that?" Ellen shifted on the chair, which caused her breasts to wiggle.

"We both know that Leah Frazier's the culprit here, but I haven't been able to prove it."

Ellen stood abruptly. This time her entire body shook. "Well, prove it or . . . " She paused and stared at J.T., one lip curled slightly in contempt.

He flushed and wiped his face again. "Or what, Mrs. Thibodeaux?"

She didn't hesitate. "Or else I'm going to get you fired. Is that clear enough, Mr. Partridge?"

Sweat oozed out of every pore in J.T.'s body. He really ought to get the air conditioner checked in his office. But he knew it wasn't the a/c that had him sweating. If this woman succeeded in costing him his job, he'd have two bitches to get even with.

"I'll get the goods on the Frazier woman. Meanwhile, you're going to have to be patient. She's in deep financial trouble, and sooner or later she's going to fence those jewels for cash. You mark my words on that. When she makes her move, I'll be on her like a dog on a june bug."

"See that you are." Ellen reached for her Gucci handbag, then jutted her chin. "Oh, and don't make the mistake of underestimating me and my influence in this town, Mr. Partridge. I may be old and overweight, but when I talk, people still listen."

J.T. quelled the urge to roll his eyes. Just because she had money and lived in a mansion didn't mean she was better than he was. The only problem with that was she thought she was. Right now he couldn't think of a way to tell her off without jeopardizing not only his promotion, but the job itself.

He must've been drinking when he took this case. But he'd been certain it would be cut and dried, that the Frazier woman would have made her move long ago.

Why the hell hadn't she?

"Another thing," Ellen said, having moved to the door. "Did you know that Leah Frazier has landed a great job?"

"I suspected as much." J.T.'s tone was quarrelsome.

Ellen smiled a sarcastic smile. "I thought you said you were on top of things?"

"I am," J.T. said defensively.

Ellen merely looked at him. "Well, now that she's working again, I figure she'll hang on to my jewels for no telling how long."

The sweat running down J.T.'s body felt like slithering snakes. He walked from behind his desk. "No, no, she won't."

"You'd better hope she doesn't."

With that Ellen Thibodeaux jerked open the door and walked out.

J.T. was hardly aware that she was gone. His mind was in turmoil. So that Montgomery dude had hired her. How the hell had she pulled that off? One thing he'd always prided himself on was not getting caught with his fly open. Lately that seemed to be the order of the day.

J.T. pounded his forehead with his fists. "Shit, shit, shit!"

He should've still been grieving for his dead father. After all, it had been only a month since he'd buried him. Dalton grieved, only not for Parker.

At this moment Leah Frazier was the primary source of his grief.

He twisted his chair so that the sun from the window wouldn't scald his back. He knew the air outside would feel like copper pennies that had been baked. Inside, the new air-conditioning unit hummed.

Still, Dalton was uncomfortable with the predicament he'd gotten himself into. Hell, he hadn't expected her to look so good or for that matter smell so good, as if she'd just wallowed in a bed of roses.

The phone rang. He flinched, then gave a bitter laugh. Saved by the bell, he thought, and reached for the receiver.

"Montgomery."

"How's it going, my friend?"

Dalton straightened. "Hello, Norm."

Norman Thornhill was his banker and one of the smartest men Dalton knew, smarter than a fox in a chicken coop.

"How's it going with you?" Dalton asked, playing it cool.

"Great, just great."

"So, what can I do for you?"

"Oh, nothing, not really. Just thought I'd check and see how things were progressing."

Like hell that's all he'd called for. Old Norm was getting antsy about his money. He figured that the estate settlement should've been finalized and that Dalton should now have his father's millions. If he only knew . . .

But Dalton wasn't about to tell him the truth, nor was he going to sweat yet. He still had time before the bank note was due. By then he'd *have* access to that money, thanks to Leah Frazier.

"Well, things are progressing real nice," Dalton finally drawled. "In fact, I've hired an architect and designer, and we're about to get the project rolling."

"I see. Well, you keep me posted, you hear?"

"Sure thing, Norm. Meanwhile, you hang loose in this heat. Don't let it get you down."

"Yeah, right. You do the same."

Dalton chuckled when he heard the dial tone. Nosy old fart. However, that chuckle soon faded as he realized his situation was no laughing matter. He could panic if he thought about the wringer his tail was in. But he still had confidence in his ability to get that money—*if* he could control his libido around Leah.

When she had walked in on him half naked and he'd watched her eyes peruse his body, heat had stirred in his lower abdomen. If he hadn't been mistaken, he'd seen a responsive flicker in her eyes.

To make matters worse, when he'd moved close to her at the table, his thoughts had turned to the insane idea of what it would be like to fuck her on the kitchen table.

Thoughts like those were worse than dangerous; they were suicidal. He had no reason to insinuate himself in Leah's personal life. To do so would muddy the waters and make the legalities more difficult when he got ready to obtain custody of his son.

Besides, he couldn't forget about DeChamp. After that phone call the other day, Dalton knew he had a problem. But he felt confident he could handle the attorney.

He would make his move in his own sweet time. Hell, he hadn't even met his son; and until he did, no one, least of all DeChamp, was going to bully him into anything.

Sophie smiled at Louis, who lay beside her. They had just made love, even though it was in the middle of the afternoon.

Louis had taken the day off, and he'd talked her into doing the same.

"So tell me, how's Leah's job going?"

Sophie smiled. "Good, as far as I can tell. If anyone needs a break, she's the one."

"So this is really that break, huh?"

"Let us pray." Sophie crooked an elbow and propped herself up. "She's in hock up to her neck; but at least now she can keep Rufus in that facility for a while longer, and that's really important to her."

"Have you met the new boss?"

Sophie trailed a hand up and down his flat, hairless stomach. Louis trapped that hand in one of his, then played idly with her fingers.

"Nope, not yet."

"You don't sound like you're looking forward to it, either."

Sophie frowned. "It's not that. It's just that I hope he's legit, that he's not taking her for a ride."

"Ah, don't worry. Leah's a savvy businesswoman. Surely she can recognize a con artist when she sees one."

"Under different circumstances I'd agree with you; but now with Rufus in such poor health, she's not thinking clearly."

"Well, she can check him out, you know."

"She's not the one who's worried. She met with him a couple of days ago, and he told her to get started."

"Which goes to show that you're worrying needlessly."

"Maybe so, but I know for a fact that when things seem too good to be true, they usually are. And Mr. Dalton Montgomery fits that rule to a tee."

Louis didn't respond. Sophie peered at him. His features were sober—no, "troubled" was the correct word. Her heart faltered. She had sensed something was wrong even during their lovemaking, that his performance was more mechanical than passionate. But she hadn't worried about it, until now.

"What's wrong, Louis?"

He blinked. "What makes you think something's wrong?"

"Come on, don't give me that. I know you better than you know yourself. And something *is* wrong."

"I got the job today."

"What did you say?"

"You heard me. I got the job at Crestview Hospital today."

Sophie scrambled to her knees and let out a whoop. "All right!" Then she leaned down and planted kisses over his face and chest.

"Whoa," he said, pushing her away. "Don't."

"Why? That's cause for celebration. Why are you acting like

someone just died? I'm delighted. After all, that's what you wanted, right?"

"Yes."

"So what's the problem?"

"I got the results of my physical."

She giggled. "So what'd they tell you, that you needed to gain some weight?"

"No, they told me I was sterile."

His words were so unexpected and spoken so brutally that Sophie felt the air swish out of her lungs. She grappled to speak.

Louis's mouth turned down. "Don't think that news didn't knock the wind our of my sails, too. Before I could even be considered for the position, I had to go through a battery of health tests." He swallowed hard, then went on, "But I decided, while they were at it, I should have a sperm count done. My having mumps in my teens has done me in."

For a moment the room was quiet. Sophie heard his labored breathing beside her and wanted to cry, not for herself, but for him.

"So, you're sterile," she said at last in a "it's no big deal" tone.

Louis bolted upright, turned, and sat on the side of the bed. "Dammit, how can you be so . . . so—" He broke off. "Hell, I can't even find the right word."

"So blasé, is that what you're fishing for?"

"Yeah, that'll do," he flung back over his shoulder, his tone nasty.

She scooted up behind him and rested her head on his shoulder. "That's because I am. Sure, I'd love to have babies, and so would you. I won't deny that, and it hurts that we can't have our own. I won't deny that, either. But nowadays there are lots of ways to get babies. We'll just have to change our plans, that's all."

Louis swung around, his eyes wide. "You mean you'd still consider marrying me?"

She bit him on the shoulder, then grinned. "Maybe."

Louis turned, grabbed her, and held her against his heart. "For now, that's promise enough."

Nineteen

"Leah Frazier, meet my assistant, Tony Watson."

Leah smiled and held out her hand. Tony returned both her handshake and her smile, the latter forging the dimples deeper in each of his cheeks. Besides those awesome dimples, his eyes were kind; he reminded her of Rufus.

"Hello," she said softly, shifting her thoughts.

"Pleased to meet you." Tony's smile remained in place as he faced his boss, who was perched on the edge of the desk, dressed in jeans and T-shirt and swinging a booted foot. "So what's up for today?"

"For starters," Dalton said, "check with the gaming commission and see how our permit's coming along. We still don't have the damn thing."

Tony gazed at Leah. "Ah, but we have plenty of time, right, Mrs. Frazier?"

"Please, call me Leah."

"All right, Leah."

"Doesn't matter about the time frame," Dalton put in. "I want that piece of paper in my hands the second it's available. It's what's going to make this operation one hundred percent legit."

"Whatever you say, boss," Tony replied with a wicked

wink at Leah. "I probably won't be back until late this afternoon. I thought I'd check out several electrical engineers, mainly to see which one can get to us first."

"Do you have a preference?" Leah asked.

"No, do you?"

"Yes, as matter of fact, I do. There's a particular company in Gulfport that I've worked with and think is excellent." She reached for a notepad and scribbled the name, then handed it to Tony."

Tony nodded. "Much obliged."

"Talk to 'em," Dalton said, slipping off the desk.

"Consider it done." Tony waved, then turned toward the door. "Check y'all later."

Once he'd gone, silence filled the room. Leah tried not to notice how overwhelming Dalton's presence seemed and how his casual dress accented his masculine appeal. He'd apparently just showered; the ends of his hair were still wet and sparkled like the sun on early morning dew.

"Well, shall we get started?" she asked in what she knew was a prim tone. But at least she'd forced her mind back onto business.

Dalton looked at her for a moment, his lips twitching, then pointed toward an open door adjacent to the large room. "Your humble office, ma'am," he said, a mocking lilt in his voice. "I know you're just dying to check it out."

"As a matter of fact, I am."

Inside the cubbyhole was a desk, two chairs, and one window with a skewed green miniblind covering it. She frowned.

"That color looks like the stuff you blow outta your nose, doesn't it?"

"What a great analogy," she said drolly.

He laughed. "Sorry, I spoke before I thought, but you'll have to agree—"

"You're right, both the window shade and the color are awful, but I can live with them for now."

After she seated herself behind the desk, Dalton plopped down on the other chair. "So, did you study the plans?"

"Yes, in detail, and everything here, in the club, looks to

be okay, except maybe the plumbing and the electrical, which Tony is already checking into."

"I'm sure everything's going to have to be rewired. The building is ten years old and will fall far short of the city's stringent codes."

"Speaking of stringent codes," Leah added, "don't forget about the fire codes. They're the strictest of all and will take top priority."

"You won't get any argument from me on that." Dalton shook his head. "The thought of a fire in my or any casino is too horrible to contemplate."

Leah shivered visibly. "I couldn't agree more, and that's not going to happen at the . . . " She paused and pushed aside the heavy sweep of hair that had fallen across her face. "I just realized that neither the club nor casino has a name. Or have you one in mind?"

Dalton didn't respond right off, and Leah saw that he was watching her with an odd expression in his eyes. Did that scrutiny have anything to do with the way she looked? Perhaps he'd noticed how pale and listless her overall appearance was.

Unexplained color crept into her face. She hadn't bothered about her looks these last few days. The fact that she thought about it now was disconcerting at best.

She'd had a bad night. The nursing home had called her at midnight. Rufus, the nurse had said, had roused from his coma, but she'd been wrong. Leah had stayed by his bedside for several hours anyway, and as a result, she hadn't had much sleep.

Whether she was unattractive or tired or both was inconsequential, or at least as far as Dalton was concerned. He was nothing to her, and vice versa. She was a hired hand; when this job ended she would most likely never see him again.

"You look tired," he said suddenly, tapping into her thoughts with daunting accuracy.

"I was called to the nursing home late last night," she said with reluctance.

"I'm sorry."

"So am I."

"Your life's tough, isn't it?"

What life? she wanted to cry. The only thing that kept her existence from being a total dark and empty void was Coty first and her work second. But she wasn't about to share this with a stranger.

"Yes, but I have a lot to be thankful for as well."

Dalton sighed, then changed the subject. "Actually, I thought about calling it Dalton's Place."

She raised her eyebrows.

"So?"

"Mmm, not bad. How about the casino?"

"Dalton's Place and More."

"Not bad, not bad at all."

"I have no doubts that when we're finished with this entire project, both the club and casino will be unmatched here or anywhere else."

"I'd say you don't lack for self-confidence."

If he heard the sarcasm in her voice, it rolled off him. "You're right, I don't."

His swaggering ego was astonishing, but at least it served to keep her own grudging awareness of him at bay.

"So keep that thought in mind when you're working on the decor."

"Do you want one theme carried throughout?" Leah asked, relieved they were back on a business footing.

"Maybe, maybe not. But then that's why I hired you. I want you to come up with ideas that will knock the socks off our patrons."

"The club will be easy to work with," Leah said, unrolling the scaled drawing and peering at it. "There are no structural problems, and the layout is okay as is."

"What about my apartment idea?"

"It's not a good one, if you're still thinking about adding it overhead."

"I figured you'd say that."

"What we can do, though, is extend that corner room with the adjoining bath or, for that matter, add two rooms."

Dalton rubbed his chin. "Maybe I'll just scratch that idea for a while until I see how the money's going to hold out."

Leah didn't say anything. Instead she reached for the boat

layout, glanced at it before lifting her eyes to Dalton once again.

He frowned. "Don't tell me there's a problem there as well."

"Not a problem as such, but I do recommend that the kitchen be moved and a deli added."

His mouth fell open. "And you don't call that a problem?"

Leah's lips twitched. "Well, maybe a tiny one. But it can be done relatively easily. Besides, the boat doesn't need that big a kitchen since you want to encourage your patrons to dine at the club. Still, the casino does need a place for them to grab a quick meal, especially when they're deeply involved in a game."

Dalton was quiet.

"Uh-oh, you aren't excited about that. You don't think it's a good idea, do you?"

He leaned closer, so close that he crossed his arms on her desk, then he smiled. His craggy features took on a disturbing sensuality that she suspected he wasn't even aware of. But *she* was.

"Hell, I think it's a great idea. In fact—"

The phone rang, cutting him off. He cursed; then, reaching for the tiny cellular in his pocket, he popped it open and said, "Yeah."

He listened while his eyebrows drew together in a frown. Then he handed the cellular to her. This time it was Leah who frowned.

"It's your mother."

Leah's heart skipped a beat. "Mother, what's the matter?" she said without preamble.

"Coty's complaining of a stomachache and wants you."

Leah heard the frustration in Jessica's voice. "Let me talk to him."

"He's in the bedroom crying."

"Oh, great," Leah muttered. "Leave him alone; I'll get back to you in a minute."

"Problem?" Dalton asked as he reached for the phone.

Leah leaned back on her chair and rubbed her head, which was beginning to throb. She didn't need this, not now, anyway. "Coty's crying with a stomachache."

"You act like you don't believe him."

Leah's head popped up. Was she that easy to read, or did this man have the uncanny ability to see through her? Both were scary thoughts.

"I'm not sure that I do. Last night upset him. I had to wake him up and take him to Mother's."

"I can see where that'd be tough on a kid. So go get him."

"You wouldn't mind?"

"Heck no. If he's really not sick, bring him here. I'll show him the paddle boat; that ought to cheer him up."

Leah was flabbergasted.

Dalton chuckled. "Just because I don't have any kids doesn't mean I want to drown them all on sight."

"Well, all right, if you're sure."

"I'm sure. Go on."

Well, he'd done it. He'd taken the bull by the horns, devised a way to meet his son. Suddenly Dalton shook like someone who had the palsy. His flesh and blood would soon walk through that door.

God! What could he say to the child? He didn't know the first thing about conversing with a kid. What if Coty despised him on sight? It didn't matter. It was the money he was after and not the child's affections.

Yeah, right, Montgomery, he told himself. In the beginning that was the case, but no longer. Not only did he want to see the person he and Leah had created, but he even wanted his son to like him. Now, wasn't that a helluva note—Dalton Montgomery going soft?

He felt his breath gurgle in his chest while he faced the door. And waited.

Fifteen minutes later Leah was back with a smiling Coty in tow. But moments before, he *hadn't* been smiling. When she had arrived at her mother's, his sniveling had stopped instantaneously. Leah had seen the tears for what they were, a ploy to get her attention.

Her first thought had been to spank him, but then she'd

changed her mind, as she'd known the reason behind his faked illness. He missed Rufus, plus he sensed how upset *she* was. However, she had scolded him for deceiving his grandmother and made him apologize.

Now, as Coty scampered alongside her, his eyes took in everything around him. Leah had the urge to shake him, yet she wanted to hug him, too.

When they entered the makeshift office, Dalton was standing at the window.

"We're back," Leah said, hearing the uncertainty in her voice. She still didn't feel comfortable about bringing Coty here. After all, the job site was no place for a child. Yet Dalton had said to bring him.

Dalton swung around. His eyes darted to Coty and stayed there for what seemed to Leah like a long time, but in reality it was only seconds. More than the time element, it was the way he looked at her son, a look she couldn't begin to decipher.

Dalton suddenly crossed the room with a broad smile on his face and held out his hand to Coty. "Hi."

Coty peered up at Leah, a question in his eyes.

"It's all right," she said, nudging him. "Mr. Montgomery's my new boss." She smiled. "He's the one with the big boat outside."

Coty's face came alive, and he stepped forward and placed his hand in Dalton's.

In that unexpected but poignant moment, Leah again wondered what it would be like to walk into Dalton's arms and have him hold her as a friend and tell her that everything was going to be all right.

Since that was *not* going to happen, she shook herself and watched as Dalton dropped Coty's hand, then leaned down and asked in a conspiratorial tone, "Wanna see the paddle boat?"

"Wow! Do I?" Coty glanced up at Leah at the same time Dalton sought her eyes.

"Oh, all right, go on. I'll stay here and work."

But Leah made no move toward her desk. Instead she stood still until the tall man and small boy had walked out the door.

If only Rufus . . . No, don't think about that. But she couldn't help it. She missed her husband, and Coty missed his father. She blinked back tears, squared her shoulders, and marched into her tiny cubicle.

Twenty minutes later Leah heard the door open. She walked around her desk just as Coty ran to her. His face was flushed, and his eyes were flashing.

"Mommy, Dalton said I—"

"Mr. Montgomery to you, young man," Leah interrupted, her tone stern.

Coty's face fell. "But . . . but he said I could call him Dalton."

Leah lifted frustrated eyes to her boss.

"That's right, I did."

"If that's what you want," she said, but her attention was focused back on her son. "So did you like it?"

"It's awesome! And Dalton said I could help him and those men work on it."

Leah shook her head. "Oh, I don't think so."

"Why not?" Coty asked in a petulant tone.

"Maybe that's something you should talk over with your mom," Dalton put in. "Anyway, we have plenty of time to worry about that."

Coty brightened. "Okay."

"Look, why don't we . . . you call it quits for today?" Dalton's eyes were on Leah. "Take Coty and go on home."

Leah raised an eyebrow. "Are you sure you don't mind?"

"I don't say what I don't mean." He paused and held her gaze. "You'll soon find that out."

Leah lowered her head and latched on to Coty's hand. "Let's go, cowboy."

They were just about out the door when Dalton said, "Do you have someone who can watch Coty?"

Leah swung around.

He was leaning against the desk, his dark eyes unreadable. "When?"

"This evening."

"I . . . I guess so."

"Good."

"Why? I . . . mean—" Leah realized she was stuttering and

hated herself for it. But that request had come out of left field and knocked the props from under her.

"Business. I want you to see what I like and don't like in a casino. I'll meet you at the Lucky Seven at eight o'clock." Dalton paused. "Any problem with that?"

Leah expelled her breath in a rush. "No, no problem."

"See ya, then."

"Can I go?" Coty asked.

"No."

"Why?" Coty whined.

Leah grabbed his hand and pulled him out the door into the hall.

"Ouch, Mommy! You're hurting my hand."

"Hush," she said in an unsteady voice, "or I'm going to hurt something else!"

Twenty

Leah stepped into the shower; instantly the water mixed with her tears. She rubbed her face, as if that gesture would wash them away.

After she and Coty had arrived home from the club, they had played catch until the heat and the mosquitoes had driven them inside. She'd fed Coty and left him with Sophie, who had agreed to watch him, though Leah had sensed something was bothering her friend. She'd almost asked, but since she'd wanted to stop by the nursing home there hadn't been time for a chat.

She had sat by Rufus's side for over an hour, creaming his body with lotion, talking to him, making it a special point to include the stunt Coty had pulled.

"I wanted to throttle the little bugger," she'd said to the pale listless figure in the bed, all the while caressing his hand.

"You wouldn't have thought it funny, I know, that our son was able to pull one over on me like that." She'd paused and swallowed around a lump in her throat. "He's growing up, darling. I wish—"

Her voice had broken and she hadn't been able to talk anymore, but she had continued to sit with him until time had forced her to go.

Now, as she stepped out of the shower, Leah fought off another bout of self-pity. She didn't want to go with Dalton to a casino, but she had to. So to boost her own confidence, she wanted to look her best.

She recalled what Sophie had said to her when she'd come by with Coty.

"Just try to relax and enjoy yourself, okay? I know Rufus is sick and that you feel a ton of guilt, but you have to go on with your life."

Leah's eyes darkened. "How can I, when . . . ?"

"Because that's what Rufus would want. This is part of your job. You have to think of your future and Coty's. You can't afford to jeopardize either."

"You're right, but . . . "

"No buts. Hell, play a slot machine."

Leah wrinkled her nose. "I think I'll pass."

"You're impossible, Leah Frazier."

"I know."

Sophie laughed, then her features turned somber. "Look, I know now's not the time, but later, when you have a free moment, there's something I'd like to ask you."

Leah was taken aback. "My, but that sounds ominous."

Sophie's smile was lame at best. "Not ominous, just serious."

Curious, Leah said, "If it's that important, I can make time now."

"No, you can't. I'll catch you later. It's no big deal, really."

It was a big deal, Leah thought as she finished her toiletries. Something was wrong; she'd seen the anxiety in her friend's eyes. For now, though, she had no choice but to thrust aside that uneasy thought.

Thirty minutes later she was dressed and standing in front of the mirror for one last peep at herself.

"Not bad," she mused out loud, especially for someone who had just cried her eyes out.

She'd chosen a simple black linen dress, black hose, and heels. Silver earrings dangled from her ears. "Understated simplicity" were the words that came to mind. Not that either mattered, she reminded herself; this outing was work and nothing more.

Then why was she so uneasy?

Twilight had descended, painting the sky a beautiful lavender. Inhaling the scent of the ocean breeze, she made her way toward the casino. She paused inside the two-story entrance and looked around the atrium.

The Lucky Seven was packed. Shoulder-to-shoulder gamblers hovered near tables like vultures waiting to pounce if and when a space became available.

Leah blinked against the smoke that hung in the air like a wall of thick fog as her gaze wandered around the premises. The noise from the row after row of jangling, gaudy slot machines, into which players were frantically feeding quarters and nickels, fascinated her.

When a machine close by suddenly sang, *kathunk*ed, then dumped a pile of quarters in the tray, Leah smiled as the lady who had won let out a yell. But then Leah looked at the lady's hands, saw how black with grime they were, and winced, knowing instantly that this type of existence was not for her.

"Well, what's the verdict?"

At the sound of husky spoken words, Leah turned. "I didn't see you," she said with difficulty.

Dalton chuckled. "No, I'm sure you didn't. But I saw you, taking everything in with wide eyes."

"You're exaggerating."

"Wanna bet?"

She smiled reluctantly, conceding that he spoke the truth. The entire spectacle was rather overwhelming, including Dalton himself, who looked great but daunting in a pair of black jeans, black shirt, and dress boots.

"Yeah, just another night on the Mississippi coast, where the roll of dice and the flip of cards are music to the ears of the city fathers. And I can't wait to get my fair share."

"Well, I hope you'll include a nonsmoking area."

He looked at her for a second, then laughed. "Leave it to a

woman to think of that. But I have to agree; this smoke's the pits."

They were silent for a moment, as the burgeoning noise would have prevented further conversation anyway.

"Come on," Dalton finally said, "let's go upstairs to the restaurant, where we can get both a drink and some quiet. Then I'll give you a tour, show you how the other half lives."

Leah frowned inwardly. He made her sound like some backward housewife who still made bread the old-fashioned way. Just because she didn't believe in gambling didn't mean she was a misfit. Apparently he thought so.

Once they were seated at the casino's full-service restaurant, a waiter appeared at Dalton's elbow.

Dalton raised his eyebrows at Leah.

"I'll have Perrier with a twist of lime, please."

"I'll have a beer."

The waiter nodded, then disappeared.

"By the way, you look great in that outfit." He smiled as he opened the conversation.

That smile drew her gaze to his mouth. His lips were full and parted over even white teeth. Leah felt out of her depths as her eyes collided with his probing gaze. Flustered, she turned her head.

"Would you like something to eat?" Dalton asked at last.

Food was the last thing she wanted. "No, I had to feed Coty, so I ate with him."

"I'm not hungry, either." Dalton was quiet for a moment, then he said, "You have a great kid."

Leah's spirits lifted. "Yeah, I think so, too." Then, realizing how that must sound, she added sheepishly, "Sorry, I know you're not supposed to brag about your own."

"Why not? He's something to brag about."

"I want to thank you again for this afternoon, for being so understanding."

"I gather you're still shocked by that 'understanding,' right?"

His blunt question momentarily caught Leah off guard. But the waiter appeared and brought her a reprieve. Not for long, though.

"Well?" he pressed when they were alone again.

She smiled grudgingly. "Well . . . "

"Okay, so 'kids' aren't my thing. I'll concede that."

"That's understandable."

He shrugged. "On the other hand, I do try to accommodate."

"You certainly impressed my son."

"But not you?"

Another question out of left field, but always at close range. Though his tone was casual, there was nothing casual about the tension that leapt between them. He was probing—delicately, with silken words—but probing nonetheless.

He was dangerous, and she was defenseless. As long as he didn't pick up on that weakness, she would be just fine.

"So what do you think about this operation?" Dalton asked in a tone that placed them and the conversation back on solid ground. She hoped her imagination had just worked overtime, and he'd meant nothing by what he'd said.

"Frankly I find the whole operation amazing."

"I agree. To think that one can take an old riverboat, complete with smokestacks and paddle wheels, and transform it into what looks like a land-based casino *is* an amazing feat."

"I guess that's what I find so incredible; they float, but they don't."

"And that's what makes them so lucrative and enticing," Dalton added. "With boats, no property taxes are required because of the fact that they *are* on water and not land.

"Another advantage is that there's just so much room and no more."

"Which means the cost and staff can be held to a minimum."

Dalton seemed taken aback by her perception. "Exactly. To date the biggest draws are the slots. Table games, with the exception of blackjack and poker, are scaled down, again because of the space factor."

"Well, I think we can better utilize our space and upstage this casino with no problem."

Again Dalton seemed surprised at her analysis, which irritated her. "Look, I told you I intend to do my job, despite the fact that I know nothing about gambling."

"Nevertheless, you look down your nose on those who partake in the sport."

"That's not true," Leah snapped. "Besides, we've had this conversation before."

He leaned closer. She smelled his cologne. She stiffened and looked away.

"We'll probably have it again, too. You think people like me, who gamble seriously, are pond scum."

Leah turned back around, her features pinched in fury. "How dare you put words in my mouth? You don't know me well enough to judge what I think."

Dalton leaned back; his eyes were inscrutable, but his mouth was tight.

Leah felt impending doom. How had the conversation gotten out of control? It was as if someone had dropped a bomb in their midst and started a war. She couldn't afford to let that happen. Nothing must derail this job.

"Look, I know you're still concerned that I won't do a good job because I don't indulge, but that's simply not the case." She tempered both her tone and her words.

"If I had thought that, you wouldn't have gotten the job," Dalton said flatly.

Then why do you keep throwing it in my face? she wanted to ask, only she didn't get the chance. A man approached their table.

"Well, if it isn't Dalton Montgomery."

Dalton turned, stood, then held out his hand to the man who smiled at him, though Leah noticed the smile was insincere at best.

"Hello, Phil, how's it going?"

"Couldn't be better. Couldn't be better."

"Phil Chapin, Leah Frazier."

Phil nodded and gave her a polished grin, only this time that grin seemed wholeheartedly sincere. "Mrs. Frazier, welcome to the Lucky Seven."

Leah couldn't help but notice he stressed the "Mrs." as his eyes targeted her wedding ring. "Thank you."

Dalton remained standing and said, "Phil's the marketing vice president here."

"It's a lovely place," Leah remarked.

"Do you gamble, Mrs. Frazier?"

Dalton grinned, which made her want to kick him under the table.

"No, no, I don't."

"Too bad. Anytime you'd like to, just say the word."

"She works for me, Chapin," Dalton said in a rough tone.

"Ah, so that's what brings you here. You're checking out the competition."

"Yep," Dalton said with unabashed candor. "Why not? You'd do the same thing."

"So when do you plan to open?"

"ASAP."

"Well, good luck in your endeavor," Phil said. "And do enjoy your visit." Though he spoke to both, his eyes were on Leah.

"Thank you, we will."

Dalton watched him walk off, his jaw set and his eyes hard.

"He doesn't like you, either."

With a start, he faced her, then smiled as only he could smile, that slow, burning smile. "You're right, he doesn't."

Their gazes held for another moment. Dalton cleared his throat and said, "Come on, let's see how the rest of this place is laid out."

"Fine," Leah's voice was light, but she heard the tremor in it. She just hoped he hadn't.

For an hour they circulated, watched patrons enjoy the slots, which Leah found the most fascinating, looked on as the dealers arched cards, retrieved dice, spun wheels, and scooped chips in fluid movements.

Yet for all the attention she paid to these activities, her mind was more on the layout and the decor of the casino as a whole.

"So, what are you thinking?"

Because of the boisterous noise and large number of people, Dalton spoke close to her ear. His warm breath fanned her neck and sent chills down her spine.

"I'm thinking what a challenge it's going to be to make your casino better than any of the others on the strip."

"That's exactly what I was hoping you'd say."

Feeling his warm breath again, Leah stepped quickly to his right.

That was when it happened.

A group of rabble-rousers chose that moment to thrust their way through the crowd. The beefy guy in front bumped into Leah.

"Oh!" she cried, feeling her breath leave her lungs and her legs buckle.

"Sonofabitch, watch where you're going!" Dalton's threat rang out at the same time he circled her bare arms and anchored her against his body.

"Are you okay?" he demanded, his tone harsh but unsteady.

Leah jerked away, her face scalded.

He dropped his hands and, with his teeth ground together, said, "Come on, let's get the hell out of here."

Twenty-one

Dalton was sweating like a field hand, but he didn't care. The harder he ran across the sand, the more he dripped. During the last few weeks he'd developed this warped habit of beating up on himself both mentally and physically, thinking that he could outrun the demons chasing him. No dice.

His heart rate increased each time his Nikes slapped the sand. His eventual target was the boat, the point at which he'd begun this marathon. But thirty minutes in the humidity, even at seven o'clock in the morning, made the jog seem like the equivalent of climbing Mount Everest.

The paddle boat was within yards when his legs suddenly gave way. "Sonofabitch!" he muttered as the white powder rose up to meet him.

Seconds later he lay facedown in the sand, his mouth filled with grit. He rolled onto his back and swiped the back of his hand across his mouth, then spat to one side.

Still, he didn't get up. He remained unmoving, then laughed, a deep belly laugh that had nothing to do with glee. Butt deep in the sand, he forced himself to face the truth.

He wanted Leah Frazier in his bed, which was the one thing that *wasn't* going to happen. His plans would not be derailed by sex.

Touching her had been the fatal mistake. But the assault on his body had started before that jostling incident. When he'd sauntered into the casino, he'd been confident that this was just an evening with an employee, who just happened to be attractive. Then he'd seen her, and that scenario had been brutally shattered.

He blamed his downfall on that little black dress. While not even tight, it nevertheless had left no doubt as to the curves hidden beneath. And when she walked, the sway of her hips had been damned hypnotic.

Why couldn't she have been ugly? And why couldn't he keep in mind that she was married? That fact hadn't previously been a deterrent, however. He'd had his share of affairs with married women, not that he was proud of himself. In retrospect there wasn't a lot about himself or his life he *was* proud of. However, that would change when he got his hands on the money.

And the kid? *His kid, for chrissake!* Why did he have to be so likable? Why couldn't he have been an obnoxious monster like so many kids his age?

Dalton wanted to get close to both mother and child, make himself a part of their lives, but with no strings attached, certainly no sexual strings.

"Ah, shit," he cried to the skies, then rolled over and up.

This kind of mental abuse was getting him nowhere. Part of his problem was that he was horny. Maybe he'd give Tanya Delisle another call. Maybe that would make him feel better. Then again, maybe it wouldn't.

He'd told Leah to come to work at ten. He planned to be long gone by then. Today was not a good day to see her.

Chicken! a voice taunted, but he ignored it and stomped through the sand to the club.

Bill DeChamp passed Dalton on the beach. Of course, Dalton hadn't recognized him. He'd made sure of that, having donned a baseball cap and the darkest sunglasses he could find.

Dalton was obviously pissed about something, DeChamp thought as he paused and watched Dalton enter the club. Good. DeChamp hoped to hell Dalton's life stank as badly as his, but he doubted it. Some things never changed, and Dalton's luck was one of them. Lack of his old man's money hadn't stopped him from going ahead with his casino.

Yeah, Dalton Montgomery had it all—looks, money, prestige—while others, like himself, had nothing, except the crumbs dribbled to him by his wife.

Sweat poured down DeChamp's face, and he removed his cap. He was careful, however, not to remove his glasses. Even though Dalton was no longer in sight, he wasn't about to take any chances.

The reason for his venture onto Dalton's turf was hope of catching a glimpse of the kid. He had seen the boy and his mother enter the club a few days ago. He'd had business in Biloxi and couldn't let the opportunity pass to again spy on Dalton.

Maybe a closer look would reveal that the brat was a dead ringer for his daddy. DeChamp almost laughed out loud. Now wouldn't that be justice. Whether or not he favored Dalton didn't matter. What mattered was obtaining proof that the kid belonged to Dalton.

That wouldn't be easy, DeChamp knew, as volatile as Dalton was. Even though it galled him to admit it, DeChamp continued to fear Dalton. He was capable of anything, especially violence, when crossed.

Still, DeChamp was determined not to be thwarted. He had a plan of his own; and if Dalton didn't make his move toward settling the estate soon, then he would. He'd use that ace he had up his sleeve.

By the time DeChamp reached his car, he was actually whistling.

Dalton had just stepped out of the shower and stuffed his shirt in his jeans when the phone rang. "Dalton," he said in a clipped tone.

"Ah, yes, this is Cooper Anderson."

For a moment Dalton's mind went blank. Cooper Anderson? Then he remembered. The architect who had come to his office. He remembered something else, too. He hadn't liked the s.o.b.

"So what can I do for you, Mr. Anderson?" Dalton asked, hearing the chill in his voice.

"It's what I can do for you that prompted this call," Anderson responded eagerly.

Dalton picked up on the syrup in the architect's tone and wanted to puke. He hated it when grown men begged, and he felt that was exactly what Anderson was doing. Was his firm in financial trouble? Was that why he wanted Dalton's job so badly? Or was it because he hadn't wanted Leah to have it? If so, why not?

The answers to those questions eluded him. Still, Dalton was getting a whiff of something that smelled foul; he just didn't know what it was. Yet.

"Mr. Montgomery?"

"Look, I'm sorry I didn't get back to you." Hell, he wasn't sorry at all, but it sounded good, anyway.

"So you've hired someone else?"

This time the chill was in Anderson's voice. In fact, it was downright icy. Dalton smiled. "Yes, Leah Frazier."

Silence throbbed through the phone line.

"I see," Anderson finally responded. "Well, that's too bad. I feel you've made a grave mistake."

"Now, just why is that?" Dalton drawled.

"Like I told you before, she can't handle a job of that magnitude." He paused. "You know that and I know that." He chuckled suddenly. "So remember when you need someone to clean up her mess, I'm available."

That'll be a cold day in hell, you bastard, Dalton thought. When he spoke, however, his voice was polite and even. "I'll keep that in mind, Anderson."

"I expect you will." He chuckled again, then hung up.

Dalton slammed the receiver back on the hook.

"Sure glad that I wasn't on the other end of that line."

Dalton looked up and watched as Tony ambled into the room, his muscles bulging underneath his T-shirt and Dockers slacks.

"He hung up first."

"Who's he?" Tony asked, stopping at his desk and leaning against it.

"Cooper Anderson, the architect who wanted this job."

"Must've said something that pissed you off."

"The man in general pisses me off."

Tony smiled a lopsided smile. "I gathered that." Then, changing the subject, he asked, "So what's on the agenda today?"

Dalton focused his thoughts back on business. "There's so much, I don't know where to start. But first, I guess, we'd better go work on an equipment list for both the club and the casino."

"I've already done a little of that," Tony said.

"So who's the best manufacturer for what?"

"Bally for slot machines and the Bud Jones Company in Vegas for chips." Tony rubbed his chin. "At least that's the consensus along the strip."

"What about the gaming tables?"

"I'm working on that but don't have anything concrete."

"Keep at it, then check on the security. Those damn electronic eyes are going to cost a fortune."

"Yeah, boss, but they'll save you big bucks in the end."

"I know, and I'm not bellyaching. But what I am bellyaching about is this pile of job applications that's two feet high."

Tony grimaced. "Now, that's going to be when the real trouble starts, knowing who to hire and who not to."

"I guess we'll both just have to take a bite of that elephant one piece at a time, though I have to say, I've had some calls from some of the best in the business. Dealers especially."

"Let's hope that trend continues."

"By the way, I want you to oversee the club, then help me with the casino. How does that sound to you?"

"You mean you're going to actually manage the casino yourself?"

"Yep. For now, anyway."

"Hell, you know I'll do whatever you want."

"Thanks." Dalton grinned. "I'll raise your salary."

"When, in your next life?"

They both laughed.

"Is Leah coming in?" Tony finally asked.

"Yeah, around ten, but I won't be here. As soon as I make a few calls, I'm heading for Bogalusa."

Tony was quiet for a moment, then he said, "Mind if I ask you something?"

"Nope."

"Why did you hire Leah Frazier? I mean, it's obvious she doesn't have the kind of experience . . ." His voice played out, and he shrugged. "By the look on your face, I've stuck my big foot in my mouth."

"Not really. I think she's the best person for the job."

"You're the boss."

"That's right."

Tony sighed, walked to the cubbyhole that was his office, and shut the door.

Dalton cursed, picked up the pencil in front of him, and threw it across the room. This day hadn't started off well, not well at all.

Exhaustion failed adequately to describe how Leah felt. Every muscle, every joint, ached. Was she coming down with the flu?

Coty was already in bed, thank goodness, even though it was only eight-thirty. He'd been out of sorts as well, whining about everything. She'd held on to her patience while he'd had his bath and had read him a story when she tucked him in bed.

Part of everyone's short temper was the August humidity. But at least she'd been spared Dalton's presence at work. He'd left town, which made her wonder if he wanted to avoid her as well.

Leah took a sip from her glass of iced tea, then frowned. The instant the liquid hit her stomach, it congealed. Disgusted with herself, she sank onto the couch and curled her feet under her. She couldn't ignore what was zapping her energy, but she was loath to admit that even to herself.

He shouldn't have touched her. She shouldn't have *let* him touch her. But the incident in the casino had happened so fast, who could've seen it coming? No one.

Before his illness, Rufus had been a gentle and considerate lover, always concerned more with her needs than his. Passion was a word she knew nothing about—yet when Dalton's hard, callused hands gripped her bare arms, her body had come alive. She had felt such a sharp stab of longing that her mind had snapped under its impact.

She refused, however, to give in to that longing. She was *not* attracted to Dalton Montgomery. Nonetheless, she felt guilty and soiled, as if she needed to wash her mind and heart with a bar of harsh soap.

The doorbell chimed. Leah jumped, and when she did, her elbow knocked over the glass of tea and the dark liquid spewed everywhere.

She swallowed a curse. The doorbell rang again. Throwing up her hands in defeat, she rose and rushed to the front door, fearing the noise would awaken Coty.

She switched on the porch light and asked, "Who is it?"

"Sophie."

Stunned, Leah unlatched the dead bolt and jerked open the door. "What on earth . . ." The remainder of the words died on her lips. Her friend's face was ravaged with tears, and the fear in her eyes reached out to Leah.

"May . . . I come in?" Sophie asked, her voice raspy.

Instead of saying a word, Leah held out her arms. Sophie dove into them. Leah held her for a long moment, then gently pushed her back, reached around her, and kicked the door shut with her foot.

"Look, I hate to bug you at this time of night, but I need a shoulder."

"Are you all right? I mean—?"

"No, I'm not all right." Sophie took a deep breath. "I need to talk. But if it's too late—"

"Oh, for heaven's sake, it's only nine o'clock. Anyway, I wouldn't care if it were three in the morning. Come on, let's sit down. Want a glass of tea? Or maybe coffee?"

"I don't care." Sophie's voice shook. "Whatever you're having."

"Well, I *was* having tea, but when you rang, I knocked the damn glass over."

A shadow of a smile altered Sophie's stiff lips. "I can count the times on one hand that I've heard you curse."

Leah felt encouraged. When she had opened the door to her friend's tear-ravaged face, she had feared the worst. Now she felt that Sophie's problem was probably nothing more serious than a disagreement with Louis.

Once Sophie was settled on the couch, Leah disappeared into the kitchen, then returned to the living room a few minutes later with a glass of tea and a towel to mop up her mess.

That chore soon out of the way, Leah sat beside Sophie. "Feeling better?"

"No."

"Well, at least you're honest. What's wrong?"

Sophie drank a sip of tea, then set her glass on the coffee table and looked at Leah. "Louis got the administrator's job."

Leah grinned. "That's great. So why are you crying?"

Sophie licked her lips and avoided Leah's probing gaze. "Louis had a physical and found out that he's . . . he's sterile."

"Oh, dear, I'm so sorry." Leah reached over and covered her friend's hands, which were clasped tightly in her lap.

"Me too."

"But it's not the end of the world, you know. There are ways to get a child."

"I know."

"So did you dicuss that?"

"Not yet. Louis is still trying to come to grips with the blow."

"Again, I'm so sorry."

"I hate to ask you this, but . . ." Sophie paused.

"Oh, pooh, you can ask anything you like." Leah smiled, hoping to make Sophie lighten up.

"Well, I feel awful burdening you with my problems when they're insignificant compared to what you're going through with Rufus."

"Still, it's important to you. So ask."

"It's not something you like to talk about."

Leah should've seen it coming, should have been prepared, only she wasn't.

When she remained silent, Sophie plunged forth. "Would . . . would you mind telling me what it was like to be artificially inseminated?"

Twenty-two

Artificial insemination. Leah's palms turned sweaty, and her mouth tasted suddenly like rubber. She took a deep shuddering breath, rose from the sofa, and walked to the middle of the room.

The ticking of the grandfather clock in the opposite corner seemed to calm her nerves. She felt Sophie's eyes on her; she wanted to turn around and reassure her, only she couldn't.

AI was a painful subject, one that Leah had crammed into the back of her mind. Rarely had she allowed herself to relive that part of her life that had brought both joy and pain. Now, though, a friend who had stood by her needed help. She couldn't ignore that.

But dear Lord, she didn't want to think about that period in her life, much less discuss it.

As if the lingering silence were simply too much to bear, Sophie whispered, "Look, I'm sorry. Forget I asked."

Leah whirled around just as Sophie stood and started walking toward the door. The knot jerked tighter in Leah's stomach. "Hold on. Where're you going?"

"Home," Sophie responded in a small voice.

"No, you're not. Sit down."

"But—"

"Forget the buts. Just sit down."

Sophie still didn't move. "I don't—"

"You sure don't take orders very well, do you?" Leah forced a lightness into her tone that she was far from feeling.

Sophie shrugged, yet her features lightened somewhat. "That's always been my problem."

"Well, now's as good a time as any to change."

They both knew what kind of game they were playing. They were determined to put things back on an even keel before they broached the touchy subject again.

"I guess you're right," Sophie said, and made her way back to the couch. Once there, however, the glum expression returned to her face.

Leah had never seen her friend in such a shape. Sophie had always been the eternal optimist, the one who always lifted Leah's spirits when problems were overwhelming, as they had been lately. This side of Sophie was frightening.

Leah voiced her thoughts. "I've never seen you so down."

"Believe me, I've never been so down. When Louis dropped that bombshell in my lap, I was stunned, of course, but not devastated."

"But he is."

"He . . . was . . . is like I've never seen him. He acts like he's been handed down a death sentence, and he's going to die tomorrow."

"I know."

Sophie sighed. "I know you know. That's why I asked, but if you don't feel comfortable discussing it, then say so. You know I'll understand. After all, that subject isn't something you go around discussing, for heaven's sake."

"No one except you knows I was artificially inseminated," Leah said quietly.

Sophie's mouth parted. "You mean your mother doesn't know?"

"She's the last person I'd tell."

"Right. I should've known that."

"The doctors are sure?" Leah asked, then berated herself for asking such a stupid question.

"Well, they seem to be, said having the mumps had done irreversible damage."

"I guess I was just hoping for a miracle. Medical science can do so much now, except . . ." Leah's voice faltered.

"Cure Rufus," Sophie finished for her. "That's why I feel like a heel whining about my problem when it pales in comparison with yours."

"Don't. It's okay, really."

"You know," Sophie said whimsically, "I didn't realize just how much I cared about that Yankee until this happened. Now, I know that I love him with all my heart."

"But do you still want to marry him?"

"Yes, at least that's what I told him."

"Yet you're still not sure?"

"Right, but my hesitancy has nothing to do with the fact that he's st—" She broke off.

"Sterile. Go ahead and say it. You can't deny it, nor can you not discuss it. That would be the worst thing that could happen."

"So was Rufus sterile?" Sophie's tone was once again hesitant. "Was that his problem, too?"

Leah took a deep breath. "No. His sperm count was just terribly low."

"So how long did you give it before you considered other options?"

"Not long, because Rufus desperately wanted a child." Leah's face looked tormented. "It's almost as if he knew something terrible was about to happen and that he, that we, didn't have a moment to waste."

Another silence invaded the room.

"So why didn't you just adopt?"

Leah didn't answer right away. She walked back to the couch and sat down beside Sophie. It wasn't that she was ashamed of what she'd done. She wasn't. It was just that the subject was so very private, so intimate, that she felt by discussing it openly she was betraying Rufus. Deep down she knew better. Rufus was an unselfish person who would want her to share the information. It had been she, Leah, who hadn't wanted anyone to know, because she'd wanted to protect Rufus.

"Look, I'll say it again, if you'd rather not talk about this, if you think Rufus—"

"No. Rufus never asked me to keep it a secret. I'm the one who never thought it was anyone's business. But then, you're not just anyone."

Sophie smiled a fleeting smile. "So what it boils down to is that Rufus was all for using a donor?"

"Yes."

"Even though he knew that another man's sperm would father his child?"

"That's how badly he wanted a baby."

Sophie fell back against the cushion. "Louis wants 'children,' but somehow I don't think he'll ever be as open-minded as Rufus."

"Keep in mind that at the time, Rufus was much older than Louis. That has a lot to do with it. Louis's manhood is severely threatened, and younger men seem to have more trouble dealing with that than older ones."

"You're probably right; at the moment, Louis is feeling lower than whale shit."

Leah rolled her eyes. "You and your similes; they slay me."

Another smile flickered across Sophie's lips. "So back to my original question. Why donor insemination rather than adoption?"

"First off, Rufus and I sat down with what we referred to as our mental ledger. Across the top left side of the page, we put AI, then on the right we put Adoption. Under each we listed the pros and the cons."

"Do you still remember what you wrote down?"

"Yes, but I can tell you that AI won hands down. First, *I* would have the child; its heredity would be partly mine. Second, it would be easier than adoption because of Rufus's age and the lack of newborns. Third, it would be financially, medically, and legally easier than adoption. And last, donors were handpicked from top-notch medical and graduate students."

"Ah, so that's where the donors come from?"

"Most always."

"That would be a plus, especially since Louis is in the hospital business. So go on."

"Then there's the obvious fact that Rufus could share in the Lamaze classes, then in the actual birth itself. But, to my mind, the most important point was that everyone would think the baby belonged to my husband."

"But the big minus is that another man gets you pregnant."

"That would bother Louis?"

"Big time." Sophie got up off the couch, then stared down at Leah, her eyes wet with tears. "In fact, I'm sure he'd never go for it."

"Are you going to talk to him about it?"

"Not right now. Maybe later, maybe after he has time to come to grips with it."

"Let me warn you that it won't be easy," Leah said. "He'll probably be hell to live with. And the best thing you can do is give him space."

"I know," Sophie whispered.

Leah rose and hugged her friend long and hard. Then, pulling back, she said, "I have some books on the procedure itself. I'll dig them out of the attic and let you peruse them. It's certainly not a decision you have to reach anytime soon."

"Is it complicated—the procedure, I mean?"

"No, not really," Leah said in a rushed voice. "In a nutshell, a doctor places the donor sperm into the vagina and cervical canal with a syringe."

Sophie frowned, then shivered. "Doesn't sound like very much fun."

"Well, as I said, you don't have to worry about that now."

"I . . . I feel much better, though I'm sure Louis doesn't."

"And he may never. That's a possibility you have to face, only not now. You're exhausted. What you need is a good night's sleep. Things won't look so grim in the morning."

"Is that how you face each day?" Sophie asked softly.

"Yes." Leah bit down on her lower lip.

Sophie made her way to the door, then turned. "Good night, dear friend, and thanks."

Leah stared at the ceiling and prayed that sleep would come. She had a long day tomorrow, but she couldn't sleep. She couldn't get her mind off the pain that conversation with Sophie had resurrected.

"Count sheep," she murmured out loud, turning and punching her pillow as if somehow it were at fault.

Her mind wouldn't rest. It seemed determined to replay those days long ago when she'd walked into that doctor's office. . . .

The day before she had been almost giddy. She had told herself over and over that tomorrow was the big day, the day that she'd receive the first injection of sperm.

She'd decided to take a bubble bath so she could relax. But instead of relaxing, she'd thought about the man whose sperm she would receive.

The doctor had shown her and Rufus a donor's catalog. From it, they had chosen the donor who fit the physical and mental qualifications best matched to theirs. It hadn't been an easy decision; they had agonized over the catalog for hours.

Once the decision had been made, she hadn't been able to get him off her mind. She'd wondered what he really looked like, in the flesh, how he dressed, where he worked, what he did with his spare time, whom he dated, *whom he made love to.*

While up to her neck in bubbles, that wild and forbidden thought had raged out of control. Maybe it had been the warm sudsy water, the lethargic feeling it had created. Whatever the reason, she hadn't been able to let the image go. Was it because he hadn't made love to her or to any other woman? *He had masturbated,* in a cup, for heaven's sake.

She remembered how that thought had upped her heart rate and made her stomach roll. She had never seen a man masturbate, nor had she wanted to.

Once the panic inside her had quieted, she had gotten out of the tub and gone to bed. But even with Rufus's arms around her, she hadn't been able to sleep.

As a result, when she'd entered the doctor's office the following day, she'd been a bundle of exhausted nerves.

"Relax, my dear," Dr. Raymond said in a soothing tone.

After she'd gotten on the table, the nurse placed her feet in the stirrups and covered her lower body with a sheet.

"I am relaxed," Leah said, though the tremor in her voice said otherwise.

"Do you want Rufus to come in and stay with you?"

"No. We agreed that he would wait outside."

"Fine, whatever you want." He smiled then and reached for the syringe. "Stay relaxed and this won't hurt a bit."

He had been right. The procedure itself hadn't hurt, but what followed was a painful nightmare.

Dr. Raymond had then placed a cup filled with additional sperm over her cervix. It had to remain there for several hours to keep the sperm from slipping back into the vagina. The device had a string attached that was used for the purpose of pulling out the cup. The problem was that the suction held the cup in place, and she hadn't been able to remove it.

Rufus had had to perform that task. After much maneuvering on his part, it had finally come out, but not before she'd cried out in pain.

"Oh, honey, I'm so sorry I hurt you."

Weak and trembling from the pain inside her, Leah had whispered, "You couldn't help it. Don't worry, I'll be all right."

And she had been, but the memories of those times had not faded. Now, as she relived them, cold chills suddenly covered Leah's body.

Stifling a cry, she tossed back the covers, jumped out of bed, and padded down the hallway. Seconds later she sat beside Coty, who was sleeping soundly.

She didn't know how long she remained there or how long she stared at his beautiful face before she leaned over, kissed him on the cheek, and whispered, "You're my miracle, and I love you."

When she lifted her head, his skin bore the imprint of her tears.

Twenty-three

Leah couldn't believe that she'd been on the job for a month now. Time had passed like an out-of-control forest fire. Yet it had crawled as well, because she felt guilty at having to spend so much time away from Rufus. She tried to compensate by getting up two hours earlier and visiting him before she went to work, then again afterward. There had been little change in Rufus except that he drifted in and out of a coma.

Dr. Bolton had told her that Rufus had the strongest will of anyone he'd seen, that he was fighting death with everything he had. With Dan Bolton's influence, she had worked out a temporary financial arrangement with the nursing facility to keep Rufus there a while longer. Even with the generous salary Dalton was paying her, it would still be only a matter of time before she had to bring Rufus home.

During the long, hot August days, Leah had refused to dwell on that thought, taking each day as it had come and working as hard as she could on relocating the kitchen and designing a deli on board the casino.

Along with Tony, she'd also spent hours with the engineering company. As Dalton had predicted, neither the plumbing nor the electrical work was up to standard. She'd also spent hours on the phone with manufacturing representatives from carpet and furniture companies. But she'd barely scratched the surface as far as getting the club and casino operational.

And the surfaces that she had scratched were more often than not undermined by Dalton.

On drafting paper, she placed the kitchen and the deli where she thought they should go. He wanted *them* moved. She also positioned the gaming tables, the slot machines and other equipment, on paper as well. He wanted *them* moved. Somehow she had managed to clamp down on her tongue and keep her sharp rebuttal to herself. But it was frustrating to have spent hours on something, only to have someone completely undermine the hard work.

Dalton was the boss, a hands-on one at that. She had no choice but to capitulate to his wishes because she had to have the job. Thus, on several occasions she had swallowed her pride along with a sharp retort.

What disturbed her more than the undermining of her work was Dalton himself. He was always *there*. Every time Leah looked up, he was either watching her or walking toward her desk, where he would lean over and monitor her work.

"I thought you'd be long gone."

Startled, Leah looked up to find Dalton standing in the doorway to her office. Despite the sultry heat and despite the fact that he'd been on the boat's upper level supervising the rebuilding of the deck, he looked fresh and fit, she thought churlishly.

Leah transferred her gaze to the clock and saw that it was indeed five-thirty. "That's rather obvious, isn't it?" she said with a twist of sarcasm.

His lips tightened slightly. "Go on, get out of here."

"There are some things I wanted—needed to go over with you."

Dalton batted his hand. "Not now. They'll keep until tomorrow. I'm bushed and so are you."

"Do I look that bad?" she snapped before she thought, then felt a flush cover her face.

His eyes roamed her body. "No, as a matter of fact, you

look great." He paused, and when he spoke again, his voice sounded rough. "But then you always do."

Furious with herself and with him, she lashed out, "I wasn't fishing for a compliment."

He remained unruffled. "Weren't you?"

With a still-warm face, Leah ignored him, hastily put her desk in order, then grabbed her purse. "I have to pick up Coty," she said, "and I'm already late."

"Leah?"

"I'll see you tomorrow."

He didn't say anything. Instead he merely slouched against his desk and watched as she walked out the door.

Damn Dalton Montgomery.

"Mommy, where're we going?"

Leah stared down at her son's towhead. "Back to the club. I forgot my briefcase, and I need to do a little work tonight."

Instead of going to her mother's straight away, Leah had stopped by the nursing home and sat with Rufus for about twenty minutes. After that loaded exchange of words with Dalton, she'd wanted to see her husband, whose gentle manner always put her feet back on solid ground.

Next she'd made her way to the grocery and purchased something to prepare for supper. When she'd stopped by the house to leave the cold items, she'd taken the time to change her clothes. She'd slipped into a pair of denim yellow walking shorts, matching sleeveless T-shirt, and sandals, improving her mood considerably. "Ah, shucks, that means I don't get a story tonight," Coty was saying.

"Of course you will. You know I never neglect that. Did Grandma read to you today?"

"Nah, she just fussed at me all afternoon," he said in a forlorn voice.

Another surge of fury darted through Leah, leaving her feeling more drained than ever. "Well, we all have our bad days, you know. Maybe Grandma'll be feeling better tomorrow."

"I don't think so," he responded with childish candor.

Leah didn't, either, but she refrained from saying that.

Sometimes she'd like to shake her mother. Now was one of those times.

"Can I go on the paddle boat?"

"No, not this time. We'll just run in and grab my briefcase."

"Then can we go to McDonald's?"

Leah sighed as she glanced down at his upturned face. "You're a real piece of work, cowboy. All right, I'll forget about cooking. McDonald's it is."

He giggled.

A few minutes later Leah pulled into the parking lot at the club, and she and Coty made their way into her office.

She'd just finished stuffing her case with work when she heard Coty shout, "Hiya, Dalton!"

Leah's heart sank. He was the last person she wanted to see any more of today. How had she failed to notice his car?

"Well, hi yourself, cowboy," Dalton replied.

Leah fumed at his having adopted her pet name for her son, as if it were the most natural thing in the world.

"Where's your mom?"

"In there."

Leah jerked on the handles of her briefcase and walked out of her office, only to pull up short. Dalton stood in front of her clad only in swimming trunks, and she couldn't stop staring. He returned that stare, and instantly the tension crackled.

"Are you going swimming?" Coty asked, breaking the silence and the tension.

Dalton peered down at him and smiled. "Yeah, thought I would."

"Gee, I wish I could go with you."

"Coty!"

Dalton ignored Leah and winked at Coty. "You can."

"I can?"

"Hey, you two, don't forget who's boss here." Although she spoke to both of them, her gaze was on Dalton. It was not friendly.

He merely shrugged. "So, what's the verdict, boss?"

Leah heard the mockery in his tone, and her blood pressure shot up another notch. "No."

"Ah, Mommy," Coty whined, "why not?"

"Coty, don't start. I'm tired, and I have work to do."

"Screw the work," Dalton cut in.

Coty's eyes widened at the same time he placed a hand over his mouth.

"Sorry," Dalton muttered. "I'm not used to having to watch my language."

Leah counted to ten. "Look—"

"Please, Mommy, lemme go."

"For thirty minutes, say?" Dalton asked.

If Leah hadn't known better, she would've sworn she heard a pleading note in Dalton's voice.

She dropped her case, and after it hit the floor with a thud, she threw up her hands. "Heavens, if it's that big a deal, go."

"Oh, boy!" Coty cried, grabbing Dalton's hand and pulling him toward the door.

Dalton didn't budge. "Too bad you don't have a swim-suit," he drawled nonchalantly. But there was nothing non-chalant about the way he was looking at her.

Color stole up Leah's entire body before she averted her gaze to her son. "You'll have to wait until I run to the car and get your suntan lotion. I don't want you in the water without it."

"No problem. I have some here." Dalton walked into the bathroom and returned with a tube in hand. "Ready, cow-boy?"

Coty giggled and ran out the door. There was nothing for Leah to do but follow.

The longer Leah sat in the sand at the water's edge, the higher her snit factor rose. First off, Dalton looked like some sun-bronzed god. She'd tried not to notice how his tan had increased since the last time she'd seen him without his shirt. Not only was his upper torso brown, but so were his muscled thighs. She wondered if . . .

She shut down that thought but still had to endure watch-ing him cater to her son's every whim, not to mention the laughter the wind whipped her way.

She didn't begrudge her son's having a good time, but it

galled her that it was with someone other than Rufus, someone whom she considered an enemy.

Leah paused in her thoughts, admittedly shocked by them. Enemy? When and why had she suddenly thought of Dalton as an enemy? Was it because he'd made no effort to hide his attraction for her or his friendly interest in her son? But what motive lurked beneath that bold facade? Nothing good, she'd bet—the heart of an enemy, which made him all the more deadly.

In spite of the heat, Leah rubbed her arms, feeling about as confused and guilty as she'd ever felt.

"Mommy, Mommy!" Coty yelled. "Watch Dalton body surf."

As if she could ignore him, Leah thought snidely, feeling that familiar tightening of her stomach.

She smiled and waved, even as she dwelled on how seriously gorgeous Dalton was, how gracefully and lithely he moved.

"Well, well, if it isn't the cunning little thief out for sunshine and surf."

Leah bolted to her feet, jerked off her sunglasses, and glared at J. T. Partridge. "What are you doing here?"

J.T. didn't so much as flinch at the venom in her tone. "Last time I checked, it was a free country. Besides, I particularly like to stroll on the beach at this time of the day."

"Like hell you do," Leah spat, taking in his fat gut overhanging a pair of walking shorts.

He grinned, then chomped down on his cigar. "When you gonna give back the jewels?" he drawled casually. "My patience's running out." He sent a puff of smoke straight into Leah's face.

She wanted to gag but wouldn't give him the satisfaction. She held her ground. "For the one hundredth time, I don't have the jewelry."

"I wish I could believe that." J.T. paused and looked toward the water.

Coty chose that moment to jump up and down and wave to her again.

"Nice kid you got there."

Leah's insides froze. "You stay away from my son! Do you hear me?"

"That wouldn't be a threat, now, would it?"

"Just leave us alone!" Her voice shook, but she didn't care. She had to get this vile creature out of her life.

"Tut, tut, the lady has claws." J.T.'s grin broadened, then he ambled by her, only to stop and turn around. "Don't think you've seen the last of me, 'cause you haven't." He tipped his head. "Have a nice evening."

"Ohhhh!" Leah curled and uncurled her hands while striving to keep from screaming her frustration aloud.

"Who was that?"

For the second time in a matter of minutes, Leah was blindsided. She whirled around into the face of a dripping wet Dalton, who was holding her son's hand.

She didn't know which angered her the most—his closeness to her or to Coty. It didn't matter. "No one you need to be concerned about."

Dalton sucked in his breath at her blatant rudeness.

"He sure is fat," Coty said.

"Coty, that's not a nice thing to say." Leah heard the quiver in her voice and knew that Dalton had, too. A muscle worked overtime in his jaw.

"Ah, Mom."

She pulled Coty toward her. "We have to go now. What do you tell Dalton?"

"Thanks for taking me swimming."

Dalton tore his gaze off Leah and onto Coty. "Anytime, buddy."

"Maybe I can learn to body surf. Reckon?"

Before Dalton could answer, Leah tugged at Coty. "Come on, let's go."

"You're not going to tell me who that man was?"

Leah stopped in her tracks. "Don't you get it? It's none of your business."

Despite the fact that Coty was standing within hearing distance, Dalton cursed, then said, "One of these days—"

The remainder of his words fell on deaf ears as Leah grabbed Coty and hurried toward the car.

Twenty-four

"Becky, honey, is it hot in here to you?"

Becky Childress stopped in her tracks and turned around slowly, her features pale. "Excuse me, Mr. Anderson?"

Cooper grinned. "In private, you can call me Cooper."

"I'd rather not, if you don't mind," the secretary said in a cool tone.

Cooper's eyes narrowed. "How long have you been working for me now, Becky?"

"Three months, sir."

"Ah, yes, three months. Surely you know by now there's a little game I play with some of my favorites."

Color replaced the paleness. "Look, I have work to do."

"It'll keep, honey. Only I won't. How 'bout I pick you up tonight, say, around eight, and we'll grab a bite to eat. Then if you want, we'll talk about that work."

"I'm sorry, but I'm busy tonight."

"Cancel your plans, honey. Oh, and bring me a cup of coffee."

Once he was alone, Cooper felt like punching a hole in the wall behind him. Nothing had gone right lately.

The look of repulsion on Becky's face hadn't escaped him. Damn, was he losing his touch or what? He knew what was wrong. He was still smarting over losing the Montgomery contract to that bitch Leah Frazier. Apparently he hadn't done

186

enough damage to her reputation. He'd have to do something about that. *And more.* She needed to be put in her place, and who better to do that than himself?

Cooper reached for the telephone directory.

"Hi."

"Hello."

"So how was your evening?"

"Fine, thanks," Leah replied, proud of her steady voice, although she had dreaded coming to work.

Dalton stared at her hard, as if he wanted to say something about their clash on the beach yesterday. She hoped he'd mind his own business. She would do just about anything to avoid another confrontation.

Last night had been sheer hell. She had been so knotted inside after watching him in the water that she'd tossed and turned into the wee hours of the morning. That hadn't been the worst of it. She'd had an erotic dream of Dalton thrashing naked on the bed, longing to hold her, touch her, kiss her . . .

"Was that a cop who hassled you yesterday?"

When she didn't respond, Dalton went on, "I know, you still don't want to talk about it."

"You're right, I don't." Maybe her bluntness would get the message across.

"So was he a cop?"

Leah sighed. "He was an insurance investigator. His name is J. T. Partridge."

"What seems to be his problem?"

"Me. He's convinced that I stole that jewelry."

"He's full of shit, too."

Leah couldn't help but smile. "I wish I had the nerve to tell him that, only I don't."

"I'll tell him."

She didn't doubt that for a moment, if the steel in his voice was anything to judge by. "Thanks, but no thanks. Actually, he's harmless. He's just a big-mouthed little man who has a chip on his shoulder."

"Well, if you need—"

She cut him off. "I won't. I can handle him."

Dalton looked far from convinced, but this time he didn't argue. He rubbed his forehead as if she'd given him a giant headache.

"I need you to go over the new scaled drawings of the kitchen and deli."

"Fine," he said roughly.

What a way to start out the day, she thought with added despair. With both of them in a bad mood, she didn't see how anything would get done.

Dalton looked as if he hadn't slept, either, which should have made her feel better, but it didn't. His face was drawn, and his eyes had dark circles beneath them. He hadn't even bothered to shave, either, but that didn't lessen his appeal.

Without breaking the silence, Leah set her briefcase on the table in the outer office, opened it, then spread out the drawing. Dalton sat down and studied it, while she went into her office and checked her "to-do list" for the day.

"It looks good, but there are still some changes I want to make."

Leah walked back into the room and paused in front of the table. "All right," she said, fighting back her anger, convinced she'd never please him. She didn't know what she was expecting, but it was certainly something more than this lukewarm response.

"I'll add my two cents, then we'll go over it again later."

"Fine," she said flatly.

Dalton's eyebrows rose, but he didn't say anything.

"I've also jotted down some ideas for a theme for both the club and casino."

"So, let's have them," he said.

"First, I have a friend who left my old firm and who now designs casinos in Vegas. I called him and he sent me some plans. After looking them over, I think his arrangement is savvy as well as different."

"Ah, that's the key. Different."

"While we're on the subject of different, my friend also mentioned a showroom in Vegas that he thought I should visit." Leah paused and fingered the gold chain at her neck. "He said the company would even pay my way out there."

"Call 'em, but tell 'em to make reservations for two."

"Two?"

He stared up at her. "Surely you didn't think I'd let you go alone?"

"I don't see why not. I'm a big girl."

"I'm not arguing that," he drawled. "But I'm still going. Two heads are better than one."

Despite the drawl, Leah heard that same note of steel. Only this time it made her furious.

"Besides, we don't have a minute to waste."

"I never thought we did."

He ignored her sarcasm. "So let's hear your ideas on the theme."

Leah eased onto the chair beside him, careful to keep a safe distance. Then she cleared her throat and said, "I've come up with three possible scenarios. First is an island decor, since we're on the water."

"Go on."

"Second is that of a floating plantation house." She inched forward and for a moment allowed her eyes to meet his, which she instantly regretted.

He didn't so much as move, but she suddenly felt as if he'd touched her. He had, with his eyes.

It was all she could do to continue in a normal tone. "That idea is to promote what we're famous for—our southern hospitality."

"Mmm, that's interesting, but too damned costly. So what's the third one?"

Leah leaned back, feeling a different kind of tension invade the premise. "A French château."

"Nope, that's definitely out."

"Well, so am I—out of ideas, I mean." Leah's tone was as cold as the icy band that had formed around her heart.

"It just so happens I'm not. I think we oughta go with a country-western theme. We—"

Suddenly Leah stood and, with as much dignity as she could muster, said, "We? There's no 'we,' Mr. Montgomery."

"What the hell's that supposed to mean?"

"Let me finish," she said tersely. "You've known all along what you wanted to do with the club and casino. So again, why did you hire me?" A quiver afflicted her voice. "You haven't liked anything I've done. As far as I'm concerned, I'm wasting my time, time I don't have to waste!"

His eyes narrowed, and his face turned white.

Without giving him a chance to speak, Leah turned and marched toward the door.

He lurched to his feet, and when he did, the chair crashed to the floor.

Leah didn't so much as pause. Her mission was to put as much distance between them as possible.

"Where the hell do you think you're going?"

"Anywhere but here!"

She didn't realize how close behind her he was until he grabbed her arm and swung her around. "Oh, no, you don't!"

In her efforts to get loose, Leah pressed her back against the door, only to realize that she'd trapped herself.

Dalton's face was only a hairbreadth from hers.

"No, please." Her raw whisper was barely audible.

"Yes," he said violently.

Before she could shift her head, he splayed his hands on each side of the wall and covered her lips with his.

She pushed against his chest with both hands, but to no avail. He was an immovable object who was intent on making her respond. As if they had a will of their own, her lips parted, and his tongue found hers.

Nothing she had ever experienced prepared her for that bittersweet assault. The kiss wasn't gentle, neither was it brutal; yet it unleashed a hunger inside her so intense that she lost all control. Hope of stopping him vanished, especially when she felt his blatant arousal. Her legs gave way, and she clung to him.

Only after Dalton moved his hand from the wall onto a breast did reality surface with a vengeance. Dear God, what was she doing? What was she letting him do?

Even if she'd wanted him to touch her, he couldn't. She was married, and her husband was dying! To let another man suck her into a maelstrom of wild passion was insane.

"Stop!"

Dalton pulled back with an expletive.

She opened the door and stepped into the hall. That was as far as she could go without stopping to calm herself. But she wasn't worried about his following her.

The dark agony she had seen in his eyes told her that he had his own demons to fight.

Twenty-five

Dalton stared at the numbers. They didn't add up. He had borrowed millions from the bank, and according to the figures, he was already running short. Dammit, he should have known there would be a cost overrun. Every day the prices on materials and labor rose.

He couldn't ask the bank for more money. He flinched at the thought, yet he was confident that he could hold off his banker until the estate was settled. His daddy's name still carried a lot of weight at that institution.

He felt another surge of hot fury burn his stomach when he thought of the man who had sired him, who had put him in this untenable position of having to sweat blood, to manipulate, in order to get what should've been rightfully his. But anger was futile; it wasted effort that he needed to see his plan through.

He'd been pleased with the unfolding of that plan—until a week ago, when he'd kissed Leah. If someone had told him that he would lose his head over a woman, any woman, he'd have laughed in his face, especially when so much was at stake.

Well, he wasn't laughing now. He was scared shitless.

When Leah was around, his gut felt as if it had a grenade

in it. If he allowed her to light that fuse, his whole future would be blown to smithereens. And if she ever suspected the truth . . .

She wouldn't, he assured himself, because he would damn well get control, and she'd never know his intent until the time was right to tell her that Coty was his son and that he wanted custody. By then he would've lost his fascination with her and could proceed with a clear conscience. One thing in his favor was that lust had no sticking power.

He wasn't ready to pat himself on the back just yet, especially as he would be spending two days with her in Vegas. They were due to leave the following morning.

Today at least he was free from the strain and tension of Leah's presence. He'd given her the day off to get ready for the trip. Too, he felt she was due; she'd been working long hours, then taking work home, which meant time away from her family.

He didn't want to think about the family bit, either—not her son, and certainly not her husband.

Hell, he just wanted this farce to be over and done with.

Dalton's lips curved into a bitter smile at the same time he picked up the pencil and returned to the figures. Thirty minutes later he had fared no better.

He couldn't focus his mind on business, not when outside problems kept interfering. If Leah and his financial doldrums weren't enough, there was the ever-annoying Bill DeChamp, who Dalton figured was getting edgier by the day.

He stared at the figures a moment longer, cursed, then slammed the folder shut. He'd had it for the day. He was going to the gym. That would make him feel better. It always did.

The second Dalton walked outside, the heat rolled over him like a steam roller. Even the breeze off the water seemed nonexistent. He struggled to get his breath. That was when he saw DeChamp.

"Speak of the devil," Dalton muttered under his breath.

DeChamp pushed away from his car and walked toward him. When he was in touching distance he pulled up short, then grinned.

Dalton fought the urge to knock that smug grin off his face. "Make this quick, DeChamp. I'm running short of time and patience."

"You think your shit doesn't stink, Montgomery. But I have news for you, it does."

"You know, you've become a real pain in the ass."

DeChamp's grin widened. "I've seen the kid, you know."

Dalton's features turned ugly. "I told you—"

"I don't care what you've told me. All I want is proof that he's yours."

"People in hell want ice water, too."

DeChamp took a step closer. "Does that mean you don't intend to claim the kid?"

"I'll do what's necessary in my own good time. Got that?"

DeChamp's eyes narrowed. "Look, I don't know why you're pussyfooting around." He paused. "Unless you've suddenly gotten the hots for the woman, but—"

DeChamp never finished his sentence. Dalton's fist smashed into his face, knocking him to the ground.

At first DeChamp looked as if he couldn't believe Dalton had actually assaulted him. He touched his nose with a finger, and when he saw the blood, he yelped, then scrambled to his feet.

"Why, you bastard," he spat at Dalton.

Disgusted with the whole scene, Dalton turned and stomped toward his car.

"You haven't heard the last from me!" DeChamp shouted.

Dalton stopped dead in his tracks, then whipped around. "For your health's sake, take a hike!"

"You'll pay for this!"

This time Dalton ignored him and kept on walking. Both the banker and DeChamp were nothing but vultures, waiting to pick his bones. When would it end? Only after he went to court to get custody of Coty Michael Frazier, *his* son.

Dalton wondered why that thought soured on his stomach.

Leah couldn't believe she was on a plane to Las Vegas with Dalton beside her. Even harder to believe was that she was still working for him.

She wouldn't have been if he hadn't apologized for his behavior. But what about *her* behavior? She still hadn't come to terms with her part in the fiasco. How could she have betrayed her husband in such an uncharacteristic way? She could only rationalize her temporary loss of sanity by blaming it on the pressures of Rufus's illness and her bleak financial situation.

Still, those were no excuses, and that was why she'd decided to stick to her decision to quit. She'd even gone so far as to tell Sophie what she'd done without admitting the underlying truth.

Sophie had backed her, although Leah suspected she sensed there was more to her unhappiness than Dalton's criticism of her work. However, Sophie had refrained from saying that. But Leah didn't care what anyone thought. She couldn't work in that pressure cooker any longer, couldn't further taint her marriage vows, even if she had to declare bankruptcy.

That thought had been very much on her mind the next evening when the doorbell rang. She'd been reading Coty a story.

"I'll get it," he'd said, scrambling off her lap and racing to the front door.

Shaking her head, Leah stood and followed him.

"Hiya, Dalton," she heard Coty say, and instantly Leah froze.

"How's it going, kid?"

"Okay. Will you come watch me play ball?"

Coty's invitation jarred Leah into action, thinking how she'd like nothing better than to put a muzzle on her son's mouth.

"Coty, it's bedtime," she said, walking into the entryway.

"Aw, Mom."

"Coty!"

He hung his head, turned, and sulked down the hall.

"Don't you think you were a bit hard on him?"

Leah's eyes flashed. "That's no concern of yours!"

"You're right, it isn't. Still—"

"What do you want?" she lashed out. The band around her chest was so tight that she had difficulty breathing.

"I thought maybe we could talk."

"We have nothing to talk about."

"Look," Dalton said, "things have gone too far for me to change personnel midstream. Besides, you need the job."

She couldn't help hearing the pleading note in his tone. Damn him, he wasn't playing fair. Yet she felt herself capitulating.

As if he sensed that as well, he hammered the point. "If I promise to keep my hands to myself—"

Leah fought the urge to cover her ears. She hated hearing those words spoken. They sounded so glaring, so sordid. She ached to stop up her ears.

"Leah, please." The strain was still evident in Dalton's voice.

She tightened her fingers around the doorknob. "Do you think it's possible for us to work together again?"

"Damn straight I do."

Leah almost sagged against the door. "All right. I'll give it another try."

"I promise you won't be sorry."

That conversation had taken place a week ago. And during those intervening days, she hadn't been sorry. Dalton, Tony, and she had pulled together as a team, and progress had definitely been made.

Yet Leah took nothing for granted, least of all her fragile mind and heart, especially with Dalton so close.

"We're here."

Leah forced her thoughts back to the present. Her eyes riveted to the window. Sure enough, the DC-10's tires were screeching down the runway. When she turned to Dalton, he was busy unbuckling his seat belt.

She followed suit, wondering again if this trip would turn out to be another mistake in a long line of many. But if she was to continue working for him, she had no choice. Besides, Rufus's doctor had urged her to go, as had Sophie, who had volunteered to keep Coty.

"Ready?"

Leah nodded.

"Hey, you're not going to the gallows, you know," Dalton said with a grin.

For an instant that grin dazzled her, and she realized that she had merely won a battle and not the war.

"Well?"

Leah stepped into the aisle and felt his big body close in behind her. *Careful, Leah, careful.*

Twenty-six

The day was crammed so full that Leah felt as if she'd been running uphill. Yet she'd enjoyed the time spent at the wholesalers' showroom.

The floor representatives had given her and Dalton the royal treatment, showing them a staggering number of samples of carpeting, fabrics, furniture, fixtures, and wallpaper, all tied into a country-western theme.

But even the lowest-priced items seemed outrageous, and Leah hoped that Dalton's coffer had no limits. By day's end, though, his features had become more drawn. She suspected that he was pinched for money after all.

That thought depressed her. Then she told herself she shouldn't have been surprised. She'd known from the onset that Dalton was a gambler in every sense of the word, that even if he didn't have the bank roll or confidence that he pretended to have, no one would ever know.

Besides, she had no doubt that eventually he would get what he wanted. What concerned her most about that tenacity was that he seemed to want *her*.

What about herself? No matter how hard she tried she couldn't dismiss that deep, hot, sucking kiss they had exchanged. Nor could she dismiss the fact that she'd wanted him to kiss her. No matter; such an exchange wouldn't happen again. That assurance had given her the courage to make this trip, even though the guilt associated with that moment continued to gnaw at her.

So far Dalton had behaved with exemplary decorum and treated her politely, if not coolly, which suited her just fine.

That was why, later that afternoon, over drinks at the hotel, his words stunned her. "I have a surprise planned for this evening."

"Excuse me?" Leah said, under the impression that they would each have dinner in their rooms, then go to bed early. After all, tomorrow promised to be another grueling day, as they were to visit another wholesaler. She planned to compare items and prices, then make her choices before they left.

At the moment, however, Leah was dog-tired, and nothing appealed to her except checking on Rufus and Coty, followed by a leisurely bath.

"I said I have a surprise for you." Dalton paused and looked down at his watch. "In about an hour. Will that give you enough time?"

Leah struggled to curb her impatience. "Enough time for what?"

"I told you, it's a surprise."

"What if I don't like surprises?"

"Ah, everyone likes surprises."

"Look," she said, forcing a smile, "I appreciate whatever you have in mind, but you don't have to entertain me. In fact, I'm exhausted and was looking forward to an early evening."

"That's too bad," Dalton said in such a dispirited tone that she felt guilty.

"Okay, so what did you have in mind?"

He smiled suddenly, and when he did, she drew in a sharp breath. He heard her, and for perhaps a second his black eyes unmasked.

Leah refused to acknowledge what she saw there. Instead she shifted her gaze and watched as the atrium, drenched in the late afternoon sunlight, created patterns on their table.

"Have you ever been to a carnival?"

She lifted her head. "Carnival?"

"Yeah, carnival."

He reached for his beer and over the rim eyed her carefully, though she sensed he was smiling.

"Of course."

"Fun, wasn't it?"

In spite of herself, Leah smiled. "I guess so. But what's
the point? Surely you aren't thinking of going to a carnival?"

"Sure I am. Tonight."

She gave him an incredulous look. "Well, count me out."

"Ah, come on. It'll relax you. Besides, it'll be something
you can tell Coty about. He'll think it's a hoot."

"That's a given, but—"

"Hey, what've you got to lose?"

"Aren't you tired?"

"No."

The brightness in his eyes, the childlike quality that for a
moment reminded her of Coty, tugged at something inside
her, something she couldn't put a name to. Leah sighed. "Oh,
all right, but only for a little while."

"No problem. We'll ride a couple of rides, eat some junk,
then return to the hotel."

It all sounded so innocent, so harmless, that Leah felt like
a priggish schoolmarm for objecting. Maybe it would do her
good. Maybe for a while she could set aside the pain and
heavy burden that she constantly bore.

She felt his eyes on her. Pleading eyes.

What could it hurt? Just this one time, couldn't she indulge herself and do something wild and different? Or was
she deluding herself? What gave her that right when Rufus
was barely clinging to life? How dare she allow herself a
moment of fun?

Then again, what could it hurt, *just this once?*

Later, in his room, Dalton questioned his judgment. Why
hadn't he let her finish her Perrier, agreed that they would go
their separate ways as she'd suggested?

"You sonofabitch, you just don't fucking get it, do you?"

Only he did get it. He'd sleep with her in a minute, even if
that made him a genuine lowlife and cost him everything. He
simply couldn't rid himself of how her quivering lips had felt

under his or how her breasts had swelled against the palm of his hand.

Right now Dalton felt as though his nuts were on a hot plate. And the only saving grace he could conjure up was that when he actually did go to sleep, the ache in his crotch, along with his warring code of ethics, would find relief.

What he ought to do was call and say that he'd changed his mind, that he'd decided to work. He paced the floor for a moment, only to falter in his tracks.

Maybe he was approaching this all wrong. Maybe he shouldn't fight that ache after all. Maybe he should use it as a plus. If he could win over Leah, then perhaps when he made his move to become a permanent part of Coty's life, it would be easier.

Neither ploy meant he had to get involved, not with his heart, anyway. The other side of that scenario couldn't be ignored, either, which was the possibility that once he made love to her, he couldn't walk away.

But hell, wasn't that what gambling was all about?

"Oh, please, no more."

"Ah, come on," Dalton said, grinning down at her even as he yanked off a piece of cotton candy and stuffed it in his mouth. "Where's your sense of adventure?"

Leah stood in the middle of the plush hotel room and stared out at the city, whose lights twinkled with such intensity that they almost blinded her.

When they had gotten back from the carnival, Leah had asked him for some information that he'd stuffed in his briefcase. She had explained that she wanted to study it the following morning over coffee.

She hadn't planned to go to his room, but since she'd made the request, she'd had no choice.

Now, as Leah felt him watching her, she crossed her arms over her chest, realizing that being here, in his room, was not smart.

"I hope you had a good time," Dalton commented in a lazy voice.

She hadn't realized he was behind her. She flinched.

"Sorry. I didn't mean to startle you."

He was too close. Again. Her mouth went dry.

"You didn't," she whispered.

"I still think you're a chicken for not riding the Ferris wheel."

The teasing in his tone drew her around, and she angled her head. "And I think you're weird, Dalton Montgomery."

He threw back his head and laughed.

Leah felt a breathless excitement rush through her. She suddenly wanted to tease, to flirt, to be young and carefree again. And while that thought frightened her, it also tantalized her.

Then all too quickly, Dalton's laughter stopped. The room pulsed with something else, something even stronger than tension, something so strong that Leah was powerless against its pull.

"Leah?"

She heard his breath; it seemed to rattle in his throat.

His eyes fell to her lips. She knew he wanted to kiss her; she knew because that was what she wanted, too.

Guilt reared its ugly head. She had to get away. She didn't have a moment to waste. Yet she couldn't move. Emotions, both confusing and heady, prevented that.

"Leah," Dalton whispered again, this time in such a raw voice that she brought her eyes up to his.

The moonlight streaming in the window, combined with the lamp burning softly in one corner, allowed her to see his face. It was bloodless and tight. But his eyes were on fire.

"You deserve so much more, Leah. You deserve to be loved."

"No." She shook her head violently. "I'm married, and nothing can change that."

"Does that mean you can't be happy, that you can't appease the loneliness that comes from being tied to a very sick man?"

"I can't betray him." Leah's voice broke. "I *won't* betray him. He's so good, so kind . . ."

"You deserve to be loved with more than kindness. You need to feel a man inside you. . . ."

Leah backed up, her eyes wild. "No!"

"Yes." Dalton's eyes begged her.

Her lips parted just as the phone rang.

Leah's heart slammed back in place while Dalton cursed, then he stalked to the phone. With his back to her, he lifted the receiver. "Yes."

He didn't respond again for what seemed the longest time. Finally, in a muffled tone, he said, "I'll take care of it."

Leah didn't know what made her suspect something was wrong. Perhaps it was the defeated note she heard in his voice. Her heart, which had just settled back into place, dislodged once again.

"Dalton?" Her voice was a hoarse croak.

He turned around, his face and body taut. "It's . . . your husband."

Leah placed a hand over her chest while her head swam. "He's . . . he's dead, isn't he?"

"I'm sorry."

Her lips moved, but no sound came out as she felt the carpet rise to meet her sinking body.

"Leah!"

Dalton's cry was the last thing she heard before that dark void blessedly claimed her.

Twenty-seven

Six months later, March 1995

Leah couldn't believe that Rufus had passed away six months ago. In many ways it seemed like six years. Her life was different; yet it was the same.

Thanksgiving, Christmas, and Coty's sixth birthday had all come and gone. Through all the hullabaloo, she had done what was expected of her. She'd gotten up every morning and prepared Coty's breakfast before taking him to "real school," as he called it, then gone to work.

Coty was now a proud and boastful first-grader who had adjusted much better to Rufus's death than Leah had thought possible. But then Coty had been shielded, she reminded herself. Because Rufus had insisted on entering a nursing home, Coty hadn't been a witness to his father's final days of agony.

Leah hadn't had that luxury, nor did she have the solace of a guilt-free conscience. Guilt festered inside her like a rusty nail that she'd swallowed. It poisoned both her body and spirits.

The only time she pulled herself out of her funk was when she was around Coty. For his sake she forced herself to smile, to read to him, to talk to him about school, to hold him, to *love* him, fighting off the crazy fear that she might lose him as well.

If only she hadn't been in Las Vegas, with Dalton, when Rufus had passed away. If only she'd been by Rufus's bedside, where she'd belonged, holding his hand, touching him, *loving* him.

But she'd been gone, with *another* man. To make matters worse, she'd been in his room when the call had come from Sophie. She had never asked Sophie why she'd called Dalton's room. She'd just assumed that Sophie had tried hers first or that she'd wanted Dalton to be with her when she learned the crushing news. Although nothing had been said, Leah knew her friend must wonder about the circumstances. It grieved Leah to think that Sophie thought badly of her.

Even that worry, along with all the others, failed to matter when the ramifications of Rufus's death finally hit her. The day of the funeral, Leah had sat in the small church, flanked by her mother and Coty, and stared at the coffin, draped with a huge bouquet of summer flowers.

She'd sat dry-eyed, zombielike, as if she were outside herself and this was happening to someone else. Later, when she'd stood at the gravesite and placed a single rose on the casket, she'd known her life with Rufus was over. Those stolen moments with Dalton were over as well. Only Coty mattered now.

Leah had stumbled back from the coffin, her throat so full of tears that she had feared it would rupture. Then she'd felt her son lean against her and place his hand in hers. She had straightened. Rufus would want her to go on, to make Coty's life as rich as possible. For Coty's sake only, she'd promised that.

She hadn't seen Dalton until after the minister had given his final condolences. He'd been standing off to himself. But when she had begun walking toward the car, he'd walked toward her. She'd paused, only because she'd had no choice.

"Look, if there's anything I can do—"

"I know," she'd whispered, wanting to scream at him to get out of her way, *get out of her life.* She could do neither. For one reason, Coty stood beside her. Another was that Dalton remained her employer and she needed the job, now more than ever.

Leah remembered little of what had happened after the call came, except that she had regained consciousness in the hotel infirmary, with an anxious Dalton hovering over the doctor's shoulders.

Once she'd collected herself, she and Dalton had gone straight to the airport and boarded a plane. Even now Leah could count the words on one finger that had passed between them. She'd sensed that Dalton had wanted to comfort her, but she would've rebuffed him. He had seemed to know that and kept quiet.

At the funeral, as Leah had watched him speak to her son, she'd longed to grab Coty and run. She hadn't. She'd stood and endured.

"I'm sorry about your daddy." Dalton had bent to Coty's level so that they were eye to eye.

"Me too," Coty responded in a muffled tone, all the while poking the toe of his boot into the soft ground.

"You're the man of the family now, you know."

Coty's head came up. "That's what Mommy told me."

Dalton peered up at Leah, only Leah averted her gaze. She couldn't bear to look at him for fear of what she'd read in his eyes. "Well, your mommy's right," Dalton finally said in a tight, controlled tone.

"My daddy's in heaven with the angels."

"I'm sure he is."

"My mommy said I'll see him again when I get there."

Dalton cleared his throat. "I'm sure of that, too."

"Do you have a little boy?"

Leah stiffened, then shifted her gaze onto her son, horrified. "Coty, I—"

"It's all right," Dalton interrupted, talking to Leah but looking at Coty. "Uh . . . no I don't."

"Why?"

"Coty!"

"There are a lot of reasons, but your daddy was real lucky to have a son like you."

Coty didn't respond for a moment. He just looked at Dalton, then asked out of the blue, "Since my daddy's in heaven, would you come watch me play basketball sometime?"

Leah sucked in her breath and held it until she felt her chest would burst. Still, she didn't scold Coty, not this time. There was such a forlorn, pathetic note in his voice that she wanted to grab him and promise that she'd take him to the ball game, but that wasn't what he wanted. He wanted Dalton to watch him play, which complicated the situation that much more.

"I wouldn't miss your games for anything." Dalton looked up at Leah again. The expression in his eyes seemed to dare her to take issue with that.

She didn't. Instead she grabbed Coty's hand. "Come on, son, we have to go."

With as much dignity as she could muster, she walked toward the car, but her lower lip quivered.

Coty squeezed her hand and peered up at her. "Don't cry, Mommy. I love you."

Her son's sweet declaration of love that day had been the only thing that had gotten her through the weeks and months that followed.

She had felt empty, as if someone had taken a shovel and removed everything inside her. If only she had that same luxury with her thoughts. If only she could close out what had nearly taken place in that hotel room the night Rufus died.

If Dalton had touched her, she was sure she would have succumbed to his passion, would have let him bury himself inside her as he'd longed to do.

She lunged off the couch and stomped into the kitchen, where she opened a can of Coke. While sipping the cold liquid, she stared out the kitchen window.

Dark clouds filled the sky. Leah expected it would rain soon. She frowned. Coty had gone to a basketball game with a friend and his parents. They had asked her to join them, but she'd declined, needing to work.

She had used work as the palliative for her heartbreak. That hard work had paid off. Dalton seemed pleased with her decorating skills as well as the plans for the deli. Lately he'd been all business.

Still, she had felt his eyes track her. She'd also been aware of them darkening when he'd approach her, and she would move quickly to avoid touching him.

Once when that had happened, he'd lashed out, "Will you stop flinching! I'm not going to throw you down on the floor and jump your goddamn bones. So give it a rest, will you?"

He'd turned then and stormed out of the room. She had sunk onto her chair, completely drained. She had known then, just as she knew now, that Dalton smoldered inside and that it wouldn't take much to set him off.

That tense conversation had taken place two weeks ago, but his words still had the power to shake her. So lost in thought was she that she didn't hear the doorbell until whoever was there rang it without mercy.

Frowning, she hurried into the entryway. "Who is it?"

"Your mother."

Stunned, Leah groped to unbolt the door. Jessica stood on the porch, her mouth pinched as raindrops splattered on the steps behind her.

"Get out of the way and let me in," Jessica demanded, pushing past Leah.

Leah swallowed a sharp retort, closed the door behind her, then followed her mother into the living room, where a small fire burned in the fireplace. Her mother backed up against it, shivering.

"What on earth are you doing out in this weather?"

Jessica shoved a strand of damp hair behind her ear. "I think it's time we had a talk."

Leah raised her eyebrows.

"Where's Coty?"

"At a basketball game with friends."

"Good. That means we won't be disturbed." Jessica looked around. "I assume that's a correct assumption."

Leah didn't like what her mother said or the tone in which it was spoken. "I hope you didn't come here to pick a fight, because frankly I'm not in the mood."

Jessica laughed an ugly laugh. "Just what are you in the mood for?" Without giving Leah a chance to respond, she went on, "Have you looked at yourself in the mirror lately?"

"What's your point, Mother?"

"My point is that you look terrible."

"Thanks a lot."

"Well, you do. You're skin and bones. And your eyes—they look dead."

"How I look is my business," Leah said in a dull tone, refusing to rise to the bait her mother had dangled.

"Not entirely. You have Coty to think about."

"And I haven't neglected him," Leah said, her eyes sparking now.

Jessica snorted. "Maybe not, but you're neglecting yourself and *your* life."

"You've already said that."

An uncomfortable silence descended over the room. Then Jessica said, "I've been thinking that maybe you should sell the house and you and Coty move in with me."

Leah's stomach flip-flopped. "I don't think that would be a good idea."

"Why?" Jessica snapped. "Is it because you're sleeping with that gambler?"

Leah gasped. Then something inside her rebelled, and she wanted desperately to get back at her mother. "What if I am?"

This time it was Jessica who gasped, then, unexpectedly, shrugged. "Well, he may be a no-good gambler, but at least he's got money."

If the whole entire conversation hadn't been so ludicrous and sad, Leah would've laughed. Her mother didn't have a clue what Leah was all about. She never had and she never would.

"Money. That's all you've ever cared about, isn't it?"

"That and your happiness."

"Really?"

Jessica's face turned red. "Yes, despite what you think. I've always wanted you to have what I didn't—the pretty things that only money can buy."

"Why can't you understand," Leah wailed, "that I don't want *things.* I wanted you to simply l—" She broke off, thinking there was no use. This conversation was just another verse of the same old song. Besides, she wouldn't say the word *love* to her mother. It stuck in her throat.

"If only you hadn't married Rufus."

"Don't you dare say that ever again!"

Jessica's chin jutted. "It's the truth."

"No, it isn't." Leah walked toward her mother, rage burning inside her. "Rufus saved my sanity, if not my life. If you'd been there for me after that man . . ." Again Leah's voice failed while Jessica's face turned deathly pale.

"I told you not to ever mention that incident again." Jessica's voice was as hard as a whiplash.

Leah, struggling with her own bruising memories, turned her head and strove to regain control. But she was shaking.

She didn't know how long she could keep herself from splintering apart.

"So I guess our moving in together is out," Jessica said in her normal tone, as if the past had never been mentioned.

Leah faced her. "I'm going to hang on to the house as long as I can."

"In that case, I think you should close your business and go back to the Anderson firm."

Leah let out a breath. "That's not going to happen."

"Why?"

"For one thing, I have a job, one that pays extremely well. For another, I have an obligation. We're about to open the club. In another month or two the casino should be ready."

"Then you'll be out of a job, right?"

"That's my problem." Leah's tone was flat and reserved.

"Actually, I spoke with Cooper Anderson today on your behalf."

"You did what!?"

"You heard me, Leah. And you don't have to shout."

"How dare you do such a thing?"

"Well, someone has to take charge; apparently you have no desire to do so."

Leah could only stare at her mother with her mouth agape. How could she stop this woman, who had given birth to her but who had never loved her, from continuing to steamroll over her?

Thunder rumbled loudly, but Leah didn't notice. She looked her mother directly in the eye and said, "Stop interfering in my life or I'll never speak to you again."

"Oh, for heaven's sake, don't be so dramatic. Of course you'll speak to me again, especially when you need me to keep Coty." Jessica paused and looked Leah up and down. "Meanwhile, I hope you come to your senses."

Before Leah could answer, Jessica headed toward the door. With her hand on the knob she turned and added, "I'd rather see you sleep with that gambler than watch you wallow in your own self-pity."

Jessica slammed the door behind her.

"Damn you!" Leah cried, feeling the first emotion she'd felt since Rufus's death.

Twenty-eight

Dalton took a can of beer out of the club's refrigerator, popped the top, leaned his head back, and downed two healthy swigs. Then, with the back of his hand, he wiped his mouth.

Damn, but he was tired. Every bone in his body ached, but it had been worth it, he thought with a cynical smile. He'd mastered that filly, but it hadn't been easy. The lady had put up one helluva fight.

Dalton grinned again, thinking how she'd tossed him off her backside twice. By the time he'd made his way back into the office, that grin had faded. The frown that he'd worn for months now etched his features.

He shouldn't have taken the time to fool with the horse. Yet he'd needed to make the trip to Bogalusa and check the home front. Helping Tom, who attended to the grounds and the stables, break the filly had been a spur-of-the-moment venture. Dalton had enjoyed it; it had succeeded in working some of the kinks out of his uptight body, for more reasons than one.

While there, he'd also learned that DeChamp had suffered a crippling stroke, which explained why Dalton hadn't heard anything from him. Despite DeChamp's vow to get even after having been punched in the nose, Dalton felt DeChamp no longer posed a threat.

Now he was no longer sure of that. Gossip had it that DeChamp had fully recovered but was in deep financial trouble. Too, there had been rumors he was involved with a woman. Just the thought of that weasel dipping his wick made Dalton chuckle. He didn't believe it, though. DeChamp was too afraid of his wife. Still, it was a card he planned to hold close, if DeChamp got out of line again.

Aw, to hell with DeChamp. He was the last person he wanted to think about. He didn't want to think about her, either, but he couldn't help it. Her perfume was everywhere. *She* was everywhere.

Dalton flopped down onto the couch in his newly decorated office and chugged a little more of the beer. But even if he drank twelve beers, it wouldn't help. He was exhausted. He was broke. And he was pissed.

He wanted a woman he couldn't have, and he was lying on his ass, crying in his beer.

At first his goals had been so simple and so attainable. Find the woman and the child, then sue for custody and show himself a good parent. He'd known the court procedure wouldn't be a piece of cake. But he'd been confident of the outcome in his favor because fathers now had rights of their own. Besides, with the name Montgomery behind him, how could he fail?

Then he'd met Leah, and the ground rules had changed. Oh, he still wanted custody of Coty because of the money, but he wanted Leah as well. Wanted. He didn't love her; he wanted to fuck her, which in itself was a major problem and one he hadn't counted on.

Working closely with her every day, watching her grieve for her dead husband, kept his insides stripped like raw meat. Still, he'd kept his distance. It had been hard, though, and it got harder every day. For one thing, he was reluctant to cause her more pain and sorrow. Also, he admired her strength in the face of so many problems and, again, felt terrible about adding to them.

Right now Dalton felt as if he could bite a ten-penny nail in two. He finished the beer, chucked the can in the trash, and looked around. He'd have to hand it to Leah. This place bore no resemblance to the dump it had been. She had decorated this big room in pale burgundy and green. It was now the official office for both the club and casino. While each retained a personal cubicle, here was where they planned and carried out the majority of the work.

The club was almost ready, thank God. He hoped to have it open within a few weeks, if not sooner, with the casino to follow in short order. The only problem was, the coffers were empty.

He was going to have to ask the bank for more money. His gut tightened a notch. Maybe if he jostled the figures once more, he could find extra cash. He jostled but found nothing.

He could open the club and operate it, but without more money he couldn't finish the casino.

He hated the squeeze put on his balls. He trudged to the fridge and got another beer.

By the time he decided to leave the office, he felt no pain. He knew that wouldn't last. When he got home and into bed, visions of Leah, naked, beside him would drive him into the bathroom for a cold shower.

Grimacing, Dalton started across the street—just as the car came out of nowhere. He paused, swung around, and watched as a vehicle with glaring headlights traveled toward him.

"Sonofabitch!" Dalton hollered, and dove for the pavement. The instant he made contact with the concrete, the car whizzed past.

He didn't move.

"It'll work out," Leah said into the receiver. "I just know it will."

She had been visiting with Sophie on the phone for quite a while, first about the small office project that was near completion, then about Louis and their ongoing problem.

"I hope so," Sophie responded, a glum tone in her voice. "But I have my doubts. Now that I've decided I definitely want to marry Louis, he *won't* marry me."

"Give him time, Sophie."

"I'm not sure that's the answer."

"Yes, it is. He'll have to come to terms with his sterility on his own."

"And if he doesn't?"

Leah sighed and curled her legs tighter under her buttocks. "Then he's not the one for you."

"I guess you're right, but it's hard not to want to hover, to— Oh, hell, I don't know what I'm trying to say. It's just that he's so withdrawn, so uptight, especially when we make love."

"I know some of what you're going through, and again all I can say is that you can't rush him."

"And you know how hard that is for impatient me."

Leah smiled into the receiver. "That's part of your charm."

"Yeah, right."

Leah chuckled.

"Still, I feel like a heel for dumping my problems on your shoulders."

"That's what friends are for. Besides, you were there for me when Rufus died."

There was a slight pause. "How are you doing, really?"

"I'm working hard, trying to keep my head above water financially."

"If only that bitch Ellen Thibodeaux would pay you for that job."

"Yeah, that'd be nice, but that's not going to happen, not until that jewelry is found."

"Is that jerk investigator still hanging around?"

"Yes."

"What you ought to do is get an attorney and go after Partridge's ass."

Leah chuckled again. "I don't know what I'd do without you."

"Ditto." Sophie paused. "So how's Dalton?"

"Fine," Leah said cautiously. She knew Sophie suspected something other than Rufus's death had her upset, and that that "something" had to do with Dalton. But Sophie hadn't asked, and Leah hadn't confided in her. Some things she could share; some things she could not. Besides, her feelings concerning Dalton were in such turmoil that she couldn't define them herself.

"Well, I'm looking forward to the club opening," Sophie said. "It should be loads of fun."

"That's what we're hoping."

"Look, it's getting late, so I'll let you go. Let's have lunch soon, okay?"

"Sounds good to me. I'll be in touch. And Sophie, try not to worry. You and Louis are going to be fine."

"Thanks," Sophie whispered, then hung up.

Leah got off the couch with the sole intention of going to bed when the doorbell rang. Her hand froze on the lamp switch. Who on earth would be ringing her doorbell at eleven o'clock at night? She knew this time it wouldn't be her mother.

Irritated, she flounced to the door. "Yes?"

"It's Dalton."

She took a steadying breath. "What do you want?"

"Please, let me in."

Knowing that she should do anything *but* that, Leah complied with his request, though her fingers trembled as she unfastened the bolt.

"Look, would you please—" She broke off and stared at him.

Something terrible had happened. He looked as though he'd been in a fight and lost, which caused her heart to race for an entirely different reason. Even under his five o'clock shadow, his face was pasty; but it was his eyes that concerned her the most. They were red-rimmed and filled with an emotion she couldn't identify under the dim lighting. Was it pain?

That was when she looked down and saw his blood-soaked arm.

"Oh, my God," she whispered, stepping aside.

Once he was in the middle of the living room, he turned and, with his hand massaging the back of his neck, stared at her.

"What happened? Were you in a fight?"

His lips quirked. "Of sorts."

"It doesn't matter, not now, anyway." Leah pulled her eyes off his. "That arm needs attention."

"I'll live."

"That's beside the point," she said in a husky undertone. "That arm still needs attention."

His eyes darkened, and for another long minute they stared at each other.

"Are you volunteering?" he asked in a weakening voice.

Leah took a steadying breath. "I'll . . . I'll get some antiseptic and bandages."

"Thanks." Dalton walked to the couch and practically fell onto it.

She rushed to his side.

"Guess I'm not as tough as I thought."

"Are you going to be okay until I get back?"

"I'll be fine."

Once she reached the bathroom, Leah gazed at herself in the mirror. A face with very little makeup stared back at her. But that wasn't the worst part. She had on threadbare jeans, a long-sleeved T-shirt, and no bra. She could see her nipples poking against the fabric. But now was not the time to worry about her state of dress. Dalton could lose consciousness at any moment.

Leah dashed back into the living room, only to stop abruptly. He had gotten up and removed his shirt. Before, when she'd seen him in that same state of undress, her pulse rate had shot up. It did the same now, only more so.

As if he sensed her trepidation, his lips twisted with a bit of humor. "Sorry, but I didn't think you could work on me fully clothed."

Leah moistened her lips. "No problem." But it was a problem, and he damn well knew it.

He sat back down, and when she saw the nasty abrasion that ran from his shoulder to his elbow, thoughts of what his bare flesh did to her body ceased to matter. "You should see a doctor."

"I'll be okay."

"What happened?" she asked again, sitting beside him and dabbing at the wound with an antiseptic-filled cloth.

He winced.

"Sorry," she said.

"Don't be," he said thickly. "I'm tough."

"Tough enough to tell me how you got this?"

"You don't give up, do you?" he asked, his breath ruffling her hair as he peered down and observed.

"No." Leah didn't dare look up. With fumbling fingers she concentrated on cleaning the wound. "I know I'm hurting you."

"No, you're not."

She didn't believe him, but she didn't argue. Once she'd removed the grime from the wound, it was much worse than she'd thought. Yet she didn't know if her stomach churned more from tending the nasty gash or the fact that she was so close to his body.

"A car nearly hit me."

Her head came up with a jerk. "What?"

He looked sheepish for a second. "My mind wasn't on what I was doing, and I was about half lit to boot."

"You could've been killed."

"Only I was too quick for him."

"How do you know it was a him?"

An eyebrow shot up. "Are you saying some woman might've tried to deliberately run over me?"

"I wouldn't have the slightest idea about that."

A smile lurked around his gray-tinged mouth. "Like hell you don't. If I didn't know better, I'd think you were jealous."

"Then it's a good thing you know better," she responded hotly.

"Yeah, right." His face contorted as another jolt of pain hit him.

She'd been ready to kick him out the door for his brazen statement, only now she felt concern for him. "Please, let me take you to the emergency room."

"Hey, it's all right," Dalton said close to her ear. "I've survived much worse. I've been a hell-raiser all my life. I sustained enough injuries from barroom brawls and bucking horses to last a lifetime." He held his breath as she put more pressure on the wound with a fresh piece of gauze. "But I have to admit, this is the first time I've had to outrun a car.

Still, if I'd been paying attention, it wouldn't have happened."

She didn't argue with that logic, not when the pungent smell of pain-induced sweat was wringing her inside out.

"That's about as much as I can do," she said, trying to temper the huskiness in her voice.

"It was a mistake to come here, and I'm sorry."

His gruff apology came as such a surprise that Leah's head came up. Their eyes met.

For an instant neither moved, both teetering on the brink of consuming desire and warring consciences. Then Dalton shifted, and the moment was shattered. Leah stood at the same time she tore her gaze off him.

"So why did you?"

He didn't pretend to misunderstand her question. "Would you believe me if I told you I was in the vicinity?"

"No."

"Didn't think so. Okay, the truth is I just wanted to see you."

Color flooded her face, and she bit down on her lower lip.

Dalton sighed, then said, "So thanks for patching me up."

"You're welcome." Her voice was three decibels higher than normal.

He stared at her for another long moment, then grabbed his shirt and walked out the front door.

Leah moved back to the couch. She didn't know how long she sat there reed straight. Finally she forced herself to get up and walk to her bedroom.

Everything was all right, she told herself, switching on the light. *She* was all right. Nothing had happened.

This time.

Twenty-nine

Mary Mahoney's Old French House Restaurant and Courtyard was one of the oldest residences in America, as well as one of the best restaurants. Located in Rue Magnolia in old Biloxi, it was Leah's favorite place to eat, especially when she was lucky enough to dine on the glassed-in porch.

Today was one of those days. She and Sophie had just finished lunch and a short business meeting and were relaxing over tea.

On this lovely spring day, Leah looked out at the quaint courtyard that was designed to resemble New Orleans. Yet nowhere in New Orleans could they match the huge oak tree, known as the Patriarch, that covered the entire garden area.

"Lunch was delicious," Sophie said. "Thanks for asking me."

Leah faced her friend and smiled. "You're welcome. So tell me, how are things with you and Louis?"

"About the same, except that I know he's reading at least one of those books on artificial insemination that you gave me. I found it buried under the cushion on the couch."

"Well, that's a start, anyway. It's hard to imagine you married."

"I know." Sophie grinned, then shrugged. "But when the

217

rules change midstream, things take on a whole new perspective."

"That they do."

"So how's the job going?"

"Good, actually. In fact, the club's about to open. You and Louis will get an invitation."

"With the casino soon to follow, right?"

"Right, if the money doesn't run out."

Sophie frowned. "What? I thought this dude was rolling in bucks."

"I thought so, too, but apparently there's been some hitch with his father's estate." Leah shifted her gaze. "He's not very forthcoming about himself personally."

"And that bothers you?"

"Of course not. Why should it?"

Sophie gave her a strange look before changing the subject. "So how's my boy?"

Relief flooded through Leah. "He's fine."

"So there're no lasting effects from Rufus—"

"No. Right now, Dalton is Coty's hero." She paused and laughed nervously while cursing herself for bringing Dalton's name up again. Sophie was far too curious as it was. "He thinks that man can walk on water."

"I know that bothers you, so don't deny it."

"Wouldn't it bother you?"

Sophie shrugged. "I can't say, especially since I've never met the man."

"Well, it bothers me," Leah said flatly.

"Why?"

"Oh, Sophie, he's . . . he's so different from Rufus."

"So?"

Leah's frustration mounted. "So, he's a bad influence."

"Because he's a professional gambler?"

"Yes, I guess so."

Sophie smiled a teasing smile. "Somehow I never figured you for a snob."

Leah flushed. "I'm not and you know it. But Coty's all I have left, and if and when I marry again, and that's a big 'if,' it won't be to someone like Dalton Montgomery."

"Methinks you protest too loudly."

"Think what you like," Leah snapped, looking away.

Sophie chuckled. "All right, have it your own way for now." Her face turned sober. "But regardless of how vehemently you deny it, there's something between you two. I know you like a book, Leah Frazier."

"This time you're wrong."

"A woman can't go without sex forever, you know."

"Sophie, for Pete's sake!"

"Hey, don't sound so outraged. It's all right if you want to sleep with someone."

"Sophie, don't, please," Leah begged, her eyes filled with agony.

"Okay, so you don't like hearing that. But Rufus would want you to go on with your life; in fact, he told you that. Besides, you were the most loving, most devoted wife possible. You have nothing to be ashamed of or feel guilty about."

"But I do," Leah said. "Life was so much simpler when he was well and we . . . were a family."

Sophie reached across the table and covered Leah's hand. "I know, hon, but Rufus is never coming back. You have to come to terms with that, pick up the pieces, and go on."

"You sound like my mother."

"Well, this is one time I agree with her. And if Dalton's the one, then—"

"He's not!" Leah cut in vehemently. "Granted, he's attractive and I'll admit I'm not immune to that, but as far as getting involved—"

"You mean sleeping with him, don't you?"

"No! That's out of the question."

"Well, whatever," Sophie said, leaning back and sipping her tea. "But I still say you can't stop living just because Rufus has. It's not fair to Coty."

"You're right, but—"

"Uh-oh."

Leah blinked at the sudden change in Sophie's face and voice. "What's the matter?"

"Don't turn now," Sophie said in a hushed voice, "but I think I see Ellen Thibodeaux sitting in that far left corner."

Leah felt a sinking feeling in the pit of her stomach. "Oh, Lordy. Think we can sneak out without her seeing us?"

"I don't know, but we can try."

"Then let's go."

Sophie motioned for their waitress and got the check. Once that was settled, they got up and made their way toward the door.

They were just about there when a scratchy, loud voice from behind said, "Well, well, if it isn't the little thief."

Leah stiffened. Sophie cursed. Everyone within hearing distance stopped eating and looked up.

Leah turned around slowly and faced her nemesis.

"I guess you paid for your food with money you got from my jewelry."

Sophie stepped forward. "Why you—"

Leah's hand shot out and stopped her. "I'll handle this," she said, staring into Ellen's bloodshot eyes, which indicated that she'd had too much to drink. But something else was reflected in Ellen's hazel eyes—misery. This woman was drowning in misery and seemed hellbent on pulling everyone else down with her.

Her heavy breasts, evident through the tasteless silk dress that hugged her frame much too tightly, moved up and down with each breath. And while Leah felt pity for her, she couldn't forget that Ellen was vindictive and dangerous.

"If you'll step outside, I'll talk to you," Leah said in a terse but soft tone.

"Yeah, you'd like that, wouldn't you?" Ellen said, practically shouting. "Only I want everyone in this room to know you for what you are, Leah Frazier, and that's a common thief!" She sneered. "You're pathetic."

Leah reeled under the verbal assault, but when she spoke her voice remained soft. "No, Ellen, you're the one who's pathetic."

For what seemed an interminable length of time, silence dominated the room. Then, with as much dignity as she could muster and with her head held high, Leah turned to Sophie and said, "Come on, let's go."

Once outside, Sophie said, "Damn, it was all I could do not to punch that fat bitch in the nose."

Humiliated and heartbroken, Leah couldn't say a word.

Thirty

Leah rested her cheek inside her right palm and inhaled deeply. With each passing day she sank deeper into a financial quagmire. No matter how hard she juggled her checkbook, there was simply not enough money to go around.

She owed the nursing home. She owed the maximum on two credit cards. She owed the bank on a side note she'd borrowed. She owed the mortgage company. She despised her present predicament, but she was doing the best she could with what she had.

Her creditors couldn't squeeze blood from a turnip, she reminded herself ruefully; however, that didn't stop them from trying. If only she hadn't had to cash in Rufus's life insurance policy, she would've had at least that to fall back on. If only she'd get the money Ellen Thibodeaux owed her. . . .

Suddenly Leah shivered. The thought of that woman verbally attacking her in the restaurant didn't bear thinking about, but it served her better to think about Ellen than it did Dalton.

Over the last two days, his presence in and around the office had been practically nonexistent, and she'd felt as if she'd been given a reprieve. Then, last night, that newfound peace of mind had been blown to hell.

She had gone to watch Coty play in a Little Dribblers bas-

ketball game. Sophie had accompanied her. They had been sitting in the small stand of bleachers, along with several other
parents, yelling and cheering, when Sophie nudged her arm and
asked, "Do you know that man over there?"

"What man?" Leah responded absently, her eyes tracking
her son, who had the ball. "Shoot!" she cried, then groaned
when the ball slipped through Coty's hands and another player
stole it.

"The one who keeps staring at you," Sophie pressed.

Leah's instincts jumped into overdrive. Was it possible
that— Nah, Dalton wouldn't have come to this game. He
wouldn't have even known about it. Unless . . . Again Leah's
mind faltered, even as she turned her head.

Dalton stood just inside the door, one booted foot propped
against the wall. Something akin to panic gripped Leah. She
must have communicated that panic to Sophie, who leaned
over and whispered, "I was right, wasn't I?"

Leah could only nod.

"I take it you didn't know he was coming?"

"That's right," Leah said in a voice totally unlike her own.

"Well, honey, all I can say is that he could sure as hell eat
crackers in my bed anytime."

Leah cast Sophie a murderous glance. "You're crazy."

Sophie grinned. "Hey, that was supposed to be a joke.
Lighten up, okay."

Leah forced herself to relax, then said, "What should I do?"

Sophie laughed. "Hell, Leah, you're a grown woman. How
should I know what you should do? But if I were you and he
was my boss, I'd get off my fanny and say something to him."

Leah stood, smoothed her suddenly clammy hands down
one side of her jeans, and walked down the bleachers. Dalton
straightened and waited for her, an unreadable expression in his
dark eyes.

"Hi," she said inanely.

"Coty called and asked me to come," he said bluntly, as if
determined to head off the attack he knew was coming.

Leah's mouth gaped.

Dalton scratched his head. "Sorry. Apparently he didn't ask
you first."

"No, he didn't."

Dalton shoved a hand into a pocket of his jeans. The gesture stretched the material tighter across his thighs. Leah lifted her gaze back up to meet his.

"Do you want me to leave?" he asked in a low, tense voice.

She did, only she didn't. She wrangled with those opposing emotions until Dalton turned to walk away.

"Don't go."

He swung around.

She curled her nails into her palms. "Since you're here, you might as well come up and sit with Sophie and me."

Dalton's mouth compressed, then he shrugged. "You lead the way."

Leah refused to look right or left as she made her way back to her seat. Nevertheless, she felt as if every eye in the crowd were on her.

"Dalton, meet my best friend, Sophie."

They exchanged handshakes and smiles, then Dalton sat down beside Leah. From that moment on she was aware of little else except his presence beside her. Even her son, who was playing his heart out on the court, took second place.

She was shocked again at the primitive emotions Dalton evoked within her. All he had to do was come near her. Was it because he was so different from any man she'd ever known? Or was it because he was such a threat to her conscience, her self-confidence, and the hidden emotions that no one had awakened, least of all her husband?

"Atta boy, Coty! Now, sink it!"

Dalton's enthusiastic cheering of her son switched Leah's mind back on track just as the ball *whoosh*ed through the net. "All right!" she yelled, and stood along with Dalton and Sophie.

After that, Leah settled down and enjoyed the remainder of the game. It was only after it was over, when Coty saw Dalton and tore across the hardwood floor, that Leah's resentment resurrected itself.

Coty's face was red from exertion, but his eyes were dancing, despite the fact that they had lost the game. "Hi, Dalton," he said. "Did you see me make those two points?"

"Boy, did I. You were super!"

"Will you come to another game?"

Without looking at Leah, Dalton mussed Coty's hair and said, "You bet."

They walked out of the gym shortly thereafter, with Coty rattling on nonstop. Only after Dalton had driven away did Leah relax.

"He wants you, you know," Sophie said, standing by the car but out of hearing range of Coty.

"That's your imagination."

Sophie snorted. "Why don't you just go with the flow and see what happens?"

"Because I don't trust him, that's why."

Sophie held up her hands. "Okay, okay. But I don't see why not."

"At first you weren't so high on him yourself." Leah couldn't keep the sarcasm out of her voice. "If I remember correctly, you called him a ladies' man."

"Well, it's a woman's prerogative to change her mind."

Leah rolled her eyes.

"Still, I don't see why you don't trust him now, after having worked for him."

Long after Leah had gotten home from the game and put Coty to bed, she thought about Sophie's statement.

She didn't know why she didn't trust Dalton. But what she did know was that he had succeeded in turning her life upside down, and she didn't know what to do about it.

Bill DeChamp walked around the grounds of his home, feeling as if the world had caved in on him. Not only had the stroke he'd suffered several months ago crippled his body, it had further crippled his pocketbook. As a result, he'd been forced to steal from the cash reserve his wife kept in the safe.

The baby was due at any moment; and while Sylvia's threats to tell his wife had been empty ones, he didn't trust her. So he'd had no choice but to give her some hush money. However, the thought of Terri finding out about the stolen money before he could replace it brought on the fear of another stroke.

If only he'd received the money due him from the Montgomery estate, he wouldn't be in this predicament.

Damn Dalton Montgomery and his shenanigans. If only he'd kept his pecker in his pants and stayed away from that sperm bank, he, DeChamp, wouldn't be in this situation. He'd already have the megabucks due him and wouldn't have to work another day of his life.

He'd earned it. His health was on the skids, and he was tired of dealing with nothing but sniveling women who wanted divorces. Hell, he'd like to get a divorce himself, except he knew that would never happen. His wife wasn't about to let him go because divorce would tarnish her family image.

Besides, he didn't have anywhere to go; that was the demeaning part of the scenario.

Now that he was on the mend healthwise, he intended once again to pressure Dalton into settling the estate. This farce had gone on long enough. He wanted his money, and he aimed to have it.

Besides, he owed Dalton, personally. No one hit William DeChamp and got away with it.

"Bill. Oh, Bill."

DeChamp paused with a frown, then twisted around. His wife stood on the veranda. "What?"

"Telephone."

"Whoever it is, tell 'em I'm busy."

"It's a woman; she says it's urgent."

Sylvia. Like hell it was urgent!

DeChamp stalked toward the house, asking himself why the hell he hadn't kept *his* pecker in his pants.

Dalton felt as if his head were about to split. Once he'd left the ball game, he'd gone home and tied one on. Now, this morning, all he wanted to do was nurse his ill humor, but he couldn't afford that.

Time was money, and both were in short supply. First off, he had a meeting with his banker. He was out of money, and he owed contractors and suppliers, not to mention his employees.

Added to that heavy burden was his constant rehashing of the accident that had left him battered, bruised, and madder than hell. Then, going straight to Leah had been a big, fucking mistake.

But so was last night. He shouldn't have gone to the game, only he hadn't wanted to let Coty down, which in itself had added to his frustration. He didn't want to care if he let Coty down or not.

Hell, if he had any decency whatsoever, he'd end this bloody charade right now. He'd tell Leah the truth and forget about getting custody of Coty. After all, Coty was Leah's most priceless possession.

But then Coty was his as well.

By the time Dalton reached the office a short time later, he didn't think his mood could get any darker. Then he heard Leah talking on the phone.

"I promise I'll have it later this month," she was saying, desperation lowering her voice. "You have to grant me another extension."

Dalton paused; then, when he heard her hang up, he opened the door. She was at the table in the outer office. She looked up. Tears clung to her lashes.

His gut clenched even more. "Trouble?"

She averted her gaze. "It's personal."

That rankled, but he let it pass. "If it's financial, then perhaps I—"

Leah stood, then came from around the desk. "What it is, is none of your business."

It wasn't so much what she said, though that in itself was a putdown. What set him off was the way she said it.

In two strides he closed the distance between them, stopping just short of touching her. "What if I want to make it my business?"

She held her ground. "Then that's your problem, not mine."

"But what if I want to make it *mine?*"

"I don't want your help!" she lashed out as she stepped back.

He reached out and encircled her wrist. "Then just what the hell do you want from me!?"

Leah glared at him. "Let me go."

"Answer me, damn you."

"All right! I want you to leave me *and* Coty alone!"

"That's a bald-faced lie, and you know it." He jerked her against him and instantly felt her firm, full breasts.

For an instant neither moved, but their breaths came hard. Dalton muttered an expletive and was about to push her away, only to look down suddenly and see that her blouse had parted. When he saw the luscious valley formed by her breasts, he groaned and swallowed against the mounting heat in his belly.

He'd had no intention of touching her again, but when she'd

told him to leave her and Coty alone, something had snapped inside him.

Now, it would have been easier to die than to let her go.

Leah's throat moved convulsively. "Don't . . . please." There was a pleading note in her voice that matched the one in her eyes.

He understood that raw fear. He knew how it could chew a man up inside, knew how it could blindside his judgment. He knew because that was what Leah had done to him. Yet he also knew that the only way to purge that fear was to meet it head on. But something he couldn't identify stopped him.

God help him, he still couldn't turn her loose. "What if I don't want to leave you alone?"

"What you want . . . doesn't matter," Leah whispered. "Please."

The last word was barely audible as she closed her eyes, then swayed ever so gently toward him. But it was enough to send her burgeoning nipples into his chest.

A current shot through him, and he was lost. "I can't."

She moaned, just as his mouth claimed hers.

Like the last time, it wasn't a gentle kiss. But when her lips parted under his, and his tongue licked at her teeth, nudging them apart, she stopped resisting. His tongue deepened, urgent, coaxing, hungry.

She shifted suddenly, as if to better accommodate his body, which allowed one of his legs to slide between hers. Instantly his hand drifted to her buttocks, and he pulled her closer. He began to move, to rub, hot and hard, against her.

Leah moaned while his lips continued to plunder hers with that raw, sucking hunger.

Then, as if they realized simultaneously where they were and *what* they were doing, they broke apart and turned away, each fighting for their next breath.

Dalton was the first to speak. "It'll be a cold day in hell before I apologize for something we both wanted!"

Leah simply stared at him.

Later, when he got into his car, he refused to think about the pain and confusion he'd seen in Leah's eyes.

Thirty-one

Leah couldn't believe that she was already at work and it was scarcely six o'clock. She hadn't been able to sleep; and since Coty had spent the night with her mother, she had decided to come in to work.

Now, as she walked through the deserted club, she congratulated herself. The interior had come together much better than she'd dreamed possible. For someone who had never taken on a project of this magnitude without the backing of a huge firm, the job wasn't half bad, she thought, giving herself another pat.

While she'd been miffed at Dalton for undermining *her* ideas and choosing his, she had to admit now that the country-western theme was a brilliant one. She just wished she'd thought of it.

Still, it was her talent and hard work that had made his idea come into being. The club definitely had her stamp on it, as would the casino soon to follow. The casino was where her unique talents would stand out. The rustic design in the wallpaper, carpeting, gaming tables, and deli would be complemented by the sound system that would provide as background the voices of famous artists such as Wynonna and Diamond Rio.

Despite the projected success of both the club and the casino, Leah sensed something was bothering Dalton. She attributed that trouble to lack of cash flow. He spent a lot of time on the phone with his banker, and when he'd hang up, she would notice a pinched look on his face. Yet whenever she had a cost overrun and asked for extra money, he never balked, which kept her confused.

Had he inherited his father's millions? If so, had he squandered much of it away at private gaming tables? While she had no proof that that was the case, her instincts, which had served her well in the past, warned her of trouble. Too, she couldn't forget that Dalton was still a professional gambler.

Leah wished she could ignore the niggling feeling that something about him simply didn't ring true. Maybe she should follow Sophie's advice and give in to the strong, passionate feelings Dalton stirred within her, ride the wave, so to speak, see where it took her.

She couldn't. She wanted love with responsibilities. He wanted sex without responsibilities.

Still, the thought of experiencing real passion with Dalton was as heady as it was frightening. And she couldn't continue to play sexual tag with him. One of them had to put a stop to it. She doubted Dalton would, especially after his harsh statement that he had no intention of apologizing for his actions last night, which meant she would have to. The question was, could she? His hot, breathless kisses had merely skimmed the surface of her hunger.

As if she could calm her thoughts, Leah went into her office. Soon the club would be a beehive of activity, and so would the riverboat. Tony had scheduled an employee meeting. Carpenters had last minute work to do, and they would be frantic. Freight continued to arrive.

Leah sat at her desk and looked at her list, which was the length of her arm. At the top of that list were calls to several manufacturers who hadn't as yet delivered the promised items. Rather than let Dalton's secretary take care of the matter, Leah preferred to do it herself. It was, after all, her responsibility.

As for Dalton—she had no idea what he would be doing

that day or even if she would see him. When he was around, her mind was on him and not her work.

Leah lifted the phone and made several calls. Afterward she pulled out the blueprint for the casino and checked it again for placement of the forthcoming items.

Finally her shoulders ached so that she got up and walked into the main office to the coffee bar. Once there she realized she was out of French vanilla.

"Drat," she muttered. She had some in the car. Should she take the time to go get it? She was mulling that over when she heard something. She couldn't identify the sound, but she knew she was no longer alone. Chills feathered down her spine.

She swung around and almost dropped the cup she was holding. "How did you get in here?" she managed to ask.

J. T. Partridge, cigar and all, lounged against the door frame, while his eyes toured her body. Then he smiled, a leering, "gotcha" smile that made her want to cross the room and slap his ugly face.

Yet caution took precedent over that urge. She feared this man. But she refused to let him see that fear because that would supply him with the ammunition he needed to further intimidate her.

"How did you get in here?" she demanded again, much more in command of her voice.

J.T. grinned but didn't move. "The door was open."

"That's a lie. I locked it behind me."

"Sure 'bout that?"

"You picked the lock, didn't you?"

J.T.'s grin faded. "Why, sugar, that's a mighty serious charge."

"Stop playing games with me, and get out before I call the law."

"Now, why would you go and do a thing like that?" J.T. drawled.

"Because you're breaking the law," she countered hotly.

"So are you."

"Then why haven't they arrested me?" Leah's eyes challenged him.

"They will. It's just a matter of time."

"You don't believe that," she scoffed, suddenly feeling as if she had the upper hand, "or you wouldn't be here."

J.T. wrangled the cigar to the other side of his mouth, then stepped closer. "I wouldn't go gettin' too cocky, if I was you."

"As long as we're into advice, I'd suggest that you stop calling me, then hanging up."

He smirked. "Sorry, honey, but that's not me. Must be one of your other secret admirers. I don't have to stoop that low."

Leah laughed with no humor. "Oh, so you don't call following me stooping low?"

The color in J.T.'s face heightened. "I want that goddamn jewelry you've stashed, and I want it now."

"For the hundredth time, I don't have any jewelry. And if you don't leave me alone, I'm going to hire a lawyer and get a restraining order against you."

"I wouldn't advise that, either."

Leah winced inwardly against the threatening note in J.T.'s voice; yet she still refused to let him see how she felt. "Get out of here and don't come back. For the last time, I didn't take those jewels."

J.T.'s eyes lighted with anger. "Listen up, you little bitch. I'm outta patience." Then, without warning, he closed the distance between them and reached for Leah.

Leah put up her hands to ward off his attack.

"I wouldn't do that, if I were you."

J.T.'s hand froze in midair.

Having recognized Dalton's voice, Leah almost wept with relief.

J.T. swung around. "Who the hell are you?"

"Doesn't matter."

Dalton's voice remained calm, too calm, Leah realized.

"The hell it doesn't! This is between this lady and me. So if you'll kindly butt out, I'll—"

Dalton moved with the agility of an athlete, grabbed J.T. by his necktie, lifted him off his feet, and slammed him against the wall.

Leah cried out while J.T.'s eyes bulged as Dalton's distorted face bore down on him.

"Are you crazy! Let me go!" J.T. scrambled to get his footing against the back of the wall.

Dalton's hold merely tightened.

"You're choking me, you bastard," J.T. squawked, his face turning redder by the second.

"That's not all I'm going to do if you ever come near Mrs. Frazier again or this property."

"You don't frighten me."

"Oh, yeah?" Dalton jerked him out from the wall, then slammed him back again. Harder.

Sweat bathed J.T.'s puffy face, and his tongue protruded. Yet he ground out, "She stole the jewelry. She—"

"You just don't know when to give up, do you?" Dalton bounced J.T. into the wall again.

J.T. hollered as his neck lobbed sideways like a broken flower stem. Leah winced.

"Now, listen up real good." Dalton was nose to nose with J.T. now. "Do as I say or next time I won't just bounce you off the wall. I'll beat the living shit out of you. Understand?"

J.T. nodded, not once but three times, as stark fear seemed to have replaced his cockiness.

Dalton eased J.T. down, calmly reknotted his tie, then patted him on the shoulder. "Good boy."

With his eyes still bulging and his belly heaving, J.T. edged toward the door. Once there, he dashed across the threshold and disappeared.

For another moment the room was filled with silence. Finally Dalton spoke. "So he's the asshole at the beach, the one who thinks you have the jewelry."

Leah felt sick and wanted to grab her stomach. No. She wanted to run to Dalton, feel his strong arms around her, not in a sexual way, but in a comforting way, the way Rufus used to hold her. But Dalton wasn't Rufus, and if he held her, it wouldn't be for comfort.

"Leah, are you okay? He didn't hurt you, did he?"

The rough fear in Dalton's voice raked her already weakened defenses. She started to shake inside. "No," she whispered.

He stepped closer. She stepped back. A pulse jumped in his throat as their eyes met and held.

"I don't think he'll bother you again," he said in a flat voice.

"I could've handled him," she said, lifting her head a trifle defiantly. She had to regain the upper hand before she did what she yearned, which was beg him to hold her.

Dalton's hot gaze trailed up and down her body. But when he spoke that hot flare turned to cold grimace. "Yeah, right. You could've handled him."

Without another word or glance, he walked into his office and slammed the door.

Leah sagged against the nearest chair and sank her nails into the cloth. She wanted to go after him, to tell him she was sorry for behaving like an ungrateful bitch, that she did indeed thank him for rescuing her from what could have been a horrid situation.

Fear held her back, but it was fear of a different kind. Leah got up, walked toward her own office, and tried to ignore the crushing weight on her chest.

She couldn't.

"Well?"

"Well, what?" Louis asked.

Sophie tried to ignore the dull eyes that stared back at her by averting her own gaze. "What's going to happen with us?"

Sophie actually felt like crying, but this restaurant was not the place. She and Louis had gone to a movie, something they rarely did. Lately, though, rather than be alone, they sought outside company and entertainment.

If only he hadn't looked at that article and decided to get his sperm count checked, then they wouldn't have known that he was sterile until after they were married or until they tried to have children. No matter. When that bombshell was dropped, it would've been the same—devastating.

Sophie knew they couldn't keep on behaving as if they were strangers, especially in bed. Making love to Louis these days was like making love to a robot. She shivered.

"You cold?" Louis asked, staring at her over the rim of his coffee cup. They had just finished sharing a piece of cheese-cake that Sophie thought tasted like sawdust. Now they were supposed to be enjoying their coffee, only it, too, tasted foul.

"No." Sophie switched her gaze to the view outside. It was a lovely March evening. They were sitting next to a long bay window, and she could see the multitude of stars that rained down on the waters of the Gulf.

"Do you want to call it quits?"

Sophie turned around. "Do you?"

"I don't know what I want."

"Obviously it's not me." Sophie didn't bother to hide her anger or her disgust.

"That's not true. It's just that I can't give you what you want. I'm no longer a man—"

"That's bullshit, and you know it! And I'm tired of hearing it, too. I don't care if we ever have any children. It's you I want."

"Well, I want you and children."

They glared at each other for a long moment.

"Okay, so once we're married, we'll adopt, if the donor route is offensive to you."

"Isn't it to you?"

"No."

"Only because Leah had it done."

"What Leah did has nothing to do with us."

"Oh, yeah? She's the one who put that crazy idea in your head." He leaned across the table. "Well, no way am I going to let some stud who jacks off in a bottle impregnate my wife."

"Fine. Whatever you want. I don't care. I just want my friend and lover back."

Louis reached for her hand. Sophie felt his agony in his touch, saw it in his eyes. She squeezed his fingers.

"You're still willing to marry me?"

Sophie's heart almost stopped beating. "Yes, on the condition that you'll consider adoption."

"Okay."

Sophie blinked, not at all sure she had heard him correctly.

Louis smiled a sheepish smile. "You weren't hearing things. So let's do it; let's tie the knot."

"All right!" Sophie cried, leaning closer so that their lips could touch. "It's about time you came to your senses, you jerk."

Louis chuckled.

Thirty-two

"Count me out."

"Aw, come on, Montgomery, you can't quit now, especially since you're winning."

Dalton took another swig of beer and smiled at his old friend Burt Ingram, who like other professional gamblers had followed the lure of the Mississippi gaming tables. There were also three other men at the table as well, men Dalton didn't know personally.

"That's exactly why I'm quitting, Burt. You oughta understand that."

"Shit, Dalton, a thousand dollars? That's nothing. Why, I've seen you blow that on a broad in one night."

They had been playing five-card stud in one of the private gaming rooms atop Gulfport's Grand Casino.

"Those were the good old days, my friend," Dalton drawled. "Now that I'm a legit businessman, I've reformed."

Burt almost choked on the sip of beer he'd just taken, then gave Dalton an incredulous look. "You reformed. Ha, that'll be the day."

Dalton shrugged. "It's true."

"I guess we'll see," Burt responded with a belly laugh. "As the old saying goes, The proof's in the pudding."

"If Montgomery's bowing out, Burt, then so am I," a heavyset man said.

Another looked at his watch. "Count me out, too. It's one o'clock."

"Well, shit. Looks like I'm playing with a bunch of gutless wonders."

"You'll survive," Dalton said, standing and shaking hands with the three men. "Good game. Thanks for including me."

Once Dalton and Burt were alone, Burt pulled out a cigarette and lit it. Dalton frowned. "Do you have to smoke that piece of crap?"

Burt chuckled, then snuffed out the cigarette in the nearest ashtray. "Wanna another beer?"

"Nah, I really should be heading home."

"Why?"

"I told you, I'm no longer a free spirit like you. I have responsibilities, big ones."

"Yeah, I know. I think you're nuts for tying yourself down to a casino."

"And club, don't forget."

Burt shoved a hand through his thinning red hair and relaxed back on his chair. "So when's the grand opening?"

"The club's due to open in a couple of weeks. The casino should follow shortly thereafter."

"Well, if I'd had a father that was loaded, I might do the same thing."

Dalton's face turned grim as he extended his hand. "It's been fun, old buddy."

Burt scrambled to his feet. "Yeah, it has. I'll see you at your place soon."

"You'd damn well better. If I catch you losing anyplace else, I'll break your arms."

Burt laughed. "I hear you."

A few minutes later Dalton made his way out of the private room and stopped, suddenly in awe of his surroundings. The casino reminded him of Mardi Gras in New Orleans. The atmosphere was wild and partylike.

The huge casino was located on a 730-by-125-foot barge. Spread over three floors, it boasted two restaurants, a child care center, a video arcade, and, of course, slots and gaming tables galore. The Grand was the largest casino between Atlantic City and Las Vegas.

Dalton's Place paled in comparison with this luxury and grandeur, but at least his casino would be different. His patrons would gamble all right, and party, only in an authentic country-western atmosphere.

Thinking of that atmosphere brought Leah to mind. She had left for New Orleans earlier to visit the gallery of a famous western painter. She hoped to purchase several of his paintings for both the club and casino. In addition, she wanted to commission him to paint a mural in the main gaming room.

Dalton shifted his thoughts quickly, Leah being the last person he wanted to think about at the moment—not that he ever stopped, he reminded himself with disdain. Having her in bed had become his private obsession. And hell.

Later, as he made his way through the crowd toward an outer door, Dalton paused and squinted his eyes. A man whose backside looked awfully familiar was walking up the escalator, as if in a hurry.

Dalton frowned. The man looked very much like Bill DeChamp. Nah, he was imagining things. DeChamp wouldn't have a reason to be here, at the Grand. Or would he?

It was an interesting question that plagued Dalton far into the night. That same question was still on his mind when he arrived at the office the following morning.

"You look like hell," Tony said, already in his office working.

"I feel like it, too. I played poker at the Grand last night."

"And you lost your ass, right?"

"Wrong. I actually pocketed a thousand."

"Good for you. But in your world, that's chicken feed."

What Tony said was true. Ordinarily Dalton would not have stopped until the ante was much higher and he'd either lost all or won big. But that was before he'd become legit, before he'd met Leah. He'd never thought the day would come when a woman usurped his desire to gamble. To his way of thinking, that was a sorry state of affairs.

When Dalton didn't elaborate, Tony said, "There are some things I need to go over with you."

For the next two hours they talked about casino personnel, security, and advertising for a red-ribbon golf tournament Dalton had decided to sponsor several days after the grand opening of the casino.

Once Tony had gone, Dalton's eyes wandered toward Leah's empty office. Dammit, he missed her already, missed the way she smelled, missed the way she paraded around the office, unconsciously showing off her tight ass and great legs.

"Ah, to hell with it!"

The words were no more out of his mouth than the phone rang. He reached for it. "Montgomery."

"This is the nurse at East Ward Elementary. May I please speak to Mrs. Frazier?"

Dalton tensed. That was where Coty went to school. "I'm sorry, she's out of town for the day. Perhaps I can help. I'm Dalton Montgomery, her boss."

"Then you know where I can reach her."

"Of course, but if there's an immediate problem, I'm sure I can help."

The nurse hesitated, then said, "Well, there's been an accident and Coty's in the hospital emergency room."

Dalton's heart skipped a beat. "Hospital? What happened?"

"He fell on the playground and cut his head."

"I'll be right there."

"But—"

She was still talking when Dalton replaced the receiver and tore out of the building.

"You're behaving like a champ, cowboy."

"But it hurts," Coty sniffled, his huge eyes on Dalton.

"I know it does," Dalton said, staring at the child who sat in the middle of the gurney, looking lost and shaken.

When Dalton had arrived at the emergency room, both the school principal and the nurse were hovering over an inconsolable Coty. Though Coty's face had lightened somewhat on seeing Dalton, he'd still cried, "Where's my mommy?"

Dalton had explained that Leah was on her way home and would soon be with him. He had called the artist from his car phone and learned that Leah had indeed left.

Now, as the doctor reached for the needle and other items needed to stitch up the wound, he turned to the school officials, then to Dalton. "If you'd step out of the room, please."

"No!" Coty wailed. "I want my mommy."

"Hey, you're doing just fine." Dalton forced a grin, though his own stomach rebelled. "Besides, if your mom were here, she'd probably faint."

Coty smiled a feeble smile, then said in a disgusted tone, "Yeah, most girls do."

Dalton's lips twitched as he squeezed Coty on the shoulder. "So let's surprise your mom and show her what a big boy you are, okay?"

"Will you stay with me?"

"You betcha."

"Mr. Montgomery," Dr. Hazelton began, "I must insist that you leave."

Dalton faced the small-framed doctor, his eyes hard. "I'm not budging." Even if he'd wanted to leave, he couldn't have. Coty had a lock on his hand like a vise.

"I want Dalton to stay," Coty cried.

"All right, son," Dr. Hazelton said, moving the needle closer to the gash in Coty's head.

The child pulled back and whimpered. Then he peered up at Dalton, his eyes wide and pleading.

"It'll only hurt for a minute, I promise." Dalton gave a thumbs-up sign. "You're tough. You can handle it."

And he did, though Dalton wasn't sure about himself. For a moment he thought he might be sick, as emotion after emotion charged through him, ones he'd never felt until this moment.

So this was what it was like to be a parent? If he could have taken Coty's place on that table, he would have, in a heartbeat. Sweat popped out on Dalton's upper lip and under his arms. The feelings this child stirred in him had nothing to do with money. But they had everything to do with love.

No! He didn't want to care about this kid other than as a means to an end. But then he hadn't wanted to care about Coty's mother, either.

"All done, Coty," the doctor was saying.

Coty's eyes locked on Dalton for praise and consolation, only Dalton wasn't sure he was capable of giving either. Not only did he still feel faint, but he thought he might vomit as well.

"Did I do good?" Coty pressed in a proud but shaky voice.

Dalton expelled a heavy breath, but not before he pulled Coty's small body next to his and simply held him. "You bet you did good."

If the doctor hadn't been looking at him, Dalton felt he might've cried like a baby.

"Boy, Mommy's gonna be real mad."

"Why, because I picked the lock?"

"Uh-huh. You're not supposed to do that."

"I know, only you were with me. And since you live here, that makes it okay."

Coty thought about that for a moment. "Well, I guess I am the man of the house now. Aren't I?"

Again Dalton felt a squeeze on his heart. "Right."

That conversation had taken place over an hour ago. Now, Coty had awakened and was demanding that Dalton read him a story.

"You pick the one you want."

Coty reached for a big book of fairy tales that lay on the coffee table and handed it to Dalton. Having never read a story to a child, Dalton cleared his throat, then began reading, thinking he must sound as awkward as he felt.

Coty, however, didn't seem to think anything was amiss. In fact, Dalton had read only two pages when he noticed that Coty had fallen back to sleep, a smile on his pale face. Dalton suppressed a sigh and closed the book. It was at that moment he heard the car in the drive. With a feeling of dread, he got up and walked toward the kitchen.

"What are you doing here?" Leah demanded the instant she walked through the door and saw Dalton. Then, before he could respond, a look of stark fear crossed her face. "It's Coty. Something's happened to Coty!"

"Yes, but he's all right now."

Following a muffled cry, Leah swept past him.

"He's asleep on the couch," Dalton said to her retreating back.

When Dalton reached the living room, Leah was kneeling beside the sleeping child, her head on his chest as if to make sure his heart were still beating. Dalton had to look away.

After a moment Leah gazed up at him, her eyes filled with unshed tears. "What happened?"

Dalton explained; and though he felt he'd taken the proper action, he wasn't sure she thought so. In fact, he knew so. Her lips were tight and her eyes a degree colder.

"You should've tried harder to find me," she said in a terse whisper.

Dalton curbed his frustration at female logic. "What was I supposed to do, get in the car and drive up and down the highway, for God's sake?"

"Don't be ridiculous."

"Aren't you the one who's being ridiculous?"

Leah rose, turned her back, walked to the fireplace, and rested her head against the mantel. Dalton watched her shoulders shake, and he had never felt so helpless. It was all he could do not to cross the room and haul her into his arms. But if he gave in to that urge, he'd be committing mental and physical suicide. They were both too vulnerable.

"Leah, he's going to be fine."

She turned around, her face a mask of pain. But when she spoke, her voice was strong. "Would you carry him to his bed?"

Once Coty's clothes had been removed, and he was tucked in, still without having awakened, Leah leaned down and kissed him on a pale cheek. "I love you," she whispered, stroking that cheek.

Dalton's throat worked as he suddenly yearned to ask Leah about Coty's birth father. But since she'd never hinted that Coty had been conceived through a donor, he didn't have the nerve to ask. Even if he had the nerve, he couldn't have said a word. To do so would mean cutting his own jugular, since it would alert Leah as to who he really was.

For an insane moment the urge to tell her the truth, to bare his soul, resurfaced. But he hadn't been able to say the words then, nor could he now.

Leah straightened and quietly left the room. It was all Dalton could do to follow her.

When they reached the living room, Leah stood in the middle of the floor and crossed her arms over her chest. "Don't think I don't appreciate what you did, because I do, but . . ."

She paused, and Dalton, sensing the hammer was about to fall, jammed his hands into his jean pockets, and said, "But what?"

Leah's chin tipped in defiance. "I don't want you getting any ideas that you can replace Rufus. That's not going to happen."

Dalton didn't know which appealed to him more—throttling her or kissing her. Definitely the latter. So before he did anything stupid, he'd best get the hell out of there.

Yet he couldn't resist one last parting shot. "Don't you think it's about time you stopped living with a dead man!?"

Thirty-three

She should quit. She should just tell Dalton to hire someone else to finish the project. People did that all the time, Leah told herself. But not responsible people, she added bleakly. Dalton had hired her to do a job, and she had an obligation to complete it.

But at what cost?

She didn't want to care about Dalton. She didn't want Coty to care about him. Yet she cared, and so did her son, especially after Dalton had taken charge at the hospital. "Dalton" this and "Dalton" that ran freely from Coty's mouth, although it had been two weeks since his accident.

The next morning Leah hadn't gone into work. She'd kept Coty home from school to make sure he had suffered no ill effects from the wound or the medication. Also, she hadn't wanted to face Dalton. She'd been too jealous and angry—jealous that he'd won Coty over and angry that he'd accused her of clinging to Rufus's memory.

He was right about the latter, and she knew it. If only she could get past her guilt for having been attracted to Dalton while Rufus was still alive. Still, the time had indeed come for her to stop living with a ghost.

Having reached that conclusion, however, would do little to heal the breach created by their heated exchange.

Leah massaged her right temple, then peered into her makeup mirror one last time. Did she look all right? She moved closer and scrutinized herself with a more critical eye. At least the dark circles under her eyes were covered. Thank goodness for concealer.

She smiled, though it held no warmth, then stood. Her eyes surveyed the entire picture. With Sophie's help, she had bought this dress just yesterday.

When Leah had walked out of the dressing room at the boutique, Sophie's eyes had widened. "Whoa! That's a body-conscious dress, if there ever was one."

Leah wrinkled her nose. "Exactly what is that supposed to mean?"

Sophie laughed. "It means that you'll have every man in the club salivating."

"You're nuts," Leah flung back. "But don't you think I should choose something more western?"

"Hey, those tassels on the front give the dress a western look. It won't matter, anyway. Women will have on everything from Rocky Mountain jeans to beaded dresses. Besides, you don't want to look like everyone else."

At the time she had agreed with Sophie. Now she was having doubts. Maybe the dress was a little much. Beginning with the low, just-off-the-shoulder décolletage, the black cotton knit followed every curve of her body. The tassels and tulip-shaped hem that ended well above the knee added to the dramatics.

She shouldn't have bought the dress; it was too expensive. But Sophie had insisted, pointing out that the club's opening was cause for celebration.

Leah sprayed shiner on her wildly organized curls and tried to quell the butterflies that fluttered in her stomach.

What if no one came? What if Dalton's gamble didn't pay off? Granted, the western craze had swept other parts of the country, but that didn't mean it would score here. If she was nervous, she could imagine how Dalton must be feeling.

If the night wasn't a success, it wouldn't be from the lack of hard work. Leaflets had been placed on cars in the downtown area and on the beaches. Advertisements had run in the local papers, on TV, and over the radio for weeks.

Deciding she couldn't improve on her looks, Leah reached for her bag and walked out the door. Unfortunately the butterflies went with her.

Leah pulled into the parking lot and listened as the music blared from the club. She couldn't have asked for a lovelier evening. Even though it was only just past the middle of March, the weather was already warm, but the breeze blowing off the Gulf would temper that warmth.

Her mother had agreed to keep Coty, for which she was grateful. She anticipated a long evening, which in the end she suspected would be draining as well as tiring. Yet she looked forward to it, especially as she was proud of her part in the project.

Though the club wasn't supposed to open for another hour, she noted the number of cars already there. She smiled. Maybe her fears were totally unfounded.

Leah paused inside the door. A Diamond Rio tape belted clearly through the elaborate sound system while psychedelic lights above the dance floor made the couples appear almost ethereal.

Excitement laced with pride rushed through Leah. Bright, airy, and smoke free, the interior glittered with class, she thought, swallowing a giggle. Heretofore she had seen the lights, the bar stocked with liquor, and the plants positioned in their proper places. What she hadn't seen were the patrons, who were laughing, dancing, drinking, and talking.

"Hi."

She hadn't realized Dalton was anywhere near until she heard his low, rough voice.

Leah swung around, and the butterflies that had disappeared from her stomach fluttered anew. She licked her lower lip. "Hi, yourself."

Dalton's dark eyes swept over her. "You look lovely."

"So do you."

He chuckled. "I've been called lots of things, but never that."

"Well, there's always a first time for everything," she said, her eyes taking in the way his black western suit hugged his frame. She was tempted to add the word *gorgeous* to the description but didn't want to appear more interested than she already was.

"I like your dress."

His low, raspy voice cut into her thoughts with a jolt. "Thanks," she said, noticing that his eyes had dropped to the creamy tops of her breasts and were in no hurry to shift.

"Everything looks great," she said almost desperately. "Don't you think?"

He raised his eyes to again meet hers, and this time he made no effort to hide the desire that flared in them.

Although he didn't touch her, he might as well have. She recognized the pool of warmth in the pit of her stomach for what it was and averted her eyes.

That was when she saw Sophie and Louis enter the club. Without turning back to Dalton, she said, "Ah, there are my friends. Come on, let's go welcome them."

"Oh, Leah, honey, you outdid yourself," Sophie said, grabbing and hugging her. "It's absolutely wild."

Leah grinned. "Yeah, it is, isn't it?"

"And gorgeous," Sophie gushed, her eyes on Dalton.

"Hello, Sophie," he said, extending his hand. "I was hoping you'd come."

"Are you kidding? Wild horses wouldn't have kept us away." Sophie turned to Louis and added, "Dalton Montgomery, my fiancé, Louis Appleby."

After handshakes were completed, Louis said, "Nice place you got here, Montgomery. Ought to do well."

"I'm counting on it," Dalton responded, his eyes touring the room before coming back to rest on Leah. "She's responsible for the way it looks, though, not me."

Leah flushed, this time from his praise.

They chatted over the loud music for another minute, then Dalton said, "I should circulate. Have a great time, you two, and if there's anything you need, don't hesitate to holler."

"We'll have to," Sophie said drolly. "If we want to be heard, that is."

"Right," Leah said, smiling. "The music's already bouncing off my head."

"Ah, but that's what makes it fun."

Before Leah could respond, Dalton leaned over and whispered, "I'll see you later."

His warm breath caressed her ear, adding to the warmth in the pit of her stomach. She managed to nod, then moved out of harm's way.

Sophie gave her a knowing grin.

"Put a lid on that vivid imagination of yours right now," Leah snapped.

Sophie merely laughed, then linked her arm through Louis's and walked toward the dance floor.

Leah shook herself and headed toward the restaurant. Although her job was finished here, she nonetheless felt compelled to work. So, with a smile, she made the rounds, making sure that everyone was having a good time.

It was eleven o'clock before she looked at her watch. She felt ready to drop in her tracks, but it was a good tired. The opening had been an unqualified success. At every moment the dance floor had been jammed and the restaurant packed. And at every turn she'd received compliments, especially when Tony or the other employees singled her out as the architect and interior designer.

"How 'bout this dance?"

Leah pulled up short, though she couldn't have bolted had she wanted to. Dalton blocked her path.

She gazed beyond his shoulder at the still packed dance floor and lifted eyes filled with uncertainty. "Oh, I don't—"

"Come on," he said with authority, grabbing her hand. "It's time you relaxed."

The thought of relaxing sounded great, but that wouldn't happen, not with his arms around her. Unless she made a scene, however, it appeared she had no choice. He took her in his arms to the sound of Wynonna Judd's "My Strongest Weakness."

Dalton peered down at her and smiled. "Relax."

I can't! she wanted to scream, not when her body seemed to fit his as if they were two pieces of a jigsaw puzzle.

They danced in silence for what seemed an eternity.

Finally Dalton drew back and peered down into her upturned face. "Have I told you how beautiful you look?" His tone had a husky edge to it.

"Yes," she whispered, her gaze held by his.

"Mind if I tell you again?"

Leah's pulse worked fearfully in her throat, even as her nipples swelled against his chest.

His arms tightened, and she knew with dismay that he felt them, too.

"Leah, Leah," he said, drawing her closer, "you have no idea what you do to me."

She did know because she was as aroused as he was. She felt his hardness press against her. Suddenly she began to struggle. "Please, I—"

"No, don't," Dalton said, his hold on her tightening, his eyes glazed with suppressed passion. "Feel how much I want you. And you want me, too. Admit it."

"No!" Leah cried in a muffled tone. Then, realizing how vulnerable she was, she wrenched out of his arms and fled.

Exactly five minutes later she sat behind the wheel of her car, but she didn't leave right away. She couldn't. Every nerve in her body felt stretched to the breaking point. Finally, it was the fear that he'd look for her that forced her to compose herself enough to start the car and drive off.

That trembling feeling was still with her when she jammed the key into the door of her house. All she could think of was shedding her clothes and falling into bed.

Leah thrust open the door, only to stand on the threshold in stunned dismay. "No, no," she whimpered, staring at her living room, which now looked like a hellhole in war-ravaged Bosnia.

Pictures were off the wall, on the floor. The drawers of her desk were open with their contents strewn everywhere. Even the cushions on the couch were slashed and gutted.

In fact, the destruction was so widespread that Leah's eyes couldn't take it all in. "Dear Lord, why?" she cried, tears almost blinding her.

Who could have done such a thing? She forced herself to step inside, only she just stood there, until she saw the phone. Her legs unlocked and she ran to it. Sobbing openly, she punched out the club's number.

Dalton. She wanted Dalton. He would know what to do.

Thirty-four

"Mrs. Frazier, do you have any idea who would do a thing like this?"

Dalton watched Leah, who looked as though she'd been through a wringer-type washing machine. Her face was white, her lips were drawn, and there were violet-hued smudges under her eyes. Whoever had brought her this pain deserved to have his head torn off. Dalton would've liked nothing better than to administer that just dessert.

"Yes," Leah finally said in answer to the officer's question.

The officer was a bear of a man with a large black mole on his left cheek. He raised his eyebrows. "Oh? And just who might that be?"

The prick didn't believe her, Dalton thought, quelling the urge to vent his boiling rage on this young bozo. How could he not believe her? She looked scared, confused, and lost.

When Leah had called the club and Dalton had detected the controlled hysteria in her voice, he had dashed out of the building as if it had been on fire. But that fire had been doused when a friggin' train had caught him. He'd sat behind the wheel and cursed; that hadn't done any good. By the time he'd arrived, the police were already there.

Now, as Dalton listened to the questioning, his need to give Officer Duke an attitude adjustment grew. His need to hold Leah and promise her that everything was going to be all right grew as well. But he wasn't sure everything would be all right. The person who did this damage might return. He didn't know who the crazy was, but he had his own suspicions.

"Mrs. Frazier," Duke pressed, "who do you think did this?"

"J. T. Partridge."

"Why would he do a thing like this?"

"It's a long story."

"I've got lots of time."

Leah leaned against the desk and for another moment closed her eyes. When she spoke, her voice sounded faint and far away. "Partridge . . . is an insurance investigator who's been tailing me." She paused.

"Go on," Duke said.

Leah explained about the jewelry theft.

Afterward the officer rubbed his chin. "Ah, I remember that case now, although I didn't work it. But I do know it's still being looked into."

"How do you know that?" Leah asked, terror leaping into her eyes again.

"I saw the folder on the chief's desk."

"Oh, my God," Leah whispered as her eyes sought Dalton.

That need to hold her was eating him up. "Hey, you know the case isn't closed, but you can't worry about that now." Duke cleared his throat. "So you think the investigator did this?"

"I certainly do," Leah said with conviction.

Duke turned to Dalton. "What about you? How are you connected to all this?"

Nosy bastard to boot, Dalton thought. "Mrs. Frazier works for me."

"Do you know this Mr. Partridge?"

"I sure as hell do. In fact, I almost tore him limb from limb when he came on my property and threatened Mrs. Frazier."

The officer raised his eyebrows higher. "So you think he

might've taken matters into his own hands, hoping he might find the jewels himself?"

"That's a good possibility." Dalton looked at Leah again.

She returned his stare for a second, then shifted her gaze back to the officer. "I think it's more than just a possibility," she said, a tremor evident in her voice. "I think it's a fact."

"Well, I'll certainly have a talk with Mr. Partridge and see what he has to say. Meanwhile, I'd suggest you be careful. Would you like me to send a plainclothesman to watch the house?"

Leah made a face at the same time Dalton watched her swallow hard. "I . . . don't think that'll be necessary, especially if you talk to him. Maybe that'll put the fear of God into him."

"I don't agree," Dalton said, his voice cold. But when he turned to Leah, he softened his tone. "Let him send someone for a few days. It can't hurt, although I doubt the bastard'll be back anytime soon."

Duke shrugged, his eyes swinging from one to the other. "Whatever you think best."

"All right," Leah said.

Her face was flushed, and her eyes were filmed with tears. Again it was all Dalton could do not to go to her. But he feared if he touched her now, the already volatile situation would explode sky-high.

The officer asked a few more questions, then let himself quietly out the front door. Leah stood with her arms folded across her chest. Dalton ground his teeth together, though it was he who finally ended the silence.

"You shouldn't have come in here, you know."

A defiant light suddenly sprang back into her eyes. "What do you mean?"

Dalton's dark eyes clicked with electricity. "You know what the hell I mean. Whoever did this could've still been in the house."

"But he wasn't."

"Not this time. But what about next time?"

Leah's arms tightened across her chest. "Please, if you're going to holler at me, I'd rather you go."

"Dammit, Leah! You just don't get it, do you? He

could've taken the knife he used to destroy your furniture and used it on you. That thought makes me crazy."

"Stop it!" Leah lifted her hands to her ears and covered them, while her eyes filled with tears. "If you're going to make matters worse, just go. I can't . . . take much more." She began to shake.

Dalton's heart hammered against his rib cage, and before he realized what he was doing, he closed the distance between them. At that, he stopped just short of touching her. He didn't dare touch her. If he did, he knew he wouldn't let her go.

As her trembling increased, so did his inner agony.

"Oh, Lord, Leah, I didn't mean to make you cry," he whispered, his voice revealing his misery.

She peered up at him. Her eyes were wide; her lips were parted and moist. Her burnished curls were slightly damp with perspiration, and she was lovelier than he'd ever seen her.

"I'm . . . so scared," she whispered.

Then she did something he was totally unprepared for—*she* touched him. Reaching out, she splayed her fingers on his broad chest.

God help him, no matter how much he'd wanted to, he hadn't intended to touch her. But her touching him was altogether different. Later, he couldn't remember quite how it happened, but the next thing he knew, their arms were around each other, tight and demanding.

Leah's fingertips dug into his back, while his mouth sank into hers, parting her lips. He felt on fire as he licked, caressed, sucked, faster and hotter.

A moan escaped from deep within as his hands moved down her partially bare back, and his fingers fumbled with the zipper. Soon the top of her dress draped around her waist, which gave him access to her breasts, high, full, and lovely.

Despite his trembling, he surrounded both and closed his eyes. He massaged the burgeoning nipples with the pads of his thumbs and felt something happen inside him, something akin to what he'd felt after the accident when they had put Coty to bed, something close to a shocking need for more than sex.

His mind cringed against what hovered on the outer edges. But the thought wouldn't let go. It pushed its way into his conscious mind. Love? For the first time in his life, had he fallen in love? No, he told himself again. That wasn't possible. He was immune to love.

He only knew he couldn't control his raging desire. "I want you," he ground out into her lips. "Now!"

"Yes, oh, yes."

"Then help me!"

With his mouth now suckling a nipple, Dalton used his free hands to lift the bottom of her dress, to find that she wore panties and a garter belt. He tugged the panties down and immediately covered her mound with his hand, then sank two fingers inside her. She was wet and ready.

He backed her against the wall and heard her deep moan. That excited him that much more. He grabbed her hand and placed it against him. "Feel how much I want you."

"Yes, and I want you," she whispered urgently. "But what about protection?"

"I'll take care of that."

Leah unzipped his jeans, and moments later he lifted her high against the wall, then down onto his hard penis.

"Oh, Dalton," she cried as her warmth surrounded him like a tight-fitting glove.

"Am I hurting you?"

"Yes, no," she babbled, her face drenched with sweat. She wrapped her legs around his buttocks.

He moved up and down, slowly, then with a frantic pace that soon drove them both over the edge. When their orgasms hit, they cried simultaneously.

Afterward, Dalton had only the strength to cradle her in his arms and hold her like a baby.

"Where's the bedroom?" he asked when he could get his breath.

Wordless, Leah pointed down the hall.

Something was wrong. Something was hurting her. She was a girl again, defenseless and petrified. She could feel her heart beating like a violent hammer. Someone lurked in the shadows. *Someone was touching her*. A hand. A hand was on her breast, rough, and hurtful. She wanted to cry out, only she couldn't. Another hand was over her mouth to keep her from doing just that.

Still, she struggled from side to side to try to break his hold. He merely chuckled at her exertion, while he lowered his head to that breast he'd been touching. . . .

"No!" Leah cried out loud, and lurched up in the bed.

"Leah, Leah, wake up," a distant voice pleaded. "Shh, you're all right. You're not alone."

Leah blinked several times, then tried to calm her racing heart by taking deep, shuddering breaths. Where was she? And who was with her?

"Leah, it's all right," the soothing voice repeated. "You've just had a bad dream."

With the help of the moonlight streaming through the open blinds, she twisted her head and saw Dalton's face. Suddenly it all came back to her—the break-in, the destruction, Dalton holding her, then backing her against the wall and making love to her.

Or had that coupling been more like two animals in the throes of heat? Was that what had brought back the dream that used to haunt her relentlessly?

"Leah," Dalton whispered.

Her eyes wandered over his naked body before she looked away. She scarcely remembered their going into the bedroom or disposing of their clothes. What she did remember was how they had lain together on the bed and held each other until they had both drifted into a satisfied sleep.

"Are you all right?" he asked. The tip of a callused finger traced up and down her arm. "When you cried out, you scared the hell out of me. It's the break-in that caused it, isn't it?" Dalton grimaced. "When I think of him pilfering through your things, I want to kill. And if and when I get my hands on him, I'll—"

She reached out and placed a finger across his lips. "Shh, don't say that. I know J. T. Partridge did this, and I'm confident the police will get him." She paused. "Only it's not the break-in that caused my nightmares." She couldn't meet his eyes.

"Leah, did someone hurt you?"

Tears gathered in the corners of her eyes. But she refused to let them trickle down her cheek for fear that the shame that festered inside her would win.

She couldn't bear that. She'd spent too many years keeping it locked away.

"Don't cry, please," Dalton pleaded. "It rips me apart."

"You're right. Someone . . . did hurt me."

"It wasn't Rufus, was it?"

"No." She struggled to continue. "Never Rufus."

Dalton reached for her then and gathered her close against him.

Unwittingly the words poured from her lips. "When I was ten years old my mother took in boarders to help supplement our income. My daddy had died and left us virtually penniless."

She paused and drew a deep breath.

"If this is too painful, stop," Dalton said, placing his lips against her neck. "I'll understand. We all have skeletons in our closet. Some are better left buried."

Leah shivered against the feel of his mouth grazing her skin. Yet she couldn't seem to keep the ugly past from spilling out of her mouth. "One . . . one night I was in my bedroom and had just finished reading a book and turned off the light when I heard the door creak. I . . . I couldn't see because it was so dark in the room. We'd had a storm that night."

Dalton tensed beside her as if he knew what was coming next.

"Then, before I knew what was happening, a man was sitting beside me. I opened my mouth to scream, but he was quicker than I was. He covered my mouth with his hand."

"Did the sonofabitch . . ." Dalton's voice faded as if he couldn't say the vile word that hovered between them.

"No, he didn't rape me," Leah said in a dull tone, "but . . . but he put his hands all over me." She shivered while the tears saturated her face.

"Oh, baby, I'm so sorry," Dalton whispered, "so sorry."

"I don't know how it happened, but I managed to get away and run from the room." She paused again and sniffled.

"Where did you go?"

"To my mother's room. I told her what happened."

"And?"

"She kicked the man out of the house, then told me to forget about it, that nothing bad had happened."

Expletives spewed from Dalton's lips.

"To this day my mother refuses to discuss that night, determined to pretend it never happened. Her reasoning was that if we . . . if *I* dwelled on it, then it would ruin my life." Leah laughed a cold, mirthless laugh. "You see, all she ever wanted was for me to marry well and have material things. That's all that ever mattered to her, but not to me, never to me."

"Is that why you married Rufus, a man so much older than you?"

"Yes. He was so kind and gentle. He taught me that love and pain weren't synonymous."

"Do you still love him?" Dalton asked, drawing back so that he could look at her.

She met his eyes unflinchingly. "Yes, but not in the way you mean. I never loved him passionately." Not the way I love you, she almost said. The one thing she vowed would never happen had happened. She had fallen in love with Dalton Montgomery, a man who wanted her but who didn't love her.

"Leah." She heard the desperate note in his voice, and though she didn't know what it meant, she didn't care.

"You're not afraid of me, are you?"

"Yes," she whispered. "You terrorize me, but in a different way."

He kissed her neck. "And you terrorize me. I know I should never have touched you that first time, but now that I have—"

"I know," she whispered as his arms tightened.

She gave in to the yearning those arms incited. Tomorrow she'd sort through the mess that was now her life, but not at this precious moment, not when his tongue was sliding its way down her quivering flesh.

She lay unmoving until the heat forced her to act. She dug her fingers into his scalp when the soft pads of his fingers scraped the insides of her thighs. Then, incredibly, his tongue sank into her warmth. Her legs jerked; her thighs turned to liquid as all control deserted her.

"Please, no more," she cried as the relentless pleasure became unbearable.

He paid no need to her cry but continued with his gentle assault.

Leah's chest felt as if it might burst as her lips parted and her hips bucked. "Oh, please," she groaned when one orgasm after another made her quiver in sweet pain.

He lifted her on top of him and grunted with pleasure as she sank onto his hot flesh. She rode him until they were so weary, they fell into an exhausted sleep.

Thirty-five

Coty sat with his hands folded in his lap.

"Time to go, cowboy," Leah said, smiling at him. He didn't smile back. Leah frowned.

"What's the matter?"

"Why doesn't Dalton like me anymore?" Coty mumbled.

Leah's heart sank. "Oh, honey, he still likes you. It's just that he's . . . we're frantic to get the casino open."

"What's frantic mean?"

Leah smiled and flicked his chin. "Never mind. I'm sure you'll see Dalton soon."

"Can I call him?"

Leah's throat tightened, but she managed to say, "Sure."

"Oh, goody." Coty grabbed his knapsack, kissed her on the cheek, and scooted out of the car.

Once he was inside the school building, Leah drove off. But she wasn't ready to go to the office and face Dalton. Her face burned when she thought of their lovemaking last night. She'd awakened at dawn and realized that she was in the bed alone. However, a note had been pinned to the pillow. It had read: "The detective's outside, so don't worry. I'll call a cleaning service to repair the damage. See you later. Dalton."

Leah had swallowed her disappointment, then sat up, only

258

to groan as she gazed around her bedroom that was as ravaged as the living room. The thought of that creep J.T. rum-
maging through her things was unacceptable.

She should be frightened, but she wasn't. She was boiling
mad. Something had to be done about J.T.'s continued invasion of her privacy.

She got up and put the house in order as best she could,
thankful that Dalton had been thoughtful enough to call a
cleaning service. Time was short. She had to pick up Coty at
her mother's, take him to school, then go to work.

Yet in the shower Leah had dallied, her thoughts returning
to Dalton, especially when she noticed the marks on her
breasts from his day's growth of beard.

Those same erotic thoughts remained up front in her mind,
even as she headed for the office. She didn't know what
made her pull off the side of the road and stop. Maybe it was
a knee-jerk reaction to those thoughts. Or maybe she just
needed to calm herself.

She kicked off her sandals and got out of the car. The mid-
March morning was a gem. The air was moist and warm,
with sunlight coloring the water a dazzling blue green. For a
while she simply walked, opening her mouth and breathing
in the salty air, feeling it soothe her turmoil. She listened to
the waves whisper against the sand while birds scooted
across the sand in front of her.

Leah smiled, then suddenly cried out, "Ouch!"

She moved her foot and realized she had stepped on a
multicolored shell, so fragile that when she picked it up and
held it in the sunlight, it looked like a rainbow. She smiled
again.

But no matter how tranquil the setting, she still couldn't
completely quiet her heart.

"You're a fool, Leah Frazier," she tossed to the wind.

All her life she'd wanted someone to love her, really love
her. Rufus had fulfilled that need, but now he was gone. And
she missed him, missed a man in her life. She didn't like living alone, yet she rebelled against loving a man like Dalton.

He was so volatile, so passionate, so demanding. He was
everything Rufus hadn't been. How long could she keep a
virile man like Dalton satisfied? That worry reinforced her

feelings of inadequacy. Still, she wished she could let herself go for once in her life, have an affair with him, let their relationship run its course.

Coty was one reason why she should not. Her own self-esteem was another. If Dalton were to tire of her and walk out, she would be devastated and hate herself. That fear was illogical, but it was something she couldn't conquer. She'd be wise to protect her vulnerability. As it was, he saw far too much.

Leah walked a while longer before making her way back to the car. At least some of the cobwebs had been cleared from her brain. She was ready to face the day. And Dalton.

Her steps quickened.

At first she didn't see the woman. It was only after she blocked Leah's path that Leah pulled up short.

"I'm sorry, I didn't mean to startle you," the petite blonde said, a wariness in her voice.

"Do I know you?" Leah asked bluntly.

The woman attempted a smile. "No, but I know you, or at least something about you."

"Oh?"

"I'm Becky Childress. I used to work for Cooper Anderson." Bitterness now laced her voice.

"How can I help you?"

Becky looked away. "This is extremely awkward for me, so the only way I know to handle it is to just come right out and ask. Did he sexually harass you?"

"Yes," Leah said without hesitation.

The woman seemed to wilt right in front of her. "That bastard did me, too."

"I'm sorry," Leah said softly.

"So am I."

"How can I help?"

"Would you be willing to testify against him in court?"

"So you're planning to take it that far?"

Again the secretary's lips formed into a bitter line. "If I have to. He fired me because I wouldn't have sex with him

*   *   *

He should be elated; he'd managed a reprieve so that he could get the casino open. But he wasn't elated. Dalton felt as if he'd been on a ten-day drunk. It wasn't only the banker and his money situation that had him strung out. He craved to make love to Leah again.

He tried to focus his thoughts exclusively on the road ahead. Instead he saw her face while she was on top of him. He'd experienced such potent desire that he hadn't even so much as paused to weigh the consequences of what he was doing.

With his hands on her breasts that were wet from his saliva, he'd wanted to believe that what was happening between them had the potential to last a lifetime, that if he believed hard enough, it *could* happen.

He knew better. When she found out who he was and what his intentions were, she'd spit in his face and tell him to hit the road.

To think otherwise was tantamount to blowing smoke up his ass. That was why he had to keep his hands off her and stick to his plan.

Fifteen minutes later Dalton walked into the office. Leah was alone, standing in front of a filing cabinet. When she heard him, she turned.

Their eyes met. "Morning," he said with effort.

"Hi."

She appeared to have survived the ordeal of the break-in as well as their wild, insane night of lovemaking. In fact, she looked beautiful, dressed in jeans and a melon-colored T-shirt that hugged her upper body, highlighting the imprint of her nipples.

He groaned inwardly, needing to taste them again.

As if Leah read his thoughts, she whispered, "Don't."

Still, he couldn't stop staring. That was when he noticed she hadn't come through the ordeal unscathed. The delicate veins at her temples stood out. Her face was pale as parchment. She seemed almost ethereal.

But it was in her smoky green eyes that the suffering showed the most, suffering that he had brought her. Only he couldn't say the words she wanted to hear. He couldn't make that almighty commitment.

At the same time, he was desperate to say something that would diffuse the silence and her pain.

"Look, Leah, I—"

She turned abruptly. "We'll talk later, okay?" She didn't look at him. "I'm due at the casino. I'm expecting a furniture shipment shortly."

Dalton wanted to tell her not to go, to stay so that they could talk, maybe hash things out. But he couldn't. It was as if the words had frozen on his tongue.

She looked at him one last time, and he saw the humiliating despair in her eyes. "Leah—"

She swept past him and walked out the door.

Dalton winced as if she'd struck him. Maybe he'd have felt better if she had.

Thirty-six

"Oh, Sophie, that's wonderful."

Sophie gave her a crooked grin. "Yeah, I'm kinda excited myself."

Leah hugged her friend. When they pulled apart, their eyes were glazed with tears.

"Come on, let's get some coffee. We'll have a toast."

Sophie shook her head. "Can't, not right now."

"Why not?" Leah peered at her watch. "It's only seven o'clock, for heaven's sake."

"Well, maybe I do have time for one cup."

"Good. By then it'll be time for me to wake Coty."

"By the way, how is the cowboy?"

Leah grinned. "Fine, but . . ." Her voice faltered, and her grin faded.

Sophie sat at the dining room table while Leah prepared the coffee. "But what?" she pressed at last.

"He misses Rufus, and . . ." Again Leah paused.

"Dalton. That's the word you're trying to spit out, isn't it?"

"Yes." Leah's tone was sharper than she intended.

"You're in love with him, aren't you?"

265

Leah jerked her head around and stared at her sober-faced friend. "Of course not."

"Liar," Sophie said softly, although there was the semblance of a smile on her pert features.

"It's just that—"

Sophie waved a hand. "You don't have to explain. I know. He makes you crazy, makes you want what you know you shouldn't have."

"You're right, and it's scary."

"Why? You're free and over twenty-one."

"He's . . . he's nothing like Rufus."

"So, that's good."

"No, it's not. Besides, he only wants me. He . . . doesn't love me."

"How do you know?"

"Because men like Dalton Montgomery don't fall in love. Besides, I have Coty to think about. Living with a professional gambler would not provide the stability I want for my son. As it is, Coty thinks that Dalton hung the moon, even though it's been a while since he's seen him."

Sophie looked on as Leah poured their coffee and brought it to the table. She sat down, and for a moment they sipped the hot liquid.

"So what are you going to do?"

A bleakness appeared in Leah's eyes. "I don't know. I honestly don't know. If I thought we had a future, I might go for it. But he's showed me these past three weeks that that's not possible."

"How?"

"He's been aloof and moody, which proves he's sorry that he . . . that we—" Leah broke off. She didn't want to admit even to her best friend that she and Dalton had slept together. First, it was none of her business, and second, it was too private. And last, she still felt she had been unfaithful to Rufus.

"Ah, he's probably uptight about the casino's impending opening," Sophie was saying.

"Dalton's just so different. And as you know, when it comes to men, I don't have any experience."

Sophie peered at Leah over the rim of her cup, her eyes

narrowed. "All I can say is that if you love him, and he makes you happy, go for it."

"But how do you know that?" Leah asked in a troubled tone.

Sophie placed a fist against her stomach. "Gut. It's something in the gut and the heart. Only you can know it."

"Well, enough about me," Leah said, knowing that no matter how much they discussed Dalton, he was her cross to bear and she would have to work it out herself. "When's the wedding?"

"We haven't actually set a date yet, but I suspect it'll be soon."

Leah hesitated. "So what about children? Have you reached a compromise?"

"We'll probably adopt." She sighed. "He refuses to even consider artificial insemination, says he's not about to let some man—" This time Sophie broke off with a flushed face.

Leah leaned across the table and covered her friend's hand. "Hey, it's okay. You can say the words *jack off*. That doesn't bother me. When you go the donor route, that's exactly what happens. Some men can handle that, others can't."

"Well, Louis can't. The thought drives him apeshit."

Leah had to grin. "Well, if that's the case, then you're wise to drop the subject."

"But it would be nice to have a baby," Sophie said, a faraway expression in her eyes. "I'd like for my belly to swell, but if it means losing Louis, I guess I'll have to settle for someone else's tummy swelling." She smiled lamely. "Then I get the baby."

"Atta girl," Leah said. "At least you won't have to endure donor insemination. It's not fun."

Sophie squirmed on her chair. "From what you told me earlier, that's a given."

"Whatever you decide about children, I'm thrilled that you two have worked out your differences. And I can't wait for the wedding."

"Would you be my matron of honor?"

"Just try and stop me."

Sophie grinned. "Well, that's settled, so now I guess that leaves work."

"What about work?"

"I'm not going to be able to help you out anymore. Louis wants me to come to work at the hospital. With the long hours he keeps, he feels we won't get to see each other. And since the office project is finished, I thought now would be a good time to make the move."

"I understand, especially when I don't know when or if I'll get another job."

"Don't worry, after the club and casino, you won't have any trouble."

"I wish that'd be the case, but with that theft thing still hanging over my head, I have my doubts."

"Ah, Dalton'll come through. He'll give you a great recommendation.

"We'll see."

"Speaking of the theft, don't you think it and the break-in are connected?"

Leah's features darkened. "I certainly do. I told that cop who I thought had broken in."

"That toad insurance investigator, right?"

"Right."

"Knowing that he'd be the prime suspect, why would he do something so stupid?"

"Who knows," Leah said. "Desperation, that's all I can figure."

"Well, I hope they nail his butt to the jail floor."

"Dalton says the same thing, only he'd like to do the nailing."

Sophie chuckled. "I told you, he's my kinda man."

Leah didn't respond. Every time Dalton's name was mentioned, her heart wrenched, which was ridiculous, as he had made it quite plain that he regretted sleeping with her. And though his rejection was like a slap in the face, there wasn't anything she could do about it. She'd have to find a way to cope until the project was finished.

Sophie stood, breaking the silence. "Look, kiddo, I gotta run."

Leah stood as well. "Thanks for stopping by. I'll talk to you soon."

Once she was alone, Leah stared out the window and watched two bluebirds splash in the birdbath. The day was shaping up to be one of those rare ones that made her itch to be outdoors rather than cooped up inside.

She was considering how she could manage that when the phone rang. She crossed the room and lifted the receiver.

"Hello."

"Leah."

Dalton's strong voice sent chills down her spine. "What?"

"Look, I know you're going to think I'm nuts, especially with all we have to do, but . . ." He paused and drew a deep breath. "I have to go to Bogalusa to check on a filly, and I thought maybe you and Coty might like to ride with me. Reckon he could miss a day of school?"

Leah sat down. "Oh, I don't think—"

"Please," he cut in, and Leah heard the desperate note in his tone. "Coty will love it."

Leah closed her eyes. "All right. When . . . time?"

"How 'bout an hour?"

"We'll be ready."

After he hung up, Leah held the receiver and stared at it, unable to control the excitement that raced through her at the thought of spending a day with Dalton.

"So what's the verdict?"

Leah smiled as she faced Dalton, who sat beside her on the blanket and leaned against a tree. "I think this is as close to paradise as I've ever been."

"Really? I guess I just take it all for granted."

"That's too bad. I could never do that. My appreciation of the finer things in life comes from never having them."

"And because I've *always* had or been exposed to them, it's made me jaded."

Leah didn't respond right off. There was so much she didn't understand about him. It was as if she were constantly swimming against the tide.

But she'd been sincere when she'd said this place was

lovely, not only the site that he'd chosen for their picnic, but the entire estate. The surrounding land was covered by tall pines and oaks that seemed to brush the sky.

And the house itself was a thing of beauty, with its columns, balconies, winding stairway, and crystal chandeliers.

"Whoa, Mommy, look!" Coty had said when he'd seen the stairs. "Can I run up them?"

"Be my guest," Dalton had said with a wink at Leah, which had made her heart catch.

The housekeeper had packed them a lunch, then after Dalton had met the local veterinarian and tended to his filly, with Coty looking on at every turn, they had made their way to what Dalton said used to be his favorite hiding place.

A babbling brook that fed into a deep pond was directly in front of them. Earlier, Dalton and Coty had swum there. Both had tried to get her to join them, but she'd declined. She hadn't wanted to get wet, but more than that, she'd been slightly overwhelmed by the camaraderie between her son and this man.

Dalton had played tirelessly with Coty.

"Watch, Mommy," Coty had cried more than once when Dalton would heave him onto his shoulders for Coty to dive.

"I'm watching," she had assured him with a laugh.

Now, after they had consumed a huge lunch of fried chicken, potato salad, baked pork 'n' beans, and fried-peach pies, they were resting on two separate blankets.

Leah's eyes drifted to the blanket a few yards away and watched as Coty's chest moved up and down. She smiled, thinking how exhausted he was, yet what fun he'd had.

She turned back to Dalton and forced herself to say, "Thanks for playing with Coty."

He shrugged. "You don't owe me any thanks. It was my pleasure."

She felt he spoke the truth, which confused her more. He had more mood swings than a blues band. One minute he was sexually charged and loving, the next cold and withdrawn.

"Leah—"

The broken sound in his voice and the way he looked at

her left no doubt as to his current mood. He wanted her, only he didn't make a move to take her, and she wanted him to, so much that she did something totally out of character. She raised herself on bended knees and placed her lips against his.

She heard his sharp intake of breath, which sent another shaft of longing through her.

"Oh, Leah, Leah," he chanted against her lips while his hands clutched at her.

She kissed him again, deeper, bolder, even going so far as to sneak her tongue into his mouth. She didn't stop there. She clasped her hands around his midriff and dug her nails into the exposed skin. What she really wanted to do was rip his clothes off.

He squeezed her so tightly that she feared he would crush her. But then his hands moved to her buttocks and cupped them. That contact, hard pressing against soft, sent a jab of pleasure through them both.

"Oh, Leah!" he whispered, reaching inside her cotton top and surrounding, then kneading a firm breast.

She placed her hand against him, which sent him into a frenzy. At last she had won. He would take her on the spot.

After a few seconds he stiffened and pulled away.

She swallowed a cry, then stared at him, wild-eyed.

"Don't look at me like that!"

"I . . . disappointed you the last time, didn't I? I didn't satisfy you—"

"Jesus! Don't say that! Don't think that!" He grabbed her hand and placed it on him. "Feel how much I want you."

His penis was full and throbbing under her hand, wrestling to break the confines of his jeans. She quickly withdrew her hand, but she couldn't stop looking at him, at the anguish on his face and in his eyes.

"I've never felt with another woman what I feel with you. And I'd like nothing more than to fuck you three times a day for the rest of my life. Only I can't make that kind of commitment, and I know that's what you want."

"You don't know what I want," she snapped.

"There's so much you don't know about me."

She wrapped her arms around herself to control the shivering that was taking place inside her. "I don't suppose you're going to tell me, either," she said, unable to keep the bitterness out of her voice. What had started as a day bright with promise had turned into a nightmare.

He remained silent.

"Please, just take me . . . us home."

"It's not that easy to talk about myself."

"Don't you think I know that?" she cried. "Telling you about my past, about that creep who came into my room, was one of the hardest things I've ever done."

"My daddy was a lot like your mother, cold and self-centered."

"I'm sorry," she whispered, and waited with bated breath, unsure if he'd continue.

"He really got that way after . . . after my brother—"

"Brother? You have a brother?"

"I *had* a brother. He's dead, and my old man blamed me."

"Oh, Dalton."

He had a painful, faraway look in his eyes; she didn't know what to say or how to comfort him.

Finally he went on, "Michael was older than I was, and our mother died when we were young. Parker made no bones about which one of us would follow in his political footsteps. He picked Michael, thought he was a sure bet to make it to the White House." Dalton smirked. "As for me, I was nothing but a bloody nuisance."

"I'm sure that's not true."

"Oh, it was true all right."

"How . . . did he die?"

"When we were teenagers, he and I took our new boat out in the bay. He insisted I drive because he wanted to drink his beer. He'd become quite a lush, only dear old Dad didn't have a clue. Anyway, I don't really know what happened, except that another boat seemed to come out of nowhere. I swerved so I wouldn't broadside it, only when I did, my brother hit his head."

Dalton paused and drew a struggling breath. "He never regained consciousness. He died two days later, and my old man hated my guts from then on."

"How could he? It was an accident."

"I know that, but there was no telling him that. You couldn't convince your mother to change her mind about what happened to you, right?"

Leah nodded, tears filling her eyes.

"Well, then, you know what I was up against."

"So what happened next?" she asked in a wobbly voice.

"I turned into a hell-raiser, a first-class pain in the ass. I was determined that Parker was going to notice me whether he wanted to or not."

"What you really wanted was for him to love you," she put in softly.

Dalton's eyes narrowed on her face. "Maybe so. Anyhow, I got his attention. Boy, did I ever. I started gambling, and because he didn't want the Montgomery name sullied, he bailed me out of more jams than I can count. And he hated every minute of it, almost as much as he hated me."

"Apparently he didn't hate you as much as you thought. He left you all this land, and house, and money to boot. Right?"

Dalton scrambled to his feet and turned his back on her. "Yeah, right." Then, after a moment, he said in an expressionless tone, "It's time we woke Coty and headed back."

Another sharp pain of rejection jabbed Leah. "Dalton?"

He swung around, his eyes filled with distress.

"Where do *we* go from here?"

He rubbed the back of his neck in a helpless gesture. "I wish to hell I knew."

She knew. Leah knew that she had to get away from Dalton soon or he would break her heart, perhaps more than losing Rufus had broken it. Only this time she wasn't sure she could survive.

With as much composure as she could muster, she said, "I'll get Coty."

Thirty-seven

Dalton walked into the casino, stopped, and looked around. He still couldn't believe it. His dream was about to come true. If only you can hold on to it, that is, he reminded himself, feeling a brutal twist in his gut. But he wouldn't think about that now. Instead he'd savor the sweet taste of success.

In three days the casino was due to open, though it wasn't quite finished. Leah was in the process of decorating the top floor. Each floor had a unique western design, which had been Leah's idea, and a good one, but it also required more time and thought. The long work hours had taken their toll. He was so tired, he felt he could sleep for days.

Leah hadn't come to work today because Coty had a virus. When she'd called this morning to tell him, he'd told her to take the day off and stay home with the child. He'd heard the relief in her voice when she'd said okay.

Since the picnic they had behaved as virtual strangers while they had worked side by side. But he knew his rebuff of her had stung. Hell, it had nearly killed him. Because she was more than just a good fuck, he couldn't postpone the inevitable; he had to make his move.

The bank was on his ass big time, and Leah's job would soon end.

He paused in his thoughts, made his way to his desk, and sat down. He picked up a pen and thumped it up and down, but he knew he wasn't about to work.

Maybe if he told her the truth, she'd forgive him.

"Sure, Montgomery, and pigs fly."

Dalton peered at his watch and noticed that it was past midnight. He'd left the casino earlier and after eating at the club had spent some time there. Instead of going home, he'd come back to his office. The thought of going home to bed didn't appeal to him. But he had no choice; he'd made that bed, and now he had to lie in it.

Alone.

That thought still tormented him a few minutes later when he walked out of the club of his car. He paused by the door of his car and breathed deeply of the ocean breeze. It was a perfect evening, made for love.

"Ah, shit," he muttered at the same time he heard something behind him. He swung around. Something hard and lethal connected with his temple.

Fire shot through his head while his stomach roiled. He fell to the concrete.

Leah blew the whistle in the phone, then heard a screamed curse. Only then did she slam down the receiver.

Afterward she shook so hard inside, she fell onto the couch. Had Coty heard the commotion? She forced herself to get up and go to his room.

The shrill sound of the whistle hadn't affected the child. Coty was deep in sleep, but then she'd given him medicine earlier that the doctor had said might make him drowsy. For once she was glad it had.

Leah closed his door and returned to the living room. The trembling had eased somewhat, but that would be only temporary if she received another of those dreaded crank phone calls. That had started some weeks ago, but she knew who was behind them.

Damn J. T. Partridge. And damn her inability to do anything to stop his harassment. And while she was at it, she might as well damn Dalton Montgomery for making her fall madly in love with him, only to reject her.

So deep was she in her dismal thoughts that she didn't recognize the sound for what it was. Only after it became louder did she connect it with the front door. Someone was knocking. For a second she didn't move, all sorts of crazy notions going through her mind.

Surely Partridge wouldn't call, then show up on her doorstep. Or would he? Then her mind jumped to Cooper, only to dismiss that as pure nonsense, which left only one person brazen enough to knock on her door at half-past midnight.

Damn him! she raged. If he awakened Coty . . .

Without stopping to think how scantily clad she was, in a robe and nothing else, she hurried to the door. But when she opened the door, her mode of dress was forgotten. Everything fled her mind except Dalton and the fact that he stood on her doorstep, bleeding. *Again.*

"Oh, my God," she wheezed, taking in the gash on the side of his forehead that was caked with dried blood.

"May I come in?"

Ignoring the metallic taste in her mouth, Leah reached for his arm and steered him to the couch. Under the lamplight she assessed the damage, trying to decide what to do. "What happened this time?"

"Someone jumped me from behind in the parking lot."

"No arguing this time. You have to go to the emergency room."

"No. I'll be all right."

Leah fought for control of her emotions and her temper. "No, you won't be all right, not without stitches."

"Do you have any alcohol?"

"Alcohol?" She suddenly fought the urge to shake him. Alcohol. That was like asking for a Band-Aid after major surgery. "You need more than alcohol."

"That's what you said last time, and I survived."

"All right, hardhead, but when you pass out from a concussion, don't blame me."

"I won't," he said, an obstinate note in his voice.

Rather than waste any more time arguing with him, Leah

dashed into the bathroom and found the necessary items to patch him up while fighting off a sense of déjà vu.

His showing up at her door was getting to be a habit she didn't like and intended to stop. She went back into the living room, only to gasp. His back was to her, and he was on the phone. She stepped back, but still she could hear what he was saying.

"Eddie, Montgomery here. I have another job for you. I want to put tabs on an attorney in Bogalusa. His name's William DeChamp. Find out all you can about him."

Dalton replaced the receiver, then turned around. An odd look crossed his face, and before Leah thought, she blurted out, "Who's William DeChamp?"

If possible, his face lost more color. "Nobody you need to be concerned about."

"You're right, it isn't," she snapped as he made his way back to the couch, leaned back, and immediately closed his eyes.

While she remained curious as well as angry concerning his phone conversation, Leah sat beside him, as easily as possible.

"Ouch," he whispered as she placed the warm cloth against the tiny but oozing cut.

"I'm sorry, but you knew it was going to hurt."

For a moment he looked up at her. She met his gaze. Even though his eyes were dull with pain, she saw something else in them, something she recognized as lust.

She tried to ignore that. She tried to ignore *him*. Both were impossible. He didn't have the right to do this, to make her touch him.

Yet she had no choice. And while she might tell herself that she wouldn't let him make love to her now, she knew better.

"Why would someone do this to you?" she whispered. "One accident I might buy, but two, no way."

"Whoever waylaid me took my Rolex watch and my billfold."

Leah gave him an incredulous look. "You were robbed?"

"That's what whoever did it wanted it to look like."

"Obviously, you don't buy that."

He didn't respond, and she knew him well enough to know that it was useless to press him. She saw his reluctance to confide in her as a lack of trust, but she didn't trust him, either, which didn't speak well for any relationship. But then, they didn't have a "relationship." They had only one thing going for them—sex. They shared a hot, searing need for each other's bodies, and that was all.

Finally she had patched him up as well as she could. She stood and said, "I'll get you a couple of aspirins."

"I'd rather have a beer."

"I don't have a beer," she snapped.

His eyes slowly perused her body before settling on her mouth. She pulled in her lower lip so he wouldn't notice that it quivered. But there was no way she could protect herself when his gaze shifted to her breasts. She wanted to fold her arms over her hardened nipples, but she refrained. To do so would admit that he had unnerved her, which would be a mistake.

"All right," he said in a brusque but defeated tone, "I'll take the aspirins."

When Leah returned with the pills and a glass of water, he was sitting up straight. "How do you feel?" she asked.

"Like I've been worked over with a baseball bat." He tried to smile. "Otherwise, great."

When he wasn't wringing her inside out, his dry humor made her smile. Now was no exception. Through twitching lips she said, "Here, take these."

Once he'd downed the aspirins, he asked, "Mind if I take a shower?"

She blinked. "A shower?"

"Yeah."

"Here?"

"Do you mind?"

Her jaw dropped. "Do you mean you actually feel like taking one?"

"Sure, why not?"

Leah shook her head. "You're truly amazing. I suspect that most men who had taken a blow to the head would be in the hospital, sedated and sleeping."

"Only I'm not most men."

"That's a fact," she said begrudgingly. "So, take your shower, but don't wake up Coty."

"How is he?"

"Much better. He's asleep, like you ought to be."

"Stop nagging," he said huskily. "It doesn't become you."

Following those words, he walked out of the room.

Leah was still trying to sort through her tangled thoughts when, a while later, she heard him behind her. She twisted her head and made a strangled sound.

"Do you make it a habit of running around without any clothes on?" she demanded, disqualifying the towel that hung loosely around his flat stomach because it shielded very little.

Despite the deep lines of pain and exhaustion on his face, Dalton smiled a slow smile. Then he looked down and back up, his dark eyes unreadable. "Only around you."

"You're impossible."

"Does that bother you?"

"What?" she asked, playing the innocent, then regretting it the instant his smile disappeared and that light appeared in his eyes.

"You know what," he muttered, his voice now low and unsteady, as though he'd just finished making love to her.

She turned away, her face flushed. This wasn't working. He shouldn't have come here. She wasn't his keeper. Besides, she didn't like patching him up; she didn't like seeing his flesh torn and mangled.

She'd much rather see him unblemished and naked, with her hands on . . .

"Please, I think you should go." Her voice was a mere whisper of sound.

"You're right, I should." He regarded her through hot, narrowed eyes. "Only there's a problem."

"What?"

"I can't."

Those two words sounded as if they were dug out of the bottom of his stomach.

"Why . . . can't you?"

His eyes moved to the open slit in her robe. He swallowed convulsively before his gaze met hers again.

Leah stood transfixed while a silence stretched between them, long and painful.

"Aw, to hell with this!" he finally muttered, then turned as if to go back into the bathroom.

That was when the towel slid to the floor.

Thirty-eight

Leah's breath caught.

"Well, shit," Dalton muttered, standing still and naked as the day he'd come into the world.

Leah tried not to stare, but her eyes were drawn to his penis, which left no doubt as to his arousal. Electricity crackled in the air.

She couldn't tear her gaze away. She'd seen his body, of course. But tonight, in the veiled lamplight, he looked more enticing than ever. She wanted to make love to him no matter whether they had a future or not.

"I'll go," he said, then leaned over as if to pick up the towel.

"No." Her voice was a shadow of a whisper, but he heard it.

His hand stopped in midair, then he slowly raised back to full height. "What did you say?"

"I said no." She licked her lips. "Don't go."

"You know what will happen if I stay." It wasn't a question.

She nodded, then for some crazy reason felt tears impair her vision.

He groaned. "You rip me to pieces, you know that? I can't

280

think straight when I'm not around you, and I can't think at all when I am. My mind's on one thing, and that's stripping you naked and making love to you." He paused and drew a deep breath. "You noticed I said love, not fuck."

"Oh, Dalton," Leah cried.

As before, she never knew who reached for the other first. It wasn't important, not then, not now. What was important was holding and being held.

His arms circled her like gentle iron, and when his lips adhered to hers, they were moist, hot, and savage.

She helped him as his hands yanked frantically at the ties on her robe. In seconds she was as naked as he was. With mouths clinging they sank to the rug, onto their knees.

Then Dalton tore his mouth away from hers and surrounded a nipple. He sucked it as if he were starved, while a free hand kneaded the other nipple.

She splayed her hands in his hair and dug into his scalp, frantic to feel him inside her.

"Not now," he said in a gravelly-sounding voice, pulling her down with him so that they lay side by side. "I want to love you all over."

He eased her onto her stomach, then, beginning at her neckline, nipped his way down the center of her back.

"Oh, Dalton, Dalton." She squirmed under the heat of his lips, especially when they reached the upper crevice of her buttocks. When his tongue touched her there, fire shot through her. She bounced onto her back.

Sweat lined Dalton's upper lip, and his eyes were glazed as he peered into her face. "Didn't you like that?"

"Too much," she whispered, lowering his face back to her breasts. But again his hands weren't idle. While suckling one nipple at a time, he eased a finger inside her warmth.

Leah arched her hips and stared at him wide-eyed, even as he inserted another finger.

"Dalton!" she gasped. "I'm going to come."

"It's all right. Let it happen."

Seconds later an orgasm overwhelmed her, and she muffled a cry. He removed his fingers and cupped his hand over her until the rapture had passed.

Though limp and exhausted, she smiled up at him. "Now it's your turn."

She heard his breath rattle in his chest.

"I want to taste you." She eased him onto his back and, beginning with his nipples, sucked each until they were rock-hard pebbles. Then she tongued her way down to his penis. She paused and looked at him.

"You don't have to," he ground out as if in pain.

She didn't say anything. She merely tongued its rigid tip to his deep-throated groan, then eased the rest of it into her mouth until she couldn't go any farther. Then she slowly brought her lips back up, then down again.

"Oh, Leah, Leah, I can't stand anymore." He tugged on her arm. "I don't want to come in your mouth."

"I wouldn't mind."

"But I would." He reached for the other arm and, lifting her, eased her down onto him.

She moaned.

"Does that hurt?"

"No, it's just that you're so big."

"And you're so small and tight."

She felt as if she might split in two, but it was worth that just to be part of him.

"Ride me," he demanded, placing his hands on her breasts.

"Yes, oh, yes." She moved, first slow, then faster, then still faster, until their cries rent the air and she collapsed onto him, their hearts beating as one.

A short time later he eased her off him onto her side, then pushed the damp hair out of her face. "Are you all right?"

"I'm fine."

"You'll be sore tomorrow."

"That's all right."

He shifted slightly so that he could hold her closer. They were silent for a time, listening to the sounds of the spring night. Leah heard a cricket chirp and smiled.

"Leah."

"Mmm?"

"Do you want to sleep?"

"Not unless you do."

"I just want to hold you."

She scooted closer, and he chuckled. "If you don't be still, I'll be inside you again."

She brazenly caressed the hairs on his chest. "You won't find me complaining, although I'm not sure that will be possible."

"I don't doubt that. Your pussy's had a workout. And it's so tight," he said again.

"Is that bad?"

"Hell no, that's the best." He was quiet for a moment, then he said, "In many ways, even though you've had a child, you're like a virgin."

"Does that bother you?"

"Hey, nothing about you bothers me. You're perfect, and I can't get enough of you." He took her hand and placed it on him. He was hot and rigid.

She began to move her hand. Another long silence ensued.

"You're insatiable," she said later, against his damp chest.

"Are you complaining?"

"Never, but you can't keep showing up here in the middle of the night all battered and bruised."

"I know."

"I'm worried about that." She reached up and touched the gash.

He didn't so much as flinch. "And I'm worried about you."

"Because of J. T. Partridge?"

"Yeah, that s.o.b. oughta be locked up."

"Maybe that detective will put the fear of God in him, and he'll just disappear. Only—"

"Only what?"

"He can still make those phone calls."

Dalton stiffened, then shifted so that he could see her face. "What phone calls?"

"I answer the phone, but no one says anything. Just heavy breathing."

"Have you told the police?"

"No."

He expelled his breath.

"I know, but there's been so much going on. Besides, I'm not positive it's J.T. It could be Ellen Thibodeaux trying to intimidate me. Or it could be Cooper Anderson."

"What makes you think Anderson's involved?"

Leah sighed. "He has a problem."

"What kind of problem?"

Leah hesitated, only that hesitation came too late. Now that she'd opened her big mouth, she knew he wasn't about to let her off the hook.

"Leah?"

"He . . . he has a habit of coming on to every female in the office."

"Did he come on to you?"

"Yes."

"Did he—" Dalton broke off as if he couldn't bring himself to say the word that she knew was on the tip of his tongue.

"No, he didn't, but it wasn't from the lack of trying. He trapped me in the closet one day and . . . fondled me."

"That slimy bastard. If he ever so much as touches you again, he'll get a sample of what Partridge got, except worse." He paused. "Hell, no wonder you don't trust men. First that boarder, then Cooper."

"Who said I don't trust men?"

Dalton kissed her on the forehead. "You don't have to say anything, honey. I felt it in how you responded to me at first."

"You're right," Leah said on a shaky breath. "Trust does come hard."

He simply held her close for a moment.

"Well, let's hope Cooper's groping days will soon be over. A woman in the firm office is about to file on him for sexual harassment."

"Well, hurray for her."

"I told her I'd testify against him."

"Hurray for *you*."

"Thanks. I wish my mother felt that way," Leah added without conscious thought.

"After what you've told me about your past, it doesn't surprise me."

"It shouldn't me, either." Leah laughed without humor. "Jessica's so hung up on material things that she actually wants me to go back and work for Cooper."

"Does she know he's tried to put the make on you?"

"She wouldn't care."

"Sounds like my old man, which is no damn compliment. How does Coty feel about her?"

"Most of the time he hates staying with her because she acts the same way to him as she does me. Nothing ever pleases her."

"That's too bad. Children need grandparents, especially ones who take them to McDonald's."

She pulled away and grinned. "Were you ever taken to McDonald's?"

"Huh, are you kidding? Daddy wouldn't have been caught dead there unless he thought it might bring him some votes."

"It's a shame what some parents do to their children."

"But not you. You're doing everything right with Coty."

"I doubt that, but he knows he's loved. Rufus worshiped him. . . ." The second she spoke of her dead husband, she wished she could recall the words, realizing this was not the time or place to discuss him.

As if he sensed her discomfort, Dalton gave her a squeeze. "It's all right. Rufus was and still is a part of your life, though I can't help but feel a little jealous."

"Don't be. What I had with Rufus was totally different from what I have with you."

"Oh?"

Again she felt her face turn beet red. "He . . . he never . . ."

"Never what?"

She remained silent.

"Never made love to you with his tongue? Here? Like I do?"

He cupped her mound with the palm of his hand. Heat stabbed her; she pressed her legs together and trapped his hand.

He began to move it up and down. "Leah," he said in an agonized tone, "there's something I should tell you, something—"

"Shh." She reached up and covered his mouth. "Not now, not when my insides feel like hot putty. Make love to me."

His lips sank into hers.

Eddie Temple slouched behind the wheel of his car in front of a doctor's office in New Orleans. He'd followed Bill DeChamp here and watched now as DeChamp climbed out of his Lincoln and walked toward a very pregnant woman, who had stepped out of her car a few spaces behind him.

They met, and the woman smiled, then kissed DeChamp. If DeChamp's expression was anything to judge by, he was far from thrilled with the gesture.

"Now, ain't that some shit," Eddie mused aloud, thinking his boss was gonna love this scenario.

He punched out Dalton's number and waited.

Thirty-nine

"Mommy, where you going?"

Leah smiled at her son as she put the finishing touches on her makeup. He was sprawled on the bed, watching her. "To the club."

"Again?"

"Yes, again."

"Can I go?"

"You know you can't."

His lower lip protruded. "I bet if you ask Dalton, he'd say I could."

"For starters, young man, I'm not going to ask him. I've already said no. Besides, you'd be bored."

"Not if Dalton was there. Don't you think he's cool?"

Leah swallowed a sigh, then forced a smile. "Yeah, I think he's cool."

Coty didn't say anything for a moment, and Leah gave her nose one last pat with the powder puff. She swung around.

"Well?"

Coty looked blank.

She laughed. "I'm hinting for you to tell me that I look nice."

He made a face. "Aw, Mom, you're just like those dumb

287

girls in my class. They always want you to tell 'em they're pretty."

"Well, is your mom pretty?"

He grinned a half grin. "I guess so."

"You guess so." Her eyes glinted. "You'll pay for that, young man."

He giggled and jumped off the bed. "You have to catch me first."

"Calm down. I can't chase you now, and you know it. Go get your backpack. It's time to go."

Once he'd left the room, Leah took a deep, settling breath and once again stared at her reflection in the mirror. Did she look all right? Only "all right" wasn't good enough. She wanted to look stunning, if for no other reason than to buoy her own spirits. For the past two weeks, ever since the club had opened, she'd been down.

Her job was about to end, although the top floor remained unfinished. But right now that wasn't Dalton's top priority. Getting the casino open and having it bring in money was what Dalton lived for.

So far, he hadn't been disappointed. Opening night had been a smashing success, a mob scene, in fact. The customers had seemed to enjoy themselves.

Thousands upon thousands of dollars had been taken in, but Dalton owed millions, she knew. And the strain was beginning to tell on his face. Of course, he still hadn't confided in her concerning his personal business, which annoyed her in one way and garnered her respect in another. He didn't burden others with his troubles.

She wished he'd burden her. She wished he'd ask her to . . . She stamped out that thought. She wouldn't torment herself with the hope of marriage in connection with him. He'd made it plain that commitment was not for him. Yet she couldn't walk away, not now, anyway. And maybe not ever.

Leah picked up her purse and called, "Coty, let's go."

"I think this is the best night yet, boss. Two weeks into this thing and Dalton's Places are the talk of Biloxi."

Dalton, dressed in a western tuxedo, stared at his assistant. "Let's just pray it stays that way."

"It will. We've done ourselves proud."

"You got that right, especially you and Leah."

"I agree," Tony said with a huge grin. "This place looks great."

It sure as hell does, Dalton thought, taking in the homey yet sophisticated western setting. But more important, people were having a good time. The poker videos were going crazy, the slot machines clanging, the gaming tables packed with players. In addition, patrons were eating and drinking as if there were no tomorrow.

"Oh, by the way, see that fellow at the number three table?" Tony said.

"The one in that ridiculous tie?"

"That's the one," Tony added, "only don't let his flamboyant demeanor fool you. I think he's cheating."

Dalton's eyes hardened. "A blackjacker who thinks he's got the system beat, huh?"

"Yeah. He's hit all three shifts today."

"You think he's counting cards?"

"Yep."

"Well, don't let him out of your sight. Alert the pit boss, too, and make sure those damned cameras are working."

"You got it."

Damn. Dalton didn't want to deal with cheaters tonight, or any night, for that matter. Unfortunately that went with the territory, and he knew the idiot in front of him was just one in a long line of many.

He peered at his watch. Where was Leah? She should already have been here, he thought, eager to see her. Since that wild night of lovemaking at her house, they hadn't been alone. The casino's impending opening had consumed all their time and energy. Tonight, though, he aimed to relieve that throb in his groin. And as for thoughts of a future with her . . . well, he couldn't think about that and maintain his sanity.

But then continuing to sleep with Leah was insanity in the highest degree.

"Dalt, Leah just walked in."

He shook his head to clear it, then followed Tony's nod.

"Man, she looks like a million," Tony said, taking the words right out of Dalton's mouth.

She had on a white knit top that hugged her breasts and waist to perfection. But it wasn't the top that drew his attention, although her nipples were visible, but the black jeans that fit her as if they had been painted on. Yet when she walked, she glided as if they were made of silk. Her hair and face, under the glaring lights, glowed.

Dalton felt his dick swell to new proportions. Damn, but he'd like to take her to his office and fuck her six ways from Sunday.

Instead he sauntered toward her.

"Hi," she said when he stopped in front of her.

"You look good enough to eat." He spoke for her ears alone.

"Thanks," she whispered, staring up at him.

"Tonight?" There was an urgency in his voice that he didn't bother to hide.

"Yes."

"My place or yours?"

"Mine. Coty's at Mother's."

His eyes became temporarily unmasked. "I wish we could leave right now."

"But we can't." There was a tremor in her voice.

He shoved his hands into his pockets to keep from touching her.

"I'll see you later, okay?"

Dalton grazed the side of one cheek with the pad of his finger. "Count on it."

Leah circulated, feeling as if she were walking on a cloud. Tonight was the first time she felt that she could enjoy her handiwork. Earlier it had been too hectic, and she'd been too busy with all the last-minute details.

Now she was free to give herself another pat on the back for the bonus she would soon receive, which would help her desperate financial situation. She had Dalton to thank for that. Among other things, she thought, feeling that familiar warmth pool between her thighs.

Dear Lord, would she ever get enough of him?

She heard the sudden commotion. It came from a table near her.

"You're full of shit," a man shouted. "I wasn't cheating!"

"That's not what the camera shows, fella."

Leah recognized the voice of Gary Welch, one of the pit bosses, who patrolled the floor as a part of security. Fearing trouble, she walked toward the raised voices, all the while looking for Dalton.

That was when it happened. Without warning, a rough hand shot out and collared her around the neck.

She cried out. The man who held her tightened his grip. "Shut up, lady!" he hissed, and placed a pistol against her temple.

At the sight of the gun, no one moved, no one spoke. It was as if the room were filled with wax statues. Then bedlam broke out. Several women screamed, while scores of others scrambled to get out of the way.

Leah couldn't have moved if she'd wanted to. Yet she shook so hard on the inside that she was sure she might break apart.

"Let her go."

She almost didn't recognize Dalton's voice. It was so deadly cold that it sounded inhuman.

"No!" the man cried. "Not until you give me back my money."

"Let her go," Dalton said again.

The man's arm tightened against Leah's windpipe. Tears filled her eyes.

"Get out of my way. I'm leaving, and she's going with me."

" 'Fraid not. Not if you want to keep breathing, that is."

One of the security men, who had managed to sneak up behind him, shoved a gun into the back of his head.

The man's eyes turned frantic.

"Now," Dalton said, "let the lady go, nice and easy, or I'll tell him to blow your fucking brains out." He never raised his voice. It was as if he were saying that the weather sure was nice outside.

The man seemed to know he was in a no-win situation. He dropped the hand that held the gun, leaned over, and sobbed like a baby.

"Leah, come here," Dalton said, still in that same controlled tone.

Leah didn't move.

"Leah, honey," he whispered, and moved toward her.

She held out her hand. "No!"

He pulled up short. She backed up. Tears saturated her face, and her eyes were as frantic as the man's had been a moment ago. "Don't, don't touch me."

"Leah, what—"

Before Dalton could finish his sentence, Leah turned and pushed her way through the crowd.

Dalton cursed, then started after her. A hand detained him. He swung around. "Let her go," Tony said.

"You go to hell," Dalton lashed back. "She needs me, for chrissake!"

Tony's hold tightened. "No, she doesn't. Not now, anyway. What she needs is to be alone."

"To hell with that!"

"She's freaked out, and frankly I don't blame her."

Dalton's jawbones turned rigid. "That's why she shouldn't be by herself."

Dalton started after her, then stopped at the entrance. Maybe Tony was right. Maybe he should let her go. The only purpose in going after her was to assuage his own need.

You really are a shithead, Montgomery, he told himself as he turned and made his way to the bar.

So much for fantasies and dreams, Leah told herself. They were nothing but self-indulgent tortures. She felt the urge to scream, to rant, to rave. But that wasn't her nature. She'd never been allowed to do such an unladylike thing. Her mother had taught her to keep her emotions bottled inside her, to bury them, especially if they were untidy or ugly.

Since the violent incident at the club, she'd done nothing but think about it.

There were no easy answers, because she was confused about so many things. When that crazed man had put that gun to her temple, she had faced death, which was one of the most terrifying moments of her life.

Myriad thoughts had flashed through her mind: She would never see her son again. He would have no parents. She would never see Dalton again.

But when the incident had ended in her favor, the emotions that had charged through her had been of a different nature. One minute she had reviled herself for getting involved with a man who was a gambler and a renegade, who had nothing going for him but ambition and charm that he used to the maximum.

The next minute she'd forgiven him those shortcomings and felt that even though he'd never committed himself, he cared more than he wanted to admit. After those long sweet hours of lovemaking they had last shared, she'd thought that maybe he even loved her.

And love meant commitment and marriage.

So if the chance presented itself, could she live with a man whom she considered a walking stick of dynamite ready to explode at any moment? The paralyzing incident at the club had forced her to face that side of Dalton. No doubt he would have ordered that security guard to blow that man's head off. If the guard hadn't been willing, then Dalton would have done it himself.

How could she live that kind of life day in and day out? How could she put her son through that, a child who had already suffered?

There was no choice involved, Leah reminded herself as she stood by the window in her living room and gazed at the blazing array of flowers in the backyard.

God help her, she loved Dalton, and it wasn't that easy to reprogram her heart. Still, she had refused to see him. Her own insecurities had been too deep-seated.

When she had driven Coty to school, she had almost given in and gone to work. But she'd changed her mind and had come back home. She had bills to see about, bills that still hovered over her like a dark cloud. It was the thought of facing Dalton, however, that had kept her away. She needed more time and distance to sort through her thoughts.

Feeling the urge for a strong cup of coffee, Leah walked toward the kitchen, only to hear the sound of the mailbox opening and closing. She backtracked, opened the door, and retrieved the stack of mail.

More bills, she thought with glum despair. Still, she paused and sifted through them. A letter in a pink envelope caught her attention. It had no return address, and she didn't recognize the handwriting.

With a frown, she tossed the other mail on the nearest table and walked back toward the kitchen. Once there, she sat down, then ripped open the pink envelope.

Forty

The words leapt off the page at her.

> If you don't return my jewelry and return it
> soon, you're going to be sorry. My patience, as
> well as that of my insurance company, has run out.
> Heed my words, bitch, or you'll never work
> again in this town or any other.
>
> Ellen Thibodeaux

Red-hot anger charged through Leah, which left her unable to function. How much more could she stand? How many more persons were going to exact their pounds of flesh?

After a moment Leah straightened, though she still felt weak, violated, and furious. With shaking hands she prepared a cup of coffee, but she no longer wanted it. *She wanted her life back.* She was tired of being the victim, tired of getting trampled for something that she hadn't done. That woman and that disgusting insurance investigator had questioned her integrity, her honesty, one time too many. No longer would she be a doormat for either.

She dashed to the phone and, after dialing, waited for an answer.

"Hi, Sophie, I need to beg a favor from you."

"Are you as uptight as you sound?"

"That's putting it mildly."

"What's wrong?"

"I'll tell you later. Could you pick Coty up after school and watch him for a while?"

"Sure."

"Thanks, I owe you."

Leah grabbed her purse and raced to the car, only to mutter, "Damn!"

Leaving the engine running, she went back into the house, into the utility room. She opened a drawer in the cabinet and rifled through it. After finding what she was looking for, she dashed back to the car.

"What do you want? You're not welcome here!"

Leah stood her ground and stared at Ellen Thibodeaux, who in the afternoon light looked as though she'd been to hell and back. Her eyes were red-rimmed as if she'd been crying, or drinking—Leah couldn't tell which.

Her robe was dirty and did little to hide her full-figured body, especially her breasts. They jiggled up and down with each jerky move she made. Actually, Leah was shocked. She looked nothing like the confident woman who had lambasted her at the restaurant. The woman who stood before her now appeared almost cowed.

"I'm sure I'm not welcome," Leah said, "but I'm not budging until I've had my say."

Ellen's lips curled into a sneer, while she ran a hand through her disheveled hair. "We'll see about that, you little bitch. I'll call the cops."

"I don't think so," Leah said, then darted past the woman straight into a dark foyer.

"Why . . . you . . . you!" Ellen spluttered, and made an attempt to grab Leah's arm.

Leah dodged. She was on a mission, and nothing was going to stop her. She had known she'd be taking a chance by coming here, but she hadn't cared. All she cared about was getting this woman out of her life and her name and reputation restored.

"I didn't take your jewelry, Mrs. Thibodeaux."

"You're lying," Ellen said, her voice having risen two octaves.

"No, I'm not. Granted, I was, and still am, in deep financial trouble, but it wouldn't have mattered if I were homeless and living on the street, I would never take something that didn't belong to me."

"You can stand there like a bleeding heart forever, and it's not going to change my mind."

"Why? Why are you so sure *I* took the jewelry? Don't you think if I had, I would've fenced them for cash by now? Since I need the money so badly, what would be the point in my waiting?"

"Because Partridge is on your ass."

"Not seven days a week, twenty-four hours a day." Leah was putting up the best fight she could, but she didn't have the foggiest idea if it would work. This woman seemed hellbent on blaming her, and she couldn't imagine why.

"The cops think you did it, too."

"Oh, really?" Leah said with far more cool composure than she felt. In fact, her heart was beating so fast that she feared the woman could hear it. "Then why haven't they arrested me?"

"They're incompetent as hell, that's why."

Leah counted to ten, then tried another tactic. "Partridge broke into my house."

Ellen's face turned ashen. "I didn't know."

Maybe she did and maybe she didn't. Leah couldn't tell. Still, she intended to milk it for all it was worth, see how Ellen liked being threatened.

"Well, the police are certainly looking into it, and J.T.'s their number-one suspect. It'd be too bad if you were somehow involved."

"Stop it!" Ellen screamed. "You're just trying to turn the tables and make me the guilty party, when it's really you."

"That's not true, Ellen," Leah said softly, feeling as if she'd finally made a dent in the woman's armor. What followed seemed to come out of nowhere. The words tumbled from her lips. "You know what I think? I think *you* hid the jewels, that you've had them all along."

"Why, that's nuts! You're nuts!"

"Am I?" Leah said, maintaining her control, but just barely. "No, I don't think so. You have them, don't you, Ellen? You staged that theft just to get attention, your husband's attention. Didn't you?"

It was as if the key word were "husband." Suddenly the woman began sobbing, deep, gut-wrenching sobs that pulled at Leah's heart—but only for a second, because it was then she realized that what she'd said *was* the truth.

There had been no theft.

"Why, Ellen? Why did you do it?"

"He doesn't love me, you know," Ellen said in a lifeless tone. "He only married me for my money and . . ."

Leah wanted to scream as the woman bared her soul to her. She didn't want to hear Ellen admit that she'd made her life miserable because of her rotten husband's unfaithfulness. But that was the gist of it, and Leah didn't know whether to slap her or to sue her. Then another thought occurred to her.

"Ellen, listen to me and listen carefully. This is what I want you to do."

Later that same day Leah walked out into the harsh afternoon sunlight. She had her hand on the handle of her car when she looked up and saw another car across the street.

She recognized the car and the driver. Blood pounded in her head, though she didn't hesitate. She turned and made her way toward the car.

J. T. Partridge's office had been her destination. Now he had saved her a trip. He got out of his Ford and ambled toward her; they met on the sidewalk.

For a few seconds neither said a word. It was as if they were both gearing up for battle.

"Good afternoon, Mr. Partridge, you're just the person I wanted to see."

J.T. seemed taken aback by Leah's words. He recovered

quickly, though, and said, "Well now, isn't that a coincidence. You're just the person I wanted to see, too." He grinned a leering grin. "Must mean you're about to admit your guilt."

Leah laughed before her eyes hardened and her tone turned razor sharp. "Hardly. What I'm about to admit is that you're a lazy, no good bastard, who should be in jail."

J.T.'s features twisted until they were an ugly mass. "I'd watch my mouth if I was you, honey."

"I'm afraid those scare tactics won't work any longer." Leah smiled. "For you see, I have proof that I didn't take that jewelry."

He laughed. "Yeah, right, and I'm gonna occupy the White House at any moment."

"Oh, I'm afraid it's not going to be the White House you'll occupy, but rather the jailhouse."

J.T. edged closer, his eyes narrowed against the glare of the hot sunlight. "Now, you listen up, honey. I'm tired of shittin' around with you. You give those jewels to me now, and I'll do what I can to see that you get a reduced sentence."

"I'd like to say I'll do the same for you, only I'm going to do what I can to see that you rot in jail and lose your license to boot."

"Piss off, lady! I'm tired of fooling with you! Now you take your skinny ass back into that house and—"

He didn't see the bag coming until it hit him square in the face. He jumped, then shouted, "What the hell!"

"It's the jewelry, Mr. Partridge. Only thing, it didn't come from my house, but Ellen Thibodeaux's."

By the time he recovered, Leah had pulled a tiny recorder out of her pocket and had turned it on. Ellen's sobbing confession rang out loud and clear.

J.T.'s face turned purple with rage, then he began to shake. "Why, that bitch! I'll wring her fat neck!"

"I doubt that." Leah's voice was filled with scorn. "I doubt you'll have the chance or the means to do anything after I call the insurance board and report you."

"You wouldn't dare."

Leah laughed. "You watch."

"If you do, you'll be sorry!" he shouted to her back as she walked away.

She stopped, turned slowly around and looked him up and down, contempt written on her face. "But not as sorry as you're going to be."

She smiled and opened her car door. But she didn't get inside. Instead she turned again, looked him up and down for a long moment, then said, "Have a nice day—*honey.*"

Forty-one

Leah was hyper—wired, actually.

Following her scene with Ellen, then the one later with J.T., she couldn't settle down, even after she'd picked up Coty at Sophie's. She'd wanted to talk, only Sophie had been on her way out the door to meet Louis.

Now, as Leah looked at Coty, an idea struck her. "Hurry, go wash up," she said. "We're going out to eat."

Coty grinned up at her. "Can we go to McDonald's?"

"Oh, good grief, I guess so."

"Yippee!"

Leah shook her head. Her son acted as if he'd never been to McDonald's, but it had been a while, she reminded herself. She'd been too busy, too upset, too broke, to consider it.

"Can Dalton come with us?"

Leah gave a start. "What?"

"Can Dalton come with us?" Coty repeated, his green eyes wide and eager.

Excitement curled through Leah's stomach. Suddenly she wanted to see Dalton. More than that, she wanted to touch him, realizing how foolish she was to hold him responsible for what had happened at the club. It hadn't been fair to shut him out, not to let him share in her fear and pain. Besides, she'd known what type of man he was when she fell in love, hence she'd have to take the good with the bad.

"Mom?"

"Uh, okay, I'll call him while you wash your hands."

Dalton knew something was wrong. His sixth sense told him that. He had just walked into his condo and was dog-tired. Now, however, that tiredness fled and paranoia took over.

Then he told himself to cool it, certain he was overreacting. But hell, after that near hit-and-run and getting clobbered, he defended his paranoia. Still, the latter was the one that concerned him.

Dalton walked around the living room. Nothing seemed out of the ordinary, until his eyes reached his desk. He'd left some papers stacked there three days ago. Now they were slightly scattered. On closer observation he noticed that one of the drawers was cracked.

He darted across the room and opened that drawer. He'd bet his ass that someone had rifled through it.

DeChamp? Had he broken in, looking for information about Leah and Coty? Hell, he should've kept Eddie on his tail, he guessed. But after Eddie had called and confirmed the rumors about DeChamp's involvement, Dalton had told Eddie he no longer needed him.

He'd planned to use that information against DeChamp. Now it appeared that DeChamp had again caught him unawares. Thank God he hadn't found anything incriminating. The information Eddie and the secretary at the sperm bank had given him was at the bank, locked in a safety deposit box.

Dalton's rage soared to the boiling point. He slammed the drawer shut, then stomped out onto the deck.

The breeze was cooler now, off the water, even though the sun setting in the west still looked like a ball of fire, which was how his gut felt—on fire.

He perched on the deck railing and watched as the waves lulled toward the sand, caressing it gently, as he had caressed Leah.

"Shit!"

He had to confess to Leah who he was and that he wanted Coty before DeChamp did that for him.

"Yeah, right, Montgomery. You just waltz your ass into her house and drop that bombshell."

Dalton shook his foot and blew out his breath as though he'd been belted in the gut. He'd done so many things in his life that he wasn't proud of, even unscrupulous things. In fact, he had few scruples.

But when he dug deep inside himself and analyzed what he felt for Leah in the glaring light, he realized that she had changed him. He was amazed and even a bit awed that he could actually feel so strongly for someone other than himself.

What was equally as amazing was that she loved a hell-raiser like him in return, though she'd never said so, except with her eyes and with the unselfish giving of her body.

When she learned the truth, however, that love would turn to hate, and he couldn't blame her. Still, the truth had to come out. Too many employees and their families depended on the club and the casino for their livelihood, and he couldn't let them down.

That all sounded good, he told himself with a sneer, but it wasn't altogether true. He liked what he did and didn't want to lose it. He had groveled all his life for love, for attention, for money. He didn't intend to ever do it again.

So maybe he didn't love her enough after all. Maybe it was more lust he felt for her than love. Love or lust, what the hell? He didn't want to lose her.

Dalton lurched off the deck, his heart drumming so hard inside his chest that for a minute he felt dizzy.

There had to be another way. There had to be a way he could have his cake and eat it, too.

Deciding that a run on the beach would relieve both his mental and sexual frustrations, he walked back into the condo. The phone rang.

He made a face. The club. He figured something had gone wrong. Well, Tony and the others could damn well deal with it.

He yanked the receiver off the hook. "Yeah."

Silence.

"Montgomery," he said in a sharper tone.

"Is it that bad?"

The sound of Leah's soft voice was the same as stepping on a live wire. He jerked inside, then strove to pull himself together.

"No, now that I'm talking to you."

"You always know the right words, don't you?"

I wish. Oh, how I wish. "They're not just words, and you know it." His voice had dropped to a matching huskiness.

He heard the catch in her throat before she said, "Were you busy? I mean—" She broke off.

"No, I wasn't busy. I'd just had enough of the casino and hauled ass."

She laughed. "Are you hungry?"

"I'm always hungry."

Another silence.

"For food, Dalton," she said pointedly.

"Ah, heck," he said, "that's too bad. Any chance that could change?"

"Mmm, maybe, only not right now. Coty and I are going to dine at McDonald's. We request the pleasure of your company."

"McDonald's. Well, hell, no one in their right mind would pass up a chance to dine there."

She laughed again. "We're about to leave."

He paused a second, then asked in a low voice, "Does this mean that you've forgiven me?"

She didn't pretend to misunderstand. "It wasn't a matter of forgiving you, Dalton. It's just . . . just that when that man put that gun to my head, I had a lot to think about."

"I know, only I wanted to hold you so damn bad that—"

"And I wanted you to, but . . ." Her voice faltered.

"Hey, I understand. Don't cry, honey, I can't stand that."

"So . . . can you meet us?"

"Wild horses wouldn't stop me."

"Mommy, here comes Dalton!"

Before she could stop him, Coty ran to the side entrance of McDonald's just as Dalton opened the door.

"Hiya, cowboy," he said, smiling down into the child's upturned face.

Watching, Leah felt her heart beat just a little too fast. What if things didn't work out between Dalton and her? Coty would be crushed, but then so would she.

Dalton looked at her then and winked, and her world suddenly righted. What she saw in his eyes was more than lust; for a second she had seen love. She swallowed the lump in her throat and smiled brightly.

"So what's the occasion?" Dalton asked, easing his big frame onto the seat next to Coty and across from her.

The scent of his cologne made her dizzy with a longing that was so strong, she couldn't say a word.

"Gosh, Mommy, you look kinda sick," Coty said.

Dalton looked down at the boy. "Now, is that any way to talk about your mom?"

Coty thought a moment. "Well, she does."

Both adults laughed, while Coty looked at them as if they were both a little crazy.

"Actually, we're celebrating," Leah said, her eyes on Dalton, who looked great in a pair of snug-fitting jeans, beige shirt, and boots. Yet there was a weariness about him that the stubble on his face couldn't hide. Still, that sexual charisma oozed from him, and again she wondered what he saw in her when he could have any woman he wanted, ones who were much more experienced than she was.

For now he wanted her, and that was all that mattered.

"Celebrating what?" he asked, his gaze warm.

"Two things happened today that I thought warranted this celebration." She paused with a laugh, followed by an indulgent glance at her son. "Though McDonald's was not the place I had in mind."

"I can't imagine why." Dalton nudged Coty. "But then, everyone needs a sawdust patty every once in a while. Right, kiddo?"

Coty wrinkled his nose. "What's a sawdust patty?"

"Never mind," Dalton drawled, looking at Leah through lazy, narrow eyes. "So, again, what's to celebrate?"

"I'm hungry," Coty wailed. "I wanna eat."

"Okay, first things first," Leah said with a resigned sigh.

Dalton took their orders, then walked to the front and turned them in.

"Mommy, can I go play on the slide?"

"After you eat," Leah responded absently, watching as Dalton eased back into the booth beside Coty. He placed the tray piled high with goodies in the middle.

They ate in silence for a while. Finally Leah wadded her paper and half her burger into a ball. "I'm full."

"Me too," Coty said, slurping the bottom of his cup.

Leah glared at him. "Stop it. That's rude."

"Can I go play now?"

"By all means," she said, rolling her eyes.

Dalton chuckled as he let Coty out of the booth.

Once the child had left, Dalton reached across the table and clasped Leah's hand, his mouth slanted sensually. "I'd much rather have had you for dinner, you know?"

Color surged into her face. "That's nice."

He laughed outright. "Is that the best you can do?"

"Under the circumstances, it is," she said rather primly, feeling the other patrons' stares.

"All right," he said, withdrawing his hand. "I'll behave." His eyes turned hot again. "For now, that is."

"You're awful."

"And you're beautiful when you blush."

She kicked him under the table. He cursed.

"So do you want to hear about my day or not?"

"I'm all ears."

She told him then about the day's events, beginning with the letter from Ellen Thibodeaux.

"Why, that bitch," Dalton interrupted.

"Wait, you haven't heard the rest of the story." He listened intently, then Leah asked, "So don't you feel a little sorry for her?"

"Hell, no. It's her fault she's overweight and married a man who only wanted her money. She had no right to use you as a scapegoat for recouping her losses."

Leah's mouth turned down. "You're right, but in the end she gave me the ammunition I needed to lower the boom on Partridge."

Dalton's eyebrows shot up. "You mean . . . ?"

Leah grinned like a cat who'd just swallowed a canary. "Yep. I kicked him where it hurt the most."

"Literally."

Leah's lips twitched. "No, not literally, although I was tempted."

"So go on," Dalton prodded with a grin.

When she finished her story a few minutes later, she expected a resounding pat on the back from Dalton, but she didn't get one. Instead his expression was quite grave.

"What's wrong? I thought you'd want to pin a medal on me."

"I do," Dalton said, releasing a breath, "but that bastard's liable to retaliate in some way."

"No, he won't." Leah's voice was firm with self-confidence.

"I hope you're right. But when you get a man by the short and curlies, especially a lowlife like Partridge, he comes out swinging."

"Well, all the swinging he's going to do is in the wind. I'm planning to call the insurance board and turn him in." Leah twisted her head sideways and smiled. "So did I do good, or what?"

Something odd flickered in his eyes. "You did good."

"Well, then, say it like you mean it."

"I will, only not here. I've kept my hands off you about as long as I can. Are you ready to go?"

Leah's head spun. "Yes."

"How long do you think it'll take him to fall asleep?"

They stood in the middle of Leah's living room with only the moon as their light.

Leah smiled. "As long as it takes for his head to hit the pillow, which means he's already in never-never land."

"So does that mean we can do it?"

Leah slapped him on the chest. "You're perverted."

He laughed, only to gulp when she placed her hand on his belt buckle. "Look who's talking."

"Do you prefer the bedroom?" she whispered, her hand now on his zipper.

"No," he ground out. "It's too far away."

They made love until they were exhausted. But Dalton still wanted more—and not just sex, not just his penis thrusting inside her. He wanted inside her heart for a lifetime.

But an inner voice wouldn't let him rejoice in that thought. It kept saying, *Tell her the truth; there's no other way. Tell her now, when orgasms have her weak and pliant in your arms.*

"Leah?"

"What?" she whispered against his neck.

He was silent, except for his heart; it pounded hard.

"Dalton?"

"Leah, I—Oh, hell." He pulled back and stared down into her eyes.

"It's all right. You can say what's on your mind."

He expelled a breath. "Will you marry me?"

Forty-two

Bill DeChamp watched as the white ball suddenly swerved to the right of the hole. "Dammit, I thought for sure I had that!"

Ron Arnold, who was a judge and DeChamp's friend, laughed. "Boy, didn't your mama teach you not to count your chickens before they hatched?"

"Go to hell, Arnold," DeChamp said, taking his stance and putting the ball into the hole.

Ron laughed. "My, but you're a sore loser. You ready to call it quits or do you wanna play another nine? It's your call."

"I don't want to play anymore, that's for sure."

"Then let's go to the club. I'll buy you a drink. Maybe that'll take the edge off."

"Think we can find a secluded spot?" DeChamp asked.

Ron looked puzzled, then turned toward the veranda area. "Don't see why not. Looks deserted from here."

"Good, let's go."

Once they were seated by themselves and had their drinks, Ron asked, "What's going on? You're acting strangely, to say the least."

"I'm in a jam."

Ron toyed with the olive in his martini while focusing his

deep blue eyes on DeChamp. "Why doesn't that surprise me?"

"Ah, shit, Ron, don't go sanctimonious on me. I need some advice."

"So talk."

"You know I've been seeing someone."

"Yeah, so what?"

"She's just had a baby."

Ron's eyes narrowed around his swarthy skin. "Your baby?"

"Yep, and she's been threatening for months now to go to Terri. I've been able to put her off until now, but with my health improved and the baby born, I'm running out of borrowed time."

"Shit, man, how'd you get yourself in such a mess?"

"I thought Sylvia was on the pill, but she wasn't."

"How do you know she's not duping you?"

"Because she did one of those home pregnancy tests in front of me."

"That doesn't prove it's yours."

"Right, but proof is not even the issue here. If Sylvia goes to Terri, Terri'll know I've been screwing around and the damage'll be done. Terri'll crucify me."

"So how much does this Sylvia want to keep quiet?"

"Fifty grand."

"Greedy little bitch, isn't she?"

"You don't know the half of it. She calls me every day. Hell, she even showed up at the house once under the pretense of bringing me some papers from another attorney."

"Jesus, just like in the movie *Fatal Attraction*."

"Only this is real."

"How can I help? If it's money, you know I don't have—"

DeChamp waved his hand. "It's not money I need from you; it's a favor."

"Since I owe you, consider it done."

For three weeks following Dalton's proposal, Leah's feet had barely touched the ground. In fact, she'd been downright giddy.

She had replayed that moment over and over in her mind. To those shocking words *Will you marry me?* he'd added, "I love you, Leah. I have from the first moment I saw you."

"And I love you," she'd responded.

"So is that a yes?"

"That's a resounding yes!"

They had made love again with both a fiery passion and a tender sweetness. It had been another celebration, one she would never forget as long as she lived.

Then Dalton had left so as not to be there when Coty awakened. She would have liked to talk more about their future, but there hadn't been time, nor had there been since.

The past three weeks had been hectic. They hadn't seen each other away from work because Dalton's job as manager, in light of the casino's infancy, had been severely demanding. The casino was his baby, he'd told her, and he wanted to be part of the everyday workings.

She had understood, as she'd been busy putting the finishing touches on her work, which no longer depressed her. She knew she wouldn't be leaving Dalton.

They hadn't told Coty yet. They were waiting for a special time. Leah couldn't wait, knowing that her son would be ecstatic.

As to the sanity of all of this . . . well, Leah had refused to pursue that thought. At the same time, she wasn't fooling herself. She knew there would be tough times ahead because there was so much she didn't know about Dalton. She just knew that she loved him and had to give that love a chance.

With that thought in mind, Leah made her way toward the utility room to do a washer load of clothes. She had completed that task just as the doorbell rang. She didn't bother to answer it. When Coty was at home, he always raced toward the door, shouting, "I'll git it! I'll git it!"

It rang again. That was when it dawned on her that Coty wasn't at home. It was Saturday, and she'd taken him to a birthday party.

"Who is it?" Leah asked, vowing to get a peephole put in. Then she smiled. Perhaps she wouldn't need it. Perhaps she wouldn't be living here much longer. Oh, to be out of debt. . . . How sweet that sounded.

"It's your mother."

Leah frowned, then felt bad. She ought to be ashamed, only she wasn't. Her mother had done everything in her power to make her life miserable. Leah didn't see that changing.

She opened the door. Jessica swept past her, dressed in a pants outfit that was too big for her. But at least her hair was clean and in place.

"I've hardly seen you lately," she said in a waspish voice.

Leah bit down on her lower lip to keep back an angry retort. "I've been working, that's why."

"That's no excuse." Jessica glanced toward the kitchen. "Do you have any coffee?"

"Yes. Come on, I'll pour you a cup."

Once they were seated at the breakfast room table, Jessica sipped her coffee, then asked, "Where's Coty?"

"At a birthday party."

"So I assume you're alone?"

Leah bristled. "The last time you were here you asked that same question."

"I assume you're still seeing that gambler."

"Every day, at work," Leah said coolly.

"Ha! Don't hand me that. I know better. Coty talks about him incessantly. I know there's more going on than mere work."

Leah's eyes narrowed. "So what if there is?"

"Oh, for crying out loud, Leah, he may have money, but he's not husband material."

Leah wanted to laugh, only the situation was so pathetic that she couldn't. "Now, just how would you know that? You've never even met the man."

"I don't have to. I know his kind. My God, have you forgotten the heartbreak you went through with Rufus?"

"Leave Rufus out of this, Mother."

"I'll do no such thing. His death broke your heart, and so will this gambler, only in a different way."

"It's my heart, so don't worry about it," Leah replied with an offhandedness she was far from feeling. What she wanted to add was that her mother had never worried about her heart before. But she didn't.

"I want to sell my house and move in with you and Coty."

Jessica's words, straight out of the blue, stole Leah's breath.

"Aren't you going to say something?"

"Why?" That tiny word was the best Leah could do.

"Why?"

"Yes, Mother, why?"

"For one thing, I think it would benefit us both. You'd have a built-in baby-sitter when you go back to work for the Anderson firm—"

Leah sprang to her feet and glared down at her mother. "That's not going to happen, so forget it."

"Now, Leah—"

"For the last time, I'm not going back to that firm."

"Well," Jessica said in a nasty tone, "I think you're making a big mistake, especially when you need money so badly. But if you're determined to be pigheaded, then my moving in with you will help us both financially."

Leah sat down only because she wasn't sure her legs would hold her up any longer. "We can't live together," she said with gentle firmness.

"Even if my doctor advised me not to live alone?"

Leah was completely taken aback. Again. "What?"

Again Jessica shifted her gaze. "I . . . I have a heart condition."

Leah didn't say a word. Instead she got up and walked to the phone, placed her hand on it, then turned to Jessica. "Who's your doctor?"

Jessica's eyes suddenly turned wild. "You don't believe me, do you?"

"It's not that I don't believe you," Leah lied, "it's just that I want to talk to your doctor myself."

"It's Saturday; he's not in his office."

"He might be at the hospital making his rounds, though. I can have him paged."

Jessica's lips stretched into a thin line. "Oh, all right. My condition's not life-threatening."

"Meaning?"

"Meaning that I'll have no problem as long as I take my medicine."

"So this was just a ploy to get your way?"

"You're an ungrateful daughter, Leah." Jessica's eyes flashed. "And selfish to boot."

Leah struggled for control. "I'm going to marry Dalton."

Her mother raised herself to full height and looked at her daughter with contempt. "He'll break your heart, then you'll come crawling back to me. You wait and see."

A sadness came over Leah, and she wanted to cry. All she'd ever wanted from her mother was a kind word. She had long ago given up on a hug or a kiss. She didn't remember her mother ever holding her.

"You're welcome to come to my wedding, but if you decide not to, then that's your choice." Leah looked her mother straight in the eye. "But no longer are you going to tell me how to run my life, which doesn't mean that I'll ever abandon you. But I can't live my life according to your guidelines. I have to make my own choices."

Jessica sneered. "You're my daughter, but you're a bigger fool than I thought."

Leah heard the front door slam. She sagged against the table as hot tears stung her eyes.

Her mother and that unsettling conversation were still on her mind later that evening when she went into Coty's room for their bedtime story.

At first Leah didn't say anything. She just sat on the bed beside Coty and placed her arm around him. Touching his small, firm body that now smelled of soap and shampoo always made her feel better, somehow managed to right the wrongs in the world.

"Hi, Mom," he said in a grown-up-sounding voice.

"What are you doing, cowboy?" she asked, watching him draw lines on a tablet that was propped on his lap.

"I'm making a treehouse. Do you think Dalton'll help me build it?"

"I imagine so."

"Want to see where the stairs are gonna be?"

"Of course."

She looked on as he drew two parallel lines down the page. She didn't know what made her notice the pen, but she did. Maybe it was because she'd never seen one like it before; it was silver and extremely thin. And expensive.

"Coty, honey, let me see that pen."

He stopped drawing and handed it to her.

Without looking at it, she asked, "Where did you get it?"

"Under the buffet. I lost my Ping-Pong ball." He shrugged. "I didn't find my ball, but I found that. It's neat, isn't it?"

Without responding, Leah examined the pen. The tiny letters stenciled on one side leapt out at her: **Mutual Insurance Company.** *J. T. Partridge's employer.* When the words registered, Leah gasped out loud.

"Mommy, what's the matter?"

Leah hesitated, her brows drawn together. "Er . . . nothing, sweetie. Everything's just fine." She got off the bed, then added, "Hold on a sec. I'll be right back. I have to make a phone call. To the police."

Coty's eyes widened, and Leah laughed a giddy laugh.

"Are you sure you want to go through with this?"

"Are you kidding?" Leah said. "I wouldn't miss this for anything."

Becky Childress smiled. "Those are my feelings exactly, but I'm not sure what's going to happen."

A hard glint appeared in Leah's eyes. "I hope Cooper will get his comeuppance."

Becky had called her a few days after that scene with her mother, a scene that still shook Leah when she thought about it. She'd confided in Dalton that same night, after they had made love. He'd held her close and told her not to worry, that when push came to shove, Jessica would come through.

That show of arrogance had bought him a punch in the ribs. Still, his calmness and rational thinking had made Leah feel better.

What would make her feel even better would be to put Cooper Anderson permanently out of the sexual harassment business.

"I hope you're right," Becky was saying as they sat over coffee in her attorney's office.

"We have an airtight case," Jerry Norton said, rubbing a hand over the top of his bald head. "And we're definitely going for the jugular."

"I'm asking a million dollars in psychological damages," Becky said. "I just wish this were a criminal instead of a civil suit."

"I say get him any way you can," Leah responded.

Becky shivered. "I just wish he had settled out of court. I hate to have to get on that stand and tell what that creep did to me."

Leah reached out and squeezed her hand. "Me too, but we have to stop him, and this is the only way."

"I pray you're right."

"So, Mrs. Frazier, how can you help us?" Norton asked, settling down to business.

A short time later Leah walked toward the rear door of the courtroom. She had testified that Cooper had trapped her in the closet and left suggestive messages on her answering machine.

Her testimony, correlated with the others, had drawn a resounding guilty verdict.

As Leah continued toward the exit, she didn't know what made her pause. She looked up and saw Dalton sitting in the back pew.

He smiled and winked.

Leah hugged herself mentally. This evening called for another celebration. Perhaps they would tell Coty they planned to marry.

Leah was sure her feet had wings.

Forty-three

Sweat covered J.T.'s body. Damn, but he hated it when he sweated like a bull in heat. He couldn't control that quirk of nature any easier than he could stop that sick feeling from invading his gut.

Bitch! That word had circulated in his mind over and over since Leah Frazier had one-upped him. But Leah wasn't the only one who rated that pejorative. Ellen Thibodeaux was in the same distinctive class. They had both made a fool out of him, and he despised them.

J.T. couldn't believe that fat broad had staged that robbery just to get attention from her itchy-dick husband. It was damned criminal; that was what it was. After Leah Frazier had thrown that package of jewels in his face, and he'd listened to the tape, he'd driven to the Thibodeaux home.

Of course, the maid had refused to let him in, saying that Mrs. Thibodeaux was out of the country. Out of the country, his ass. He'd known better than that. More than likely she'd been at her lawyer's, trying to keep her butt out of jail on fraud charges.

J.T. smiled at the thought, but the smile didn't hang around long, especially when his thoughts reverted to Leah Frazier. She had guts; he'd say that much for her.

Still, it cut to the bloody quick that she had won that battle, and he intended never to forgive or to forget. Right now, however, he had a meeting with his boss.

That sick feeling in J.T.'s stomach spread to the rest of his body, and for a moment he feared he couldn't walk into the sanctum. He dug a handkerchief out of his back pocket and swiped at his face. Damned hot weather. He wished he lived in Alaska.

"Screw it!" The sound of his voice gave him the courage to kill the engine and get out of the car.

Maybe everything would be all right, he rationalized. Maybe he was blowing this meeting completely out of proportion. Maybe his boss planned to pin a medal on him for saving the company megabucks. His boss didn't have to know the entire story, especially when he could doctor his report.

Another smile appeared on J.T.'s face; this time it remained. He was also confident that Leah Frazier hadn't made good on her threat to turn him in to the insurance board. Like most of the women he knew, she was all talk and no action.

Even if she did, he could defend himself. He hadn't done anything wrong, except vandalize her house. So far the cops didn't have any evidence to pin that on him.

By the time J.T. reached his boss's office, he felt much better. The secretary sent him right in.

"Ah, Partridge, have a seat."

Joseph Seasack never failed to make J.T. nervous. That reaction stemmed from the fact that the man looked, talked, and acted like a prizefighter. He even had one of the trademarks—a flat nose.

"I was surprised you wanted to see me," J.T. commented, then wished he'd kept his mouth shut. He always seemed to blurt out the wrong thing. He sat heavily onto the chair across from Seasack's desk.

"Oh, really?"

"Well, after all, the case has been settled," J.T. said a little too eagerly.

Seasack rubbed one side of his face. "True, it has."

"So do I get my promotion, like you promised?"

"Like I promised?"

J.T. flushed. "Well, you didn't exactly promise."

"No, that's right, I didn't," Seasack said in an even tone.

"But I did save the company millions." J.T. tried again to suppress the eagerness in his tone. His future was hanging in the balance, yet he remained confident that he wasn't going to get the short end of the stick.

"Through no fault of your own, I might add," Seasack responded in that same even tone.

"Uh, I don't understand."

Seasack harrumphed. "Oh, I think you do. So let's stop circling the rosebush and grab the thorns, which is to say, you fucked up, Partridge. Fucked up real good."

J.T. bolted out of his chair. "Now, wait just one minute."

"Sit down!"

J.T. sat down.

Seasack bore down on him. "Listen real good because I'm not going to say this but once. No one embarrasses me or this company. The way you handled this case was contrary to all our standards."

J.T.'s face was once again drenched in sweat. "But you told me—"

"Shut up!"

J.T. shut up.

"That Frazier woman called the insurance board and reported you. She filled their ears full, mainly implicating you in the trashing of her house."

"She can't prove nothing."

"She doesn't have to, you idiot. All she has to do is report you. Then they call me and jump my ass. Well, that old dog don't hunt. If you're going to break the law, rule number one is don't get caught."

"I didn't get caught because I didn't do anything wrong," J.T. lied with as much bluster as he could. "I hounded her like any good investigator."

"What about breaking into her house?"

J.T. felt cold panic. Still, he continued to hold on to his blustering facade. "That's her side of the story."

"And what's yours?"

"I didn't do it," J.T. lied again, this time with more confidence. "All I did was save the company the money you wanted me to, and for that I should be rewarded."

Seasack leaned forward, so close now that J.T. could smell his unpleasant breath. Seasack laughed. "Reward. Oh, I hardly think that's in the cards." The smile fled. "Have your desk cleaned out in thirty minutes and your ass out of here."

J.T. blinked. "What did you say?"

"You heard me. You're fired. Get out of my sight and out of this office. Now!"

J.T. forced his jellylike legs upright and hardly made it out of the room before a sour belch further tainted his mouth. Leah Frazier had ruined his chance for a new lease on life. One way or another she would get what was coming to her. He'd see to that.

Thirty minutes later J.T. climbed into his car. He looked up and saw a tall man hurrying toward him, so thin he looked like a walking string bean. J.T.'s stomach heaved, bringing up another sour belch.

When the man stopped beside the Ford's door, J.T. sat paralyzed with fear.

"J. T. Partridge?" the man asked.

"Who wants to know?"

"Would you please step out of the vehicle."

"Why?"

"Step out, please." Though the man never raised his voice, J.T. knew better than to disregard the command.

He got out.

The man pulled his badge, then said, "You're under arrest."

"What the hell for?" J.T. demanded, hoping to bluster his way through this nightmare.

"Breaking and entering." The detective then read him his rights.

"You don't have any proof!" J.T.'s voice was loud but wobbly.

"That's where you're wrong. We have all the proof we need."

Maybe now that he'd been arrested, he'd finally get rid of his wife. That thought was small consolation as J.T. felt the handcuffs lock around his wrists.

"Move it," the officer said.

J.T. moved it.

"Something bothering you, boss?"

Dalton grimaced at the same time he looked at Tony. "Yeah, but it's nothing I can't handle," he responded, lying through his teeth.

"Well, if there's anything I can do, holler."

"Will do, and thanks, but this is something I have to work out on my own."

They had just finished a staff meeting in which all had gone well, though Dalton had been distracted. Apparently that had been obvious to everyone, or maybe just to Tony, who was more in tune to his moods.

Tony stood. "I'll talk to you later, then."

"Fine," Dalton said absently, then leaned back on his chair.

Dalton had thought about asking Tony to kick his butt all the way to Texas and back. Marriage? Had he lost his mind? He could have asked her to live with him, for chrissake! Or he could have told her the truth, which had been his intention.

Instead his subconscious had gotten the jump on him and played a nasty trick. Since day one the entire scenario had been nothing but gut-wrenching twists and turns. When he'd decided to put his plan in action, he had approached Leah and the child with purely selfish and coldhearted intent. He'd wanted the money and nothing else. And if someone other than himself got hurt in the battle, then so be it.

The plan had backfired, and he stood to get hurt as well. Yet the bank was breathing down his neck, and if he didn't come up with the money within the next two weeks, he would lose everything. If *that* happened, the truth would come out. He didn't want Leah to hear it from anyone but himself. He was a bastard, but not that much of a bastard.

Even though the heat index was over a hundred, a chill shook Dalton's body. To alleviate that, he got up and walked to the bar, where he poured a healthy shot of bourbon. He'd hit the sauce heavily last night in Vegas. He'd been there for a two-day casino managers' meeting.

He'd gotten back late last night and had gone straight to bed. He hadn't called Leah yet, thinking she would be at work soon.

He'd tell her then. He swore he'd tell her. Time had run out. When the phone jangled thirty minutes later, he'd had one bourbon too many.

"I still don't believe it," Sophie said, her eyes wide with shock.

Leah hugged herself. "Well, believe it because it's true. I'm getting married."

Sophie had stopped by the house unexpectedly this morning for a quick cup of coffee, with the excuse that the two friends had had so little time together lately. Leah had been delighted to see her.

Alone, with Coty having gone to day camp, they were at the table, yacking over a cup of coffee.

"And to make life even sweeter, J.T. finally got arrested."

"Well, I'll be damned."

Leah grinned and told her the story.

"I was counting on that creep getting what he deserved, but you never know." Sophie shuddered. "Enough about him. Let's get back to the subject of marriage. Maybe we could have a double wedding," Sophie quipped, then grinned.

"Maybe we could."

"Hot damn!" Sophie slapped her leg. "I was just joking, but that would be a hoot, wouldn't it?"

"It's certainly something to think about."

"On the subject of thinking," Sophie said, "have you thought about this?" Her face colored. "I guess what I'm trying to say is that you always claimed to know so little about Dalton."

"I love him," Leah said simply.

"But do you trust him?" Sophie pressed.

"I do now."

"But you haven't always, right?"

"Right." Leah's face clouded. "And there are times when I still feel I don't know all there is to know about him. But who's to say that's bad? He's so different from Rufus. Rufus never held anything back. His face, his personality, his life, it was all an open book. Dalton's not like that. He's moody at times, hardheaded at others. And if he doesn't want to talk about something, then you're wasting good energy trying to get it out of him."

"He sounds a lot like Louis. And speaking of Louis, I gotta go. It seems like I'm always on the run."

Leah got up and walked with Sophie to the front door.

"I still can't believe we're both about to get married," Sophie said. "It seems like only yesterday that both our lives were in the pits."

"I know," Leah said softly.

"Well, you have a great future in front of you. Think only of that."

"I know, and I couldn't be happier."

Sophie hugged her and walked out the door. Leah had just locked it when the phone rang. A smile lit her face. Dalton. She'd expected his call earlier. Her pulse rate skyrocketed. She'd missed him the two days he'd been gone.

She lifted the receiver. "Hello," she said in her sexiest voice.

"Mrs. Frazier?"

She straightened while her face turned red. The voice on the other end of the line was not Dalton's. "Yes."

"This is Sergeant Mays at the police department."

Her heart dropped to her toes. Dalton. Something had happened to Dalton.

"I'm afraid I have bad news."

She gripped the receiver so hard that she felt as if her knuckles would pop in two.

"Mrs. Frazier, are you still there?"

"Yes, Officer," she managed to croak.

"It's your son."

"My son!" she cried. "Oh, God!"

"Please, Mrs. Frazier, listen to me." The officer's voice

was firm but kind. "He's turned up missing from day camp. We think he might have been kidnapped."

Silence.

"Mrs. Frazier, are you there?"

The phone slipped from Leah's hand at the same time she let out a bloodcurdling scream.

Forty-four

A camp aide wrung her hands, and her voice shook so much that Leah had difficulty understanding her. "I . . . I . . . he was here one minute, then the next he was gone."

"But how could that be?" Leah cried. "How could a child just disappear into thin air?"

"Shh, hon," Dalton said, pulling her against his side. "Trust me, we'll find him."

Immediately after Leah had hung up from talking to the police, she'd called Dalton. His shocked expletive, followed by, "I'll be right there," had somewhat reassured her.

That assurance had become her strength once she'd sat close beside him in the car on their way to the campgrounds.

Now, as she stood in front of the camp director while the police combed the area, Leah's worry turned into full-blown panic. It seemed that her son had truly disappeared into thin air.

"Mrs. Frazier."

Leah swung around to face one of the officers. His name was Tom Richards. "Yes," she responded with bated breath. Dalton's arms tightened around her as he, too, stared at the young man.

"He's nowhere to be found around here."

"Is that all you have to say?" Leah demanded, feeling the urge to strip him of his calm facade.

As if Dalton knew how she felt, he hugged her closer to his side. "Take it easy."

Leah took a series of deep breaths, then released them slowly.

"Actually, there was a woman, a neighbor, who was returning from the grocery store and saw a car sitting on the side of the road. At the time, she said she thought nothing of it. We suspect that the person in that car may have taken your son."

"So you're holding to the possibility that it was indeed a kidnapping?" Dalton put in.

"Yes, sir, that's what the chief thinks, anyway. I suggest we go back to your house, ma'am, and wait for a call."

"Wait!" Leah almost screamed. "Is that all you intend to do?"

Officer Richards looked at Leah through kind eyes. "No, ma'am. We'll have officers searching high and low for your son."

Leah opened her mouth, only to shut it tightly.

"Come on, let's go," Dalton said tenderly.

With tears trailing down her cheeks, Leah walked with Dalton to the car.

"Is there any reason why anyone would take your child, Mrs. Frazier?"

Leah, Dalton, a local FBI agent named Wiley Sizemore, and the chief of detectives, Lyle Cummings, were seated in her living room. Dalton had offered to make coffee, but all had declined.

Leah certainly couldn't have drunk any. She was perilously close to throwing up, and the thought of putting anything on her stomach made it worse.

She knew Dalton was worried about her. He remained close by her side, though he, too, looked as if he'd been poleaxed. Her instinct told her that she hadn't made a mistake in her decision to marry Dalton. He would make an ideal husband and father despite the wild streak that drove him.

Leah clung to that thread of comfort as she battled through one of the darkest periods of her life. Her child. Her baby. Oh, God, if anything happened to Coty, she wouldn't want to live. She'd already lost a husband. She couldn't lose her child as well. Oh, dear Lord, please let this be a dream.

Leah knew it was no dream. If nothing else, the grim faces staring at her bore testimony to that. No, her son's disappearance was horrifyingly real, yet totally unbelievable.

It was then that she realized the agent had asked her the question again. She shook herself mentally, then said, "No, no one that I know of."

"Think, Mrs. Frazier. There has to be a reason."

Leah tried to corral her thoughts in order to think straight.

"Perhaps a business deal has gone sour?" Agent Sizemore prodded.

"She works for me," Dalton said in a clipped tone, as if that adequately answered the question.

The tall, lean agent scratched his chin, then threw Dalton a look that said "Butt out." Dalton's eyes narrowed into slits, but he didn't say anything else.

"What about debts, Mrs. Frazier? Any creditors who might pull this stunt?"

It was bad enough that her son was missing, but to have to air her dirty laundry in front of these men, even Dalton, was almost more than she could bear. But if it meant finding who had taken her son, she'd gladly tell them anything they wanted to know.

"There are definitely debts," she admitted, looking Agent Sizemore straight in the eye. "My husband was ill for a very long time. In fact, I'm close to losing my home."

"Say what?!" Dalton said. "Why didn't you tell me?"

She shook her head at him, then turned back to the agent. "But I hardly think my banker would turn to that kind of tactic, nor would the credit card companies whom I owe."

"No, you're right, I doubt they would." Again the agent scratched his chin.

"There are two other possibilities, though I'd hate to think . . ." Her voice trailed off.

"Go on, Mrs. Frazier," Detective Cummings chimed in, his voice sympathetic and encouraging.

"Well, I've been under suspicion for a jewelry theft," Leah said, then rushed to add, "Although I've now been cleared of all charges."

"Mmm, that's interesting," the agent said, rising from the couch and pacing the floor. "Give me a quick rundown."

"An insurance agent by the name of J. T. Partridge was so sure that I was guilty because of my pressing financial burdens that he hounded me relentlessly. He broke into my house, and because I was able to prove that, he was arrested. But I'm sure he's out on bail."

"So you think he might have pulled this stunt to get even?"

"If you had asked me that a week ago, I would've told you no. He's a nutcase all right, but to stoop to kidnapping—I don't know," she added in a hoarse whisper.

"He couldn't have done it."

Suddenly a hush fell over the room as all eyes riveted on Dalton, whose low, rough voice commanded instant attention.

"How . . ." Leah couldn't go on, so shocked was she at Dalton's unexpected input.

Agent Sizemore had no such problem. "You sound pretty sure of that, Mr. Montgomery."

"I am."

"How's that?"

Dalton faced Leah. "J.T.'s fishing."

Leah blinked in disbelief. "Fishing?"

"Yeah, fishing. He did indeed post bail and has been camping ever since."

"How do you know that?" Leah asked, her eyes wide.

"I made it my business to know, that's how."

"Now, why would you do that?" Agent Sizemore asked, looking more perplexed by the second.

"Because I didn't trust him not to hurt Leah, especially after that last confrontation."

"Well, that certainly clears him," Detective Cummings said, sounding let-down.

Leah was struggling to cope with her own let-down feelings when the agent asked, "Anyone else on the list?"

"Yes," Leah said, pulling her gaze off Dalton. "My ex-boss, Cooper Anderson. I just testified against him in court on sexual harassment charges."

Agent Sizemore grimaced. "Do you think he's capable of such a thing?"

"I don't know!" Leah knew she had all but shouted at the agent, but she didn't care. She was about at her wits' end as to who or why anyone would do something so inhumane, so cruel, as to take her child.

Dalton's hand tightened on her shoulder. "It's going to be okay."

Leah grabbed his hand, then looked back at Agent Sizemore. "The only other person who might have an ax to grind is Ellen Thibodeaux, the woman who faked the robbery. I called her hand on that. Maybe she's—" Leah gulped back tears, unable to go on.

Without saying a word, Detective Cummings walked to the phone and lifted the receiver. Momentarily he said, "Run a check on Cooper Anderson and Ellen Thibodeaux."

Leah stood suddenly, closed her arms around herself, and walked to the window. Only after he'd replaced the receiver did she swing back around, her face filled with torment. "Why?" she whispered. "Why would anyone take an innocent child?"

"There are all kinds of perverts in this world, Mrs. Frazier. You know that."

"Dear God, that's what I'm afraid of." She hugged herself tighter. Then, before she broke apart completely, she added, "I'll go make us some coffee."

It was all Dalton could do not to follow her. But he sensed she needed to be alone. Besides, he couldn't comfort her, not when his own insides were bleeding.

If some pervert had indeed kidnapped his son, then the courts wouldn't have to bother trying the bastard. Dalton would kill him.

Suddenly a thought hit him, and he almost choked. The

two lawmen heard him because they looked at him strangely. Dalton turned his back and walked to the window.

What if DeChamp—? No. That thought was too crazy even to consider. Oh, he wouldn't put it past the scheming bastard if he thought it would get him his money. But to kidnap Coty would defeat his purpose. He'd land in jail, where the money wouldn't do him one ounce of good.

Besides, DeChamp was smarter than that. He wanted Dalton, not the child. So who the hell took Coty, and why?

He couldn't bear to answer that question. Thank God he didn't have to. Leah chose that moment to return with a tray in her hand that was wobbling.

"Here, let me have that," he said, reaching her side and taking it from her.

He set the tray down at the same time the phone rang.

Leah held her breath. Dalton stiffened.

"Are you up to answering this call, Mrs. Frazier?"

Leah's eyes were filled with terror. "I—"

"Let me take it." Dalton's face was like stone, blank and hard.

No one argued.

Detective Cummings lifted the receiver and motioned for Dalton to take the call.

"Montgomery, here."

Leah couldn't take her eyes off Dalton, but that was the only part of her body that seemed to be functioning properly. The rest of her was completely incapacitated. What if . . . ? No! she cried silently. Don't even think it.

"That's great!" Suddenly a huge smile replaced the sad grimness on Dalton's face.

Leah's hand went to her heart, to contain it, for fear it would pound out of her chest. Dalton wouldn't be smiling unless . . .

He handed the phone to the detective, who was watching him through puzzled eyes.

Dalton's gaze sought Leah. "He's all right. Coty's all right."

Leah would have crumpled to the carpet if the wall hadn't been behind her. She sank against it like a tire that had been punctured.

"Leah." Her name was a whisper on his lips as he once again moved toward her.

She let Dalton hold her, but she couldn't say anything.

Detective Cummings replaced the receiver and turned to Leah. "Your son is indeed all right."

Leah could only nod, her throat still too full to speak. Silently she breathed a prayer of thanks.

Coty was safe, and that was all that mattered. But she wouldn't be satisfied until she touched him, held his body against hers. That need took precedence over everything else.

"How . . . where did they find him?" she finally managed to ask, still using Dalton's body for support.

Cummings smiled. "I'm not sure you're ready for this, but the little whippersnapper slipped down a ravine, and after crying so hard, he fell asleep."

"Oh, my God," Leah cried.

"Well, I'll be damned!" Dalton grinned and gave Leah a bear hug. Then, turning to the detective, he asked, "So where's Coty now?"

"On his way here," Detective Cummings said, walking to the window and peeping through the blinds. He turned back to Leah. "It shouldn't be much longer, ma'am."

Leah pulled away from Dalton, raced to the door, and waited.

"Mommy, Mommy!"

Leah heard Coty's voice and smiled through her tears. The instant the door swung back on its hinges, Coty threw himself at her. Despite his size, she lifted him in her arms and hugged him until she thought her arms would break.

For once her son didn't protest. He seemed content to snuggle against her neck.

"Are you sure you're not hurt?" Leah whispered, all the while touching his head, his neck, his back.

Coty raised his head. "Nah, but I was scared."

"Hiya, cowboy," Dalton said, walking up behind Leah and placing a hand on Coty's head.

Coty grinned.

"It's time you had something to eat, young man," Leah said. "Then it's a bath and to bed."

"Guess we'll be going now, Mrs. Frazier," Sizemore said, motioning to Cummings.

"Thanks so much for everything," Leah said, a catch in her voice.

"We're just glad things turned out the way they did," Sizemore said, then cuffed Coty on the chin. "You're a real trooper."

Coty grinned, despite the fact that his eyes were beginning to droop.

The instant the door shut behind the men, Leah put Coty down. "Take off into the kitchen. I'll be right behind you."

"Can Dalton come, too?"

"Of course, sweetie."

Once the child had disappeared, Leah straightened and stared at Dalton, her heart in her eyes. "I . . . couldn't have endured this had you not been with me."

"Oh, my darling, the same goes for me. I love Coty, too."

"I . . . know you do."

"Come here," Dalton whispered, tears now misting his eyes.

She snuggled against his chest to the jarring sound of a car door slamming.

"Damn," Dalton muttered.

Leah pulled back and said, "Who could that be?"

"Whoever it is, I hope they don't plan to stay." He smiled and flicked her on the chin. "I'll handle the door. You go tend to Coty."

Dalton waited until Leah left the room, then he ambled to the window and peeped through the blind. He sucked in his breath and held it.

Bill DeChamp was making his way up the walk and was about to step on the front porch. Pushing the panic button, Dalton dashed to the front door, yanked it open, then slammed it behind him.

DeChamp pulled up short and smiled. "Well, well, imagine finding you here, Montgomery."

"Get the hell away from here, DeChamp!"

DeChamp smiled and rubbed his chin. "Not this time. I'm going to do what I should've a long time ago."

"You open your mouth," Dalton hissed, "and I'll make you wish you hadn't broken into my house or clobbered me in the parking lot."

DeChamp smirked. "You deserved both, you bastard, especially after you hit me. But you don't scare me anymore." He paused and waved the piece of paper in his hand. "I've got the upper hand now. I'm going to tell your squeeze the truth, and—"

Dalton grabbed DeChamp's tie and jerked him so close that their breath mingled. "You keep your filthy mouth shut, you hear!"

"What's going on here?"

When Dalton heard Leah's voice, he let go of DeChamp so quickly that DeChamp lost his balance and fell to the floor of the porch, along with the piece of paper he had clutched in his hand.

For a moment no one said a word as the document landed at Leah's feet. She reached down.

"No!" Dalton's harsh command stopped her for a second. But when she peered up at him, she knew she couldn't obey.

She had never seen him look as he did in that instant, as though he were just about to be gutted with a knife. Fear routed through her so strong that her legs gave way.

Dalton held out his hand. "Leah, please, give it to me."

She moved back and clutched it to her chest. "No. Not until I've read it."

Finally she looked up at Dalton and whispered, "This . . . this is a court order for you, me, and Coty to get a blood test."

"Yeah, that's right, lady."

"Shut the fuck up, DeChamp!"

Something was happening, something that her mind either couldn't or simply wouldn't understand. Whatever it was, it was evil, and she didn't want to hear it. Yet she knew she had no choice.

She locked her eyes on Dalton. "Who is this man, and what . . . what does this mean?"

"I'm the attorney for the Montgomery estate," DeChamp put in. "And—"

"No!" Dalton yelled.

"Then you tell her, damn you!" DeChamp yelled back. "I want my money!"

"Dalton, what does this man want you to tell me?"

Her vicious tone had the desired effect.

Dalton's jawbone was rigid against his cheek. "He wants me to tell you that Coty's my son."

Forty-five

"What!?" Leah cried.

"Adios, you two," DeChamp cut in with a grin and wave of his hand. "I'll leave you to slug it out."

Leah and Dalton ignored DeChamp and instead continued to stare at each other.

"Coty is my biological son, Leah; and in order to claim my inheritance from my father, I had to find him and assume my parental responsibilities."

Leah continued to stare at him, this time not with confusion, but with a mixture of pain and hate.

Stifling another oath, Dalton stepped toward her, a hand outstretched, his eyes dark with misery.

"Don't you dare touch me!" Leah cringed against the wall.

Dalton flinched as if she'd actually struck him. "I know how this sounds, how it must look. And believe me, I had no intention of your finding out like this, but—"

"No! Don't say another word!"

She couldn't begin to comprehend what Dalton had said, nor did she want to. The sting of Dalton's betrayal was so severe, she wanted to crawl off into a hole and disappear. Yet at the same time, none of what was happening seemed real. It was as if she were a spectator watching a horror movie about her own life.

"I'm going back into the house," she said in a calm, zombielike tone, "and I want you off my property now."

"Leah, don't. At least give me a chance—"

Leah shook her head and backed up. "No!"

His eyes pled. "Even prisoners on death row get a chance to tell their story."

Her mouth curved into an unflattering sneer. "I've heard all of your story I want to hear. So just leave. Now."

Dalton's face took on the texture of marble. "All right. I'll go, but I'll be back. Count on it."

Dalton didn't know how long he drove or even where he drove. He just knew that he had to keep active or he'd crumble inside.

As badly as he wanted to blame DeChamp and beat the shit out of him for forcing him into admitting the truth, he couldn't do either. Oh, he still despised the little weasel and hoped to hell he got his comeuppance. But all the responsibility for what had happened belonged to *him*.

Dalton gripped the steering wheel so hard that he felt his knuckles might snap. He'd known deceiving Leah had the potential to explode in his face. To some extent he'd been prepared for it, but that hadn't stopped the arrow from entering his chest and going out the other side.

He had to make her understand how sorry he was. He had to have his say, and she had to listen. She owed him that.

No, she didn't, he told himself savagely. She didn't owe him a thing except a boot out the door, but he was going to do everything in his power to prevent that from happening.

Suddenly he made a U-turn and headed in the opposite direction, toward Leah's house, then broke into a cold sweat.

Perhaps he should wait. Maybe this was not the time to try to reason with her, to make her understand. Yet if he waited, he might not get another chance. He didn't trust her mental state. She'd been through hell and back, and he didn't want to leave her alone.

He wheeled into her driveway and got out. He didn't ring

the doorbell for fear of waking Coty. He tapped repeatedly on the door.

Silence.

"Shit," he muttered just as he heard Leah's voice.

"Go away," she said.

"I'm not leaving. If I have to, I'll kick down the goddamn door."

Leah unlocked and opened the door. Dalton stared into her cold, hostile face. Then, before she could slam it in his face, he swept past her.

She made her way toward the phone. "I'm going to call the police."

Dalton blocked her path.

"Get out of my way!"

"No."

They stared at each other. Leah started to tremble.

"Please, let me hold you," Dalton pleaded. "Let me hold you and convince you how sorry I am."

Leah held out her hands. "No. Please, just go. Don't you think you've done enough harm?"

Her trembling body was hard enough to bear, but the emptiness in her eyes when she looked at him was more than he could stand.

"I know I was wrong not to tell you who I was."

"And just who are you?" she asked in a dull tone.

"I'm the donor you chose out of that catalog."

Leah's hand went to her throat, and the remaining color drained from her face.

The fact that she didn't bolt gave Dalton the confidence to continue, though he knew he'd better talk fast. "I intended to tell you who I was; but after I fell in love with you, I knew that if I confessed, you'd send me away, just as you're trying to do now."

"Love? If that's your definition of love, then God help you."

He ignored another upthrust of pain and went on, "I'll admit that when I first met you, I didn't even know what that word meant. And I sure as hell didn't intend to fall in love with you. I only wanted—"

"To take my child from me so that you could get your hands on some filthy money!"

He deserved the contempt and loathing he heard in her voice. Still, he winced. "I deserve that and more, I know," he finally said, voicing his thoughts. "But you have to understand that when my father's will was read and I found out that in order to get his money I had to find my firstborn child, I was between a rock and a hard place. Finding Coty and getting my hands on the money was all I could think about."

"So you used me, you bastard! And worse, you used my son. But no more. Do you understand, no more!"

"Leah, you can't just—"

"Oh, yes, I can," she cried, her eyes wild. "I'd hate to have you arrested, but I will. Don't push me or I will, if that's what it takes to keep you away from me."

Without so much as another look in his direction, she turned and walked back toward the door.

Rage, directed at himself, combined with the fear of losing her got the better of Dalton. He started to shake inside, and when he spoke he didn't even recognize his own voice. "He's my son, too, you know."

Leah froze, turned around, then laughed, a high, hysterical laugh.

"What's so funny?"

Leah stopped laughing, and her features turned chillingly distant. "You really want to know?"

"Of course I want to know, but if this is some silly little game you're playing—"

"It's true that I was artificially inseminated with your sperm, and it took." She paused again, deliberately. "Only shortly afterward, I miscarried."

Dalton's face lost its color, and he seemed to wilt on the spot.

Still, Leah waited a moment longer, determined to let her words exact full damage. Then she smiled triumphantly. "So you see, Coty is *not* your son."

Forty-six

Dalton looked as if someone had turned him upside down and drained all the blood out of him. He reminded Leah of Rufus as he'd lain in his coffin.

She turned away and waited for the jubilation to wash through her. After all, she had delivered a mortal blow to Dalton's self-inflated confidence and visions of grandeur at her son's expense. But no jubilation prevailed. She felt vacant inside. She just wanted Dalton to go as far away from her as possible.

"If he's . . . not mine, then who's . . ." Dalton stopped, as if he didn't have enough air in his lungs to go on.

"Coty is Rufus's son."

"But I don't understand. Why . . . why were you artificially inseminated?"

"Rufus's sperm count was low, which made it difficult for him to father a child, but not impossible." Leah's voice was like a whiplash. "Following my miscarriage, we made love and I got pregnant. End of story."

Dalton regarded her through dazed eyes. "I can't believe this is happening. How could . . . ?" Again he stopped, at a loss for words. "I was so sure that Coty—"

"You were so sure about a lot of things," Leah interrupted

nastily, feeling another choking sensation fill her throat. "Sure that *my* son would be your ticket to all that money."

Dalton's expression didn't alter. "I deserve everything and more that you're dishing out. And I have no defense except to say I wouldn't have hurt either of you."

Leah laughed a bitter laugh. "You bastard! You can't begin to know what you've done to me. Now, again, I want you out of here, out of my life."

"It's not that simple."

"It is to me." Despite her bravery, Leah heard the crack in her voice. She knew Dalton had, too. If possible, his features became more twisted. She couldn't bear the thought of his touching her, and she knew if she showed the least sign of weakness, she wouldn't be able to stop him.

"Leah?"

"How could you?" she lashed out. "How could you use Coty and me like this?"

"I tried to explain that."

"Don't you have any scruples? Any conscience?"

"At first, no," Dalton said savagely. "I already told you that. At the time I was desperate. I had expected to inherit my father's estate, only to find that he'd once again cut my legs out from under me. Even from the grave, he still had the power to stick that knife in me and twist."

"My mother did the same thing to me!" Leah shouted back. "But I don't try to get back at her through others."

"Leah, please, don't make this harder than it already is. If I'd had any inkling how this would turn out, I would never have followed through with my crazy scheme."

"I don't believe that for one minute."

"Well, it's the truth."

Leah's lips curled in contempt. "Yeah, right. I don't want you to have anything to do with my son. You have no legal right or ties to him. You make that clear to whomever you need to inform. As for the money—"

"Forget about the money!"

She laughed again. "That's good. That's real good."

Dalton flushed. "Fine. Have it your own way. But for the record, I no longer give a rat's ass about the money or who Coty's legal father is."

"Oh, please."

Leah didn't see it coming. Dalton moved so quickly that she was caught totally off guard. He clamped his hand around one arm and stared into her face. "I love him, and I love you! And I'm sorry as hell about all this. Coty can have all the goddamn money."

Leah peered down at his hand, then back up. "Take your hand off me."

He removed his hand, but he didn't put any distance between them. He still loomed over her. "How can I make it up to you? Tell me, please."

She ignored the anguish in his voice and lifted her chin a notch higher. "There's nothing you can do." The scorn she felt for him burned brightly from her eyes.

"Leah—"

"My God, Dalton, you betrayed us, and for what? Greed. How can you expect me to forgive you? Better still, how can you forgive yourself?"

"Believe me, it's not easy."

"For the last time, get out of my life and stay out. I don't want anything to do with a liar and a cheat."

Blanching, Dalton turned and walked out the door.

Leah sank to the floor. She could no longer stand. She felt as if every nerve inside her had been severed.

She had loved Dalton as she'd never loved before and never would again. But he had used her in the vilest way possible, and for that she could never forgive him.

Besides, she didn't believe he loved her, that he'd ever loved her. His declaration of love was merely a facade that hid his real motives and hid the real Dalton Montgomery.

How could she have been so gullible? How could she have been taken in by a wolf in sheep's clothing? She'd thought she was smarter than that. Was it because she'd been so vulnerable and ached so badly for the sexual satisfaction she'd often dreamed about but never experienced? Was that the unvarnished truth?

The thought further sickened her. She knew that was only a part of her attraction to Dalton. He'd charmed her with his forceful personality and his smile, but it would be his warmth next to her in bed, his insatiable appetite for her body, that she would miss with bittersweetness.

Coty? What about her son? Leah's heart stopped beating. He adored Dalton. The child would be crushed when he learned that his idol would no longer be a part of his life.

Sobs tore through her. She didn't try to stop them.

"Mommy."

At first Leah thought she had imagined she heard Coty. Nonetheless, instinct made her look toward the door. He stood in the doorway and stared at her out of wide, frightened eyes.

"Mommy, why are you crying? Are you hurt?"

Leah straightened to her knees and held out her arms. "Come here," she whispered.

He didn't hesitate. Like a tiny missile, he raced into her outstretched arms. "Are you crying because I got lost in the woods?"

She held him close to her trembling body and forced herself to swallow around the lump in her throat. "Yes," she lied, unable to tell him the truth, not after what he'd been through.

He pulled back, then bracketed her face with his small hands and said, "It's all right, Mommy. I'm a big boy, so you don't have to cry."

She smiled through her tears. "I know. You're my big boy, the man of the house."

"That's what Dalton said."

She fought off the knot of agony in her chest. "Well, he's right. We're a team, you and me. And don't you ever forget that."

"You aren't going to be sad anymore, are you?" Coty asked, his voice anxious.

She kissed him on the cheek, then brushed his hair out of his eyes. "No, Mommy's not going to be sad anymore."

He cuddled close once again. "I love you," he whispered.

To hold back further tears, Leah raised her eyes to the ceiling and rocked her child in her arms.

How would she pick up the shattered pieces of her life a

second time? She didn't know. But for Coty's sake, she must.

She wouldn't think about that now. She would wait until tomorrow.

"Don't you think you should give it a rest?"

Dalton stared through bleary eyes at the casino manager of the Flying Clipper. "Ah, hell, Ed, don't get your drawers in a wad on my account."

The other men around the poker table were silent as they watched the exchange.

"You're drunk, Dalton."

Dalton laughed. "And losing money to boot."

"That's right, so that's why I'm calling this game to a halt."

"You're not going to do jackshit," Dalton countered, his eyes circling the table. "These bloodsuckers aren't through taking my damn money. Are you, fellas?"

No one said a word.

Ed clamped his hand down on Dalton's shoulder. "I don't want to have to call a pit boss to oust you, Montgomery, but I will. And trust me, tomorrow you'll thank me for saving your crazy ass. Now, get up and get the hell out of my club while I'm still in an agreeable mood."

Then Ed's eyes roamed the table. "This game's over, gentlemen."

Though they grumbled under their breath, no one countermanded his order, especially when they saw the burly pit boss standing in the door of the private gaming room.

Dalton smirked, then rose unsteadily to his feet. "You're a real shit, Ed. Did anyone ever tell you that?"

Ed didn't respond. He just motioned for his pit boss to grab hold of Dalton and escort him out of the casino.

Moments later, when the still hot air hit him in the face, Dalton shook loose the man's hand on his arm. "Take a hike."

The man's features didn't change. "It's you that's going to take a hike, partner. Let's just hope you make it home without killing yourself or some innocent victim."

"Fuck off."

*   *   *

Later, lying buck naked in bed and staring up at the ceiling, Dalton wondered how he had made it home. He hardly remembered getting into the car.

But then for the past two weeks he'd been living in a stinking hellhole filled with nothing but a bottle of booze to comfort him. He knew Tony and the others at the casino were at their wits' end as to how to cope with his behavior. He'd yelled at the pit bosses; he'd yelled at the cashiers; he'd yelled at everyone who got in his way.

Hell, he didn't give a damn what they thought. Hell, he didn't give a damn about anything. When he'd lost Leah and Coty, he'd lost his soul. He hadn't been sober since. But he knew he couldn't keep on going like this. He knew he had to get hold of himself and go on with his life.

He didn't want to. He wanted back what he'd lost, and he didn't give a damn if Coty was his child or not. He wanted to marry Leah and adopt Coty. That was all he thought about, night and day.

But that wasn't going to happen, he reminded himself bitterly, reaching for the bottle beside his bed and cradling it against his chest. He took a slug of the booze, felt it set his stomach on fire; then it did what it was supposed to do, knocked him out.

He didn't know how long he slept. He didn't have any idea even what the time was. But the obtrusive noise beside the bed now so assaulted his head and ears that he reached for the pillow and placed it over his head.

The noise still hurt his head. He released a string of profanity, then pitched the pillow to the floor and turned sunken, red-rimmed eyes toward the bedside table. That was when he realized that it was the phone ringing and not the alarm. At the same time he reached for the receiver, he looked at the clock and saw that it was nine in the morning.

He scrambled upright, only to grab his head as a pain ripped through his skull. He barely managed to say, "Yeah," into the receiver.

"Good morning, Dalton, this is your friendly banker."

Friendly, my ass, Dalton thought, the pain in his head shooting all the way down to his toes.

"What can I do for you, Norm?" He tried to keep his voice even, but under the circumstances it was impossible.

"I called the casino, and they told me you hadn't made it in to work yet."

Silence.

Norm Thornhill sighed. "All right, I'll get straight to the point."

"I'm listening."

"The board met last night, and you have a week, and not one day more, to meet your financial obligations to this bank or—" He paused and cleared his throat. "Or face foreclosure."

"Look—"

"No, Dalton. No more talking. No more cajoling. It's out of my hands now. I'll expect to see you soon, you hear?"

The dial tone buzzed in Dalton's ear before he had the chance to slam down his receiver. He sat unmoving for a moment, his mind now relatively clear. So push had finally come to shove, which didn't surprise him.

Dalton dropped his head in his hands. What should he do? Leah was lost to him. Since Coty *wasn't* his biological son, and there was no record of a subsequent pregnancy from his sperm, he did not have to fulfill that provision of his father's will. The estate would revert back to him. He was confident of that.

So should he take the money, save his business, and ignore the gaping hole in his heart? He sat on the side of the bed a moment longer, then got up slowly.

When he reached the bathroom and stepped into the steaming hot shower, he asked himself that question again.

Forty-seven

Leah placed the bouquet of fresh flowers in the container, then fell to her knees. She wouldn't cry. She had promised herself that when she'd decided to visit Rufus's grave. She knew she shouldn't have come, but she hadn't been able to stay away.

She looked up at the oaks that draped the gravesite. Their branches sagged with leaves and moss. She closed her eyes and listened to the birds chirp, then breathed, taking in the sweet smell of the May flowers.

She had hoped she'd find inner peace here. And to some extent, she had. At least she had come out of this mess with an insight into herself. Dalton was like a Texas dust storm that had blown into her life out of nowhere, sent her life flying in all different directions, then swept away, leaving her heartbroken but unsure of what, exactly, had happened.

Only now did she recognize why she'd been such an easy target for him.

After Rufus died, she hadn't wanted the responsibility of taking care of herself and Coty. She'd wanted someone strong to lean on. Dalton had been that someone. But no more. She had learned that she didn't need a man to be complete, to function. She had proved that she could rely on herself, that underneath the outer fragility, she did indeed possess an iron will.

She hadn't searched for another job, though she knew she would have to soon. The bonus, combined with the salary she had earned while working for Dalton, had saved her house. Ellen Thibodeaux had finally paid her, which had helped.

However, she still had Rufus's massive medical bills to pay. At the moment, though, she had a more pressing problem on her mind—her son. Coty couldn't understand why Dalton had suddenly disappeared from their lives. Finally she'd had to tell him, which had taken its toll on her.

"Oh, Rufus," she whispered, the tears she had promised to keep in check trickling down her face, "I didn't know what to say to him."

As she had feared, she'd bungled it badly. The last thing she wanted was to replay that conversation in her mind, but she couldn't help herself.

It had started when the school had called and said that Coty was in the principal's office. She'd been mortified, and by the time she'd arrived on campus that mortification had swelled into full-blown fear. What on earth had her mild-mannered, fun-loving son done to warrant such an action?

She'd found out soon enough. Coty had plunged into a fight with another boy at lunch over a set of baseball cards that her son shouldn't have taken to school in the first place.

She'd witnessed the principal give Coty two swats with the paddle before he was sent back to class. Then, when Coty had come home, they'd had a long discussion about his attitude. That was when he'd asked, "Why doesn't Dalton like me anymore, Mommy?"

Leah had known this was coming, but dear Lord, she had needed the time to heal herself, to reconcile the loss within her own mind and heart, before she tackled telling her son.

She could no longer put it off. If Dalton was the root of her son's sudden upheaval, and she knew that he was, then she had no choice but to tell him.

Besides, she had to face the brutal truth herself.

"I'm sure he likes you, honey."

"Then where is he?"

"For one thing, he's busy," she hedged, still unable to say the words that had to be said.

"When's he gonna get unbusy?"

"Son—"

"I want him to be my new daddy."

Leah felt a coldness creep around her heart. She pulled Coty onto her lap and clutched him close. But he wasn't in the mood for cuddling. He was in the mood for answers.

Coty had seemingly picked up the vibes from her that something was wrong, even though she'd tried to hide her misery. She had noticed him watching her with worried eyes.

The fact that he got in trouble at school shouldn't have come as a surprise; but it had, and Leah felt responsible. And Dalton. At that moment she longed to put the same knife through his heart that now jabbed hers. She could take the pain of rejection and betrayal, but Coty couldn't.

"Sometimes things don't work out the way we want them to."

"Why?" Coty, his lower lip protruding slightly.

"It's called life, my darling. And life is not always fair. It wasn't fair that your daddy died, but that's a part of life just as much as living is."

His eyes registered confusion, and Leah knew she was bungling the job. "I guess what I'm trying to say is that Dalton and I are not going to get married."

"Why not?" he asked, anger in his voice.

"Because it's not meant to be." Leah struggled for the strength to find the right words. "There are things that happened that you can't understand; that's between Dalton and me. He still cares for you very much, but I think it's best if you don't see him—"

Coty sprang off her lap, his eyes filled with tears. "Just because you don't like him anymore doesn't mean I don't. I want him to be my daddy!"

He turned, ran to his room, and slammed the door. Leah gave him a few minutes alone, then knocked on the door. Once inside, she sat on the bed beside him and again pulled him into her arms.

"I'm sorry," she whispered, holding him tightly.

He didn't say anything, but at least he didn't reject her. She didn't know if she could have borne that.

Now, as Leah looked at the leaves scattered across Rufus's grave, she thought about her life and how its pieces were just as scattered. One day soon she hoped she would find those pieces and glue them back together.

Painful as that process would be, it wouldn't be impossible. She had Coty; she had her health; she had friends, especially Sophie and Louis, whose wedding she had attended last week.

Other positive things had happened as well. Becky Childress had called and delivered some good news.

"It's all official!"

"Oh, Becky, I'm thrilled for you," Leah had said.

"Yeah, the judge socked it to that bastard. I was awarded my million dollars."

"All right!"

"Yeah, and get this. Cooper got called in by the other partners, and they told him if he ever so much as looked cross-eyed at another woman in that office, he was out on his butt."

"Couldn't happen to a more deserving fellow."

"I want to thank you again for your part in helping to sandbag that pervert."

"I'm glad I could help. I should've done what you did a long time ago."

"At the time you had your husband to think about," Becky had said softly. Then, on a brighter note, she'd added, "Of course, Cooper will appeal; and even if I don't get a dime, at least his sins are out in the open, and everyone knows him for what he is."

"I couldn't be happier for you," Leah had said. "Good luck and keep in touch."

She had grinned after hanging up the phone, thinking there was some justice in this world after all, especially as her mother, surprisingly, had also showed her some kindness.

Still, despite her newfound belief in herself, nothing filled the void left by Dalton. If only she could hate him with her heart as she did with her mind, then the healing process would begin.

She prayed that time would soon come.

"Something told me I'd find you here."

Startled by the unexpected invasion of her privacy, Leah swung around and tried to smile.

Sophie, dressed in shorts and a T-shirt, dropped onto the grass beside Leah. "Am I intruding?"

Leah shook her head. "No, actually I'm glad you came, but I'm surprised."

"Well, I stopped by the house, and when you weren't there . . ." She paused and shrugged. "Heck, I don't know. I just thought I'd take a chance, especially since you've been in such a funk lately."

"I wish it were just a funk."

"I know it's much worse than that. Your heart's broken, but it'll mend."

"It's Coty's I'm worried about. He's devastated by what happened."

She told Sophie about his getting in trouble at school and their conversation concerning Dalton.

"He has a right to be upset. That kid's gone through a lot."

"I know," Leah whispered. "And it's all my fault. If only I hadn't lost my head over Dalton, then none of this would be happening. Soph, how could I have been so stupid, so blind?"

"Maybe you weren't so stupid after all."

Leah gave her an incredulous look. "How can you say that, in light of what he did?"

"I debated about coming here."

Leah sighed. "You're not making sense. Since you brought it up, why *did* you track me down?"

"I found out something that I thought you ought to know. Now, I'm not so sure."

"Would you please stop talking in riddles."

"I have a friend who works at the bank, and scuttlebutt has it that Dalton's about to lose everything."

Leah gave her another incredulous look. "You mean the club and the casino?"

"That's what I mean."

"But why? I don't understand. Since the child Dalton would have fathered through the insemination never was born, that should've automatically voided the provision in the will, clearing the way for Dalton to inherit all those millions."

"I agree. Maybe his trouble is not about money."

Leah leaned her head sideways. "Are you sure there isn't something else you're not telling me?"

Sophie raised her right hand. "That's all I know. Scout's honor."

"Well, it doesn't change anything," Leah said, a militant note in her voice.

Sophie leaned over and hugged her. "No, I guess it doesn't, but I thought you ought to know anyway." She pulled back. "Come on, let's go."

"I'm ready," Leah whispered, getting up.

Arm in arm the two friends walked toward their cars.

Two hours later the doorbell rang. Leah put down the phone, got up, and made her way toward the door. She'd been making calls, having heard of various jobs that were in the offing. She'd already set up several appointments and, for the first time in a while, felt a tiny portion of her heart come back to life.

A man stood on her porch dressed in a Federal Express uniform. She frowned.

He tipped his hat. "Ma'am, I have a package for Leah Frazier."

"I'm Leah Frazier."

"Sign here, please."

Leah took the clipboard from his hand and scribbled her name across the invoice. He then gave her the package.

"Thank you, ma'am, and have a nice day."

"Thank you," she muttered to his back, while the frown on her face deepened.

But it was only after she reached her desk and examined the front of the package that an alarm bell went off inside her head.

The return label was that of Dalton's bank. What on earth would they be sending her? She couldn't imagine, but whatever it was, she was reluctant to open it. In fact, she wouldn't open it. If it had anything to do with Dalton, she wanted no part of it.

He had stepped on her heart, but she'd be damned if she'd let him keep walking on it. She slammed down the package and tried to make more calls, only to find she couldn't concentrate.

Finally curiosity got the best of her. "Damn," she mumbled, and reached for the envelope.

With trembling fingers she ripped it open and read the letter. Her eyes widened as shock rippled through her.

> Leah, I meant it when I said that once I fell in love with you the money ceased to mean more than you and Coty. Therefore, I have set up a sizable trust in *our* son's name.
>
> Dalton

Leah looked up and stared into space. This could not be happening, she thought.

But it was. She had the stark evidence in front of her. Dalton had given Coty a fortune, not because he had to, but because he wanted to, which meant what—that he truly loved them?

Her heart raced. If so, then she had misjudged him cruelly. Was it too late to make amends, too late for another chance?

Suddenly she smiled. After all, what was life without a few dust storms blowing through?

Leah jumped up. "Coty! Come here! And hurry!"

Forty-eight

"Mommy, where are we going?"

Leah kept her eyes on the road. "It's a surprise."

"But I'm 'posed to go to Mike's today and play."

"I know, and I suspect you'll have a chance to do just that, but later."

"Okay," Coty muttered.

Leah heard the down-in-the-mouth tone in his voice, but she didn't want to say anything because the surprise she had in mind might blow up in her face. What if she had made a mistake? What if . . . No. She wouldn't think like that. She would think on the positive side.

Finally she reached the turn that led up the long driveway. She glanced down at her son, who was applying bright red crayon to a clown in his coloring book. "Take a look."

He lifted his head.

"Do you recognize anything?"

Coty scooted to the edge of the seat, and his head bobbed from right to left. "Yeah!" he cried. "That's Dalton's big house up there on that hill."

Leah laughed a nervous laugh. "That's exactly what it is."

Coty turned toward Leah, a puzzled expression on his

face. "Why are we coming here? You told me Dalton didn't like us anymore," he said with childlike bluntness.

"I said no such thing," Leah responded, appalled. "I said that he and I weren't getting married."

"If he liked us, he'd marry us," Coty muttered, seemingly unwilling to concede anything.

Inwardly Leah groaned. She saw no way to reason with him or even to defy that logic. Yet.

She stopped the Honda in front of the house and forced a smile at her son. "You stay here. I'll be right back."

Coty didn't say anything. He merely looked at her. She kissed him on the cheek, then got out of the car and made her way up the sidewalk, telling herself that she was insane, that more than likely Dalton would . . .

Again she shut down her negative thoughts and kept on walking. Before coming here, she'd gone to Dalton's condo; and when he hadn't been there, she'd gone to the club. Tony had told her he was in Bogalusa.

She rang the door bell and waited. Nothing. She rang it again. Finally she heard footsteps but was surprised when the door swung open and Dalton himself stared back at her.

For a moment Leah couldn't say a word, not because of fear, though that had something to do with her muteness, but because of Dalton's appearance.

He looked like hell. His eyes were bloodshot and sunk so far back in his head that they looked hollow. He'd lost weight as well. His cutoffs and muscle shirt didn't seem to touch him anywhere.

"What do you want?" he demanded in a slurred voice.

Obviously he'd been drinking or was downright drunk. Leah's courage faltered. "Are you all right?"

"Do I look all right?"

"No, you look like a walking skeleton."

"Do you care?"

Tears pricked Leah's eyes. She'd made a grave mistake. "Look, I'm sorry I—" She couldn't go on. He didn't want her anymore. He might have given Coty money, but when it came to her . . . She turned and started down the steps.

"Leah!"

His bleak cry brought her back around.

"I—"

He fell silent, and they stared at each other. Leah saw in his eyes what words couldn't say. She twisted her head toward the car and called, "Coty, come here."

Her son scrambled out of the Honda and dashed up the steps, straight into Dalton's outstretched arms. He lifted him and held him close, but his eyes were on Leah.

"I . . . we love you," she whispered. "And if you want us, we're yours."

Dalton tongued his way down the center of her back to the bottom of her feet.

"Oh, Dalton," she whispered, squirming. Every spot he touched set her on fire.

"Be still."

His low, sexy drawl made her squirm that much more. "Please . . . you're driving me crazy."

He turned her over at the same time he said, "Not nearly as crazy as you're driving me. I want to be inside you all the time. I rarely think of anything else."

Having said that, he intertwined their legs and thrust deeply into her.

Leah moaned but didn't close her eyes, watching both love and passion darken his as he began to move, first slowly, then faster, then still faster, flesh against flesh, until they both cried out.

Later they lay facing each other, his penis still within her. Dalton brushed the limp, damp hair off her forehead and seemed content just to look at her.

Leah felt the same. Since the day she had walked up the steps of his house, they had been inseparable. A week later they had married. It had been a small wedding with little fanfare. Tony had stood up with Dalton, and Sophie had stood with her.

Even her mother, who seemed to have accepted that her daughter was doing what she truly wanted to do, had put on a happy face.

Leah suspected, however, that it would be a while, if ever, before Jessica would learn to like Dalton. But she didn't care. Her mother had to get a life of her own. If she didn't, that was her problem, not Leah's.

Her home had sold, which had paid off most of Rufus's debts. What was left, Dalton settled, despite her protests, citing that what was his was hers. Following the sale, they had moved into Dalton's condo, and she'd had a great time redecorating it into a home for the three of them.

Both the casino and the club were doing well, although megaproblems were usual in that business and arose every day. Dalton had to work hard to keep them solvent, especially as new casinos were popping up almost daily, offering new and innovative lures to the gambling public. But he was a fighter, and he wasn't about to be outdone.

"What are you thinking about?" he asked huskily.

"Our life and how happy you've made me and Coty."

"He's a special kid. When he came up to me and put his hand in mine after the wedding and asked if he could call me Dad, I thought I'd boo-hoo like a baby. Imagine a grown man doing that, and in front of our friends."

Leah kissed him and felt her tears mix with his.

"I love you," he said in a strangled tone.

"And I love you, more each day."

"How long have we been married now?"

"Four months tomorrow, as if you didn't know."

"How time flies."

She grinned. "Especially if you're having fun."

His face sobered. "I've never been so happy in my entire life."

"Me either."

"Even when you were married to . . . Rufus?"

"Even when I was married to Rufus."

They had not talked about Rufus since they had been married. Leah knew there were many unanswered questions in Dalton's mind that she wouldn't hesitate to answer, if only he'd ask.

She heard him release a deep sigh. "You have no reason to be jealous of him, you know," she said quietly.

"But I am, especially since Coty's not my child."

"He was almost yours."

Dalton held her close. She felt the rigid contour of his

body before he asked, "How did you feel when you found out that you'd rejected my sperm? Did you feel relief?"

"No. It was very painful," Leah said softly.

"Mentally or physically?"

"Both."

"What about Rufus?"

"He was devastated, because he had wanted a child so badly."

"So using a donor didn't bother him?"

"No, not all."

"I can almost picture the two of you poring over that catalog, looking for the perfect donor—" Dalton broke off and turned his head.

"Dalton," she whispered, "what you did was nothing to be ashamed of."

"I know, except that I hated it. I hated what they called the 'cupping' room. And I hated jacking off like some pimply-faced kid who couldn't get a girl."

She had to smile at that analogy, but not for long, sensing how distressing that time had been for him. "I know. I felt some of the same emotions while on that table, having a stranger's sperm put in me. I felt almost as if I'd been raped."

He looked wretched.

"But that feeling didn't last long. When I thought about the miracle of carrying a child in my belly, I was content and actually thanked you."

"Thanked me?"

"Well, you know, thanked you for being a donor so that I could have a baby."

"I guess that's the way I should've looked at it, but I didn't. I couldn't hack it again. It's a wonder the donor bank didn't sue my ass."

Leah laughed. "Knowing you, you wouldn't have cared."

"You're right. I wouldn't have gone back there even if that doctor had threatened to denut me." Dalton paused. "I'm truly sorry, though, that Coty's not my son."

"He is now."

"And has been, in my heart, since that day in the emergency room. I looked at him while he was bleeding and thought, This kid's my flesh and blood, and I'm using him in such a cavalier, cruel manner.

"But I fought that feeling because I didn't want to care, didn't want that responsibility. I just wanted to get even with Parker. I knew, though, that someday I would have to come to terms with those feelings for both Coty and you."

"I'm so glad you did," she whispered, hugging him.

He kissed her long and hard.

"We're going to have to stop meeting at noon like this," she whispered when she could breathe again.

"Why?"

She looked up at him and smiled. "Well, now that you mention it, I can't think of a reason."

He laughed, a deep belly laugh. "I know you want to go back to work. Is that what you're leading up to?"

"Well, yes and no," she mused. "You know I've had a lot of potential clients wanting my expertise."

"Huh, gettin' the big head, are we?"

"Mine's never been as big as yours."

"Tut, tut. The lady has claws."

She dug her fingers into his chest.

"Ouch!"

"Be nice when you talk about me."

He nuzzled her neck, then said, "Speaking of work, it helps to have Cooper Anderson's mouth sewed up. That's one reason why you're getting all those offers. You were so good on that stand, though I know how you hated spilling your guts that way."

Leah's eyes clouded. "You're right, I did, but he had to get his comeuppance."

"Speaking of comeuppance, ole J.T. sorta got his, thanks to you."

"You mean thanks to Coty, don't you? If he hadn't found that pen, then J.T. would've been let off scot-free for breaking into my house." She raised her eyebrows. "What do you mean by sorta, anyway?"

"Hell, that judge who let him off on probation was too damn liberal to suit me. I'd have sent his ass to the slammer to stay and thrown the key away."

"You would, but at least J. T. has to make restitution for the damage he did."

"Well, don't hold your breath. That s.o.b. doesn't have a pot to pee in or a window to throw it out of."

Leah giggled. "Well, pot or not, I think he'll do as he's been told or else he *will* go to the slammer, as you call it. And there's Ellen Thibodeaux. She just might end up in jail herself on fraud charges."

"You can forget that. If it ever goes that far, she'll get probation."

"Well, when you think about it, she's to be pitied, and so is William DeChamp."

"You got a more forgiving heart than I have."

"Oh, I think he's been punished for his sins, so to speak."

"Yeah, I guess you're right," Dalton conceded. "With a wife on bottom and a pregnant mistress on top, he was in deep shit." He chuckled. "And to add to his just desserts, his wife divorced him and two clients sued him for mishandling funds. So between his legal and marital woes, I'll bet the money he got from the estate is just about gone."

"Do you think he might get disbarred?"

"Possibly, but he's already so disgraced, he's had to leave Bogalusa."

"Have you seen him since that day he came to my house?"

"Nope. I would imagine he's steering clear of me. He's afraid I might beat the stuffing out of him."

"And would you?"

Dalton peered down at her. "Nah, not now. I'm through with all that hell-raising. Just the fact that DeChamp's intimidated is good enough for me." He grinned. "He doesn't have to know I've turned into a big, contented pussycat."

Leah laughed. "That'll be the day."

"Aw, come on, you know I'm telling the truth. See how good I am at nuzzling your neck?"

"You're definitely good," Leah responded huskily, "and as much as I'd like to stay here and—"

"Fuck all day," he finished for her.

She pinched a nipple. He yelped.

"That wasn't what I was going to say. Anyway, that pinch serves you right for talking nasty."

He grinned. "You love it."

"You're right, only not now. Tonight's a costume carnival at the school."

"So?"

"So, I have to bake cookies and get costumes together. We all have to dress up."

"Not me."

"Yes, you. Coty's counting on it."

"All right. I'll go as myself, a professional gambler."

"That's a cop-out if I've ever heard one."

"Beggars can't be choosers." He grinned. "What about you?"

Leah fell silent and stared into his eyes.

"Leah?"

She heard the uncertainty in his tone, as if something might be wrong. For a moment she couldn't reassure him. Her throat was suddenly too clogged with emotion.

"Leah?" he repeated roughly, fear darkening his eyes. "Why are you looking at me like that? Is something wrong?"

She smiled and placed his hand on her stomach. "No, my darling, everything's just right. You see, I thought I'd go as a pregnant woman in a maternity outfit."